THE CURSE OF CONSTANTINOPLE. THE CATALAN EXPEDITION TO THE EAST.

Book Three of The Chronicles of
The Forgotten Kingdom.

Jeremy Ottewell

Copyright © 2022 Jeremy Ottewell

All rights reserved

The characters and events portrayed in this book are fictitious. Any similarity to real persons, living or dead, is coincidental and not intended by the author.

No part of this book may be reproduced, or stored in a retrieval system, or transmitted in any form or by any means, electronic, mechanical, photocopying, recording, or otherwise, without express written permission of the publisher.

Cover. The Entrance into Constantinople of Roger de Flor, Commander of the Grand Catalan Company of Almogavers, by José Moreno Carbonero, 1888.

*To Lisa, Livvy and Luke, who have stood
by me throughout this project.*

CONTENTS

Title Page
Copyright
Dedication
Foreword
Map of the main movements of The Grand Catalan Company of Almogavers and important battle sites (cou

PROLOGUE	1
CHAPTER ONE	5
CHAPTER TWO	18
CHAPTER THREE	38
CHAPTER FOUR	46
CHAPTER FIVE	55
CHAPTER SIX	73
CHAPTER SEVEN	78
CHAPTER EIGHT	84
CHAPTER NINE	94
CHAPTER TEN	105
CHAPTER ELEVEN	113
CHAPTER TWELVE	123
CHAPTER THIRTEEN	140
CHAPTER FOURTEEN	143
CHAPTER FIFTEEN	147
CHAPTER SIXTEEN	154
CHAPTER SEVENTEEN	157

CHAPTER EIGHTEEN	166
CHAPTER NINETEEN	171
CHAPTER TWENTY	176
CHAPTER TWENTY-ONE	185
CHAPTER TWENTY-TWO	192
CHAPTER TWENTY-THREE	206
CHAPTER TWENTY-FOUR	213
CHAPTER TWENTY-FIVE	224
CHAPTER TWENTY-SIX	234
CHAPTER TWENTY-SEVEN	245
CHAPTER TWENTY-EIGHT	254
CHAPTER TWENTY-NINE	266
CHAPTER THIRTY	273
CHAPTER THIRTY-ONE	280
CHAPTER THIRTY-TWO	291
CHAPTER THIRTY-THREE	301
Epilogue	307
Afterword	309

FOREWORD

There is a historical account of this period at the end of the book but please be warned that it contains spoilers if you should read it first.

MAP OF THE MAIN MOVEMENTS OF
THE GRAND CATALAN COMPANY OF
ALMOGAVERS AND IMPORTANT BATTLE SITES
(COURTESY OF *BYZANTINE MILITARY*)

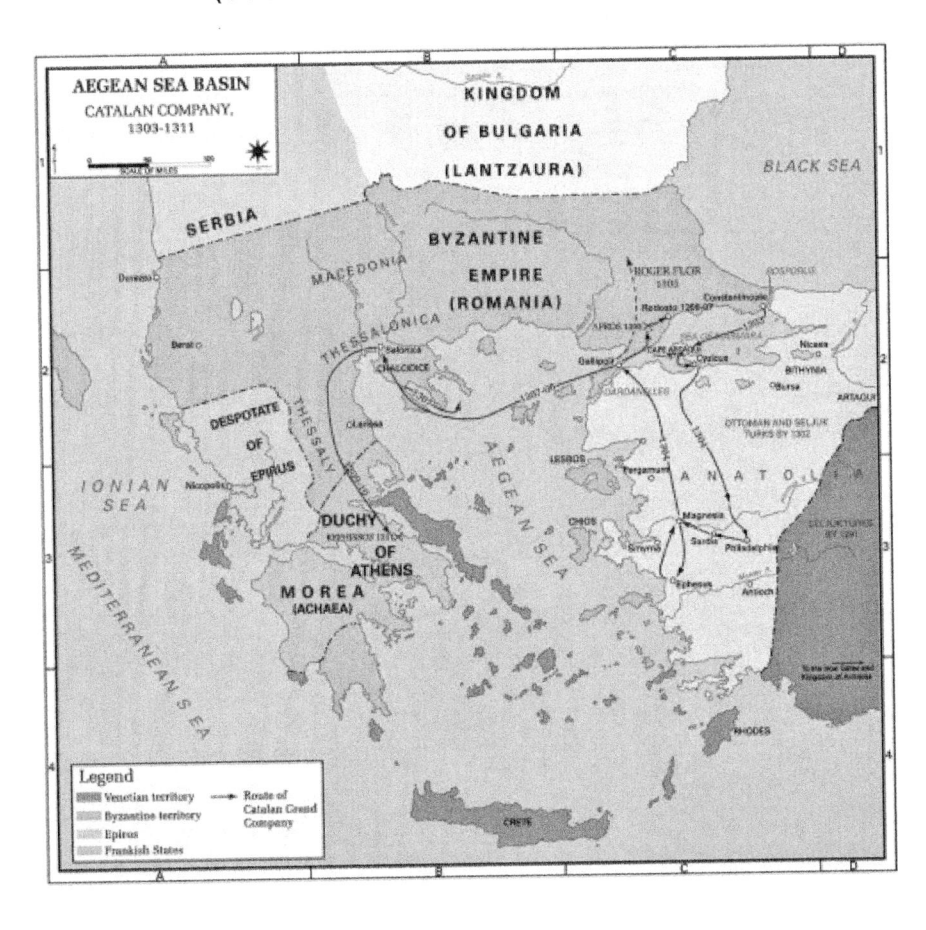

PROLOGUE

Hear me, for I am Ramon Muntaner and I have set down in my Chronicle the great deeds of the Kings of the House of Barcelona, Kings of Catalunya Aragón. Between the years of 1260 and 1320, King Jaume I, his son King Pere II and in due time, his son King Jaume II ruled with the grace of God and did His will through their dominions and were greater than Roland, Tristan, Lancelot and King Arthur of the Round Table. Let their deeds be a mirror for other kings and my history be a warning for those who would be kings. For great strife is engendered when we seek to meddle in God's work for our own petty ends, be we kings, popes, or paupers, such as ourselves. Everyone, great or small, has a reason and a price and it takes wisdom to resist temptation, to be ruled by what is right, to know when one has enough and to steer a good course.

King Jaume I the Conqueror was a mighty king regaining Valencia from Islam for Christendom and adding it to his kingdoms of Catalunya and Aragón. Yet he made one error. On his death, he divided his kingdom, giving Catalunya, Aragón and Valencia to his elder son, King Pere, who ruled in the cities of Barcelona, Zaragoza and Valencia. To his younger son, Jaume, he gave Majorca: therefore, King Jaume of Majorca, ruled in Palma de Majorca and Perpinyà. This city is called Perpignan in French and is already too close to mighty France, to our north. France was for years bound by marriage with the Royal House of Barcelona and it was so even in my own lifetime. Yet the Capets, the Royal House of France, now seek to meddle in our affairs for the benefit of their princes, namely the House of Anjou. Shall I tell you why? To satisfy the vanity of one of these princes, Charles of Anjou, and for the love of a woman.

For the wife of Charles of Anjou, Beatrice was one of the four daughters of Ramón Berenguer IV, Count of Provence, of the House of Barcelona. All four daughters were beautiful beyond compare. Yet Beatrice was said to be the most exquisite of them all and she alone was the only one who was not a queen. Beautiful, powerful and wealthy though she was, she complained bitterly to her husband about this and so the seed of a wicked desire was planted in him. For he sought a kingdom to please her and the Pope, Clement IV, who had his own reasons for doing so, was pleased to grant him the Dual Crown of Sicily in 1266 so that he reigned in Palermo and Naples.

Terrible strife was thereby engendered, as King Pere II, whose heroism and tragedy I shall recount, had for his queen the rightful heir of Sicily, Queen Constança, and once he was King of Catalunya Aragón and Valencia, he asserted her right to the throne, as the last surviving heir of the Hohenstaufen dynasty, the rightful heirs to the throne. He invaded Sicily and won it for his queen. Yet this was done because the Pope hated the Hohenstaufen dynasty because they were of the House of the Holy Roman Emperors, who vied for power with the papacy. Half of Europe was for the Pope and half was for the Holy Roman Emperor and Charles of Anjou wanted a kingdom to satisfy his wife's desire to be a queen.

What can I say? These were personal hatreds, desires and ambitions, causes unworthy of starting a war. However, the Pope preached a Crusade and war was declared against King Pere and he was excommunicated by the Pope and had to fight the invasion of his own kingdom by France in a most unjust Holy War against him. Even his own brother, King Jaume of Majorca, plotted with the French against him. For the devil lurks even behind Holy Mother Church and though there are many questions that I cannot answer, such as why the Pope wanted to curb the power of the Roman Empire in the east at Constantinople, you will hear how God's anger was against the French and the Pope for this. What more can I say? King Pere is now known as King Pere the Great. Charles of Anjou became King Charles I of Naples as half the kingdom he was offered was wrested from him and he had to be contented with Naples, the other half of the dual crown, while Sicily rid themselves of him and went to their natural queen, Constança. Thus, King Charles' wife, Beatrice of Provence, became a queen, but of a smaller crown than she had imagined, not the dual crown of Sicily but of Naples alone. Because of their wickedness and selfish plotting, they lost Sicily itself, the jewel of their kingdom, and died young. Pope Clement died but two years after offering, but failing to deliver, the dual crown of Sicily.

Now I must stop talking about the Pope and would-be kings and queens and tell you the story of a simple man like you and I. For I have watched him grow from boy to man and I feel I know him well. His name is Joseph Goodman, for that is the name his mother gave him but he is known here in Catalunya as Pere Josep Bonhom for the great services he did King Pere the Great. I know him well for we were schooled together and served shield by shield in the army and I watched him in his struggle to discover his true identity for he did not know his father. I have seen him over the years strive to rise in the service of men who inspired him deeply, his knight Pedro de Ayerbe and King Pere the Great. I watched him rise in King Pere's esteem. Suffice it to say here that when King Pere restored his wife to the throne of Sicily, this young man was there at many decisive moments in that story.

Even before Pere became king, Josep witnessed how he drowned his half-brother Ferran Sanchis when he sought to raise a rebellion of Aragón nobles against him. He witnessed the arrival of the first ambassadors from the Hafsid Kingdom of North Africa in the Drassanes of Barcelona before King Pere embarked on his mission to Sicily. Josep it was who subdued the French spy who was burning the ships in Port Fangós the very night before King Pere's fleet set sail for Sicily. We served together in Sicily and I was with him the night he set sail for Catona from Messina when his overladen boat went down and he was thought drowned.

Shall I tell you how he survived, even though you may not believe me? He was in the water fighting for his life for three days. By the grace of God, he was washed up on a beach on the island of Formentera and was rescued by a woman named Eulàlia, who was living alone on the island, and he stayed there with her for half a year. He fell in love with her and yearned to be able to stay with her but devotion drove him back to Catalunya. He was with King Pere on the Pass of Panissars between Catalunya and his treacherous brother's kingdom when the French army withdrew in tatters at the end of the so-called Holy Crusade against our country. Not much later, he was with King Pere in Vilafranca just hours before he died.

Now to rejoin our tale of the travels of Josep. In King Pere's will, Josep has been rewarded for his services to the king with a name given him by the king as well as a small stipend and a property in Trapani, Sicily. He arrived there some weeks ago and wishes to stay there and continue his service to Queen Constança and Prince Jaume in Sicily. The queen is still regent there until the coronation takes place of Alfons in Barcelona and Jaume in Sicily. Yet before Josep settles there, his heart tells him he must see Eulàlia, or Lali, again. He has arrived in Formentera to find her and ensure the woman he loves is not abandoned as his own mother was. What can I say? His heart skips a beat when he sees her. The woman he loves is heavy with child. It can only be his child. And she is fishing.

CHAPTER ONE

December, 1285.

"Do not let any of them get away!" Lali said, spearing a large mullet that was flopping its way back to the shoreline. "They may be all I have for a good while and I'll have to..."

"Hang them to dry?" Josep asked. "Is that what you were going to say? Lali, I'm back. I'm going to help you. I'm not going to leave you."

There was something in her look, half disbelief, half joy as if she could not or would not allow herself to believe what was happening.

"Do not worry about that right now. Let's just get these fish. It's hard for me to move these days and I've been at this since before dawn to catch the fish while they're still sleepy," she said.

Josep saw how heavy with child she was and decided not to say what had been on his lips to say. He picked up the spear and started working quickly.

They exchanged grunts, gestures and commands and he let himself be told what to do because he knew he was back in her place, the place where she had rescued him now more than a year ago. This was her place, he reminded himself. Yes, he had taught her things, among them this technique for catching fish, but this stretch of beach, the vantage point he had seen her from, the cave where they had lived, where she had nursed him back to life after his days of ordeal at sea, all these places were in fact hers.

"You survived very well without me," he said smiling when they had all the fish.

"Do you mean before or after you arrived?" she said.

"I'm saying I'm happy to be here but I can see you're managing just fine."

She looked at him in a way that showed he was missing the point.

"I am fine, Josep, but I'm having your baby and I was wondering if and when you might come back and look after me as my options here are limited."

He laughed. That was a little sharp, he thought.

"How long have you known?" he asked pointlessly, realising the baby was coming when it came.

She shot him a look.

"I missed my menses the month you left," she said, "so the baby is due quite soon, I think."

"My timing is impeccable!" he said.

"If anything is impeccable, it's going to be me, the birth and the baby," she said.

"Yes, of course!" It was all he could think to say. He was there just in time, he thought, but who did he think was responsible for this situation? Lali had been reticent for them to become lovers in the full sense of the word. He tried to make the mental adjustments necessary as quickly as he could and nodded to cover his embarrassment at appearing slow.

"What do you need me to do?" he said.

"Now, that's more like it!" she replied. "For a start, take the fish and prepare them for drying. I'm cold and tired and need to rest. The baby has been kicking a lot recently and I'm not sleeping well."

"When did you last eat?" he asked.

She looked at him, turned white and then green, then ran off to the water's edge and started retching. He ran to her and gave her fresh water. When she had recovered, they walked in silence back up the beach and picked their way up the rocks to the cave.

She got undressed as if he were not there, dried herself and lay down under a skin and within seconds was asleep. He was reassured when she reached for him and he lay with her, remembering the intense warmth and intimacy of her lovely naked body. He had missed her terribly. Yet he knew what she needed from him right then, apart from his warmth, was to look after her and her baby. Their baby, he corrected himself, though he considered she clearly felt it was hers more than theirs at present. She was going to be a mother and he was going to be a father and that was going to be a challenge. He knew she had been ready and able to do it on her own and she was relieved to see him but was she happy to see him? He saw it did not matter. She was the one who was going to have the baby and he had to be there to make sure it all went without problems. That was his role now. He was the help, the safety net, the provider, because, as she had said, her options were limited. To say the least, he thought. That showed her state of mind: ironic at the very least if not hostile towards him, because she was about to bring forth a new life she had known would come and she had to make sure it thrived. He wondered if she had any idea whether it was a girl or a boy. She probably knew because she always seemed to know that sort of thing. But that did not matter, either.

He nodded off, feeling he was where he should be, a little nervous but confident he was up to the task and responsibility, enjoying the warmth they were sharing.

"I'm starving!" she said suddenly. "I haven't felt hungry like this for ages. I normally cannot sleep because I'm cold, then I roll over onto my side and get to sleep and wake up with awful stomach burn."

"But do you have it now?" he said, a little confused and wanting to do whatever she wanted. She looked at him blearily but smiled.

"No, for the first time, I do not. Something must have changed."

He resisted the temptation to take the credit and she chuckled to herself because she could read him like a book.

"You haven't changed," she said and he smiled back. But he thought he had changed. He felt he had been through a great deal but he said nothing. Maybe that meant he had changed, he thought, because in the past he might have said something.

"Can I get you something?" he said as cautiously as he could. "Yes, but use your imagination, please!" she murmured. "I do not want anything with fish in it and I do not want to smell any fish and I do not want you to make it anywhere in the cave or where I could possibly smell it, all right? It's my turn to be looked after now, all right?"

He laughed and stroked her face and felt the warmth in her body flood into him. "I'll be as quick as I can," he said.

"Yes, hurry back or I'll get cold again," she said.

He piled as many rugs and skins on top of her as he could, kissed her on the forehead and murmured something about getting back beside her while it was cooking. She seemed to be ignoring him, but then he heard her snoring. He was glad she was asleep again.

◆ ◆ ◆

When the baby arrived less than two weeks later, Lali was so practical that it was a lesson in how to give birth alone, even though Josep was there. It was a girl. They were in the water bathing when there was a gush of blood between her legs. She knew what was happening but he thought something was wrong.

"Just help me out of the water!" she said. But they did not get that far. They were only in up to their knees and within two or three steps, she leant forwards and her face started to contort.

"She's coming, Josep!" She grabbed her knees through the water. "Hold me up and do not let me go under!" she gasped.

She threw her head back and screamed, long and hard, screwed up her eyes, opened them wide and stared wide-eyed at Josep. Then she grabbed his head with such ferocity he thought she was going mad.

"She's coming!" she kept saying. She gave a low grunt, there was a rush of blood again in the water and what looked like a white bag on a string appeared in the water next to her. He did not know for an instant what was going on and she looked at him with disbelief and terror in her eyes.

"Josep, get the baby out of the water, for God's sake!" she hissed. She let go of his head and hair and he linked an arm under her armpit to support her, then grabbed the bundle and held it to himself. They stumbled out of the water trailing the loop of the umbilical cord between them as they walked and she pointed at the knife.

"You have to cut the cord!" she said. "Haven't you ever seen this before? Cut the cord with the knife as close as you can to the baby without cutting the baby, too."

He grabbed the knife and unsheathed it. It was a Catalan *coltell*, brutal, somewhere between a cleaver and a fish knife. It was well kept, clean and very sharp. He looked at her in horror.

"That is what we have to do," she said. "She is out of me now. She has to be separated from me. She has to breathe on her own. Cut the cord, Josep."

He cut the cord. There was a spurt of blood and his head span and he had to struggle not to fall down. He thought for a split second he had killed the little girl.

"Well done," Lali said. "You did a nice neat cut. She won't complain when she is older."

He stared at her in disbelief, then his mouth twisted into a manic grin, his eyes bulging.

"Is she all right," he asked.

"Yes, but you have to smack her on the bottom to get her to breathe!"

"You're serious!"

"Yes, smack her on the bottom!"

He smacked her quite hard. There was a sharp wet slap.

"Again!" she said.

This time, the baby girl flung her arms out to the side, grabbed onto his left arm, in which he was cradling her, with her little fingers and pulled her legs up to her chest. She put her head back and let out a loud cry. Josep's instinct took over then. He rested her tiny body on the palm of his left hand and wiped her little mouth, from where blood and mucous were dripping. He looked at her with her blue eyes screwed up in a howl, turned her over and looked at her unfeasibly small body covered in blood and greasy white slime and he thought, "This is my daughter!" To himself almost secretly he said "I'm going to look after you and do my best to make you happy!"

"Josep, support her head! Stop daydreaming! Give her to me!" said Lali. Her fierceness caught him by surprise.

"We need to wrap her up. She's getting cold already, can you not see?" she said, not even looking at him.

Lali took her from him before he could answer, nestled her to herself and started to rock her gently. The little girl's colour changed in seconds as they watched and a thumb went into her mouth.

Josep wrapped her in the cloths and skins they had to hand and the baby became a formless bundle.

"Josep, isn't she gorgeous? I cannot believe it. She's fine. Look at her! She looks like me! She's got my eyes! I'd kill for that colour hair!"

It did not take long to get mother and child comfortable in the cave, a fire going, food ready for Lali for whenever. An hour after the birth, Lali tried her on the breast and the tiny infant latched on immediately. Lali looked blissfully happy and triumphant for a moment then had a far-away look of absolute and total serenity and fulfilment. She and her baby were going to be fine. Her man had been adequate. That was all she had wanted. He was a bit slow sometimes but he had done fine.

"Are you all right?" Josep asked.

"Yes, we are fine. And you?" Lali replied.

"I'm fine," he said, smiling.

"Well done. You did fine," she said.

"Thanks. Do you need anything?"

"I think I'll just lie here with her. Maybe she will want to feed again in a minute. That is quite a journey she has made."

"Yes, you too," he said, though he thought it sounded silly and he did not want to annoy Lali.

"Thanks," she laughed.

"I'll cover you so you do not get cold. I mean either of you, all right?"

He tucked the various coverings more snuggly around them, she settled more comfortably and he squeezed her hand. She smiled up at him.

"Thanks. You're doing a good job. Sorry if I sometimes seem moody. I'm tired and anxious about her," she said.

He smiled. They gave each other a shy kiss as if it might disturb the baby and laughed.

Ten minutes later, Lali and the baby were both asleep, there was a crackle from the fire and he could hear the waves. He felt for a moment as if time had stopped.

"It's not even dusk yet," he thought. "A couple of hours still till the sun goes down. What is the date today? December the seventh. It is going to be a beautiful evening. I am happy."

❖ ❖ ❖

"How did you know she was a girl?" he asked her later.

"Women just know these things," she said simply. "Besides, she was lying quite low in my belly and that's a sign that it's a girl."

"It's cold in here, isn't it?" he said, mystified. "I think I'll build up the fire, it's going to get colder too, I can feel the chill on that wind just outside the cave. We will be fine for a couple of weeks and the weather will continue to be all right during the day but it is going to get much colder. Do you think there's anywhere else better that we could go to?"

"This is the best place for us. It is the only place I can think of," she replied.

"Yes, but I mean my mother lives in Sant Pere de Ribes just south of Barcelona."

She looked at him expectantly as if she did not know what to say.

"She lives in a large, comfortable house with several other people, it's warm there in winter, there's plenty of food and it's safe," he said.

"But how would we get there?" she said.

"Well, that's the complicated thing," he said, "We would have to take a boat between here and Eivissa, then to Majorca and then from Majorca to Barcelona. That's the way I came anyway and then I went to Sicily but while I was coming over, I was with a lot of troops of King Alfons preparing to attack his uncle, King Jaume of Majorca, who refuses to accept him as his sovereign the way that he had accepted his father."

"That doesn't sound too good, then," she said, "I think we should avoid Majorca at all costs!"

"Yes," he said, "it would depend on us taking a boat from Eivissa directly to Barcelona."

"And how are you going to organise that?"

"Good question!" he said.

She looked at him for a moment expectantly.

"We're warm enough here at the moment and we are definitely safe." she said, coughing into her hand to disguise her surprise at Josep.

"Nobody knows about us and all we have to do is to provide warmth and food for the baby. That has to be our main concern at the moment. Also, the weather at sea is unpredictable at this time of the year."

"Yes," he said, "it was bad enough coming over in early December. I do not really think the weather at sea is going to improve for at least another couple of months."

She nodded intensely.

"So we have a war raging in Majorca, on the one hand, and we have heavy seas on the other hand. I think we had better stay here for the time being!"

"Yes," he said, "maybe you're right."

She shook her head as if to close this silly conversation.

"Yes, I really think I am, actually. Anyway, I can make this cave comfortable," she said, changing the subject. "I've been here for years. I have plenty of skins and furs that we can use. I bank up the fire. I generally eat more but now that I have you here, you can devote yourself to those things while I devote myself to the baby."

Just at that moment Pauly, her rabbit, jumped into the cave.

"Oh my goodness," Josep said, "I did not know you still had the rabbit."

"Oh, yes, Pauly is a frequent visitor. He comes and goes but we're the best of friends. We just have one stipulation. When you go hunting for food, you do not hunt for rabbit!"

"That's a deal," said Josep. "I think I'll be able to get enough fish. I can improve the nets that you've been using. They work well but the reach could be made a little wider."

"Fine!" she said, "It was your idea in the first place and it has worked well so far." He nodded expectantly, keen to hear praise. She looked down momentarily.

At that point, the baby woke up. She was lying on her back so Lali started cleaning her. She took off the skins and when she had finished put a little cloth around her and let her just lie there in the warmth of the cave. The little girl looked up and seemed to smile. Lali laughed.

"I cannot believe it! I think she recognises me already. Oh, she's so lovely."

She picked her up and put her to her breast and the little girl started sucking immediately. Lali flushed with colour and looked at Josep.

"I'm so happy and I love her so much," she said.

The fire was starting to die down and they needed more wood so Josep went into the woods to fetch more. There was plenty that had fallen or that could be chopped down easily. The sun was just going down on the horizon to his left as he walked back towards the cave.

"Right now, my life couldn't get any better than this." But he started wondering how he was going to feed Lali over the next couple of months, especially if she did not want to eat only fish.

He knew that she had a storage area just outside the cave which she had developed since he had been gone and discovered in the cavities and holes in the rocks various compartments. He found fruit: figs, grapes, some almonds and hazelnuts in one hole. In another, he found some freshly ground wild wheat flour. He knew it was wild wheat because there were still whole grains in the flour with their sharp, long bracts and next to them some carob seeds, which he knew he could grind down as well to make a sweet flour.

He mixed the wheat flour with some fruit and made it into a paste, then added a drop of the primitive wine that Lali made from the island's grapes and then made patties on a hot boulder that he pulled out of the fire and took outside the cave. He used some more of the flour to make himself some patties but this time he added a little salt water and prepared some dried fish for himself. When he had finished, he went back into the cave and sat down next to Lali who was lying there contentedly with the baby asleep in her arms.

"I've brought you some food," he said.

"Oh, it doesn't have any fish in it, does it? she said.

"No, mine does but I do not think you'll even be able to smell it."

"Just as well!" she said.

◆ ◆ ◆

The next few days followed a similar pattern. Lali was quite contented to look after the baby. Occasionally, she left the cave in order to wash and to stretch her legs but she was perfectly happy to allow Josep the run of the camp and reminded him where the larger water cistern was, where to find the best fruit and where to find repair materials for the fishing nets.

The weather was pristine. The mornings always began bright and sunny, the sun was now lower in the sky and its strength was noticeably diminished but, for all that, it gave them enough warmth but they knew within a week it would get cooler. When the sun went down, Josep busied himself maintaining stores, making sure that he harvested enough of all the different foods that Lali had carefully and cleverly organised around the camp and even decided to experiment with what he concluded was wild pumpkin. He was able to prepare a kind of wild spinach from the leaves and reserved the pumpkins for their flesh and to be used as water vessels.

He also spent a lot of time repairing and developing the fishing nets. The three original ones that they had made the previous year were still functioning reasonably well but the binding was becoming loose between the woven grass ropes that formed the weft and some of the gaps were becoming too large to be able to trap many of the smaller fish. Finding suitable materials for repairing these nets was something that only he could do and he knew he had to venture far and wide to find them. One day, about two weeks after the birth, he left everything ready for Lali and set out early in the morning before the sun was fully up and made his way east along the island shoreline and started climbing towards La Mola at the far eastern end of the island. This was where the woods were at their most dense and where he and Lali had found the materials for the fishing nets a year ago. The raw materials were there, of course, just as they had been a year ago but it was heavy work especially on his own and several hours later, although he finally had all the materials that he needed to repair the nets, he was exhausted.

It took him an hour to put everything in a bundle that he could carry back to the camp and when he arrived the sun was just about to set. Lali took one look at him and screamed.

"Josep! What's happened? Have you been in a fight? Have you had a problem with a wild animal or something?"

"No," he replied calmly, "I've just been in the forest all day and did not wear enough protective clothing and I did not have anything on my feet and I was climbing trees and chopping down branches and I did not notice at the time because I was working hard and I was hot. I just got scratched up. I'm absolutely fine. How are you two?"

"Fine!" she said. "You won't have to go back now, will you?"

"No," he said.

"I missed you. I actually got a little scared during the day when you did not get back. I thought you'd be back in the middle of the afternoon."

"I was up near La Mola in the middle of the forest so I did not notice I had lost track of time but I think I've got everything I need. I do not think I need to go back there again soon. I think I can work here now with the nets over the next few weeks."

He started the next day. To repair the nets, he twisted the vines using a stake fixed firmly in the ground and then pulled out the vines as far as he could before tying off the ends when he felt that he couldn't make the rope stretch out any further. With these different lengths of plaited vine rope he then made longer pieces of rope by tying them end to end and then proceeded first to repair the nets and then, discovering that he had plenty left, he made a fourth net barrier. These were very simple, about five feet high and eight feet long made of four pieces of wood in a rectangle. He cut the shorter vertical ones into spikes at the ends and cut the longer horizontal ones into shafts at the top and the bottom. He bound these rods together. Within this frame, he attached vertical strips of rope, which he then interlaced with longer horizontal strips, leaving holes which would be big enough to allow the fish through but small enough to stop the fish getting out again. This design had worked well for Lali, even using it by herself but he saw that he would be able to extend the range of the fishing area by using a fourth frame, too. He left the fishing frames for three days in the sun to dry and tighten up and then experimented with them a week later.

CHAPTER TWO

The sea was getting noticeably rougher as December progressed and with the waves came the wind. It was colder than it had been when he arrived but he was able to stake out the four frames and he was reasonably satisfied that the volume of fish he was able to trap and then drive up onto the shore was greater than it had been previously. He wondered at Lali's fierceness of spirit and independence that she had been able to manage the three frames and provide for herself for the eight months that he had been gone and saw just how necessary the drying process was because fishing was not the kind of labour that one could embark on every day, especially not now that she had the baby. He soon realised that he was able every time he went fishing to provide them with enough fish for at least a week if not two. It also meant that he had to build more fish drying frames.

A month had passed since the birth and the baby was thriving. Lali was eating enough of the different things that Josep was able to find for her and after a month started to find her appetite for fish again. She told Josep where the best water reservoirs were. These were natural cavities in the limestone around the island that she knew about and had known about since her earliest days on the island. They were of different sizes, the smaller ones she called *cubelles* or buckets in Catalan and the larger ones she called *sitges* or cisterns and they were simply natural fissures in the rock where rainwater collected. These were so small sometimes that you had to lower a cup on a rope to get to the water or if you were lucky there was enough room at the top of the hole to be able to lower a bucket into the water but sometimes they were actually big enough for even someone Josep's size to be able to squeeze through and get into the cavity where the water was deposited. These of course had always existed but improvements could always be made, for example, to stop small animals, vegetable matter or simply grit and stones from falling in, by covering them. In some cases, this was necessary as if you did so you were able to stop the water evaporating during the hotter months of summer. Josep also noticed that there were various other natural water basins that he could develop by covering them. They were about three feet deep by three feet wide and he was able to find suitable pieces of wood to cover them that were large enough to be strapped together to stop the water becoming contaminated or evaporating.

Just days after his discovery of several such large water basins, he deliberately left the coverings off all the water deposits big and small and the first rains of the winter started to fall so that water collected in them. He then systematically went around them all replacing the covers. They always boiled the water in order to make sure that it was totally clean but the first night that rain fell, it completely filled the deposits that John had discovered and he came back with enough water in one trip to completely fill the small basin containing about ten buckets that they had near the camp. Of course, they also left the top off this during the rainy season so that it filled naturally whenever it rained and the water was cool and instantly usable as it had only just fallen.

Lali seemed to grow more and more contented as the rainy season progressed. Between rainy days there were always sunny days and on those sunny days everything had such a clean, polished, limpid look that it made up for the cold of the rainy days. Also, having plenty of water and not having to use only salt water to wash helped in the care of the baby and meant that she did not always have to go down to the sea to bathe as there was always plenty to wash in.

The fire was always banked high and even though they felt the chill in the late afternoon and evening, they were always snug in their cave by the end of the day when they settled down to go to sleep. The baby was breastfeeding well and was beginning to grow and put on weight. Whenever her clothes were taken off, she lay there and kicked happily, held things in her little hands and looked up at her adoring mother and father. She seemed to smile at them and they felt very contented and as if they needed nothing else.

As January progressed into February, the weather worsened again and storms blew up frequently and even made it difficult to have large fires just inside the cave entrance as they had done before. Josep built a windbreak following the design of his fishing net barriers to keep out the wildest gusts of the wind and to a certain extent this also protected them from flying sparks and embers from the fire blown in by the wind but work needed to be done on the fire area if they were going to keep warm enough. Josep constructed a second wind barrier similar to the first one, which he cleverly arranged in a staggered formation at the front of the cave so that, just like at the back of the cave they had the false wall where they could retire when the weather was at its worst, they also now had at the front of the cave two sets of screens with the right and the left edges of the respective screens overlapping so that they actually had to turn in order to leave the cave. At the beginning of that small turn, Josep hung an assortment of old skins to stop the wind coming in even further. This was good but it restricted the light in the cave during the day and so he developed the fire pit as well. He dug it deeper, put bigger stones at the bottom and was able to fill it to a depth of about two feet full of wood. This not only gave them more heat but also more light.

There is no doubt that they could have continued living like this with John making improvements and improvisations whenever the need arose. He could fish even in the worst weather at least once a week and they were never short of fish but as the winter wore on, their store of fruit, including figs, carefully left to dry, began to diminish. Towards the end of February, he knew that at the end of March things would start to change but the month of March itself was complicated. They were reduced to eating a diet of only fish and small amounts of patties made from the final reserves of wild wheat. Then the food stores ran so low that they had to start making broth out of the carob seeds as well as grinding these into a sweet flour to make patties. They had enough food for two, especially as the baby was still breastfeeding, but they couldn't help thinking about how they were going to manage when the baby started eating more solid food, which was going to happen sooner rather than later and definitely sooner than they could for example get any kind of organised crop cultivation going. This was only going to get worse as the baby grew in its infancy, started walking and needed to eat greater amounts of more nourishing food.

It was the middle of March when the baby was three months old that she started to use her hands to move around and pick things up. They inevitably decided that if there was an alternative they should at least be thinking about it. Josep of course had absolutely no idea how things had developed in Majorca, which had kept them on the island in the first place. However, as the weather was finally beginning to improve, just around his own birthday at the end of March, he decided that he would investigate the possibility of taking a boat from Formentera to Eivissa. This was a small expedition but of course it required planning as he would be gone for at least a day but when he came back it was only to say that only small boats were making the crossing at the moment and they would have to wait at least a month until the larger boats started coming between Formentera and Eivissa.

As the weather improved, the notion of actually moving from a cave where their resources were extremely limited to a real home with as much variety of different types of food as one could imagine became compelling. For all the attraction that that life might appear to have from the outside, the idea contained the added advantage of increased safety. Of course, Lali had an innate sense of what her baby needed. However, perhaps she was also beginning to imagine having some more company even though she would never have claimed that she missed it: company for herself and company and stimulation for her baby.

She began to be more and more inquisitive about Josep's mother and asked Josep more questions than ever about how his mother, an English woman, had ended up finding herself in the heart of Catalunya a thousand miles from where she was from and hundreds of miles from her last closest contact. But this gave John the opportunity to tell her in greater detail than ever and perhaps for the first time about his mother's origins and how she was born in the south of England in a county called Cornwall and at the age of eighteen had had the opportunity to go and serve the Seneschal of Bordeaux, Sir John de Grailly and his wife in Bordeaux. This part of Aquitaine was an English possession and it was because her father was a senior officer in the Duke of Cornwall's army that he was acquainted with the de Graillys in Bordeaux.

Lali of course wanted to hear about many details that John just couldn't explain to her, for example how her relationship had been with Sir John's wife and Joseph said that he believed that it became quite complicated because she had started seeing the man who would become Josep's father and Sir John Grailly, though he understood the situation, was naturally discreet and was not keen for this relationship to become common knowledge. Little by little, Lali filled in the spaces herself and explained to John that perhaps Sir John de Grailly's wife suspected that some kind of relationship was developing between his mother Catharine Morris and Sir John de Grailly himself. The problem was that for the sake of his reputation and decorum, Sir John could not explain the situation completely clearly to his wife and that secrecy itself caused her to suspect him of having more than a professional relationship with Josep's mother. This of course meant that Lady de Grailly became cooler and cooler to Catharine so that when Catharine eventually did fall pregnant she did not feel that she could turn to other women in her life and although she had friends among the other employees in the Grailly household, she soon realised that the longer she hesitated to leave, now visibly pregnant, the more embarrassing and therefore difficult the situation was going to be. This was the case not only for her but for everyone around her and so, one early morning, she left.

She made her way to Barcelona and then from Barcelona to Sant Pere de Ribes in order to see the man who had introduced her to her lover in the first place. Here the story from Josep became even more complicated because he had to explain that for years even when he first met Lali, he had not known who that man was. He had not known the identity of his own father and it had not been to his own father that Catharine Morris had gone in Barcelona. It had been to find the man who had introduced Josep's father to Catharine and that man was Josep's godfather. Josep had in passing explained several times who his godfather was. That his name was Jacques de Molay and he was now the Grand Master of the Knights Templar. He then had to explain why his mother had not simply stayed in Barcelona and waited for Jacques de Molay. That was because she had been told that there was a midwife in Sant Pere de Ribes who knew de Molay and whose family had known Jacques de Molay for years. He had been known to her brothers and cousins when old King Jaume was still carrying out his reconquest of the Kingdom of Valencia in the years prior to Josep's birth in 1266 and they had all served in King Jaume's crusader army, as the Reconquest was a Holy War against Islam.

These conversations took entire evenings and Josep had to answer all of Lali's questions and had to go over certain points again and again. However, Josep refused to reveal who his father actually was until it was absolutely clear what were the circumstances that had led his mother to finding herself in Sant Pere de Ribes. He explained how it was that she had all those years ago found herself on the doorstep of a beautiful and prosperous farmhouse in the middle of the Catalan countryside asking, in broken French, the occupant of the house to believe her when she told her that she knew who she was, that she was a friend of Jacques de Molay's and that she needed her help.

It was hard for him initially to explain why it was that Clara was so cold to his mother at first and nearly turned her away. Yet luckily he was to discover that he did not need to explain those details to Lali because she was perfectly aware of how the situation must have been both for Clara and for Catharine. She seemed to understand intuitively when Josep started to explain that Clara was a well-to-do single Catalan woman who had seen her father and brothers die over the course of her life and had inherited not only the family farm, Can Baró de la Cabreta, in Sant Pere de Ribes, but also a whole host of other problems that came with the farm.

None the least of these was who were the family of Muslims who lived in and around her property whose family could trace their origins back hundreds of years to a ruined property not a hundred metres from where the farm stood. Not to mention Bru Miret. Josep had not spoken to Lali of him but now felt that it was inevitable that he would have to explain to Lali who Bru was, an Almogaver, and a cousin of Clara's and a frequent visitor to the farm.

Lali, being Catalan herself, knew exactly what an Almogaver was: a brutal killing machine, who killed for booty, never settled down and, in her opinion, never had relationships and never changed. Josep had to explain how his relationship with Bru Miret had developed over the years before he was taken away from Bru Miret's influence to be schooled as a young gentleman under the guidance of Jacques de Molay, who became his patron and benefactor. It took days and days and weeks and weeks to communicate and clarify all this information and though it was difficult for Josep to explain and try to fill in all the blanks, he was amazed at how many details Lali was instantly able to remember and also the connections that she made between the different stories and the intuition that she showed about how all the different elements in the stories affected each other and the people involved. At the end of it, she said that she could clearly imagine Clara Miret, the landowner, because she had met people like her in her part of Catalunya although a hundred miles to the south of Sant Pere de Ribes. Where she was actually from was away from the coast and up in the hills right on the border with the Kingdom of Valencia and she had met people who were or sounded quite similar both to Clara and Bru Miret.

"Catalans do not like strangers!" she said. "If you are not a friend, even if you are recognised but are not introduced to someone, you are certainly not automatically given the benefit of the doubt. Far from being considered a friend, you are considered, quite the opposite, to be a natural enemy." When John shook his head and said he just did not understand why people are like that, she said Catalans considered themselves to be mountain people first and foremost.

"Your world is limited by what you can see upto the next hill and beyond that it's the outside world and trouble always comes from beyond the hills. Mountain people are used to living in small tightknit communities with all the problems that brings, and there are many, such as ignorance, interbreeding, cruelty, abject poverty, and the extent of their acceptance is people who at least speak their own language, Catalan."

Hence, she was able to understand completely how Clara nearly rejected Catharine when she came asking for her help and the only reason that she accepted her, even more than the fact that she was pregnant was because she claimed that she knew Jacques de Molay. He had years ago recommended Clara to Catharine and at that point, Clara immediately accepted Catharine and revealed the most extraordinary depth of generosity and friendship not only to her but also to Habiba, the last remaining survivor of the Muslim family who claimed to have lived near her property for centuries. Josep explained they suspected Bru Miret at one point of being responsible for the disappearance and murder of her husband and father. However, Josep then clarified that Bru, the last time that he had seen him in Clara's house in Sant Pere de Ribes, had sworn in front of Clara, Catharine his mother, himself and Habiba that he had absolutely nothing to do with the disappearance and murder of Habiba's menfolk.

It was therefore inevitable that they started talking about leaving again. The question was not whether but where and when.

"I have a little land and a beautiful, old farmhouse, though it's purely residential, not part of the working farm. It's quite basic but I think of it as home already. Wait till you see it!"

He set about convincing her to move to Sicily. They argued and wrangled. Lali cried and Josep became nervous he was going to lose her. The idea of leaving appealed to her but represented an emotional upheaval.

"Josep, I've just had a baby and besides, remember, I'm still married!" she said.

"We can have the marriage annulled on the grounds of estrangement. You simply do not know where your husband is any more. It's not so unusual and besides the Crown wants to populate Sicily. It's in their interests to allow us to marry," Josep argued.

"But we are going to see your mother, first, are we not? I need to meet her having talked so much about her and I need all the help I can get," she said.

"Yes, of course, and we can organise the annulment of your marriage," he said.

Once the decision had been made, there was little that needed to be done. Josep left for two days and found a boat direct to Barcelona from Eivissa. They stored their nets and other possessions in the inner cave and left with enough food to last them for two days. Pauly hopped up just as they were leaving.

"I do not know if I will be back," Lali said to him, petting his head. "This cave and island have been home to me and I am grateful to you. You have all have brought me good luck and a future is now clear to me."

She smiled at Josep and they hugged with the baby between them.

"Formentera will always be here in my heart. Thank you for looking after me," she said and wiped a tear from her eye. "Look after it all for me, Pauly, and take care." The rabbit hopped into their cave and they laughed and took it as a good omen.

She was a good sailor and stood at the aft of the ship looking into the churning waters and back at Formentera as it grew more distant and only the hill at La Mola could be seen. She had seen Eivissa many years before but enjoyed seeing again the impressive castle atop the hill from the sea, invisible from Formentera, even though you could usually see the smudge of the island on the horizon even from the cave.

They were able to pick up more food easily in the port and the passage to Barcelona was calm now that it was mid-April and uneventful. No one seemed surprised to see them together or asked them any but the most basic perfunctory questions.

As soon as they could see Montjuich in the distance as they approached Barcelona, Josep explained the story of the expedition to the Hafsid Kingdom in North Africa, the prelude to the invasion of Sicily. After they disembarked and Josep had found them transport to Sant Pere de Ribes, he explained a little where they were in Barcelona.

"That is the Drassanes, the Royal Shipyards," he said, as they passed nearby the monastery of the Framenors and the convent of Santa Madrona. "I actually saw the Hafsid delegation arrive there in secret in the middle of the night as I sat sleepily waiting for my knight to finish meeting with King Pere. It was the night before my sixteenth birthday. I did not know it at the time but that moment has marked the direction of my life ever since."

"I hope it becomes a little more peaceful for a while," commented Lali, holding the sleeping baby close to her. "We could all do with some rest and recuperation for a while, couldn't we?

"I am deliberately avoiding any official checkpoints. There are more of them to enter the city through the city gates than to leave it. We'll be out of the city quite soon."

"Good, because it smells terrible around here," Lali said. "If it were not for the strong sea wind, it would be appalling."

"Yes, I am afraid that's the Caganell. The city sewers drain into the marsh around here. We'll be past it soon. Have you not been to Barcelona before? I thought you had."

"No, remember I am from the south of Catalonia so I escaped my town of Ulldecona down the dry riverbed that nobody goes along as it can flood unexpectedly. I crossed into Valencia over the hills and took a boat from the city to Eivissa. I arrived in Valencia and boarded within a morning. You remember I was on the run. I do not remember much about the city at all, just the port. I was terrified of being stopped and sent back at any moment."

"Did they not check your papers?" Josep asked. It was the first time Lali had spoken about this and leaving Formentera and being back in Catalunya brought back memories.

"I stowed away, Josep. When they caught me, all I could do was beg and work for my crossing. So they made me work like a slave but it saved my life. It is not a period I choose to remember in detail."

"Sorry," said Josep. "That must have been horrible for you."

"It is not all bad. The past is the past, isn't it? And I have you and the baby now. Hopefully good luck will be on our side," she said. Josep considered for a moment whether he felt the past was simply the past. The last year, he had seen people again he hadn't seen since his childhood and the past had become a nightmare in the present. He said nothing but put his arm

round her tightly and kissed her and the baby.
They headed for Sant Pere de Ribes as soon as they arrived, eschewing all unnecessary contact for the present. Their carriage took them out of the city south along the Via Augusta and eventually they passed the sacred mountain of Montserrat, clear and bright in the early spring air and through the stark plain of the Penedès, the vines standing bare in the chilly breeze, liked massed ranks of soldiers standing ready for action.

"We can try to persuade Mother to come to live with us!" Josep said, reaching that conclusion for the first time. Lali stifled a laugh. For her, it was the most obvious notion in the world.
They turned seaward near Vilafranca with Josep explaining when he had last been there just before King Pere had died, passed Olerdola and Canyelles, then followed the riverbed as it winds its way through the woods around his town. The first thing they saw was the Hermitage of Sant Pau, where they crossed the bridge and headed for Sitges to Can Baró de la Cabreta.

"It is pretty around here, "said LaIi. "Small vineyards and hills, little ravines, pine forest, holm oak and carob trees. I love it!"
So many comments came into Josep's mind that he was for a few minutes unable to speak. He realised this was the first time he had been in the position of showing someone new around his town. There were so many things to explain and connections in his mind that he gave up. "I'll let you know all about everything little by little," he said. "Right now, If I tried, we would be here all night. They do not even know we are coming and you must be exhausted."

She nodded and said, "Yes, and our little Cat needs to be fed."
She had started calling her that over the last few days and Josep liked it. There was something cute and catlike about the little girl with the strawberry blond, whispy locks and the wide, dark, intelligent eyes that seemed to drink everything in without blinking.

They turned into the drive leading to Clara's masia.
"I can smell the sea again," said Lali.
Yes, it is just a mile away over that hill.
"What a beautiful farmhouse!" Lali said. From where they were just a few hundred feet from Can Baró de la Cabreta, the masia was framed by the surrounding vineyards, a low hill just behind the house and Montgrós, the mountain behind Sant Pere de Ribes in the mid-distance. It was late afternoon now, the day was clear and bright and the shadows were lengthening. There was a pink orange glow to their left from the southeast as the sun started its descent behind the hills. The familiarity and strangeness of the front of the house struck Josep as if he had never noticed the details even though it had not changed, the height and solidity of the perimeter wall, the large, well-maintained wooden gate and what he could see of the house behind the gate, its walls latticed with bougainvillea vines.

They bade farewell to the coachman and tipped him well, and knocked on the big old wooden door. Clara came and there was a momentary look of surprise she quickly disguised as she realised Josep had come accompanied. She greeted Josep formally, then turned before he could introduce Lali and called Catharine. Clara did not return until sometime later, realising the momentous occasion that was unfolding in her home.

"Mother, this is Lali. I have told you about her. And this is our baby," he said almost lost for words at that moment.

Catharine's delight at meeting Lali and her granddaughter and seeing Josep was overwhelming. She was crying from the moment she saw them, hugged Josep and kissed him all the time uttering words he could not hear. Then she kissed Lali on both cheeks. Lali started speaking to her in Catalan and beamed with pleasure when Catharine replied in kind.

"Quín nom li heu posat a la noia?" "What have you called the baby girl," she asked.

They had not talked about it more than a couple of times in passing but it now seemed the most important question of all.

"We have not decided yet," said Lali. "We were waiting till we arrived."

Josep nodded. They looked at each other. "Catarina," Lali said, "after you, Mother!" she said.

Catharine dissolved into tears now and took the baby Lali handed to her in her arms and looked at her face.

"Yes, I think she looks like a Catarina," Catharine said, smiling through her tears. She touched her nose and lips with a fingertip and the little girl grabbed her finger and put it in her mouth. They laughed.

"She is hungry," said Lali. "It was uncomfortable at times in the carriage, so she is due to be fed. Is there somewhere...?" She did not need to finish her sentence as Clara, the experienced midwife, was already anticipating her request. She stepped forward and led her into a secluded part of the garden where she could sit in the shade and offered her something to drink at the same time. Habiba appeared and politely welcomed the visitors in her traditional elaborate way with bows of the head and hand gestures to show respect and welcome to honoured guests then left they thought to help Clara. All three women had started to look similar, Josep decided now, wearing similar clothes, a long heavy cotton dress, a woolen shawl against the cold and a scarf, while Habiba wore a more ornate longer Muslim headdress with tucks, folds and pins to cover her hair completely. Josep realised he was seeing many things with fresh eyes now and saw how little attention he had paid to any of them when he had last been here. He took stock now of how preoccupied he had been with the king's death and on the moves he now had to make in his own life.

Over dinner that evening, simple roast vegetables with bread, tomato and olive oil with cheese and their own wine, it was clear the three women were enchanted and overjoyed to see him and his family doing so well. Yet a knot in Josep's stomach tightened.

"I cannot wait to show you my house in Trapani," Josep said as dinner was ending.

"But how can I see it?" Catharine said lightly, without really thinking.

"That's what we want to talk to you about, Mother," Josep said, his tone suddenly changing. The smiles faded from everyone's face.

"Lali and I have thought long and hard about this and would like you to come and live with us," he said. There was a stunned silence from the three older women.

"But Josep, this is very sudden. This is my home. I have responsibilities here. What would I do without Clara and Habiba? What would they do without me?" Catharine said.

"But we feel that you'll soon be in a position of needing help as much as giving help, Mother," Josep replied.

"Josep, as you are speaking so plainly, I must remind you I've been here for years. I cannot just uproot myself because you come to pay me a visit."

"I know it will be an upheaval for you, Mother, but time moves on, Habiba is young enough to look after Clara but will find it too much to maintain the place and look after you, too."

Clara laughed with a look of surprise and disbelief.

"I do not want to speak out of turn, but I can understand what your mother means, Josep. This is all very sudden. You may well be used to a life of action and change and that is as it should be but even the war we have just waged against France barely touched us here at Can Baró."

Catharine nodded. "Three months ago you passed through on your way to Sicily or Mallorca we thought and you will understand when I say I am delighted with everything that has happened but we have not had time to get used to the new changes and think about how they are going to affect our lives."

Josep looked from his mother to Clara, groping for inspiration. He looked at Lali, who checked Catarina was sleeping and turned now to Catharine.

"This has been sudden for us, too, Mother. We only know we could not make it to summer on Formentera and needed your help. Maybe Josep means we would love you to come and live with us when everything has settled down and we have organised all the details properly."

"Thank you, Lali, well spoken," Catharine said. "We all need time to adjust." She paused and taking a deep breath, reached her hand out to Lali.

"And yet, that does not mean that he is not right, you know, Lali? Clara has said you are all perfectly welcome to stay here for as long as you need to. We have made a home for ourselves, here, perhaps not a conventional one, but it has worked. Yet sooner or later, the daily running of the place is going to become too much. We already have to get extra help tending the vineyards. I am not able to bend and stretch the way I used to. Habiba can do more than I can but even the three of us will need help to run the farm in the right way." She paused for a moment. "But I need to be active, Josep," she continued. "Much of the work around the house and the management of the vines and olive trees are done by me. What would I spend my time doing if I lived with you?"

"Mother, we now have a place of our own and believe me, it will take all Lali's energy to manage things there." He described their smallholding, which was half the size of Can Baró but still represented significant work.

"It is much less work than here, it is true, but Lali would be delighted to have you there by her side and to share your expertise, especially while I'm away."

Catharine's face dropped.

"What do you mean *"while you're away"*?" Suddenly, the conversation shifted again and Josep had to explain what he understood his commitments would be in order to receive the stipend granted by King Pere. He would have to be available for anything the queen might ask.

"And I suppose Bru has decided to stay there?" Clara asked.

"As far as I know, he has registered but I have seen nothing of him since the death of King Pere. I understand he was on active service in Murcia but I was not there."

"That is where he was when you were born, fighting on the borders of the Kingdom of Valencia along with his cousins, my brothers. Things seem to have gone full circle," Clara said.

"He hasn't set foot in Sicily since the war of the Sicilian Vespers but there is more chance of earning a fortune in Sicily than on the borders of the Kingdom of Granada," Josep said.

"I always thought he would probably retire here. He is my last remaining relative, so I intend to bequeath the house to him with its lands. Perhaps you would pass that information on to him if you should see him first. I'll have an official document drawn up. Therefore, Josep, your visit is in fact very convenient and fortuitous," Clara said.

"Bonds of blood will always prevail," Josep thought to himself. It was as well he had come to offer his mother her rightful home. He couldn't imagine her being able to live in the same house as Bru. He later mentioned this to his mother. She hung her head, looked away and pretended to occupy herself with some small matter but when they next spoke, he could see she had been crying.

"When will I see my friends again?" she asked simply and Josep realised all the more keenly what a wrench this move was going to be for her.

However, matters did not move quickly. Clara's legal document naming Bru as her heir was complicated as it was unusual but Clara had considered it would be the best way to provide for the continuing care of Habiba and the welfare of her workers to have a clear heir who knew in advance about his inheritance and would therefore act quickly to settle matters on her demise. It showed extraordinary clarity of mind. However, it took time. Nor was Catharine in any hurry to move quickly and Josep's occasional visits to Barcelona gave her the time she needed for herself and Lali to get to know each other and adjust to their new roles.

Clara returned from Barcelona one day having settled her will. News came that King Alfons had succeeded in reducing

Majorca in 1285. He cemented a reputation as a brutal adversary there. A travelling troubador sang a song Josep heard about two knights in a town called Alaró who refused to renounce their loyalty to King Jaume of Majorca and surrender the town to the Catalan king. One of them had the misfortune of being called Cabrit, or *little goat,* in Catalan. It came to King Alfons' ear that Cabrit had joked that in Alaró, Alfons was the name of a fish that swam deep in the sea, suggesting the king should do the same. When the king heard this, he flew into a rage and swore he would have his revenge. On capturing the town, he had the unfortunate knight brought before him. He was then stripped and on an open fire in the in the Plaça Major of the town, was roasted like a little goat. Except he was roasted alive.

However, in Sant Pere de Ribes, they were insulated from these developments. Catharine developed a deep love and respect for Lali and was enchanted with her granddaughter. She had never thought this could happen to her while she lived at Can Baró and that made everything much more agreeable for her when the final plans for moving came to be made. Josep and Lali met with a senior priest in Barcelona through Josep's Templar contacts and Lali's previous marriage was annulled on the grounds that she had never consented to it; her husband had physically and sexually abused her and therefore she had not wanted to have his children. Josep and Lali were married in a quiet ceremony in the church in Sant Pere de Ribes at the same time as Catarina was baptised. When the time came for them to leave, it was seen as the natural step and they looked forward to being able to visit again in future, when the situation in the kingdom stabilised.

The night before they left, they prepared the cart and the following morning the mule was there waiting and Clara told them to sell both the cart and the mule when they got to Barcelona.

"It's a present for you now," she said. "Use the money to get another cart and mule when you come to visit us."

This was a good way of dealing with the pain of leaving as it focused them on the positive aspects of their new life and future. They left early one bright September morning and Josep and Lali retraced their steps through the vineyards between Sant Pere de Ribes and Barcelona, this time accompanied by Catharine, who enjoyed the journey. Josep did not feel like a fugitive this time as he had done when returning from Formentera and they made their way quickly to the port, sold the mule and cart and found passage to Trapani and berths on the *Reina Yolanda*, a *tarrida*. She was a swollen-bellied cargo ship that sat low in the water and Josep felt the name was laughably inappropriate. They boarded and bedded down by nightfall ready to sail the following morning.

When they set sail at first light, they were all on deck watching the sun coming up over the sea in the eastern sky. Though it was a perfect day for sailing, Josep noticed that his mother was strangely tense.

"I am not a good sailor," she said to Josep. "I have not been on a boat for many years and they always fill me with dread."

Josep had not slept well but nonetheless was feeling light-hearted and confident. "Mother," he said. "What do you think is going to happen? Do you think we are going to spring a leak and go down with the ship?" Lali laughed nervously but Catharine went white, clutched Josep's arm and looked anywhere but the sea.

"I do not know why I have these feelings," she said, "but please do not tease me as I am terrified!"

Josep made his mother as comfortable as he could and later tried to explain her reaction to Lali.

"We have both always had nightmares about sailing and drowning. I witnessed King Pere, when still crown prince and fighting off competition for the crown, kill his half-brother, Ferran Sanchis, by drowning him when I was a boy. I remember my mother's horror of seeing people arrive by boat. Whenever anyone arrived in Sitges by boat, my mother always became very nervous."

What he did not mention to Lali because he only remembered later were two other incidents. The first one was when he had been with Alba his childhood sweetheart, in Navarra when he was convinced that Guillaume de Nogaret in disguise had rammed his boat at the wedding celebration of Prince Phillip and Joanna of Navarra just before the French invasion of Catalunya. Alba had been angry with Josep for this and it was an incident that marked the end of their relationship. Connected with this inevitably was his memory of the mutilation Bella, Alba's sister, had suffered when she was killed by old enemies of Josep's at the end of the French invasion. When he thought of that incident it reminded him of another incident when his friend Amauri, the simple Cathar was drowned in the waterfall of Aneto while he was still at school. They were all connected with Guillaume de Nogaret and the Comte de Foix, and water was a common theme. These events were of course disturbing but what caught his attention was why they still played so much on his mind and whether they had something deeper to do with his mother.

"Did you sleep well, Mother? "Josep asked the following day.

"No, I cannot say that I did, Josep. I had nightmares about the ship sinking and all of us drowning."

"Yes, Mother, so did I. Perhaps in time we will come to understand what these dreams mean."

A look of alarm flashed across Catharine's face and Josep put his arm around her but they did not talk about it any further. In any case the passage was impeccable and Lali and Catarina seemed to enjoy themselves and the days passed slowly but peacefully.

CHAPTER THREE

September 1286

Life on their farm, Can Pere Josep, began happily and smoothly. Josep's duties outside the house were light. He had requested this much from the Queen Constança. She seemed to understand that he had earned respite after the three years of his young life, between the age of fifteen and eighteen, that he had spent in loyal service to King Pere. He had often risked his life in the king's cause. The queen also seemed to understand intuitively, though Josep told Lali and Catharine he had never mentioned it to her, that Josep's family needed time to establish themselves in Josep's small estate.

Once, to Lali and Catharine's delight and pride, Queen Constança visited but conditions were so rudimentary that the idea she might stay was never aired.

"Make sure you wrap up warm this winter," she said amiably on leaving. "We have our fair share of storms and sea mists round here in winter. I take it the roof is sound?" Josep checked and was impressed at the Queen's observation: there were parts of the roof that needed re-tiling, which, once done, made the old farmhouse even more hospitable that winter, when Josep, Lali and Catharine spent their evenings in the kitchen next to the big old rustic fireplace, where there was always a cot. Catarina thrived, both parents got used quickly to the restrictions on their time and freedom a baby means and life went on idyllically for the first two years of Catarina's childhood.

News came whenever there was work for Josep to do which Prince Jaume and the queen preferred someone they knew and personally trusted to perform, such as the administration of taxes or the organisation of a local Almogaver militia to pursue King Alfons' campaigns. On these occasions, Josep would be away for some weeks and he always worried about leaving Lali and Catharine on their own with a little child in a foreign country, without any protection.

"But Josep, you forget I lived entirely on my own for five years before you even met me and had my own arrow trained on you the day we met. I am perfectly capable of looking after myself!" Lali reasoned a little indignantly. "When I was younger than you are now, I walked from Bordeaux to Barcelona and beyond carrying you and on my own. I can also fend for myself!" said Catharine.

Josep knew this was true but had also arranged that the local couple who had been the *masovers*, the tenant farmers, who had always looked after the property and worked part of the land, would stay on those occasions, just in case.

Eventually, outhouses were properly refurbished and the couple took up permanent residence in Can Pere Josep, Giuseppe a man in his forties and Giuliana his wife, also the local midwife, a little younger than himself. "I value them both as friends and advisers," Lali remarked to Catharine. "They do not work for me."

"You will all be in good hands when I'm gone," Josep said.

Catharine was delighted. "I continue to live with a woman of my age," she said.

Lali in the meantime occupied herself with the administration of a sizeable estate producing five thousand litres of wine a year and a thousand litres of good olive oil. The living that resulted from this was modest but solid and she enjoyed visiting the merchants in Palermo to negotiate with them and frequently accompanied Josep, taking advantage of his visits there on royal business.

Lucio was born in April 1288, much to the delight of Catarina, who was nearly two and a half at the time. Catharine and Giuliana attended. The birth was rapid and uncomplicated.

"I wonder what took so long," Catharine said to Giuliana.

"Lali asked me to help her to take precautions as she did not wish to fall pregnant until she felt settled," she replied.

Lali was recovered within a week and bursting with ideas. "I've noticed the fisherman salt their fish so they can eat them at all times of the year," Lali said to Josep the day before one of his royal visits six months after Lucio's birth. "But a lot goes to waste if they run out of salt," she wiped the oil from around Catarina's mouth, as the three-year-old devoured the wonderful salt cod meal she loved.

"Do you think you could spare a couple of men to develop the saltpans that occur naturally along the coast? It would be a matter of raising low walls to keep out storm water. If we could harvest the salt for ourselves, Josep, we could buy up the fisherman's fish that they cannot use and start salting it ourselves."

Josep loved it that Lali had turned her hand so successfully to business. He was delighted by the idea. Lali was always full of ideas for expanding her business, making things more efficient and helping the workers with their problems, despite being a mother to a new-born and a little girl.

"We could pay the fisherman a fair price for the fish, too," she added.

"And sell it back to them at a special rate," Josep observed.

"Or both," laughed Lali, her eyes lighting up.

"Why not? It's a useful service to the community," concluded Josep, picking up Catarina and tickling her in his lap. The little girl squealed with delight and laughed so much she gave herself hiccups.

"But I want to help Mummy build up the saltpans," the little girl hiccupped every third word then wrapped her arms around her father and pulled him backwards, so they could wrestle better on the grass.

Over the three years it took Lali to develop her salting industry, Lucio grew into a strong happy boy surrounded by adoring family and friends. He was physically energetic and fearless, constantly climbing up and falling from trees, surrounded by the dogs. He was also bright and funny, chatting away with anyone who came by the farm. But though he loved his parents and grandmother, his favourite companion was his sister, who, though only two and a half years older than him, seemed older than she was and always played with him, looked after him and was as lovely in looks as in nature. With their mother, they learned to fish together and knew the names of, and where to find, all the wild greens and herbs of the countryside where they lived.

"I have never seen two children so complete in their togetherness and happiness in each other's company," Catharine said to Josep. "It is a perfect childhood for them. They have all they need here: love, safety and complete freedom to roam and explore."

As his duties required his presence in Palermo every fortnight, Josep received news largely in the same way as other people on the island. He heard without knowing the details that the young Catalan Aragonese King Alfons, despite his bravery as a knight, continued to fail to appease the Aragonese nobles or bring about peace with France and the King of Naples with whom the crown of Sicily was disputed.

Alfons' fierce reputation held him in good stead with the King of England, Edward I who was keen to pursue the marriage of his daughter Eleanor to him, a betrothal that had been made years before when Alfons was but four or five years old in the reign of King Pere the Great. The resulting alliance would have protected the King of England from Navarra in his possession of Guyenne and the King of Catalunya Aragón from aggression from Navarra with France. All preparations for the marriage in Barcelona were made ready for 1291.

However, the night before the celebration of the long-awaited ceremony, King Alfons suddenly and mysteriously died. He had developed a swelling in his groin, which had spread its contagion through his body and in the morning he was dead.

Some blamed the fact that he was marrying so late in life and that his continuing virginity was too much for his body to bear. But others, once the disappointed wedding party had left Barcelona for England via Bordeaux, pointed to his will as evidence that this story was unlikely to be true. In King Alfons' last will and testament, he provided specifically for a young woman named Dolça, with whom, it was said, he had been – secretly albeit– romantically involved for some years.

The new King of Catalunya Aragón, King Jaume, was at the same time and separately King Jaume of Sicily, too. He acted promptly and deployed his youngest brother, Prince Pere, to Leon, together with tough old soldier Ramón d'Anglesola, to defend Aragon's borders in the disputed succession in the Kingdom of Castille. But he desperately needed troops and Josep was requested to step up recruitment for more Almogavers from Sicily.

The request came through Frederick, King Pere's third son, who had summoned Josep to his palace in Palermo just two months after Josep had returned to Trapani from Barcelona after the death of Alfons.

"I know you are working more than you feel is your fair share at the moment, Josep," Frederick nodded earnestly to him. "But King Jaume says that the men will be paid in advance for four months' service, so they'll be home for Christmas."

Josep felt he had to argue his case.

"My stipend comes from the reign of old King Pere and is received in recompense for saving the king's life. Do I not have a right to my own life? I struggle to make ends meet as it is. It is basically out of loyalty to Queen Constança that I have raised the troops for King Jaume anyway. Now I have to raise more troops and am busier than I've ever been," he said, wishing he had spoken about the matter with Queen Constança instead.

"Josep, we know this. The queen and I are aware of the strain it puts on you. The supply of men in western Sicily is also stretched. Be sure that Commanders Alamany and Villaragut have been asked to do the same in their respective provinces."

"Yes, your Highness, but they are from noble Catalan families and have far greater incomes than my own." "Josep, if it is a matter of money, I'm sure we can come to an arrangement."

"Your Highness, I want freedom from commitments more than money at the moment. This latest recruitment will also reduce our capacity to defend ourselves if an attack is launched against Trapani."

"An emergency force is being assembled in Castrogiovanni for that purpose, Josep. We can get anywhere on the island in a day from there."

"But my militia could repel any attack from the coast itself so that no force could even land," Josep said.

"Josep," said Frederick, still earnestly looking the older man now in his mid-twenties in the eye. "This request comes from King Jaume himself. I'm afraid your stipend could be at risk if you fail to comply."

"That's grossly unfair!" Josep replied. "It's a misrepresentation of why I receive it."

"Nevertheless, the country is again putting itself on a war footing. All shoulders – and cash – to the wheel – if I may mix my metaphors!" Prince Frederick joked, trying to dispel the tension.

"You are King Jaume's representative here so you have no option," Josep said. "I just hope he shows you the same level of loyalty and deference as you show him when push comes to shove," he said to himself.

"Thank you, Josep, for your understanding. The queen warned me you would not be happy but our hands are tied."

Josep looked away at the mention of the queen.

"It's time to untie *my* hands at least," Josep thought to himself. He cast a probing glance at Prince Frederick, scanning his eyes for clues as to any hidden intentions and saw only a young man, with little experience in these matters, without art or deception. He politely said goodbye, wished the queen well in her absence, turned and left.

Yet the war between Sicily and Naples dragged on and if it had not been for the strenuous efforts of the Admiral Roger de Llúria and his constant war of attrition on the whole of the Kingdom of Naples from the capital to Brindisi, coast and countryside, marine and mountain, there would have undoubtedly been attacks on Sicily itself.

"We are safe so long as we have Ramón de Llúria on our side," John of Procida once observed to Josep. What Josep did not see was at what price they had the admiral on their side. The war against Naples had been dragging on for so long now, since 1282, so thirteen years, that it had become his life's work.

"He has always been a favourite of mine," Queen Constança confided to Josep once. "After all, he is the son of my closest lady-in-waiting, Bella d'Amichi. He has almost seemed like a member of the family to me."

However, news came to Palermo that shocked everyone. Without consultation or warning, King Jaume had made his decision and plans were well advanced for his wedding. No explanations were given as to how or why he had come to his decision but John of Procida was not surprised.

"This has been a long time coming," began John of Procida, the grand orchestrator of the conquest of Sicily, now chief adviser to the queen and Prince Frederick.

"The king is at the end of his tether with the ongoing war against Naples. His grain trade suffers as his fleet is constantly occupied with war against Naples. He wants a commercial alliance with as many of his neighbours as possible. It is not clear how marrying into the Royal House of Naples will affect us. Presumably, the admiral has been consulted, for without him, our seafaring prowess as a martial maritime kingdom of islands will be diminished."

It was shocking that the King should marry Blanca, daughter of King Charles II of Naples, granddaughter of Charles of Anjou, against whose brutal regimes King Pere and his successors had been fighting all these years. Sicily was scandalised. It was completely unexpected and filled all Sicilians from all walks of life with dread. For they knew they were defenceless at sea and from the sea without the king's fleet. What is more, doubtless Naples would be only too keen to have Sicily back. Some years before, there had been rumours that King Alfons had contemplated the idea of marrying into the house of Naples but, beset on all sides as he was, he felt his interests were better served by developing his relationship with England than with his Italian neighbours. That English fire had in the intervening years gone cold, Princess Eleanor had finally subsequently married in 1293 and King Edward I had gone on the rampage against Scotland leaving Guyenne to fend for itself. Guyenne, the English region of south-west France, was thus suffering a protracted French invasion as a result, leading to a siege of Bordeaux. There was always a price to pay.

CHAPTER FOUR

Perhaps it was because King Jaume could not rekindle interest in an alliance with England. Perhaps it was because it had been old King Pere's grand design not Jaume's own to forge relationships north of his frontier, which seemed unnatural now to Jaume. Perhaps it was because it was pragmatic for King Jaume to sue for peace with an enemy that was now amenable. Perhaps it was for all these reasons that King Jaume decided to abandon Sicily in the interests of consolidating his kingdom.

He married Blanca of Naples, daughter of King Charles II of Naples, and granddaughter of King Pere's arch enemy, King Charles I of Naples, Charles of Anjou. Blanca of Naples was thus powerfully connected, beautiful and the right age. She was seventeen and he was twenty-eight. From a personal point of view, as well as pragmatically, it was a statesmanlike move. However, the consequences for Sicily were disastrous. As the details were revealed in subsequent missives from the King, Prince Frederick became more and more sick at heart, once turning in public to Queen Constança, who was already weeping quietly.

"It is all over for our beloved Catalan union, Mother. All we have fought for in Sicily is for nothing. We have been abandoned for a new queen and our fate has been handed back to the Angevins." He was fighting back tears.

"It is shocking. These are the brutal regimes King Pere and Alfons were fighting against for all these years."

Worse news was to come. The Pope had given King Jaume Corsica and Sardinia in compensation for Sicily. It was one thing to state this on paper, yet everyone knew Corsica and Sardinia would only be won with the spilling of much blood. Yet, the terms of the dishonourable Treaty of Anagni, in 1295, demanded the immediate surrender of all towns and castles in Sicily.

"The Sicilians simply won't accept it," said Frederick vehemently. "There will be riots before the townspeople hand over their towns or simply walk away from their houses."

However, that is exactly what the terms of the treaty demanded. The Mayor of each town was to evacuate his town, then leave the keys in the main gate and shout three times that the town was empty and could be occupied by whoever had the right. In due course, a Napolitano would come and take up residence.

"They'll have to kill us first," was the Sicilian response. "This is the stupidest thing I've ever heard. I'm not leaving my house, mistress or master, unless someone forcibly comes and ejects me," said Giuseppe. Yet those were the terms of the treaty. Sicily was King Jaume's dishonourable compensation to King Charles II for losses the Kings of Naples themselves had incurred. Furthermore, there was still the matter of the Kingdom of Catalunya Aragón to be settled, which had been signed over by the Pope to the King of France's brother, Charles of Valois. He still wanted his due and to be king of his own kingdom. He was therefore compensated with the County of Anjou, which King Charles I of Naples had possessed and had passed down to his heir. This was a huge loss for Charles II. He therefore wanted compensation himself. Thus Sicily was exchanged for Anjou and the pact further cemented by the marriage of King Jaume's sister Yolanda to Charles II's younger brother, Robert, Duke of Calabria.

"What is most distasteful, even treacherous," said Queen Constança, "is that Jaume has achieved only the maintenance of Catalunya Aragón and the lifting of the excommunication that had led to the Crusade in the time of his father in the first place."

"Absolutely!" said Prince Frederick. "It is difficult for the Sicilians not to conclude that he has abandoned them for a girl, albeit a princess. He is betraying his people, for he is still their crowned king."

"He has been their king since before Alfons was crowned King of Catalunya Aragón," said the queen. "The Sicilians never fail to remember that. He is also betraying me, his own mother," said Queen Constança, "for the Princess, once married to King Jaume, will become Queen of Sicily. Once more, we will be ruled from outside our island either from Naples, or from Barcelona but not from Palermo itself."

The situation was apt to make Sicily once more a tinderbox, ready for another explosion, like that of the Vespers of 1282, half a generation before. History was repeating itself. It could not be allowed to. There were riots in all the cities of Sicily. Work came to a standstill. All official business stopped. Messina, Catania, Syracusa, Agrigento, Trapani, Palermo, all revolted on the coast; Castrogiovanni and Calatafimi in the heart of the island. Deputations from all corners of the island converged on Palermo, begging Frederick not to abandon them. Josep was summoned to the Norman Palace in Palermo. A message had been sent expressly to him. He was handed the parchment by John of Procida himself, in the presence of Prince Frederick and Queen Constança. Josep ripped open King Jaume's royal seal and scanned the contents of the letter.

"As King Jaume is no longer King of Sicily, I have been recalled to Barcelona," Josep summarised. "My stipend will not be paid until I return to the King's Court. With immediate effect." Josep's livelihood had been cancelled at the stroke of a pen. He faced losing everything he and Lali had worked so hard to build up over the past ten years.

"This is going to end in civil war," Frederick said simply. "If we must fight brother against brother, our land of Sicily, as it has a queen, must also have a king."

"You are within your rights to proclaim yourself king," said John of Procida. "In King Pere's will, it was specified that Jaume would be King of Sicily as Alfons would be King of Catalunya Aragón. But it also said that if Alfons died, Jaume would be his heir and Sicily would have its own king. You will be the third King Frederick of Sicily, the third son of King Pere. You must be up to the challenge of history!" he urged.

"This, your brother, the King of Catalunya Aragón recognises. He has not abandoned you, my Lord. He expects you to behave like the Royal Prince that you are, to seize the opportunities the situation presents you with, to further the interests of your house and subjects without seeking self-destruction."

"You mean he seeks peace with Sicily?" Frederick shot back at him.

"On how many fronts can he maintain the war?" the old adviser asked.

"But with Sicily he does have a front open. Stop talking in riddles, Sir John."

"But has he attacked you yet?"

"No he hasn't but his family by marriage are preparing an invasion force as we speak."

"King Jaume will never truly act against you but he expects you to defend yourself vigorously." Sir John of Procida sought out Frederick's eyes.

"You mean I should attack Duke Robert of Calabria as that is where they are preparing the invasion of Sicily?"

"If you do not, they will come against you!" said the old counsellor.

"Not Naples?" Frederick asked checking he was following

closely the old man's thoughts.

"It is not Naples that is planning the new invasion," John of Procida replied.

"But Charles is behind it!" Frederick said.

"He doesn't want Sicily for himself," replied John of Procida. "He must support the acquisition of Sicily to compensate for his loss of Anjou. That is his bequest to his son, Duke Robert of Calabria. But he will leave it to his son to take it" said Procida.

Frederick had been well prepared by Sir John of Procida to deal with the proposals the new Pope Bonifaccio VIII would offer. Roger de Llúria was personally commanding the galley that took the small party to Rome, a journey of three days, in the late September winds. Josep was commanding the company of two hundred Almogavers allocated to the mission. It was a test for Frederick's statesmanship. He had to perceive the underlying pattern; he had to cut through the enticements, the temporary advantages, the flattery, the pomp, the ceremony. Above all, he had to have Sir Jonn of Procida at his side to advise him, to help him to navigate the shallows.

Rome was magnificent and the Holy Father seemed at pains to be as charming and elegant as a Caetani faced with a Hohenstauffen could be. Frederick was noticeably tense, almost irritable at the endless blandishments and luxuries he was offered, looking finally relieved when the Pope, together with an ambassador from the Kingdom of Jerusalem and John of Procida, got down to business.

On offer was the Latin throne of Constantinople. Frederick would marry the Courtenay heiress of the title. However, the throne had been lost and was presently held by the Palaiologos family.

"I have no idea how you knew anything about this but what I do not understand is how you could have supported and promoted the Palaiologos cause during Charles of Anjou's life and plotted his downfall with Palaiologos gold and now support his rival's claim to the throne," Frederick said frowning deeply.

"Because then Constantinople will permanently stay out of French hands, your highness," Sir John of Procida answered simply.

"I suppose that the Pope's offer that you can reclaim your lands on the Island of Procida has nothing to do with your enthusiasm!" Frederick said.

Sir John of Procida was utterly speechless and for the first time could not hold the gaze of the young Prince.

"My Lord, I cannot deny the rumour. The Island of Procida is of no consequence to the Holy Church or to Naples. I am now on the wrong side to request it from your brother King Jaume. I have no living heirs. I have only my wife and daughters. I satisfied my revenge when Charles of Anjou died. I simply want now what has belonged to my family. I feel it is my just reward for my service to Sicily."

Frederick seemed to relent. He saw an old man fighting for his dignity standing before him. He looked away.

"If I were a Courtenay, I wouldn't make this offer. After all, what use is a king without a kingdom to a queen without lands. You have a month to leave Sicily. Negotiate your precious island for yourself."

Sir John of Procida bowed his head, returned to Ostia and King Frederick never saw the old man again. As far as Josep knew, Sir John of Procida managed in the end to regain the island of Procida.

Less than a month later, a papal embassy attempted to land at Palermo in order to renew papal pressure on Sicily to return to the fold. Their reception was so hostile that the ambassadors and sixty staff, sailors and soldiers among them, had to turn tail and flee for their lives.

Frederick confounded everyone's plans and resisted Sir John of Procida´s subterfuge to become a puppet Emperor of Constantinaople. He was loyal to the Sicilians and to his mother and was finally crowned King of Sicily at Palermo Cathedral on 25 March 1296, five days before Josep's thirtieth birthday. While King Jaume had won the love of the islanders during his decade as their king, within six weeks, Frederick, with his boyish good looks and bellicose air, reminded many of his father King Pere.

◆ ◆ ◆

It was July 1299. King Frederick had been on the throne just over three years. He had grown in experience and confidence, some say he had become brutal, as a military commander, especially at sea, where the majority of engagements with the enemy were taking place. As he looked out to sea from San Marco d'Alunzio, Cape Orlando, on the Cefalú coast, he could see a squadron clearly bearing the Catalan colours. Josep, as commander of the Trapani militia was at his side, together with twenty or so commanders from around the kingdom. However, the ships were clearly heading from the northeast, so he presumed they were coming from the Amalfi coast. Now his consternation was apparent. Here he was again facing the Catalan fleet.

"I do not see how he thinks he can fool people like that!" King Frederick said to his admiral, Conrad Llança. "Now we'll see clearly how he sees things."
"I agree with His Majesty," replied Conrad Llança. "King Charles may tire of the Sicilian question but not so Duke Robert of Calabria. He may be married to His Majesty's sister, Yolanda, but she is also King Jaume's sister. It seems his part of the family has more influence these days. Anyway, Duke Robert is still planning his invasion and he seems to be using King

Jaume's fleet. We have to stop them now."

"But that is precisely what Duke Robert wants us to do!" Conrad Doria, the rear admiral said as calmly as he could. He continued looking straight out to sea. "This is a coded message from your brother King Jaume not to attack now. This is a decoy from the main attack which will happen in Syracusa. If they are Catalan galleys, it is Roger de Llúria commanding them and that is his favourite tactic. He lures out his enemy. Then he pounces on them."

"He is laughing at me!" King Frederick said to himself, just loud enough for Josep to hear. He was standing by now to embark with his Almogavers. Josep did not envy the King having to make that decision. In his mind, he went back over the two battles that had been fought off Syracusa in the past three years.

The Catalan fleet commanded by Roger de Llúria and accompanied by King Jaume himself had tried to take Syracuse with a fleet of Catalan and Calabrian galleys once in 1296 and again the previous winter in 1298.

King Frederick still deeply regretted the loss of the greatest admiral of the time. Yet when dispossessed of the various castles in Sicily which had been requisitioned for King Frederick at this time of shortage by Galceran Cartella and Blasco d'Alagó, Roger de Llúria had flown into a rage and raised a rebellion in Catanzaro in Calabria against Frederick. However, having scant land forces, he had been unable to maintain the town and had blazed a trail back to Barcelona, abandoning Sicily which he had been fighting for since 1282.

In Barcelona, of course, he was given a hero's welcome and immediately assumed his role of Admiral of the Catalan fleet once again. Shortly afterwards, King Jaume accompanied this time by Roger de Llúria and therefore feeling invincible, set off for Syracusa for the first time. King Jaume encountered more resistance than he had expected from his younger brother's fleet. King Frederick, bending to his advisers' opinion that his elder brother could not possibly want to wage war on him seriously, was indeed surprised by this first attack on Syracusa but had managed nonetheless to repel it.

King Jaume left the fleet there blockading Syracusa, returned to Barcelona and sent Roger de Llúria's nephew, Joan de Llúria, to assist his uncle as his rear admiral. However, Joan de Llúria's small fleet of sixteen galleys was intercepted just south of Messina by the Sicilian fleet and the rear admiral and the galleys were captured.

Roger de Llúria surrendered and begged King Frederick to spare his young nephew's life. However, Frederick, confused, angry and beset by nerves decided to make an example of Joan de Llúria and in a scene almost reminiscent of Charles of Anjou's treatment of young Conradin, his mother's usurped cousin, at Benevento, at the beginning of the Sicilian war thirty years earlier, Joan de Llúria was beheaded on the rear of his own galley in full view of Roger de Llúria. He then imprisoned Roger de Llúria but so many were his contacts and such was his prestige that he was free in a matter of days.

This time, if the Catalan fleet was sailing back to Syracusa, they were going the wrong way: across the north coast of Sicily, instead of via the Straits of Messina. De Llúria had a combined fleet of Catalan and Calabrian galleys all flying the Catalan flag. King Jaume was still playing games. "History is repeating itself," Frederick muttered to himself. The "conflictum inter fratrem nostrum" had become a civil war. Jaume refused to use the term and Frederick could not bear to. The Queen had lost all hope now, seeing her two sons, who had been so close so recently, at war. She spent her days in seclusion, mourning.

CHAPTER FIVE

Now Roger de Llúria was on his way to wreak his revenge, there was no doubt about it. Whether the fleet was heading for Syracuse again or not, the Sicilian fleet consisting of forty-eight galleys, six of which had come from Trapani, was awaiting them at San Marco d'Alunzio. Frederick and his admirals had their galleys drawn up on the beach prow foremost.

Josep had just arrived when the first attack was made by the Catalan admiral. It was a taste of things to come. Conrad Dòria had been mistaken. Far from changing course, the Catalan fleet no sooner came into view than it attacked the prone Sicilian galleys firing burning crossbow bolts from a distance of two hundred yards, causing death to scores of sailors as well as setting fire to several galleys.

King Frederick turned to Conrad Llança.

"Scramble the galleys. Chase them or we will be burnt on the beach!" he said.

Many galleys put out with great trepidation as a result of the damage they had already sustained, the ill-omened beginning of the engagement and the knowledge they were to face Roger de Llúria at his most savage. The two fleets spied each other. There were fifty-eight Catalan galleys, ten more than the Sicilian vessels. The two fleets approached each other, drawn up in half moon formation. Josep looked west from the galley he had jumped onto to the galleys that were foremost in the Sicilian formation.

"They are labouring to keep ahead of us. Their rudders are damaged and the galley slaves are exhausted."

He looked ahead of him and saw the Catalan galleys in perfect formation coming at them at great speed. If the Catalan galleys managed to sail through the Sicilian formation, it would send the weaker ships on the edge of the formation into a panic. These vessels would then be surrounded quickly and picked off one by one before the Sicilian fleet could turn and regroup in order to counter-attack. Josep knew the damaged galleys were doomed. The exhausted sailors and the galley slaves would strain every sinew to hold the line but their weakness would be seen and two or three of the enemy galleys would surround each vessel and board it instantly. Josep thought of his friends on board.

"Lord have mercy on them," he prayed silently. The Catalans were faster and smashed through the centre of their formation. As Josep had predicted, the galley on his far left was boarded within ten minutes. The other two galleys to his left, which were to have picked off weaker Catalan galleys, simply sailed on, unable to fulfil their battle orders.

The Sicilian fleet's formation was smashed and though Conrad Llançà signalled them to regroup, Roger de Llúria's fleet went into single file and like a serpent striking at its prey from the side, sailed straight at the Sicilian galleys, each one now showing its broadside, and opened fire with the crossbows. One by one, the Catalan galleys sailed between the Sicilian galleys having all the time in the world to cause the most damage possible. The Sicilian galleys desperately tried to turn south and repeat the original formation in reverse, a half-moon facing south. But the Catalan galleys were too quick, sending a hail of crossbow bolts onto the decks and decimating the Almogavers, who stood in battle formation ready to board. Sicilian galleys were burning now, the slaves screaming as they were roasted alive where they were chained to their bench and oars. The smell of roasting flesh filled Josep's nostrils. His vessel lurched west as it was rammed from the rear and they floundered in the strong breeze, unable to regain their direction, their rudder smashed to pieces. Nonetheless, Josep ordered his Almogavers to get ready to repel the attack. The next moment the grappling hooks were on the deck, the Catalan galleys came alongside, the enemy marines sprang on to the Sicilians' deck and the hand-to-hand fighting began.

"They're Provencals and Napolitans!" he shouted to his Almogaten. "They're good with the crossbow but no match for the Almogavers at close quarters. Tell the men to throw their spears and come to close quarters."

Josep stood on the raised stern defending himself as he watched the developments of the battle. The Sicilian retreat was being sounded and suddenly the Catalan galley attacking their own was isolated. The captain shouted something Josep did not understand. The invading crew leapt back onto their galley, many not making it and landing in the water. The captain of the galley Josep was on managed to catch the wind and their galley lurched around to the south and the order to row was given. Behind them the Catalan fleet had now encircled ten Sicilian galleys. Eight galleys were set ablaze and sunk in the battle, twelve were captured and twenty-eight made it back to the beach.

Later that day, a single *lleny* carrying a skeleton crew and injured noblemen who bought their freedom there and then, arrived bearing horrific news. Roger de Llúria had taken all two thousand captured Almogavers and roped them together. He then made them contemplate their fate as they watched him behead the twenty Almogatens at the stern of each ship just as their King Frederick had executed his nephew Joan. Many of the Almogavers had served with King Pere in the crusade of the 1280s or were the sons of those who had served with King Pere or Roger de Llúria himself during that war or in the intervening period when Catalonia and Sicily were still one kingdom. Some had even served with Roger de Llúria when he was Sicilian Admiral as little as three years before.

He prepared to have the bound Almogavers dragged out one by

one behind several *bots* normally used for transporting horses. It was horrifically reminiscent of his treatment of the captured French sailors fifteen years before. The order was given to set sail. As the *bots* moved off, the line of men was dragged out of the back along the fixed rope. The hands bound, there was nothing they could do to reverse their fate. Josep heard later that the admiral addressed the boat containing the fortunate noblemen before they departed.

"Your king offended the laws of chivalry by executing Joan de Llúria. Observing the laws he breaks, I have ransomed you few nobles. Tell your king I have left his side permanently, he has offended my honour and I shall fight him tooth and nail for my properties in Sicily and Calabria and shall meet force with force wherever he wishes."

The galleys that remained were then set on fire, the three thousand five hundred galley slaves still chained to their benches, an appalling burnt offering to the God of War.

Encouraged by their success, the houses of Barcelona and Naples acted quickly to push home their advantage. Duke Robert of Calabria attacked and took Catania.

"Josep, our world is imploding," the Queen said to Josep when the news about Catania was received in Palermo. "Even if my son Jaume only expects his younger brother to show valour and defend himself, his chances are growing smaller and smaller. I do not want to live to see Frederick die at the hands of the husband of my daughter and his sister. Sicily is surrounded now on all fronts. King Jaume seems powerless in the thrall of his admiral, the speed of events has surprised even him and we await the deathblow."

"My lady, the Sicilians will not allow themselves to be taken over again. They will fight the invaders to the last man," Josep said. It was the only response he could give, as he himself identified with that spirit of resistance.

"Do you think courage is any comfort to me, Josep?" The queen looked at him with bloodshot eyes.

"What a bloody inheritance I was bequeathed, that I should

watch my own sons jump at each other's throats. What devil ever inspired me to pursue my rights, bought so dear in countless lives of men and women of so many nations, all to avenge one king and his heir, all for revenge! But revenge begets revenge, blood alone can pay for blood and the blood that is next to be spilled is that of another one of my sons. Go, Josep. Take a message to Yolanda in Catania, where my daughter accompanies her husband, Duke Robert of Calabria. Tell her I wish to see her. I do not know how much longer I can endure this."

Josep departed for Catania immediately but as it was on the other side of the island, went via Trapani. He was sick at heart for the tragic Queen, whose fate it was to see her offspring destroying each other. As he neared Trapani, his old friend Giuseppe himself met him on the road. At first, Josep's mind refused to accept it. It could only mean his family had been harmed.

"No, not Lali!" he said. "Not the children!"

"It's the mistress, sir," came the reply.

"What's wrong with her? Is she alive?"

"Oh yes sir, she is alive but badly wounded in the thigh, sir. They shot her with a crossbow, sir, the invaders."

"What invaders?"

"I do not know, sir, it all happened very suddenly, but hours ago," replied the steward.

"Where is your mistress?"

"She's at home, sir, having the wound dressed by my wife. The children are with her."

"Are they hurt, too?" Josep asked, his voice a whisper, his face ashen.

"No, upon my word, sir, they are unhurt but that is the Lord's doing."

"Why do you say that?" Josep remounted his horse.

"They were all at the saltpans when the invaders came ashore, sir."

"All the workers dead then?"

"All the men either shot or hacked down where they stood, sir. They weren't armed. It was just an ordinary working day, now the saltpans are red with blood, the banks smashed down, bodies face down in the pools."

Josep spurred his horse on and sped along the road, black thoughts gathering like never before in his mind, stabs of fear clutching at his heart.

As always after a battle, there was an uneasy silence. But for the lack of birdsong, everything looked as if nothing had happened. Josep's mind not wanting to believe hoped against hope it was all a mistake.

As he dismounted, various women employed by Lali ran out to explain to him what had happened and to bring him to where Lali lay. She was pale and her face distorted with pain yet she managed a flicker of a smile as soon as she saw Josep enter the room. Catarina and Lucio jumped up as he entered. Josep stood still in confusion for a moment. Then he realised he must look almost identical to the men who had just come ashore, dressed for action if not for battle. He only lacked his helmet, cloak and shield. He had his cuirass and greaves on and his *coltell* was strapped to his waist.

"Catarina, Lucio, it is only me!" he whispered somewhat defensively. "I came as quickly as I could." He looked to Lali, who seemed to summon all her strength to say something. He laid a finger on her cold lips and noticed the damp, clammy feel of the skin of her face, normally so warm and soft.

"Catarina, Lucio, tell me what happened?" He only wanted to be with them and his wife and he wanted the report of an eyewitness. The girl of fourteen before him bravely described what had happened. Josep found himself looking at Catarina in a different way suddenly. Her big eyes were brimming with tears but she described how the soldiers led by someone who looked like a prince beached their ships near where they were working, then started firing indiscriminately on them, bringing many down instantly. Catarina snatched up Lucio and hid in a myrtle thicket. Many of the men died instantly cut down either by knights on horseback or by the foot soldiers. They rode roughshod through the pans, destroying in minutes the work of ten years of labour as wave upon wave of men and horses came ashore.

There was of course no resistance. Some of the invading soldiers were speaking Italian, some French, there were even some Catalan voices among them. Giuliana, Giuseppe's wife, managed to find Lali. She was conscious but thought her leg was broken. As soon as they got her out of the shallow water, they saw the crossbow bolt sticking out of her right thigh.

"Lucky for her it was not a foot higher," Giuliana said. "Otherwise it would have been in the stomach and she would certainly have blead to death." Catarina turned pale and the old woman stopped talking.

Catarina was sobbing now. Josep cleared his throat and sent for the doctor from Trapani. There was too much to do. Having verified from the doctor her life was not at risk, he told her he had to let the king know. Lali smiled weakly but nodded. Josep kissed her forehead, kissed Catarina and Lucio, spoke to Giuliana and left.

Within an hour, he was at the head of the local Almogaver militia, which of course knew about the invasion but nobody knew what to do and it was pointless attacking a force of two or three thousand on their own; brave though it would be no one courted suicide.

Josep sent a messenger to Palermo and Calatafimi and set out in pursuit of the enemy force. Scouts came back two hours later to say the rearguard was two leagues away and the army numbered more than ten thousand. It was spread out over several miles along the road heading south to Marsala.

When asked where they were heading, someone said they were on their way to Catania.

"But Catania is on the other side of the island completely!" Josep said in disbelief.

"They wanted to ravage the island completely before arriving there," came the reply.

"This is total madness. It's the work of an imbecile or a megalomaniac," Josep shouted angrily.

"Charles of Naples' youngest son is in charge, sir, Philip, the Prince of Taranto."

"But why did King Charles tell him to invade Trapani in order to help his brother Duke Robert in Catania? Josep asked, seething with contempt.

"Apparently, he refused to follow his father's instructions, which were to land as close to Messina and march south as quickly as possible. Despite their victory at Cape Orlando, they still do not trust their chances south of Messina."

Later, a message came from Palermo saying a force had been dispatched from Calatafimi in the centre west of the island and advising Josep to await its arrival before risking an engagement.

However, Josep's militia had swelled as news of the devastation the invaders were wreaking became known and all men of fighting age, Almogaver trained, semi-trained, experienced or not, many carrying nothing more than farming tools, gravitated around Josep's company. At dawn, the force had grown to a thousand or more and Josep, whose wife's pale image haunted his thoughts, could barely stay still with anxiety so keen was his desire to avenge his wife and get back to care for her.

"I can wait no longer for reinforcements. I must attack them now when they least expect it. We are but half a day from them. If they chose to pursue us with a fraction of their force, they could wipe us out in a pitched battle. We must attack them unawares," he said to his Almogatens.

"After all, they arrived unannounced and took no care who they cut down!" he said half to himself.

"Very well, sir," Pietro Antonelli, one of his most trusted Almogatens said. "We can surround them while they sleep. We know the terrain after all. On a given signal each Almogaver can go in and do as much damage as he can, then withdraw as quickly as possible when the trumpet is sounded again," he said.

"Make it so. Inform the other Almogatens. Total silence once deployed. One trumpet call to retreat. Understood?"

They marched through the night and, as soon as they identified the enemy, picked off the sentries and attacked the sleeping troops just before dawn. Few realised what had hit them. By the time any trumpets sounded, each Almogaver had cut the throat of three if not four of the enemy. The force was instantly reduced by three or four thousand men. There were no Sicilian casualties.

When the reinforcements arrived in the morning, Philip of Taranto's force was ready for battle despite the night raid. The two armies met at Falconaria. It was the first of December, 1299. Philip himself commanded cavalry of two or three hundred. Next to him, General Count Sanseverino, commanded a similar sized force of cavalry. The remaining depleted force numbered seven thousand foot soldiers. The Sicilian force numbering far fewer was similarly drawn up. With a desperation borne out of repeated calamity and pure mortal fear for self and family, the Sicilian Almogavers charged the enemy army. The mounted Sicilians then attacked, cutting swathes through the enemy footsoldiers. Philip of Taranto then charged.

"I thought the general would charge first," Josep said simply to Pietro Antonelli.

"Yes, sir, as did we. I think they have made a mistake," replied Antonelli.

Within seconds, the mounted Sicilians, recognising who the prince was, grouped together to isolate him. The prince had been captured. The battle was over.

Despite his tribulations, Josep had to laugh several weeks later when Pietro Antonelli reminded him of the haughty fury of the young prince on being captured.

"Lucky for him the fighting only lasted half an hour, sir, otherwise he'd have been cut down like his foot soldiers. He made a great show of fighting with his guards when he was

taken to the prison of Cefalú, where they still have him."
Josep was now able to fulfill his mission to Catania, delivering the message the Queen had urged upon him before the battle of Falconaria. It was then his duty to escort the Queen's daughter, Yolanda, Duchess of Calabria, from Catania to the Royal Palace in Palermo, where her mother Queen Constança, awaited her.
Meanwhile, Josep was finally free to take care of his wife and family. Their savings had diminished significantly. The invasion of Trapani that had led to the battle of Falconaria had destroyed the industry Lali had been building up. The wound on her thigh had healed but had left her much less physically confident than she had been. Josep, now in his mid-thirties, remembered how she had appeared to him like some kind of savage warrioress on the rocks above the beach in Formentera seventeen years beforehand, how everything in her body was taut and flexed like the bow she'd aimed at him. He reached out for her and held her close to him. He smiled at her, stroked her hair, kissed her cheeks and lips and told her how much he loved her. She levelled a look at him as if to say, "I am not the woman you met that day!" but all she elicited from him was more tenderness. He looped his arm round her waist and felt her relax in his arms and let herself be held next to him and laughed with him.
Josep and Lali renewed their closeness to each other and their love for each other that Christmas but it did not banish the worries from Josep's mind. The scar on Lali's leg was still livid and the flesh around it dipped into the leg. Lali noticed him looking at it one day.
"You think it ugly, do you not?" she said. Josep pretended to be asleep but she was not to be put off that easily and the scene repeated itself a few days later.
"The Gods have marked you out of jealousy. Otherwise, your perfection would have excited their envy," he replied, catching her unprepared and surprising and pleasing her at same time. Yet he felt he had to be careful when they made love and he did see her wince at times. He saw that she was stiff in that leg in

the morning and asked people to pick things up for her from the floor. Yet she was the only woman he had eyes for and he loved her more than he could begin to explain.

"How is it I come through all these fights without a mark upon me and you're the one who bears the scar?" he finally said to her. She laughed and she knew then that he loved and admired her for the scar.

"It's the mark a woman's worry makes when her man goes away," she said striking home with the truth. It was her anguish carved out of her own flesh. Her remark brought other practical matters to a head. They were penniless. The years of fighting on the island had depleted the royal coffers so much that only a handful of royal household servants could be retained on a salary. Josep was not one of them. One of Queen Constança's last acts had been to reward Josep with a ruby ring when he had accompanied her daughter to Palermo. Frederick as always had put Josep in charge of dividing the spoils of the encounters with the Almogavers, most recently upon his victory over Philip of Taranto at Falconaria and Josep had received a dozen harnesses for leading that engagement, especially the surprise attack. The harnesses could be sold and would fetch good money. Jewellery from the queen, however, was another matter. That could not be sold. Nor did Josep or Lali wish to sell it. Besides, it would be extremely useful when making up a dowry for Catarina.

"I do not think it will take her long to marry," said Lali. The truth was Catarina, almost seventeen, was already talking about a young Almogaten in Josep's Trapani militia, who adored her and was affable, intelligent and polite with them.

"But is that really what Catarina wants?" asked Catharine. "A soldier's life?"

The sorrow of the women around them, marked by war, loss, sorrow, anguish, injury, as Lali's literally had been, was all too apparent. War also brought disease, as Josep had witnessed when he had been with Princess Yolanda in Catania. Though only in her thirties, camp life had not suited her health.

She was painfully thin, had a persistent cough and a wan expression that suggested if not sadness then infinite fatigue and listlessness. How could a woman constantly travelling with her military husband devote herself to anything of deep interest to herself, or have any kind of cultural life? She was always attending her three infants, one of whom was there with her, or her husband, leaving her no time for herself at all. Gone was the carefree spirit Josep had known her to be years before when he had met her with Jacques de Molay in Barcelona. They exchanged a few words and she had forced a thin smile the last time they met when he accompanied her to Palermo but it was clear that for Yolanda, Josep was now the enemy, a soldier whose troops opposed those of her husband.

"What have I done to be at war with my daughter?" Queen Constança asked Josep as he left for Trapani. "What in the name of God have I done to deserve any of this? I pursue my right to my crown and vengeance upon King Charles of Naples. Yet I am forced into marital union with his family, the murderers of my own kin who left my father's corpse for the dogs on the field of battle. First, I lose my husband and eldest son to illness, then my youngest son to war. To see my sons Jaume and Frederick at war with each other is purgatory for me. But to see Roger de Llúria, the son of my lady-in-waiting and childhood confidant, plead for his nephew's life and my own son deny him still tears me to pieces. It ripped the heart out of my childhood. Pray for me, Josep. All I can do now is to atone for sins I do not know that the Lord alone knows need to be atoned for, for the good of my immortal soul and that of my sons and daughters. Heavy weighs the crown of your queen, Josep, for I am in a living hell on earth."
Queen Constança and her daughter Yolanda, Duchess of Calabria, who was suffering from cholera, returned to Barcelona from Palermo in the New Year of 1300. Queen Constança retired to the convent of Santa Clara in the Ribera of Barcelona and devoted herself to prayer. Josep never saw the

tragic queen again and she would never see her sons at peace.

When King Frederick heard that his mother, Queen Constança, had died in late April 1302, he withdrew into himself. Despite attending her funeral in Barcelona, King Frederick did not visit King Jaume II and the atmosphere between them was icy. Yolanda, their sister, who had been attending the Queen in the Monastery de Santa Clara when she died, left Barcelona following the funeral the same day as Frederick. While he headed for Palermo and his palace, she returned to the side of her husband Duke Robert of Calabria, in Catania, just opposite Sicily.

There was so much hatred between the Neapolitans and their so-called allies the Provencals and the Genovese over the Falconaria disaster, which was vaunted as the event that was to change the course of the war, that it was no longer surprising to Josep that the invading army could no longer take concerted action and hold onto its advantages. The best example of that animosity which stuck in Josep's mind was the siege of Sciaca, a month later.

In terms of wealth, the force that had entered Sicily at the quiet, half-forgotten port of Termini was immense: it consisted of five hundred nobles from the best houses of Naples, Genova and Provence, accompanied by ten times as many foot soldiers; and if these nobles were not the heirs to great fortunes, they were the younger sons who bore all the hopes of the families of winning fame and fortune in battle. These so-called Knights of Death had arrived to deal the coup de grace to Sicily's independence from the crown of Naples yet were immediately hampered by dissent among themselves as to who would lead them. They claimed not to speak each others' languages and denied even being able to understand each other. Of an initial force of five thousand, two thousand died within the first days at Sciaca after fighting broke out between the different factions.

At sea, a man called Roger de Flor was as effective as Roger de Llúria - luckily now retired - had been at hampering supply lines. Roger de Flor was an ex-Templar turned adventurer from Brindisi, the son of a German falconer in the employ of Frederick II of Sicily, Holy Roman Emperor and the last King of Sicily before the Angevines. He had therefore been fiercely loyal to Queen Constança, King Frederick's granddaughter. With a chequered but attractive past, he seemed to be turning around the fortunes of Sicily. He had made a fortune as the owner of *The Falcon*, the biggest transport vessel of its time, by rescuing many noble refugees from Acre when it fell to the Mamluks in 1291, transporting them to Famagusta in Cyprus, where Josep's patron, Jacques de Molay was based. The laden vessels were easy prey to Roger de Flor's lightning fast naval abilities and the raw brutality of the Almogavers he commanded. Ship after ship whether Neapolitan Provencal or Genovese fell into the hands of the Brindisi-born falconer's son, who ransomed those he could and set the others free once they had taken an oath never to come against him again.

Spies said the soldiers in the camp around Sciaca were dying of camp sickness and starvation. Their supplies were dwindling daily.

"Then tomorrow we attack them!" said Roger de Flor.

An hour before dawn, the Almogavers in the south-west of the island assembled. Led by Roger de Flor, Blasco de Alagón, Berenguer d'Entença, Ramón de Moncada and Josep, the five hundred Almogavers let out a huge roar and struck their spearheads against the stones.

"Aur! Aur!" came the roar. "Desperta ferro!" And their ranks were illuminated phantasmagorically as if they were calling down some magical force to aid them.

Demotivated, ill and leaderless, the allied Napolitan force was barely able to defend itself. The Almogavers went in as a group and slashed and hacked their way through the entire force, which must have numbered three thousand. It was like a plague of locusts relentlessly devouring a field of wheat, starting at one end and not finishing until every ear of corn had been stripped. In less than an hour, only four nobles remained and three thousand, nobles and foot soldiers alike, had met their fate. The bodies were piled together and burnt. The booty for the five hundred Almogavers, as usual, was huge. King Philippe IV or Philip the Fair of France, King Charles II of Naples and the Pope, Bonifacio VIII, had thrown everything they could against Sicily and had utterly failed. Once Roger de Flor retired, superior naval ability was without question a factor in the Sicilians' favour. Yet poor preparation, lack of leadership, communication problems and outbreaks of camp sickness seriously undermined the effectiveness of the attacking force. Time and time again they also overlooked the savage effectiveness of the Almogavers.

There was a tense truce between Sicily and Naples between January 1300 and May 1302, when a solution was proposed to end hostilities. Just as Jaume had married Blanca of Naples in 1295 in an attempt to bring peace to the dominions of the House of Barcelona, so King Frederick duly married Blanca's sister, Eleanor, in May 1302 in order to consolidate that peace. Yet even that peace came at a price. Officially this ended all hostilities between the Kingdoms of Sicily and Naples but there were financial conditions attached that took time to work out. As a result, Messina was permanently host to the fleet of the King of Naples, controlling imports and exports on the east of the island. Peace still evaded them.

In Trapani, on the west of the island, the atmosphere was less tense. Josep at least had a choice. He was aware that he could have gone back to Barcelona when Jaume had first left the island to be crowned King of Catalunya Aragón and again when Frederick had been made king. He wondered what had kept him. Firstly, he recalled the optimism of the young man in his early twenties. At the time, he had been busy establishing himself on the island, he'd been in love with the *finca* now known as El Corral d'en Pere Josep. Sicily was relatively peaceful at that time as the Catalan Sicilian Admiral Roger de Llúria, had effectively policed its waters keeping the Angevins at bay. He was struck as he thought about these times how innocent and carefree they felt. He was perfectly able to pinpoint when that feeling had been lost: for it was when he was summoned to the Royal Palace and earnestly told by an optimistic future king that money would no longer be forthcoming from Barcelona unless he recruited Almogavers for King Jaume's mainland wars. He had recruited faithfully for nearly ten years until the Peace of Anagni in 1295. Cut off from his stipend unless he returned, Josep experienced living on significantly less. The Almogavers, used to continuous employment since 1282 at least, had expressly broken their oath of allegiance to King Jaume II, now the ally of Naples and so the natural enemy of the Sicilians. Josep compared the carefree days of the first seven years on the island with the sombre effect lack of money had had on their lives in the last decade. With Sicily being attacked constantly from the sea, Josep had always been away commanding his company in different parts of the island until the Trapani invasion had happened. What had been a steady income from the two established harvests of wine and olive oil had dwindled as war hit the market and the small but steady profits from the nascent fish salting industry had been wiped out.

"We'll be all right, we always have been," he said, late one night in August when the heat of the day had passed and the night was a starry dome so bright they could see into each other's eyes.

"I love your optimism," Lali said, "and I love you for it, Josep, but there's no point assuming things are going to get better. At this rate, the island could be overrun, our *finca* taken from us and we could be turned out of house and home."

"Well, there's no reason to put such an optimistic gloss on

things!" Josep replied with a little more sarcasm than he had wanted to and turning a way.

"Josep, you've got to face up to the realities of the situation," Lali replied turning him round to face her. She looked tired and worried and she knew he could see it in her eyes.

"Josep look at me."

"What?" he said gruffly, avoiding her eyes, faking a laugh.

"Look at me. You know what I'm capable of. It ahs been wonderful having your mother here. She and I have a loving and considerate relationship and the children love her being here. But I'm not sure I'm really up to all the bending and stretching the *finca* requires."

"We can get more help," Josep said.

"Not unless we can pay," Lali countered.

"We'll have a profit-share system then."

"That's all well and good but we have to rebuild the business from the top down, too. There just isn't the market for our wine and oil anymore. Illicit trade continues between Sicily and Catalonia and Sicily and Naples and the other cities of the kingdom but it's risky and profits are poor because the merchants, Catalan, Aragonese or Valencian alike are quite happy to exploit our desperation and pay the least they can. The whole island is in dire straits, Josep. It's terminal. They have us in a stranglehold."

Josep had rarely heard her talk in such absolute terms and he agreed.

"Heaven help us, then" he nodded. "Things are even worse than I thought."

"That's what I'm trying to tell you!" said Lali, looking him earnestly in the eye.

"I'm sorry, I was not trying to ignore you, quite the opposite. I do not want you to have to worry."

"I know, Josep, but I'm telling you, for all your instincts to protect us, things are only going to get worse now."

Josep took in a huge breath and pulled her to him. He had so much respect for her. He knew she wouldn't have said anything unless it was absolutely imperative now and his reluctance to talk had delayed their taking a decision about things.

"I only wanted a little peace and prosperity to raise my family," he murmured in her ear.

"Josep, I have spoken about it with Giuliana and I do not think I can have any more children," Lali whispered back.

"We have two children and I only ever wanted a small family," he said looking up at the heavens as if looking for an answer to an ineffable mystery. "But you are everything I can hope for as their mother."

She kissed him and looked into his eyes, pleased, surprised and moved.

"They take joy in their existence because of you, you know?" he said, looking up at the stars. "You make them realise that they are alive and being alive is amazing!"

He now looked so deeply into Lali's eyes he could see the clear blue of the stars of her irises. It was like looking into the heavens. "They see their life is now, unique and individual, but also somehow sense that something about it is immortal and unchanging." He paused, surprised himself by what he was saying. He did not know where it was coming from. "You as their mother deepen their understanding and joy in their own existence."

Lali gave a little choked laugh and he could see she was weeping. They sat holding each other under the night sky and the myriad stars above them, sensing the unchanging universe, the silence of the never-ending present, and their love that enfolded them.

CHAPTER SIX

July, 1302, Palermo.

"Who would ever have thought the demand would come from within the islands?" Josep laughed with true mystification at how rapidly fortunes could change.

"Well, nobody even knew who he was a couple of weeks ago but Roger de Flor is determined to sell himself to the highest bidder and he has an amazing business sense," Lali laughed back, checking off the produce as it was rapidly loaded up onto a whole fleet of carts.

"We've sold our entire wine and oil reserves from the past two years in one go!" she said grinning from ear to ear one morning.

"But it's wheat he really needs," Josep said.

"I know, and we had a little money put aside, so we bought up quite a bit the millers in Trapani and Marsala had before Roger de Flor could contact them himself, so I got a really good deal on that, too!" Lali babbled excitedly.

"They must be kicking themselves!" Josep beamed back.

"That's the importance of rapid information, Josep. It's business. Anyway, they've managed to sell the vast majority of their reserves at a good price and now they have a buyer in the future and it was me who put them onto Roger de Flor in the first place."

"He really understands business," Lali said, pulling the cords holding the sacks of flour in place on the carts.

"Messina has grown rich over twenty years of conflict, a city of pleasure for the Almogavers on leave and their coffers are groaning. What's money when it cannot buy anything, though? So they spent it all in Messina and the Messinese in turn have their coffers stuffed with gold but after these months of siege by land and sea by Naples, they have nothing to spend it on and now there are even people starving," Josep said.

"But what about the Peace of Caltabellota?" Lali asked.

"The devil is in the details," Josep replied. "King Charles does not want to withdraw his ships from Messina until he has extorted enough money out of the inhabitants. The blockade keeps all other exports out so the Messinese are short of food as all other supplies in Sicily are running out."

So the idea is he'll break the blockade and feed the starving Messinese who will be effectively a captive market and only too willing in their gratitude to pay him whatever he charges?"

"Exactly!" replied Lali.

"Brilliant! And he's a brilliant sailor, too. You should see him jumping around the masts, sails and rigging of the ship he's now got. It's like watching a monkey with a candle under its backside!"

"Josep!" Lali giggled.

"Actually, I'm just repeating what I've heard other people say. He's a couple of years older than me but he is ten times more agile!" Josep said.

Lali patted Josep's ample tummy. Times were hard but food had never been scarce and Josep had always had a good appetite.

"So when does he intend to sail?"

"They say he's going to run the blockade as soon as his ships are loaded," Lali replied.

The Neapolitans must have known what was being planned but had dismissed the plan as ludicrous. How could anyone break through a blockade that had been impenetrable for three months? Besides, who had the resources to plan and execute the operation of smashing through the Neapolitan flotilla, then organise the logistics and sale of food for a population of thousands? But Roger de Flor's plan had worked, the Neapolitan ships had scattered and the remaining Neapolitan troops around the city had been forced to surrender now their supply line had been cut.

"What they did not realise was what a brilliant entrepreneur he is. He was the person who was astute enough to rescued all the rich merchants from Acre while the city burned, for a price," Blasco d'Alagó, concluded wryly as he signed off the papers for the payment of Josep's militia.

"Let's hope he doesn't change sides when the next wave of troops invades," Josep added.

Josep's sources told him King Charles of Naples was so furious the blockade of Messina had failed, coming as it did after the humiliation of Falconaria and the imprisonment in Cefalú of his youngest son, Prince Philip of Taranto, that he had made one final appeal to the French Royal Court to assist and his request had been taken up by Charles of Valois, the King's younger brother. King Charles of Naples is said to have argued that it was to compensate Charles of Valois that Naples were still fighting in Sicily.

"Yet he will not kill a single person if he can help it" Josep heard Blasco d'Alagó say to Berenguer d'Entença. They were talking again about Roger de Flor. It was now mid-May.

"But death is the inevitable consequence of war, my dear Count" said the venerable old gentleman, in his clipped aristocratic Aragónese tones.

"But as his aim is more mercantile than military, he would rather cultivate goodwill than fear and by sparing lives he actually puts people in his debt. He has built up a huge network of contacts and loyalties and he commands huge sums of money, which he spends freely on paying his navy and troops loyal to him, for six months at a time," Blasco d'Alagó said.

"It's virtually unheard of," Berenguer d'Entença replied,

laughing.

"Exactly!" Blasco d'Alagó continued. "Four months is generous! But as a result, everyone who has the good fortune to be in his pay is prepared to do the work of two men."

"He's effectively revived the economy of the whole island then!" Berenguer d'Entença concluded, slapping his friend on the back. "That's good news for everyone."

"King Frederick is absolutely delighted with him. There seems to be nothing he cannot do. Once Duke Robert of Calabria was warned to withdraw his troops from the ring of castles he had around Messina back to Catona, Roger de Flor had the expertise and the courage to run the blockading flotilla during one of the worst south east gales Messina could remember. And do you know what?" The Aragonese noble, who had spent his life in military service, actually paused for dramatic effect.

"He was leading the four ships that got through himself in his own galley, the *Olivetti*, yet with his lateen mainsail furled and only his small sails up he managed somehow to squeeze through the Calabrian boats."

"But did not they resist?" Berenguer d'Entença asked logically.

"It was such a storm, it was as much as any of the crew could do just to remain upright. They were clinging on to the rigging themselves for dear life. Quite a few of them were swept overboard and some drowned. The lucky ones had rowed back to shore when the gale blew up," Blasco d'Alagó said. "And of course, once through, he immediately set up a wheat market."

"He must have been wretched, exhausted... and mobbed!" chuckled Berenguer d'Entença.

"Totally! But the most extraordinary detail of all is that he could have sold the wheat at double the price but he wanted to show his largesse so even the poorest citizens could afford to eat. He is being worshipped as a saint in the harbour area where the shipwrights, carpenters and fishermen live."

"So, he'll be broke before long!" Entença observed acidly.

"Well, that's what I thought. And this takes some believing but he managed to get the flour at such a low price a couple of weeks ago that he still turned a profit!" explained Blasco d'Alagó

"How much?" Berenguer d'Entença asked

"He doubled his money all the same."

"The man is a genius!" said Entença.

"Is it any wonder King Frederick has made him a member of the Royal household already and Rear Admiral of the Fleet?"

"Is there anything he cannot turn his hand to? The King had better hang on to him," Entença laughed.

CHAPTER SEVEN

King Frederick was awoken before dawn on the 29th of August to be told his sister Yolanda had died the night before and that Duke Robert of Calabria was prepared to come to terms on behalf of King Charles II of Naples at Caltabellota. Here, on the 31st of August, peace, significantly advantageous to King Frederick, given his comparatively weaker position, was signed. He was to receive Sicily as his kingdom for his lifetime but on his death it would revert to the house of Naples and would be called the Kingdom of Trinacria, an old name for Sicily long in disuse. He was also to receive one hundred thousand ounces of silver, the equivalent of a handsome royal income for five years. In return, he would relinquish all his properties in Calabria.

"He negotiated a very favourable deal," Lali commented to Josep.

"He was very ably advised by Roger de Flor and Berenguer d'Entença. Berenguer d'Entença is now charged with redeeming the castles in Calabria on behalf of King Charles II of Naples. That will not make him a popular man," Josep commented.

Josep finally met Roger de Flor at his triumph in Palermo the week after the treaty of Caltabellota was signed. The conversation would forever stay in Josep's mind.

"I understand this situation has been unfavourable for you and your family, Josep," he began.

"Well, until you came, the economy had disintegrated so completely we couldn't find buyers for our produce," Josep replied

"I'm glad we were able to help you. The islands woes are not over, I'm afraid. You do understand that, do you not? he asked, looking Josep earnestly in the eye.

"How so?" Josep asked.

"You have two generations of warriors who have been born and bred into guerilla warfare as a way of life!" Roger de Flor answered.

"You mean the Almogavers?"

"Indeed I do! Can you imagine what will happen to the island if they are to remain here?"

"But they can settle down like everyone else has to," reasoned Josep.

"But can you really see that happening? They've had ten, fifteen, twenty years of war, the last five years some of the most bitter of all. There is a momentum with this force that needs an outlet. They are an unruly, boastful, bloodthirsty bunch and you know it and the only thing that keeps them happy is fresh booty."

"They've made far more out of this war than their commanders," Josep added.

"That is up to the individual commander, Josep. There are some, who, like yourself, prefer to be discreet and others who grow exceptionally rich on the spoils of battle," replied de Flor.

"For example?" Josep asked slightly disconcerted if not embarrassed this matter was even being discussed.

"Roger de Llúria! He has amassed an absolute fortune and benefited from the generosity of his monarch," Roger de Flor smiled.

"You mean on account of his new properties in Valencia?" asked Josep.

"Indeed I do! I believe, and it is merely a personal opinion I add, that this was King Jaume's incentive to Roger de Llúria to retire from the Sicilian war thereby giving King Frederick at least a chance to fight his corner."

Josep nodded. This assessment not only accounted for the failures of Conrad Dòria and Conrad Llança who had been routed at Cape Orlando but referred to de Flor's own expertise and success as demonstrated by his handling of the Messina blockade.

"Yet he is an irascible fellow and those properties have brought him into conflict with Bernat de Sarrià, the King's Chancellor. When two great Lords like those to come into conflict, it becomes a question of honour, not just power and wealth."

"But Roger de Llúria was not born into high nobility," Josep pointed out.

"In his own opinion he was. His mother, Bella d'Amichi, after all was Queen Constança's nursemaid, lady-in-waiting and life-long companion. His family had standing."

"Nevertheless, he has achieved great success in his own right. He has become the greatest Admiral Catalunya Aragón have ever had" said Josep.

"Each man is different but there seem to be grades along two scales. There are those who desire advancement and those who are satisfied with their lot," continued Roger de Flor.

"I belong to the latter," said Josep.

"But there are many who belong to the former. Mark my words, the king will have trouble taking back from their present commanders their castles in Calabria. There will be several outraged nobles there, not to mention depleted fortunes," he explained.

There was a pause. "All this means there are going to be many ambitious soldiers who are still trying to make their mark or young Almogavers who do not know what else to do than raise hell. We need people like you, Josep, to lead these men, principled people not driven purely by material gain, de Flor said."

"What do you mean? I haven't thought about leaving the island. You can guarantee I shall not raise hell here!" Josep replied, a little warily. He did not like where this was heading.

"But we need men like yourself to bring common sense to the discussions among the commanders. and we need men of integrity that the soldiers can trust to lead them," said Roger de Flor.

"You mean, I could carry on doing what I've been doing for the last fifteen or twenty years? I was looking forward to getting away from all that."

"But your economy is now your main enemy, isn't it? Your finances do not really allow that, do they?" Roger de Flor reasoned. Josep was almost offended at the impertinence.

"What I'm offering you, Josep," Roger de Flor suddenly turned and said, "is wealth beyond your wildest dreams and within a year or two, you can be back here and live out the rest of your days in comfort and ease."

"Carry on," Josep said simply.

When Josep explained Roger de Flor's offer to Lali and his mother, Lali tried to seem calm and cheerful but Josep could see she was deeply upset.

"Constantinople? Our economic situation will not improve until you return and meanwhile it will suffer by your not being here to help," she said finally. It was the last thing Josep wanted to hear.

"But I'm doing this because of our economic situation," said Josep. "I've foregone my stipend from the Catalan crown by fighting against King Jaume II in the war. Now that the Treaty of Calatabellota has been signed and we are at peace, our source of income from King Frederick has also ended."

"We can manage," was all Lali would say.

"It's not enough," replied Josep. "This opportunity will set us up for life!"

"Or you could lose your life! What then?"

"Lali, you'll make me lose confidence in myself!" Josep replied. Catharine tactfully said nothing but when Lali turned to her, she simply opened her arms and hugged her. Josep could see Lali was crying.

It was not just the economic situation that motivated Josep. He was aware that he had been feeling restless since he'd heard about the Queen's death. She was the last link with his young adult life that he had had close to him. She had known him as a young squire, had seemed to understand him, had motivated him, consciously or not, to aspire to more than he might naturally have contemplated. He realised that he had depended for direction in his life on the fortunes of the Royal family, no less. Now that peace had been established between Jaume and Frederick, he felt somehow alienated from them. Again, that was the price he was paying for peace, a peace he had deeply desired. He wondered how close he would ever be again to either of the two brothers. There was an enormous amount of lost time to be made up between them; negotiations and treaties to hammer out, disputes to settle, future directions to be discussed. His own legal problem, the fact that he felt he still had a right to claim his stipend from the Catalan crown, would be small fry compared to all the other legal problems the court in Barcelona would be deliberating on.

He contacted a notary and set in motion the case he intended to present to King Jaume's Chancellor. Yet he knew that it would take months, if not years to settle. He was well advised to put in an appearance at the Royal Palace in Barcelona and he determined to return to Barcelona to do so.

CHAPTER EIGHT

September 1303.

As Josep had decided to travel to Barcelona before going to Constantinople, he registered with Roger de Flor, who was delighted Josep would be joining them when he had finished his business in Barcelona. The night before the Catalan company sailed, they spoke. A fortnight later the company was in Constantinople. It was September, 1303.

It felt odd for Josep to be back in Barcelona on his own after all these years. He had passed through quickly with Lali en route to Sant Pere de Ribes just after Catarina's birth and then together with his mother when they all embarked fro Sicily in 1286. That was now the best part of two decades ago already,. He headed to the Templar headquarters, which he had last visited before sailing with King Pere in 1282, when he had been but eighteen years old. Of course, he did not know anyone there but when he announced who he was, he was rapidly admitted and given comfortable lodgings.

"I have not heard from my godfather for years," he said that evening when asked about Jacques de Molay.

"Many things have happened, not least of which was the fall of Acre in 1291," replied the old Templar attending him. "However, our relationship with the Khans could bear fruit. The Mongols are fierce warriors and could hold the key to winning back the Holy Land. They won an important victory over the Mamluks in Homs three years ago."

"Fascinating!" was all Josep said, and so it was, but his mind was on so many other matters at that moment, he couldn't find room for a lesson on present-day Middle-Eastern diplomacy. He said as much, apologetically.

"Never fear, young man, I'm sure your godfather will bring you up to speed!" the venerable old monk said.

It was odd to be referred to as a young man but considering the years of the wizened old soldier warrior opposite him, he figured it was a relative term.

"Your Mother lives with you in Sicily, does she not?" the old monk said, as if reading his mind,: "That is good. A parent roots us in our childhood. We truly start to feel old when both our parents have died."

Josep was struck by the truth of what he said. Until that moment, he had felt children made their parents feel younger, more connected with life. But what the old soldier-monk said was also true. Your parents make you feel younger as you get older as they connect you with your childhood. What is more, it was not only true about his biological parents. He suddenly realised the effect that the various mother and father figures in his life had had and continued to have on his life. He had felt sad, exhausted and directionless when King Pere had died. He felt overwhelming pity for the Queen while she lived and when he had learned of her death, yet he had also felt strangely disorientated. He now realised what he had felt was a readjustment each time, as if another level of understanding was being laid down. The sense of loss and nostalgia were partly the subconscious realisation of alienation from his childhood self.

"The past is another country," he said to himself, without really understanding what he was saying or remembering when he had felt it before.

"Indeed!" said his aged companion, about whom Josep had momentarily forgotten. "And it grows stranger and stranger. In the same way, as we get older and older, we can become stranger and stranger to the next generation and those we bring into the world. The link to the present is through childhood. Once that link is cut, we drift into the past. Yet those who do not cherish their parents while they can and do not see that they link them to their childhood, those who do not have any experience of the past, do not realise the past is gone for the old because we have lost our parents and do not realise their own loss until it is too late. For that reason, it is always good for the young and the elderly to share each other's company. We were all young once and if we were lucky had parents whom we made feel young and who kept us feeling young as we got older as they connected us with our childhood. Our shared experience of childhood makes the present more meaningful." They both laughed because what the old warrior monk said was complex, sad and charming all at the same time. He had obviously been dwelling on the issue for a long time. In a flash, Josep imagined him as a younger man, perhaps married with children, then losing his wife and family and entering the ranks of the Templars late in life. He felt an aching empathy with the old man but he did not want this to happen to himself.

He was well-received the next day by King Jaume's Treasury officials and given to believe by his lawyer that his case for continuing to receive his stipend would be successful. This was due to the circumstances of his long service and loyalty to the Counts of Barcelona, even though he had ended up on the wrong side in the war between King Jaume and King Frederick The fact is that he had proof of the award to him by King Pere and in view of his good services recruiting for King Jaume during his campaign in Murcia between 1291 and 1295, his case was also fairly straightforward and likely to be heard within the next six months.

However, the conversation with the Templar had made Josep realise he wanted to see his mother more. It made him want to know his father more. It made him want to see Jacques de Molay more. And he wanted more than ever to square the circle and be able to live a contented life with his family. He looked into the future and saw it was possible but he had to go through this next stage first. He had a feeling of gathering excitement in his belly. Many strands of his life, he felt, were being pulled together and neatly tied.

One afternoon, the Treasury official attending Josep, Eiximen de Plegamans, mentioned in passing that news had been received of the Catalan expedition, which had now been in Constantinople and the Roman Empire for six months.

"They are as fierce as you would expect an Almogaver force to be. The amount of pent up energy, the desire to prove themselves up to the task to the Emperor, the Greeks and the invading Turks probably spilled over a little in my opinion," the sharp-faced accountant whispered confidentially.

"Why? What exactly has happened? They haven't started fighting among themselves, have they?" Josep asked, his imagination suddenly seizing him.

"No, no, not as far as I know, anyway, but the Greeks, it seems, are a fractious, unpredictable bunch. Apparently, the Almogavers were given a mixed reception when they arrived."

"Well, a three-week voyage doesn't leave anyone looking at their best!" Josep joked.

"No," the Treasury official said, grimacing at the imagined prospect. "Apparently, a lot of the Greek upper-class were actually scandalised by their appearance. The Greeks seem very particular about appearance and the Almogaver army was not what they had expected. They say some of them volubly expressed their horror and disappointment that these were the people who were supposed to deliver them. Their clothes of course were absolutely filthy, even more so than usual, when they paraded in front of the Emperor's Palace at Blachernae, where they anchored their fleet. They left in twenty galleys and countless smaller boats and transports so there were about six thousand of them."

Josep nodded as the images cascaded through his mind.

"You have to imagine the Emperor Andronicus there with Kor Michael, his eldest son and the entire court dressed in their finest clothes. The splendour of the occasion must have been incomparable and the contrast between the opulence of the Constantinople court of the Emperor and the Almogavers could not have been sharper," added Eiximen. *"Is this the army of the man who is to become the Grand Duke and marry the Emperor's niece?"* They asked themselves, apparently," continued Eiximen. *"They do not wear armour, they have string shoes, short spears and a fish knife for weapons. Woe is me, if these are the men who are to protect us from the fearsome Seljuk Turks."* Eiximen's imitation made Josep laugh.

"It sounds like the reaction they got in Messina at the beginning of the Sicilian war," Josep pointed out.

"Exactly so!" the official agreed. "However, the wedding did take place as planned between Roger de Flor and Maria Asanina, daughter of Ivan Assèn III of Bulgaria and Irene Palaiologina, sister of the Emperor Andronicus. However, at the height of the festivities, a messenger came to tell one of the leading Catalan knights, Corberán de Let, that the Genovese from the opposite shore to Blachernae at Pera, had crossed over the Golden Horn and set up their standard in front of the Royal Palace."

"The Genovese: a thorn in the side of the Catalans during the Catalan Crusade and the wars in Sicily. They have always vied with us and been against us," said Josep.

"Obviously, a terrible fight broke out. Who could contain that many Almogavers who still hadn't tasted battle and were spoiling for a fight? None of the nobles could hold them back nor could the Almogatens or Aldalils," Eiximen went on. "The long and short of it is that they slaughtered three thousand Genovese, together with their leader Rosso di Finar. The Emperor, far from admonishing the Grand Duke, who of course was now a member of his family, congratulated him on the success of his unruly and highly strung cohorts."

"Well, they were provoked, as you say," said Josep, indignantly, defending the Almogavers actions.

"Yes, yes, without doubt they were provoked," continued the Treasury official, "but the extraordinary aspect for me was how unconcerned the Emperor seemed to be at the fate of the Genovese."

"Why should he have cared that much?" Josep asked.

"Because this was the Genovese colony in Pera that had lived with the Greeks for centuries as their business class and bankers. They were a pillar of the community. For me, Andronicus showed himself to be ruthless and fickle," Eiximan said.

"Qualities perhaps necessary in a ruler of a besieged kingdom!" said Josep.

"Yes, yes!" said Eiximen, a little impatiently. "But he could at least have made a show of encouraging restraint out of regard for their long-standing service."

"Yes, I see what you mean," said Josep. He dwelt on that information all night. "So the Emperor is mercurial and not to be trusted!" he concluded to himself.

Further news of the Almogavers came through Bernat de Sarrià, King Jaume's Chancellor himself. Josep was summoned into his presence a week later.

"I have had word from Berenguer d'Entença that you may embark with him in September for Constantinople. He has been delayed but feels there is a lack of leadership at the higher levels of the Catalan expedition to the east and is keen to be under way. He tells me he has received your name from the

Admiral of the Catalan Company Roger de Flor, requesting that he offer you passage." Josep was both thrilled and amazed that his name had come to be known by two other such illustrious courtiers.

"I am extremely grateful to you, my Lord, and will embark with Berenguer d'Entença."

"I suppose you have heard the news?" Sarrià asked.

"No, my Lord. I was told about the arrival in Constantinople by Eiximen de Plegamans but he only got as far as telling me about the massacre of the Genovese of Pera," answered Josep.

"Ah, yes. I'm afraid this news is also rather shocking. I wonder what you make of it. I've heard that once the Almogavers left Constantinople, they sailed to Artaki, which is a promontory on the southside of the Sea of Marmoris, well-known for its rich agricultural land. Between Artaki and Birsa, the ancient capital of the Roman province of Bithynia, Kor Michael, the son of the Emperor Andronicus and Co-Emperor, had twelve thousand cavalry and a hundred thousand infantry troops at his disposal."

He took Josep over to a table in his rooms and showed him on the map.

"Nevertheless, this promontory was completely overrun by the Turks. Well, the Almogavers of course were delighted to be on a mission at last and secretly landed at the town of Artaki, the harbour on the western side of the promontory," he said pointing.

"There they quietly awaited instructions. Spies were immediately sent out to reconnoitre the position of the Turks and discovered them to be less than six leagues away, a distance that can be achieved in six hours' quick march. So at night they left to find the Turkish enemy. The spies also reported that the Turkish force was between two rivers, one major one called Gonen Çayi, which ends at this lake here, some twenty-five miles south of there, " he said, pointing it out to Josep so he had a clear idea, "and a small river, the Tatu Deresi, just north of a town called Gebeçinar, next to Misakça, just here. This meant of course that there was no escape if the Turkish force was attacked as they were encamped between two rivers and the distance to the sea, as you can see, and between the two rivers is not great. So, very convenient for the Almogavers and a perfect opportunity for a surprise attack. Well, the Almogavers fell on the enemy camp before dawn while they slept in their tents. The fighting was savage. The Almogavers were outnumbered and the Turks, though surprised, fought fiercely for they are a martial race and besides they had no option, hemmed in as they were. Also, they travel with their wives and families so they were desperate to protect them. They say that the entire Turkish force in that area was wiped out that day."

"How many were there?" asked Josep, following closely but a little mystified as to the point of the story.

"It depends on whom you count," Sarrià lowered his head and watched Josep from under his eyes for his reaction.

"What do you mean?"

"Well, this is what I want your opinion on," replied Sarrià.

"After dealing with the ten thousand troops an instruction was issued that no quarter was to be given."

"In other words, no prisoners," Josep checked.

"Yes that's right."

"So they executed the injured?" Josep asked again.

"Yes," replied the Chancellor.

"If that is what you want my opinion on, my Lord, I have to say that unfortunately that is normal procedure, especially if the force is mobile and would be hindered by having a train of prisoners behind it," Josep elucidated, holding his hands palm open as if beseeching comprehension.

"Yes, yes, I know that, Josep," said the Chancellor a little impatiently. "It's like an open invitation to attack. I've had experience of the Almogavers myself in Sicily. But that's not my problem. What bothers me is this. They showed no quarter to all boys of ten years and above. Slaughtered them all."

Josep looked away and shook his head. He remembered what Lali had said. "I hope there are no children involved." How had she known?

He looked up and saw Sarrià still watching him intensely.

"It's very extreme," said Josep. "I can't imagine it could have been Roger de Flor's idea. He is known for his mercy in battle."

"Perhaps provided they are his people," the Chancellor ventured. "I can't imagine he specified this. He must have been under instructions. Either from the Emperor," he paused.

"...or the co-Emperor, Kor Michael," Josep finished Sarrià's sentence for him. "So though he was unable to take on the Turkish force himself, he nevertheless gave instructions to kill children too," Josep said, looking shocked and appalled.

"Yes, so it seems, if what they say is true. I haven't got to the bottom of it yet but shortly afterwards, Eiximen d'Arenós, the Admiral, left the main body of the Almogavers. Apparently, there was an incident between himself and Roger de Flor," Sarrià continued.

"So where is she now?" asked Josep.

"He's in Athens with the French Duke of that city, to whom he went to offer his services," replied Bernat de Sarrià.

"To a Frenchman?" asked Josep. "My goodness, he really must have been disgusted. I'm glad I wasn't there. I couldn't have participated in the murder of children," Lali's words again rang eerily in his mind again.

"Is this the kind of war I'm volunteering for?" Josep asked himself. He stifled the thought and the obvious answer.

The following day, Eiximen de Plegamans contacted him. A reduced stipend had been granted to him. He communicated his acceptance and left for Messina, where he helped Berenguer d'Entença fit out the nine triremes King Frederic of Sicily was contributing to the mission. He sent a message to Lali that his negotiations had been successful but avoided any mention of the children in Artaki.

"It's good to know who you are working for," said Josep casually one day. Berenguer d'Entença did not reply immediately. "King Jaume has been generous with me but I feel if I had not presented my case to Bernat de Sarrià, I might have lost my right to a stipend all together," he explained.

"It's a difficult matter to work for two Kings," came the unexpected reply.

Josep did not continue the conversation but it lodged in his memory all the same. He regretted the comment he had made as clearly Entença knew his history in detail and was keen for Josep to understand that his loyalties were and always had been clear. He was the servant of King Jaume.

"I'm glad I'm not working for either of them," Josep now thought. His understanding was that he was under the orders of Roger de Flor and that his fortunes would depend on him, not on King Jaume or King Frederick. He frowned as he recognised the chill the cynicism leaked into his heart.

Messina was as busy as ever, the shipyards deafening, ringing with the endless hammering of metal on metal as the triremes were readied. It was curious to hear the mix of Catalan, Sicilian, Neapolitan and Provençal in the port, as these new times of peace meant all comers were welcome.

CHAPTER NINE

They finally set off from Messina for Constantinople at the beginning of September 1304.

A steady breeze from the south made for choppy seas but good sailing and the coastline they hugged at a distance of no more than a league though beautiful at first became monotonous and Josep lost interest in it.

The dolphins swam with the nine triremes and occasionally a pod of small whales surfaced within seeing distance, letting out huge blasts of air from their blowholes, then cruising again before disappearing into the deep. Long days of the voyage to Constantinople were broken only by the stories of the boatswain of their trireme, a garrulous Catalan from Begur, Dalmau de Peratallada.

"We are all billeted with host families," he began. "You cannot respect the locals though because they just give you anything you want. It's all dirt cheap, anyway, but we still do not have to pay for anything!"

The hollow boasting of relative wealth and disregard for the value of things, which were conversely not at all cheap for the local population supplying it, were unfortunately familiar to Josep and he found it irritating.

"Are the men showing any restraint then?" Josep asked looking hard at Peratallada. "I do not suppose anyone really has any idea of the value of things there. I suppose there's an endless supply of food and wine. How are the hosts to be paid?" he asked reasonably.

"Oh I do not know! You'll have two ask the quartermaster

about that!"

"And who is the quartermaster?" asked Josep.

"Ramón Muntaner, his name is," the boatswain replied.

"Great! I know him well. He is an old friend."

"Well, he'll organise your food and accommodation. You'll live like a king, and why not? That's why we are here after all! Constantinople needs warriors like us because they cannot defend themselves and you need to feed and water warriors well, do you not?" he said, looking nervously now at Josep for affirmation.

"Well, I suppose so but there are limits!" Josep said pointedly. The boatswain looked bored now, this was not the light-hearted banter he was used to. Josep had the impression the Almogaver army was living it up.

"How much is the allowance of the Almogavers and the other troops?" he asked Berenguer d'Entença.

"It's set at an ounce of silver per month for an Almogaver, which is about two sous a day and up to four ounces a month for a knight, who has to look after his horse, too."

"That's a small fortune. A sou a day is ample to feed yourself. You can save on two! And that's just the expenses! What about the salaries?"

"The Almogavers get an ounce which is fifty-six sous a month, so about seven hundred sous a year, the Almogatens get three times that and the knights, four times that," replied Entença.

"My goodness, that's astronomical," gasped Josep. "My stipend is three hundred sous a year and a senior functionary working for the King earns about three thousand."
"And then there's the share of the booty on top of that," added Entença.

"How can the Emperor continue to pay that?" asked Josep.

"He's banking on the job being done quickly but I think he was expecting a smaller force. I think he was expecting four thousand Almogavers and there must be six thousand, if not already there then on their way. And there must be between one thousand five hundred and two thousand knights all told. Anyway, I'm sure Roger de Flor has negotiated something acceptable to both sides."

"Well, that's what I wanted to say to you earlier," the boatswain said peevishly. "They pay good salaries because we're the only troops capable of getting rid of their vermin."

"By vermin, you mean all the Turkish tribespeople around Constantinople and its empire?" Josep asked acidly. Entença gave Josep a swift glance and raised an eyebrow a fraction. Josep heard the boatswain tut to himself.

"The various tribes or *gabellas* have been attacking the big cities of what they call the Empire of Rum, or the eastern Roman Empire to us. Big cities like Philadelphia, Magnesia, Tyre, important cities with provincial governors, all loyal subjects of Constantinople and therefore good taxpayers. Over the years the Turkish tribes have lost their fear of the garrisons that are supposed to defend these cities," said Entença.

"So the local garrison simply submits to the Turkish forces?" asked Josep

"It's a complex question," replied Berenguer d'Entença. "The cities are used to being besieged, like any city. But unlike a typical siege, where the city would have ample stores of food, the odds are heavily stacked in favour of the besiegers in Anatolia at the moment. The countryside is so overrun by the Turkish tribes that food is scarce at the best of times. Farmers are constantly at risk of attack outside the city walls as the city garrisons are ineffective" Berenguer d'Entença continued.

"But I thought all that changed after Roger de Flor's victory at Artaki?" Josep said.

"The biggest Turkish force was wiped out, that is true, but then the winter was so severe between December and March that the Catalan company simply stayed where it was until May," Berenguer d'Entença replied.

"But May is after spring has begun! Why had not they begun campaigning?" Josep said.

"Because the row between the Almogavers and the Alan mercenaries blew up," chipped in the boatswain, Peratallada.

"Yes, that's right, and apparently that took a lot of sorting out," agreed Berenguer d'Entença. "Then, there was quite a long delay before Roger de Flor finally travelled to Constantinople to negotiate payment of the troops and their hosts in the Artaki peninsula. So he did not return until mid-April or the beginning of May."

"But April and May are two important campaigning months. There's only June and July after that, are not there? I guess no fighting can take place in August as it's simply too hot," Josep ventured.

"Exactly," agreed Berenguer d'Entença. "Hence the Emperor was so keen for the army to get moving, leave Artaki and begin the Anatolian campaign."

"So when did they finally set off?" asked Josep

"They marched on the first city, Philadelphia, not long after Roger de Flor returned from Constantinople so the end of May beginning of June. By then, any refugees from the Turkish defeat at Artaki had made their way south to the Turks besieging Philadelphia."

"And the garrison inside Philadelphia did nothing!" Josep laughed. "And what about the Imperial army under Kor Michael?" Josep asked.

"They were decimated by disease on the coast of the sea of Marmara and incapable of any significant military action."

Berenguer d'Entença replied.

"Why?" Josep asked incredulously shaking his head.

"Basically, because the troops had been recruited by force from the towns of the Empire and did not have any military background and couldn't be trained. Hence Kor Michael, the Emperor's son, though apparently a worthy commander, could do nothing and had to cede the offensive to Roger de Flor, in the meantime allowing the Turkish tribes to overrun the whole of Anatolia."

"So no food was produced," said Josep.

"That`s right and not only for the cities of Anatolia, where much of the grain of the Empire comes from but also for Constantinople," said Berenguer d'Entença.

"So the powers that be needed action quickly!" said Josep.

"Exactly, and they got it. Roger de Flor went from one city to the next wiping out or putting to flight the besiegers, then punishing the besieged."

"Punishing?" Josep asked.

"Yes, for not putting up more of a fight. In Germe, he had a number of Imperial officials hanged. The Imperial governor was only saved by the insistent supplications of the rest of the townspeople. Then following the battle of Aulax, by the time the Almogavers got to Philadelphia the besieging Turkish force had scattered. By now the tide was turning and the Almogavers were received like heroes despite their appearance."

"Presumably their reputation preceded them by then," Josep interrupted.

"Exactly. People were fleeing from them in abject terror. but who wouldn't, facing a force of one thousand seasoned cavalry and four thousand Almogavers? Not to mention a whole town of hundreds of camp followers, cooks, merchants, Almogavers' wives -and they are a fearsome bunch- and families following behind them."

They had been at sea for a week now and were approaching Monemvasia, the first great Peloponnese port of Latin Achaia, at the extreme west of the Frank-controlled Greek state.

The nine triremes anchored for the night just outside the huge rocky port and they were warmly welcomed by the townspeople.

"Your colleague was the last visitor here," said the Mayor, welcoming them on behalf of William, Prince of Achaia, and offering them a delicious glass of Malvasia, which was produced locally.

"I do not know who you mean," replied Berenguer d'Entença.

"Rocafort, Bernat de Rocafort, he was here three months ago," the Mayor replied.

It was clear from Berenguer d'Entença's face that this was not good news. The Mayor mumbled some kind of apology and disappeared.

"Is this bad news my Lord?" asked Josep.

"I had something to do with that cut-throat in Calabria. I do not wish to make his acquaintance again soon."

Their voyage now took them past Hydra as they hugged the rocky Achaean coast then sailed out into the beautiful islands of the Cyclades, skirting round the southern coast of Kythnos, Syros and Tinos. From dawn till dusk, they sailed past these serene-looking gems in the endlessly churning sea. Autumn lent the air around the islands a limpid clarity, each one protected by a thin layer of high-altitude cloud. The sailing was good, the winds were always fresh, and the sun shone.

Fresh fish was caught off the back of the triremes, the sailors sang at night and even rum was given to the galley slaves on the lowest deck, where Josep never dared to go. Apart from that, life at sea seemed idyllic.

The following day, Josep spotted the island they were heading towards.

"Chios," said Peratallada, "where Admiral Ferran d'Aunés has his base. We'll skirt around the south then head North up the eastern side of the island to Chios port and city. If you look out to starboard, you'll see the coast of Anatolia. That's where the Almogavers have been operating for the past year."

Smaller vessels came and went as the nine galleys crossed the eastern Aegean from Tinos to Chios. Josep had the impression that as soon as the Greek boats realised they were so close to Catalan Sicilian galleys, they scudded away as quickly as their lateen sales could take them. Each Greek vessel was brightly painted in blues and reds and bore an Egyptian-looking eye on the prow. Josep considered this charm and the apparent dread of the Greeks toward the galleys and concluded the fleet symbolised fear rather than liberation for the fishing boats.

"These islands are under Imperial rule, are they not?" Josep asked without meaning to invite discussion.

"Chios, Lesbos and Lemnos are, yes sir," replied the boatswain. Josep could see what a beautiful island Chios was with high lands to the north of the island and an undulating, red-soiled plain, full of orchards and small shrubby trees to the south, nearest to them.

As they entered the generously proportioned harbour of Chios, they passed imposing fortified lighthouses and on disembarking were immediately struck by the perfume of the Aegean.

"What is the scent in the air?" Josep asked one of the captains of the other galleys as they congregated in the main square of the port, having tied up the vessels.

"The strong smell of musk is rock rose or cistus. It is typical of these islands. They make a painkiller from it that they mix with a gum called mastic you can probably smell too and it eases all aches and pains."

Josep filled his lungs with the strong smell, feral, earthy, carnal. It reminded him of making love.

"And the other, sweeter smell?" he asked.

"The other smell is jasmine," the captain replied.

"Of course it is," Josep said remembering the smell from his nights on Formentera, where the whole island seemed to smell of it. Suddenly he remembered Lali and realised how much he missed her. Making love with her was the best way he knew of easing aches and pains. He was missing her badly.

"I recognise it now but the combination is new for me. It smells great here."

"I'm glad you like it. It's the smell of the islands," replied the captain.

They were met shortly by the Admiral himself, Ferran d'Aunés, a hearty, stocky man in his fifties, who had heard that Josep was a friend of Ramón Muntaner's and was travelling with Berenguer d'Entença.

"Ramón Muntaner is looking forward to seeing you again. He asked me to bid you welcome and hopes you have had a good voyage. I trust you have?" the Admiral asked cordially.

"The sailing is exquisite!" said Josep. "Everything here seems to be going well. Our wishes seem to have been granted."

"The company have been very successful and the Emperor is delighted with our work," replied the Admiral.

"But where is the company now?" Josep asked. He had been half hoping Ramón Muntaner would meet him himself so he could ask him.

"At the moment, they have gone on a fact-finding mission into the heart of Anatolia, to see the extent of the Empire's dominions. They are expected back imminently," replied the Admiral.

"Has the whole force gone?" Josep asked.

"The Grand Duke is under instructions from the Emperor to penetrate as far as possible into the land held by the Turkish tribes east of here to the so-called Iron Gates which lead through Alana and Tarsus to Lesser Armenia and Syria. That is the route the Crusaders take overland to the Holy Land and the Crusades," replied the Admiral.

"I wish I were with them. It would take me closer to my Godfather, Jacques de Molay!" Josep replied.

"He is in Cyprus, is he not?"

"Exactly so, sir, as far as I know, he is mainly in Famagusta but is also often in Limassol."

"Waiting for the opportunity to take Acre back!" laughed the Admiral. "It's easier to get there by sea, let me know if you need passage!"

"Thank you, sir, I see you have every kind of vessel at your disposal. Is the entire fleet here?"

"Yes, it is. We have just returned from Anaia. You'll have heard that Bernat Rocafort has arrived from Calabria? The Admiral asked. Josep nodded. "He was sent to Anaia to meet us after presenting himself and his force in Constantinople. The company had completed its operations around the Hermos River Valley. It's a wild and beautiful part of the country, apparently, littered with ancient cities like Pergamum, Magnesia, Smyrna and Philadelphia, all back under Imperial control thanks to our efforts."

"Have there been many casualties on our side?" Josep asked.

"Far fewer than we had expected and nowhere near as many as theirs. They cannot fight against our infantry. They are completely unused to it. We can move in tight formation unbothered by the arrows of their famous archers. Our troops drive into the midst of their cavalry, their horses come down and the riders are unseated and in their heavy gear are easily picked off."

"How is it that we can withstand their archers?" Josep asked.

"We have our small shields and battle coats made of thick leather which we wear for the first part of the assaults. Also, we wear our helmets at all times. It is an especially important point since Alet's death."

"Corberán de Alet is dead?" Josep was shocked.

"One of the few casualties but of course devastating. He was the Seneschal of the Almogavers."

"And engaged to be married to Roger de Flor's daughter," Josep added.

"Indeed, you are well informed. Your Godfather must know her, as she was sent for from Cyprus."

"How did he die?"

"It happened at a city called Thyateira, between Magnesia and Pergamon. The Turkish cavalry was in full rout and the troops were fleeing in disorder into the hills around the city. Alet was at the head of the Company of Almogavers giving chase as usual with Ramón Muntaner closely behind him. They fought their way to the top of the hill and the enemy was utterly vanquished. The sun was beating down and it was incredibly hot. The troops were still in full battle gear, including the heavy leather overcoat. Corberán stopped to catch his breath, exchanged a few words with Muntaner, then inexplicably unfastened his chinstrap and took off his helmet. Before anyone could do anything about it, an arrow from a sniper hit him on the temple, killing him instantly.

"What a waste of an outstanding man!" said Josep.

"But the question is who will Roger de Flor choose to replace him? Many think it will inevitably be Bernat Rocafort!"

"Yes, that would be an obvious choice," Josep replied tactfully but he made a mental note to pass on this information to Berenguer d'Entença.

CHAPTER TEN

The following day, the entire fleet set sail to rendezvous with the returning company in Anaia, as they returned from their mission to the very limits of the now Turkish occupied Empire of Rum, as the Turks called the Roman Empire. No sooner had the fleet arrived than an Imperial messenger was ushered in to see Aunés, as the most senior officer commanding in the Grand Duke's absence. Josep attending Berenguer d'Entença was present.

"The Emperor informs you that the army is required urgently in Thrace as the Emperor of Thrace, who is the Father of Grand Duchess Maria, Roger de Flor's wife, has died. He has left two sons to inherit his throne but power has been seized by his brother."

Consequently, exhausted though they were after their journey across Anatolia, the Catalan company, laden with spoils from yet another crushing victory against the Turkish tribal armies, were quickly required to march again.

It was the first time in this campaign that the Grand Duke Roger de Flor, Bernat Rocafort, Ferran d'Aunés and Berenguer d'Entença had been in the same room on this campaign. As ever Josep was in attendance to Berenguer d'Entença.

"Forgive me, my Lord Entença, that we are unable to receive you and welcome you as your rank deserves!" began the Grand Duke. Josep noticed Bernat Rocafort cough and shift uncomfortably.

"May I introduce Bernat Rocafort, Commander of the Company, my Lord" Roger de Flor said to Berenguer d'Entença.

"Your reputation precedes you," began Bernat Rocafort, taking the initiative and reaching out to shake Berenguer d'Entença's hand. The old Catalan noble stiffened and made no move to take his hand. The snub was immediately noted by everyone and Roger de Flor shot both Rocafort and Entença a disparaging look.

"You gained a reputation in Calabria," Entença replied to Rocafort. "Duke Robert of Calabria will wish to adjust your last transaction with him when you return to Italy," he added icily.

"He can keep his castles but he cannot have his money back because it's already spent!" Rocafort forced a laugh, half turning to his Almogatens, who nodded and smirked behind him. Yet he had paled visibly.

"Nevertheless, you have caused him significant expence," replied Berenguer d'Entença.

"You can tell him from me he's welcome to sue me!" he replied, unable to disguise the petulance in his voice.

The sniping was embarrassing and the atmosphere highly charged. Both men were livid now, bodies tense for rapid action, Bernat Rocafort's eyes locked on Berenguer d'Entença's aquiline features, haughty and inexpressive.

"Gentlemen, gentleman!" Roger de Flor breathed as calmly as he could. "Let us not become a forum for litigation that belongs in the courtrooms of Naples on the other side of the Mediterranean Sea. We have important matters to deliberate on. The Emperor demands our urgent presence in Thrace. How quickly can we turn around, Commander Rocafort?"

"The company at present is at its toughest, my Lord, and will be ready tomorrow morning." he growled, not taking his eyes of Entença.

"But what about your sick and injured?" de Flor asked, genuinely shocked.

"Malingerers and whingers will be singled out and can do what the devil they like, my Lord," Rocafort replied.

"We can hardly leave them here in Anaia!" answered Roger de Flor.

"Then drop them off along the way to garrison the cities we'll lose unless we man them, my Lord!"

Roger de Flor looked at him as if he had gone mad. Josep couldn't belive he was addressing roger de Flor in this tone. Berenguer d'Entença sniffed.

"Manning the retaken cities is an important consideration, Grand Duke, but I suggest it be done by the able-bodied!" he said.

Bernat Rocafort snorted. "I was only joking. Can you not take a joke?"

"How many do you have with you my Lord?" Roger de Flor asked Berenguer d'Entença doing his best to ignore Bernat Rocafort's comment and bowing deferentially to the Catalan noble. Entença was slowly shaking his head.

"We have a thousand Almogavers and a hundred and fifty knights, Grand Duke," Berenguer d'Entença replied courteously. "But should we not present ourselves to the Emperor first before deploying our troops in his territory?"

"Indeed. It is a question of protocol," replied Roger de Flor, "You are wise to remember how crucial all such matters of form are in Constantinople, my Lord."

"I am glad that we see eye to eye" said Berenguer d'Entença quietly. "I am here to serve you as well as I can."

Bernat Rocafort coughed self-consciously. "Well, if that's settled, then, can we get down to business and sort out the details please?" he said abruptly.

Berenguer d'Entença looked away and Roger de Flor paused momentarily before he continued talking to the noble, glancing once in annoyance at Bernat Rocafort.

"My Lord, your presence is most appreciated and on behalf of the Catalan company and the Emperor, whom I, as Grand Duke, represent, I welcome you."

"I am most gratified and will do my utmost to serve both the Grand Duke and the Emperor." Berenguer d'Entença replied.

"Shouldn't that be the other way around?" Bernat Rocafort interjected, sniggering and half turning again to his Almogatens, one of whom was Gispert de Rocafort, his brother, who winked at him sharing the joke.

"My Lord Entença, excuse us if you would be so kind. Tempers are frayed and worries accumulate…"

"I'm not worried!" laughed Bernat Rocafort, swaggering a little now, oblivious of his vulgarity and the embarrassment he was causing both men.

As warmly as he could, Berenguer d'Entença grasped Roger de Flor's hand, thanked him for his gracious welcome and departed.

Josep, who had witnessed the entire exchange, was astonished by Bernat Rocafort's rudeness and blatant insubordination. Luckily, Berenguer d'Entença marched quickly away but Josep stayed just long enough to hear the door to the council chamber slam shut and Roger de Flor's voice raised loud enough for him to hear as he dressed down his second-in-command.

"Is he really thinking of making him his Seneschal!" he asked himself almost out loud. He caught the eye of Ferran d'Aunés and they exchanged a look but said nothing.

"We shall be sailing directly to Constantinople tomorrow morning, Josep," Berenguer d'Entença announced later that afternoon.

"My Lord, I have already warned Ferran d'Aunés that he should be prepared for that. He has already instructed the captains under his command to provide any equipment and victuals we may need for the three-day voyage."

"Very good, Josep. You have saved me several hours work and I am loathe to venture too far from our ships lest I should come unexpectedly across that jumped-up bailiff!" replied Berenguer d'Entença.

"Yes, my Lord. My Lord?"

"Yes Josep, speak."

"My Lord, it is some urgent intelligence that I feel you should know. I have heard that as Corberán de Alet has died, the Grand Duke must appoint a new Seneschal."

Berenguer d'Entença stiffened and looked coldly and steadily at a point between and just above Joseps eyes. It was disconcerting.

"My Lord, my point is that if you do not stay here, the Grand Duke will be obliged to appoint Bernat Rocafort as his Seneschal," Josep said barely daring to meet the noble's eyes.

"Josep, Josep, Josep! Is that all? I thought you were about to reveal a plot to scuttle our boats!" He laughed, clapping Josep on the left shoulder.

"I shall keep my men as separate from him as he shall keep his from mine. Then he can be Seneschal to his heart's content for the Company as it is at present. I am sure you are right and that this will be communicated to the Emperor before we even arrive in Constantinople!" he said.

In fact, apart from a handful of occasions Josep was mercifully spared the mayhem, barbarity and vulgarity that accompanied Bernat Rocafort's tour. As galleys that accompanied Entença's force rowed out of the elegant, perfumed port of Chios, they passed an island a little way from the coast on which innumerable flocks of birds screamed their deafening, discordant song, wheeling and diving in a seemingly pointless and unnecessary fight for a scrap to land on. Josep found himself transfixed with fascination and wondered to himself when he broke off his reverie what he had found so fascinating.

"Once they take to the air, another comes to take its place," said the garrulous ship's Captain Dalmau de Peratallada. "For me, it's like a battle but, unlike the birds, we leave troops on the ground to hold the land." Josep was struck more by the similarities than the differences.

Passing Samos, they lost sight of the coast as they headed for Lesbos, the widest stretch of open water they encountered that day. The sea, previously dark blue, now turned blue black.

"This is deep, deep water around here!" Entença commented. "Here dolphins may rescue you otherwise you are dragged down to the depths of Neptune's kingdom.

Josep shuddered as old fears of drowning threatened to engulf him and in a flash he saw Entença dead in his imagination but himself alive. He was deeply disturbed.

As Josep's galley sailed past Lemnos, he noticed the landscape on the coast was becoming significantly flatter. There was a strong wind blowing offshore and the triremes had to use their galley slaves to hold a course parallel with the coast. There was nothing but open countryside as far as the eye could see all the way to low hills in the distance. "Do you have any idea what you are looking at?" Berenguer d'Entença asked him. "This is the plain of Illias, where the Trojan war was fought."

"I'm familiar with the story because Jacques de Molay delighted us at home many times with his renditions of different episodes from the story. Sometimes, he would act out scenes, such as Paris and Helen in love, using my mother as Helen." He now remembered how like lovers they had seemed.

"They say this is the place where the city of Troy was, a fine place for a city, surrounded by farms and fertile land, with easy access to the sea and controlling the routes to the Sea of Marmara and beyond."

"But easy to attack!" pointed out Josep.

"It was surrounded by such a huge wall!" Entença replied.

"No wall is impregnable!"

"Indeed you are right, Josep!"

"And Constantinople, does it have walls to compare?"

"Mightier still some would say! The city is indescribably huge!"

They sailed past the island of Tenedos to the west and at sunset steered east and turned into what they called the Boca d'Aver, the mouth of the Sea of Marmara although the captain pointed out this more accurately referred to the estuary of the Avros, or Evros, river.

"Actually, it sounds a little like the Ebro," Josep said a little whimsically. He was missing home.

Now that they had turned east, they sped along with the southeast wind blowing fresh behind them. "This is Madytos. We're now in Thrace, peaceful territory," the captain called out, pointing to a huge castle on the left-hand shore. An hour later, he signalled also on the left

"This is Gallipolis, the castle is smaller but the harbour is deeper." As they continued their journey, they came to the beautiful port of Rodostó, where they harboured for the night. The town was welcoming, most of the main public buildings up flights of steps, giving good views over the harbour and surrounding countryside. Prominent in the town was the meat market, where prize cuts were displayed and haggling was fiercely in progress. There were stalls of every kind arranged around the market.

"We are but two days from Constantinople here," said Berenguer d'Entença, "so do not spend too much money here.

The choice is bound to be much greater in the capital." It felt as if they were idle wayfarers without a care in the world.

CHAPTER ELEVEN

Josep's first impressions of Constantinople were to stay with him in for life. He was used to seeing huge cities contained within great walls, just as Barcelona was, but the size of this city was colossal. Even from a distance, one could make out where the gleaming, sun-bleached, marble walls demarcated the city's sea-wall defences, coming all the way down to the sea of Marmara itself. In the distance, beyond the walls, he could see religious buildings with elegant cupolas, churches with intricate designs, monuments projecting into the sky the glory of the city twice the height of the ship's mast, a patchwork of warm-coloured, terracotta roofs housing, Josep imagined, hundreds of thousands of people. Dotted here and there, were green areas on the low hills and straddling the city from west to east a bridge-like structure with colonnades, one above the other, on five or more levels.

"It's the Aquaduct of Valens," said the captain, noticing Josep's fascination, "and it dates from the earliest times of the city."

"It's magnificent. I've seen similar in Tarragona but nothing on that scale. It's truly spectacular!"

"Well, prepare yourself for more architectural splendour," said the captain. The palaces are enormous!"

The seawalls broke off to give way to a huge commercial harbour and public buildings. Smaller boats, heavily laden and low in the water, sped past them in all directions. The scene was chaotic but unforgettable and the air was shrill with the cries of gulls, which wheeled round the towers, spires and lofty crenelations.

"Are we docking here?" Josep asked hopefully.

"No, we're heading for the Golden Horn. In a moment you'll spy a dramatic sight," came the reply from the captain.

"Even more than this?" Josep asked, staggered. As they came closer to the walls, Josep could see a beautiful palace, complete with a private harbour and steps leading all the way down to the water's edge. On either side of these steps, he could clearly see what looked like two enormous white marble sculptures of lions, impressive daunting sentinels.

"What is this place?" he asked in amazement.

"This is one of the smaller, older royal palaces. They call it Boukoleon. Before the fourth Crusade, they had bulls there as big as the lions, hence the name, Bull Lion Palace." It was relatively small, Josep thought, and seemed more intimate and he could imagine the Emperor being brought by royal barge to the imperial jetty in front of it.

Their galley now lurched to the left and the walls of the city could be seen to cut in sharply to reveal a wooded area running down to the water's edge, fringed by another low wall and as Josep looked, he could see beautiful, landscaped gardens, mansions, churches and monasteries on many different levels, all vying with the next in elegance and opulence. On Josep's right-hand side, on the other side of the so-called Golden Horn, the city continued with acres of residential suburbs, sprawling behind another seawall. One tower was prominent.

"Galata Tower," said the captain. "That's Pera, the Genovese quarter. They are the ones who provoked the Almogavers into a fight when they had just arrived."

As they finished their manoeuvre and took up a position equidistant from both sides of the Golden Horn, Josep now saw the most spectacular of all the sights he had so far witnessed. This was not a church or a cathedral, this was architecture in the praise of God at its highest apogee of expression. Josep was speechless as he contemplated the only building he could have named in Constantinople before he arrived: the Church of the Hagia Sophia, The Holy Wisdom. The structure was huge yet because of its pink sandstone hues in the afternoon light, it appeared unfeasibly lightly placed amid the trees and gardens surrounding it, as if it were floating on rather than dug into the highest part of the city. The design was an exercise in Romanic symmetry, the central cupola balanced by two other cupolas on either side. Each cupola was inset with windows and Josep could imagine how much light must be streaming into the church and how the sun's rays must burst onto the altar at sunrise.

He looked around him and let out a shout of amazement and pleasure to be here at last. Constantinople was arguably the greatest Christian city on earth with an uninterrupted Christian history dating back a thousand years.

They continued sailing up the Golden Horn, the water's edge bejewelled with stunning churches, decorated with geometric patterns of red and white tiles. Finally, they came to the furthest end of the city wall, several miles in from the sea of Marmara. Here they weighed anchor just opposite some huge gates in the city walls.

"This is where the Emperor now lives, the Palace of Blachernae," the captain said.

Josep was speechless. The city was of proportions he had never before seen; of an antiquity that staggered him; of a beauty that was beyond compare. As he gazed out over the side of his galley, the sun was setting behind the imperial residence, bathing walls, towers, palaces, halls and cupolas in pink and golden light.

Berenguer d'Entença was unusually reserved, not his normal hearty self in noble company. Josep had noticed immediately on mooring a certain reticence on his part to leave the galley.

"I do not mind taking a spin around the harbour area to get away from the stench of the galley," he joked but Josep suspected his reluctance was somehow connected with his status. No imperial craft had come out to meet them, night had now fallen and no one seemed to be coming. It seemed he was offended.

"I thought *we* were the ones who did not follow protocol," he joked with the captain who was keen to disembark to allow his sailors the days-off they had not been given in Chios and Anaia.

"I shall inform the authorities of your arrival my Lord. There has clearly been some oversight," the captain said. Berenguer d'Entença affected indifference but just as the captain was casting off from the galley, the nobleman signalled to Josep, who was accompanying the crew.

"Make sure he brings back safe-conducts with my name and titles on them please," he said. The *"please"* alarmed Josep considerably as it betrayed a certain diffidence in the request, as if he were expecting a problem or a delay.

In any case, Josep was relieved to get off the fetid galley. This for him had been his destination since he had left Lali and his family in Sicily. Now his imperial adventure could really begin. He had greatly enjoyed the Aegean and the Turkish coast but that was not why he was there and he had been seabound for weeks now and needed to reacquaint himself with the pleasures of dry land and walking on solid earth. As soon as the crew were processed by the port authorities, they were given temporary passes to enter the city. Josep left Berenguer d'Entença's papers with the officials, having checked that a safe conduct could be drawn up with the specifications Berenguer d'Entença wanted, to be collected later.

That evening, when Josep returned to the galley, safe-conduct in hand, he was surprised by Lord Berenguer d'Entença's reaction. Josep had spent a long time wandering around the exclusive quarter of the Palace of Blachernae and had thoroughly enjoyed stretching his legs but he had left himself plenty of time to get back before it was too late to pick up the safe-conduct. Everything seemed to be in order and Josep had been impressed by the efficiency of the Imperial Guard. However, Berenguer d'Entença was both moody and evasive with him when he handed him the document, called in Greek a *crisobul*. It was of course written in Greek.

"I asked the guards what it means and they showed me where you are named," Josep said, showing him the appropriate paragraph.

"I cannot possibly travel safely with a document I cannot read!" replied Entença with finality, turning away from Josep.

"What am I to do my Lord? Should I ask them to re-issue it in Catalan?"

"If you wish," came the reply.

The following day, Josep was up early to carry out his task. He returned to the Imperial Guard and requested to be taken to a more senior officer. As the Imperial Guard knew who he and Berenguer d'Entença were and remembered how quickly the *crisobul* had been issued the previous day, he surmised there was a serious problem and therefore made arrangements for Josep to be taken to the commanding officer in the gatehouse of the palace itself.

There, Josep explained the situation and made his request. Within four hours, he had the document handwritten in good enough Catalan and he therefore returned to Berenguer d'Entença in high spirits.

A similar scene to that of the previous night was then played out. Berenguer d'Entença took the document moodily, scanned it and thrust it back into Josep's hands.

"My Lord?" Josep asked simply.

"It is not acceptable."

"But... but...why not?" Josep thought that the question sounded childish but he was genuinely flabbergasted.

"It does not correspond with my position." Entença replied, looking away.

"My Lord I do not know what you mean," Josep said.

"I am not a "Hyparchon", whatever that may be!" he said.

"I see, my Lord," Josep said as tactfully as he could. "What would you like me to ask them to refer to my Lord as?"

"I do not know, their hierarchy or the names of their ranks are a mystery to me. Also, this letter does not bear the Emperor's personal seal, I believe, but that of the Imperial Bodyguard."

Josep carefully held the old noble's gaze without showing any reaction that might betray how at a loss he was. As soon as he could, he took the document and bade Berenguer d'Entença good night saying that he would deal with the matter first thing in the morning.

Josep undertook to do what he could the following day but he knew his limitations. He could hardly demand to see the commanding officer's superior. He had been politely dealt with thus far and felt frankly embarrassed to demand refinements he did not understand. However, he dutifully, to the best of his ability, again tracked down the commanding officer of the regiment guarding the Palace of Blachernae and explained the situation.

"Syntagmatarchis is my rank," replied the commanding officer, recognising Josep from the previous day. This corresponds to a senior knight commander. I am in charge of some one hundred officers and more than two thousand men."

"Syntagmatarchis," Josep replied, "Lord Berenguer d'Entença is a noble from an illustrious aristocratic Catalan family. He has recently been ambassador to King James II of Catalunya Aragón. I am not sure that a military rank corresponds to his position," Josep argued tactfully. He was suspected the officer had assigned him a rank lower than his own but that was beside the point. He had the impression even if they gave him the rank of *strategos* or general, this would still not be enough.

"He is a close friend and associate of the Grand Duke, Roger de Flor. In addition, he claims the seal is insufficient. He says it should be issued by the Emperor himself."

The translator took some time to relay this to the perplexed officer, a good fifteen years senior to Josep, whose expression shifted from the incredulous to the amazed, then finally the deeply worried.

"I will make the arrangements. This will take some time," the syntagmatarchis replied.

Several days later, without any announcement, a boat arrived and drew up alongside Lord Berenguer d'Entença's galley. Decorated in the Emperor 's colours and flying the imperial flag, the vessel caused a cessation of all activity in the Imperial Harbour for some time. It was clear that this most gracious means of transport was intended to bear Berenguer d'Entença to the Imperial Palace, a distance of five hundred meters.

"Have they prepared the *crisobul* with the appropriate title and safeguards?" Berenguer d'Entença asked Josep.

"My Lord, I hardly think the captain would have come without the appropriate documentation. If I may be so bold, my Lord, I feel that they will be most affronted if my Lord were not to accept their invitation to court now."

A cloud of irritation swept over Berenguer d'Entença's face as he put his chin out and his nose up and simply said "Check that the captain has the appropriate document and I shall be pleased to accompany him."

Josep went to the captain and did his best to explain the situation.

"I have no such document," replied the captain, "as this is the personal barge of Emperor Andronicus II Palaiologos."

"I am afraid I have to tell you Lord Berenguer d'Entença cannot accept without the *crisobul* issued by the Emperor himself as requested a week ago."

Finally, the Imperial barge left the galley without its occupant and returned to the Imperial Port. Josep was becoming desperate. He had not expected matters would go so badly as this. Finally on the tenth day after their arrival in the Imperial Port of Blachernae, the Emperor's barge arrived as before, carrying even more regalia and bearing Princess Maria Assèn, the wife of Roger de Flor herself.

"Your highness," began Berenguer d'Entença, "I am honoured to meet you. Forgive my stubborn behaviour but I fear for my safety unless all protocols are observed fully."

"You are wise to arrange matters thus, my dear Lord Entença! I have the *crisobul* here with me bearing the Emperor's personal seal. The Emperor is very keen to meet you and has arranged that his closest advisers should attend court today to greet you," Maria Assèn replied in good Catalan.

"May I thank you for the great courtesy you show me," replied Berenguer d'Entença, looking very pleased and relieved.

Berenguer d'Entença passed the document to Josep, who read the *crisobul* written in perfect Catalan addressing Berenguer d'Entença as Ambassador of the Catalan Company. Then matters moved on quickly. In an extraordinarily ornate ceremony, Berenguer d'Entença was greeted by the highest officials of the court of the Emperor Andronicus. The following day, another ceremony was performed in which he was made a senator of the court. Following that ceremony, he was invested with the title Grand Duke Berenguer d'Entença and clothed in the official regalia of that title. No sooner had he received that title than he was seated "but a palm lower" than the Emperor himself.

Suddenly, a new arrival was ushered in. Fresh from his success in quelling the appetite for war of the Bulgarian monarch, Roger de Flor was given a victor's reception in the Great Hall of the Palace of Blachernae. At length, the Emperor entered surrounded by courtiers and greeted him in person, addressing him now as megaduke. After the delay of the previous fortnight, Josep's head was spinning with the speed at which events were moving. Yet it seemed to him all the clearer that the person who had stood on ceremony most had been Berenguer d'Entença.

"As soon as the Catalan Company arrived within a day's march of the Bulgarian army, their monarch sued for peace," began Megaduke Roger de Flor. King Svetoslav will be on the throne of Bulgaria only so long as Emperor Adronicus wishes it so." There was polite applause.

"If the empress so wishes, the throne shall be returned to its rightful heirs, the sons of Ivan Asen, my wife's deceased father!" Flor continued.

"It will have nothing to do with the fact that they are now related to him by marriage through his wife," an anonymous Catalan speaker whispered in Josep's ear. Before he could turn, the bearer of the message had melted back into the crowd of courtiers. Nonetheless, Josep felt the incident and the message had been quite deliberate.

"My Lord," Josep began carefully and quietly, addressing Grand Duke Berenguer d'Entença. "There seems to be some controversy about Roger de Flor's strategy to return the throne to the Assèn line."

"Why should there be any doubt that it should belong to

them?" Berenguer d'Entença asked in turn.

"Because as far as I understand it, the last member of that family on the throne abandoned the country and fled to Constantinople twenty years ago. The country has known four monarchs since then," Josep replied

"The descendants of King Ivan nonetheless have the right to pursue their inheritance against the usurpers, do they not? Be that as it may, Megaduke Roger de Flor will do as the Emperor bids him," Berenguer d'Entença drawled.

Josep was not sure if this analysis of the rights and wrongs of the situation was accurate but agreed with the statement of *realpolitik* the Catalan openly expressed. It suddenly occurred to Josep that Grand Duke Berenguer d'Entença was imagining future scenarios for himself to play a part in and resolve.

CHAPTER TWELVE

The next day, the day before Christmas Eve, in the most lavish of all the ceremonies Josep had witnessed, Roger de Flor was made the Caesar of the Empire, a title that had not been held for several centuries. Berenguer d'Entença was diplomatic but Josep was getting to know him well: he was disappointed and slighted. Roger de Flor seemed utterly amazed and suggested he had not been expecting this great honour. However, in the opinion of the various Catalan speaking courtiers prepared to discuss the matter with Josep, it would seem to be fitting reward for Roger de Flor's most recent successes and confirmed him as the closest, the most trusted adviser Emperor Andronicus had. Presumably, Josep thought, these courtiers who spoke to him were fulfilling their role of explaining imperial policy to those who could then circulate it. It was diplomatically deft and gave the impression there was nothing but absolute endorsement of the Emperor's decision, that there was nothing but seamless unity and harmony.

Whether it was prompted by jealousy or simply fair comment, Grand Duke Berenguer d'Entença's words later struck a chord with Josep.

"There will be dissent among the higher echelons at court, you mark my words," he said. For all the pomp and ceremony, I could sense it. There was seething resentment from the higher officials that a position fourth in the hierarchy should be bestowed upon a falconer's son!" he snorted.

Josep, a man in his late thirties, a father, a husband, a soldier and worldly-wise, was deeply shocked. It was the first time he had heard Entença refer to Roger de Flor in those terms. He had seen how class-conscious Berenguer d'Entença was, both with those of his own standing and those like Bernat Rocafort clearly beneath it, but this reference to the origins of the leader of the Catalan Company and the military star of the moment betrayed Berenguer d'Entença's real attitude and arguably his loyalty to Roger de Flor. Could it be that he felt that he had more right to the honours accorded to Roger de Flor, that he was actually competing with him?

For reasons he did not divulge, Entença declined comfortable quarters and stayed on his galley in the Imperial Port, where Josep also felt obliged to stay, to attend him. The Catalan Company in the meantime were garrisoned within the walls of Constantinople. Reports of their drunkenness and vulgarity were circulating around court. Again, the same system was used that Josep had noted before. Josep would be drawn into a conversation about who he was and what he was doing there and the subject of the Catalan company would arise. Then the opinion would be given. *The Catalans were not behaving acceptably. This was a highly cultured city, the Catalans should show more respect.* Each time it was an unknown face, nothing remarkable about the interlocutor, a member of a corps whose purpose was to mix invisibly and insinuate opinions effortlessly. It was polished and highly effective; imperial opinion and policy were disseminated without disturbance or the need for attention-grabbing pomp and ceremony. But who was orchestrating the messages, Josep wondered? Presumably someone close to the Emperor.

Following the Christmas celebrations, there were some working days before the New Year when Roger de Flor was absorbed in negotiations with the Emperor.

"He is demanding too much!" the message seemed to be through the invisible, inscrutable imperial channels. Then, more clearly, Josep was "allowed" to overhear a conversation among senior courtiers. The conclusion was clear.

"There are now eight times as many Almogavers as were originally requested and enlisted. The Emperor cannot pay for a force of that size."

Josep began to worry about the Almogaver mission in Constantinople, and that he had made a financially unsound move in coming there in order to serve with them. Would he ever receive anything? Would he see action of any kind? Various opinions started to circulate at court that the Catalan Company needed to continue its successes in order to deserve its salary. Most recently, a battle had been averted with the Bulgarians. But was a battle averted the same as a battle won? Could the Almogavers be paid a salary for simply acting as a disincentive to the enemies of the Empire from attacking the Empire? The fact that this idea was being discussed indicated that it was a consideration at high levels, perhaps even indicated the personal opinion of the Emperor After all, it was with the Emperor that Roger de Flor was negotiating.

Hours before the official announcement was made, the idea that was floated at court in the usual way was that the Hyperper was to be devalued to broach the costs of payment to the Almogavers. Berenguer d'Entença was furious at the news and several times had to be distracted by Josep so as not to physically accost the courtier imparting this information to him.

Yet the final decision was taken by not only Emperor Andronicus but also Commander-in-Chief of the Catalan Company and Caesar of the Empire, Roger de Flor. It occurred to Josep how adroit the Emperor had been in giving Roger de Flor such high office in the empire. He now, quite literally, had to wear two hats: one the blue one, part of his ceremonial regalia when in consultation with the Emperor, when the most delicate, most intimate matters relating to the welfare of Constantinople were discussed. The other, of course, was

Roger de Flor's iron helmet as worn by commanders of the Almogavers in battle. The final outcome of the negotiations was that the Hyperper, for centuries the most stable currency in the Mediterranean world, was to be devalued. In view of the huge cost of the company, the coin used to pay the mercenaries of the Empire would be 3/8ths the value of the original.

The extraordinary scene that took place the following day could only have been orchestrated. Emperor Andronicus not only gave the information in court himself but also bitterly attacked Roger de Flor on behalf of the empire and especially the people of the Artaki peninsula and the citizens of Magnesia and Chios, for the intolerable rapaciousness and cruelty of the Catalan Company.

"Rape and pillage are unseemly upon one's own people!" The sentence rang out and Roger de Flor stood head down and acknowledged that the Emperor was right and he was responsible.

"We expect a more civilised line in future!" the Emperor concluded.

"What is supposed to have happened in Chios?" Josep later asked a courtier he had become friendly with. The courtier coughed quietly.

"Roger de Flor's critics claim that he was denied his spoils in Magnesia when he was recalled to defend the empire against Bulgaria. Therefore, when he arrived in Lesbos on his way to Bulgaria, he took a counsellor who happened to be from Magnesia but had fled and lost everything and threatened to kill him unless he paid a ransom of five thousand gold coins. He claimed that this was a punishment for this man's involvement in losing a castle under the control of Lesbos to the Karasai Turks. But in view of what happened next people started looking for other motivations, hence the rumours started."

"I do not understand," said Josep. "What did happen next?"

The courtier quickly checked no one else was looking. He looked Josep in the eye.

"The man was called Makhrames. He couldn't pay the five-hundred-coin ransom. So he was strapped to the butcher's pole in the market and his throat was cut. De Flor's men then threatened to do the same to each member of the Council who had had anything to do with the loss of the castle."

Josep had by now heard so many similar stories of such extortion and arbitrary barbarity that he had to start believing that some, if not all, of the details were true.

It disturbed him that the Almogavers were becoming embroiled in situations that destroyed their image as respectful, professional protectors of the empire. He was horrified by the high-handedness of Roger de Flor's treatment of the Emperor's administrators. Who were they supposed to be fighting, after all? Who were they supposed to be protecting? Roger de Flor was acquiring a reputation as a bloodthirsty commander and a law unto himself. Josep remembered the days of the French crusade against Catalonia and the awful atrocities committed against the Catalans by the invading army. Senseless and sickening though the idea was, barbaric acts carried out by an invading force on the enemy population were at least comprehensible as acts of war against the enemy. The Angevins' cruelty to the Catalans in the crusade was paid back when the French army retreated over the Pass of Panissars. They had then been killed as they had killed, and the Almogavers involved in that massacre were fighting to expel an unjust and wicked enemy, so even if there was little honour in those deeds there was at least some sense. The whole resistance to the French invasion had felt to Josep at the time honourable. Josep then realised matters had changed since those times. These tales of summary executions, the accusations of wanton theft and destruction, the hair-raising, spine-chilling stories of young girls going about their business being abducted, raped and then slaughtered in cold blood turned Josep's stomach. Were the Almogavers no better than the people who had raped and slaughtered Alba's sister, Bella? The twists and turns of the protracted Sicilian War, for so long fought against Anjou and Naples, who were now allies under the Treaty of Anagni and Caltabellota, had left him with the unedifying sense that from one day to the next your enemies had to be considered your friends, and quite likely, the opposite could happen, your friends could become your enemies. Since the treaty of Anagni in 1295, Josep's main motivation had been the maintenance and preservation of his family. The fierce feelings of loyalty he had felt towards the House of Barcelona in the person of King Pere II had, he realised, become more and more watered-down. He recognised in his heart of hearts that his motivation for joining this mission, though dressed up in honourable language about defending Christendom from the Islamic threat, was purely financial. He knew his loyalty to his leader, though he had met him and liked him, was based on being paid and, as if that weren't enough, the honour of the force he'd identified with for his whole life, the Almogavers, was being dragged through the mud. This leader, who at one time had been known for his vision and humanity, was now considered self-seeking, ruthless and cruel. Josep could not even say he it was essential he was there for his family. He was receiving expenses but had not been paid yet and had little hope of partaking in the rich rewards Roger de Flor had promised him when he had sold him the idea. He was beginning to wonder not only why he was there at all but also how he was ever going to get out of this mess alive.

Such was the present undercurrent of antipathy towards the Almogavers and their commanders that despite his investiture as Caesar of the Empire, despite his success against the Bulgarians, despite the fact that Anatolia was back under imperial control, Roger de Flor was being hurried to leave the Imperial City of Constantinople as quickly as possible and establish himself in Anatolia. It was even being suggested that he should consider Anatolia his own "reward" in accepting the Emperor's harsh criticism and financial chicanery.

Of course, on the surface of things and in the eyes of the ordinary people of Constantinople, life went on as usual, with parades past the Emperor seated in all his glory, wearing his formal robes of red and gold and his red enclosed mitre crown adorned with the gold cross. During one such parade, Josep noticed Co-Emperor Kor Michael, also dressed in gold but wearing a white mitre with the gold crown, which was the mark of his office, looking askance at Roger de Flor. It was only momentary, just as Roger de Flor passed the Emperor's canopy, just as the fanfare for Caesar Roger de Flor began to sound, but it was long enough for Josep to notice.

As usual all positions in the parade had been studiously organised. Every nuance had been considered, as usual. Every move was symbolic. Berenguer d'Entença was to the right of Roger de Flor and slightly behind him. Co-Emperor Kor Michael, was to the left of Roger de Flor and slightly ahead of him as he passed the imperial enclosure. Roger de Flor was blocking Berenguer d'Entença's view of the co-Emperor but Josep, riding to the left of Berenguer d'Entença, had a clear view of him. It was a look missed by the Emperor, who was bowing his head to Caesar Roger de Flor. Yet Josep was sure Co-Emperor Michael's move was rehearsed, planned and executed for the other high functionaries who attended the Emperor, namely Despot, Sebastocrator and Great Steward, the latter bearing the Emperor's imperial parasol. All three high officials were looking directly at Michael, not at Roger de Flor, waiting for the look: it was baleful, contemptuous and sly. He had him in his sights, was the message that Josep understood; he had him in his sights and had him marked for destruction. He now also understood that Kor Michael was the brain behind the subtle dissemination of information at court, the head of public relations for his busy father, Emperor Andronicus, the person responsible for the presentation of imperial policy, with all the actual power pertaining to that function.

It was therefore with a great sense of relief that Josep left Constantinople together with the majority of the Catalan Company present there at the time, in accordance with the instructions of Emperor Andronicus to take up their positions in Anatolia and leave the imperial city. Deeply impressed by the greatest city on earth, Josep was equally perturbed by its secretiveness and worn-out by its insistence on forms and protocols.

"These rituals must have taken hundreds of years to develop and must reassure the citizen population by their ostentation of the permanence of the empire. Yet they seem to me empty symbols of past glory. Not to mention the huge expense the Imperial Household must represent to the public purse when all public events are preceded by such pageants. It must be a huge drain on resources!" he happened to comment to Berenguer d'Entença. His response was very telling.

"Money that could be better spent on an effective army," came the reply. He had just returned to his galley from Court and had taken off the red ceremonial hat and coat, the Scaramangion, symbol of his rank as Grand Duke and, not having a means of cooling himself in the late afternoon sun, was using the priceless imperial garment as a bucket, scooping up water with it to douse himself down on deck. It showed how much respect he had for his ceremonial role in the empire and regard for the expense of the imperial accoutrements, in Josep's opinion. As the gown was made of exquisite pressed felt, it was fairly water resistant and with the sleeves tied shut, held a considerable quantity of water. As it slid under the clear water and was brought out, it filled and took on the form of a corseted human torso, without head and limbs. Josep dreamed of drowning that night as well as dismembered human body parts.

When, two days later, they weighed anchor in Gallipolis, Ramón Muntaner was the first to come aboard, Josep thought to welcome him but, in fact, he was seething with fury.

"I've had the army in virtual insurrection here since we heard the Emperor and Caesar have agreed to pay us less than half we are owed!" he hissed at Berenguer d'Entença after greeting him with the least ceremony possible.

"How did you hear?" asked Berenguer d'Entença coolly.

"We have people coming and going between here and Constantinople constantly," he said dismissively, waving the question away, determined not to be deflected by side issues.

"Well, as you say, you'll have to take that up with the Emperor or his Caesar," Berenguer d'Entença drawled, pausing a little too long on the second title. Josep noted the contempt in the jaw thrust out and the nose turned up. "I was not consulted, therefore I cannot be made responsible."

"But you are his closest counsellor and the second-highest ranking commander after him in the Catalan company!" replied Ramón Muntaner.

Josep noticed a fleeting look of pleasure cross Berenguer d'Entença's face on hearing himself referred to in these terms.

"Nevertheless, I was not included in those deliberations. Had I been there, I would not have stood for the public shaming the Caesar was subjected to. He seemed to take it very well, if it was news to him."

"You mean he had already struck a deal with the Emperor? What did he get in return?" Ramón Montaner persisted.

"Anatolia, it seems. That's why we are here…, apparently…" he said vaguely.

"The men need to be paid what they are owed, they have run up huge debts here already!" Ramón Muntaner tried a different tack.

"The only cure for gluttony is to consume less," Berenguer d'Entença replied.

"That's all very well for the future but how are they going to pay now?" Ramón Muntaner said, sounding exasperated.

"The Hyperper is to have the same value as it had before," replied Berenguer d'Entença testily, as if merely repeating orders.

"The townsfolk won't accept it!" Ramón Muntaner said his voice rising again.

"Then tell them to complain to their Emperor. He is the one who minted these new coins. Tell the rabble to be contented. They should know by now the Almogavers help themselves where and when they like."

Ramón Muntaner glared angrily at Berenguer d'Entença, whose comment went to the heart of the matter. It was contemptuous of the Greek population and the Almogavers alike and was helpful to neither.

Overnight, prices doubled. There was a sudden run on staples as panic buying pushed prices up to triple what they had been two days before. Those who in good faith had meant to pay their debts suddenly found themselves facing financial ruin if they kept their word yet in rare cases, the deal was honourably observed. In the majority of cases, the increased demanded destroyed the negotiations and both sides lapsed into bitter acrimony. In many cases, Almogavers now used to indulging their insatiable appetites for wine and food, now overindulged even more shamelessly as if the tomorrow they thought they'd never see had finally come. The violent mood spread like wildfire. Farms went up in flames and food and wine stores were ransacked, consumed or wantonly pillaged and destroyed. If only goods were all that were destroyed, Josep thought! Yet just as the out-of-control drunken lout destroys what he cannot have, likewise whatever of value couldn't be owned or finished was sampled and then discarded. The town of Gallipolis was in riot, houses and stores were sacked and looted, wives and daughters gang raped, their menfolk cut to pieces as they desperately tried to preserve the honour of their women.

"Where is Rocafort?" Roger de Flor was shouting within minutes of arriving from the capital. "Tell him to report to me at once." But he was nowhere to be found. "He is the seneschal, it's his responsibility to control the men." There was a new look on Roger de Flor's face: it was a mix of disbelief and fear.

"Prepare to march. I need three hundred knights and a thousand Almogavers to come with me. We need a distraction. I shall march to Adrianople to take my leave formally of Co-Emperor Kor Michael. When the rest hear where we've gone, they'll calm down and feel left out. Just as they deserve!" Roger de Flor said.

Roger de Flor's wife, Maria Assèn, pleaded with him not to go but he was adamant, saying he should have thought of it earlier.

"It was remiss of me not to have taken my leave formally of the Co-Emperor. I must act immediately or this lapse will be interpreted as a slight," he said.

Of course, nobody could understand how at this moment of absolute need of leadership, Roger de Flor capriciously chose to abandon his troops to the worst of their instincts. Yet within a day the trouble subsided.

"It is strange that the trouble begins and ends when Roger de Flor appears and exits. He has become a conduit for excess," Berenguer d'Entença opined archly.

Then, a few days after Roger de Flor had marched to Adrianople, Rocafort reappeared.

"You filthy rascals!" He was clearly poking fun at Berenguer d'Entença's diction. "You've left nothing for me," was his comment. Rumours started to circulate that he had been with Arenós, the disgraced Admiral who had left the force during the Artaki incident, who was now in the employ of the French in Athens.

"Perhaps he's paving his way in case things go awry here," commented Berenguer d'Entença in earshot of Josep.

"Perhaps he's always been in the pay of the French," said Guillem de Siscar, one of Berenguer d'Entença's close advisers.

"What would be the point of that?" asked Josep. It was the first time he'd heard the idea. It had not even crossed Josep's mind that the Catalans could be hatching plans with the French.

"It was not so long ago that Constantinople fought a secret war through John of Procida against the Angevins in Sicily to stop an invasion of Constantinople and the re-establishment of the Latin Emperors," Josep said, as if that were the final word on the matter.

"But the Angevin king who pursued that policy is long dead," replied Berenguer d'Entença swiftly.

"He is long dead but his children and grandchildren are now the King, Princes and Dukes of the Kingdom of Naples. They are cousins of the Capet Royal House of France. Their ambitions cannot be underestimated," said de Siscar.

"But how strong is the connection between the French Dukes of Athens and the French royal houses?" asked Josep.

"The present duke, Guy La Roche, was born and raised in Athens," replied Berenguer d'Entença. "But the point is they would all prefer to see a Latin Emperor back on the imperial throne." He was speaking very quietly now.

"They would have to be incredibly discreet about their plans, wouldn't they? One whiff of that and the Imperial Army would sweep into Athens and wipe them out," said Josep.

"Like they have the Turkish menace, you mean?" said de Siscar sarcastically.

"It's hardly the same," said Josep. "The Turks hugely outnumber all of us including the French nobility and their forces in Athens, that's why we've been called in."

"But while the Almogavers and the Imperial Army are fighting the Turks, Constantinople lies defenceless, easy pickings for a well-orchestrated attack!" Entença said.

"That's a possibility, I suppose," said Josep, "but it seems risky. After all, the Emperor can command the Almogavers to fight anywhere against anyone as they did last time against the Bulgarians in Adrianople."

"But if renegade Catalans are in fact in league with the Duke of Athens? What would happen if the empire suddenly faced an attack from Athens and part of the Catalan Company? That is why Emperor Andronicus is keeping Co-Emperor Michael and his forces in Adrianople, not sending them to fight the Turks in Anatolia," de Siscar replied.

"Do you think Rocafort is in league with the Duchy of Athens, my Lord?" Josep asked Berenguer d'Entença.

"He's a thug and a lowlife and he is capable of anything. But if he is, he'll have to be very careful. Remember the connection is more between the Duchy of Athens and France and Naples than the Duchy of Athens and ourselves and there are many people who hate Rocafort in Naples."

"Why would anyone in Athens trust Rocafort anyway?" asked Josep.

"You could ask the same about Arenós," replied Entença.

"True," replied de Siscar, "but he also came with a fleet. He's useful to them. Rocafort, on the other hand, comes with a reputation of deceit and brutality. I'd keep him at arm's length. Besides, he only has a thousand troops. Even if they are Almogavers, there's only so much damage one can do with a thousand troops. But if he became the Commander-in-Chief of the Catalan company..." he broke off, suddenly realising how indiscreet this comment was in the presence of Berenguer d'Entença.

It must have been the idea of Roger de Flor no longer being the Commander-in-Chief of the Catalan company that brought the thought to Josep's mind but he suddenly said:

"What if Co-Emperor Michael believes he is under attack from Roger de Flor? I saw his face at the official departure parade as Roger de Flor passed the Emperor and the fanfare for Caesar Roger de Flor started, it was so full of hatred for him."

"And that it is a prelude for a concerted attempt to put a Latin Emperor back on the throne!" de Siscar said, jumping to his feet and glad to hide his gaffe a moment before.

"Girgon the commander of the Alan mercenaries is with the co-Emperor. He has sworn to avenge his son's death, which he blames on Roger de Flor during the Artaki campaign. If the Alans have an opportunity to kill him, they will. It will be one thousand five hundred Alamogavers against ten thousand or so Alans, Greeks and Turcopoles, Christianised inhabitants of the empire with mixed Turkish and Christian parentage. Not even the Alamogavers can cope with odds of seven to one. They will be cut to pieces!" de Siscar concluded.

The news from Adrianople took its time coming. A calm had descended on Gallipolis. With Rocafort's return, a certain order within the ranks of the Company was maintained. All trust between the Company and the townspeople of Gallipolis had vanished, needless to say. The stores salvaged from the abandoned farms that littered the area were starting to dwindle and Ramón Muntaner, the quartermaster, was beginning to get anxious. It was possible for Josep, when he rose early in the morning and watched the sun rise over the Sea of Marmara to the east, to make-believe for a moment he was in a dream that he could wake up from. But reality always returned fast and he knew he was in the clutches of powers he had no control over but which held his fate in their hands.

"So this is what it feels like to be a mercenary," he thought to himself. "A paid warrior no one can trust, who must be treated with absolute suspicion and prejudice and disposed of as quickly as possible when too threatening." Something shifted in his mind. He was not going to kill for money. He'd rather go home empty-handed. He watched the sunrise, imagining Lali and the children watching the same sun, being warmed by the same rays on the other side of the sea.

"How much does a man needs to live?" he asked himself. "I should have withdrawn my application when I heard my stipend was to be renewed. I suppose they are receiving it already. What a fool I have been. I must leave at the earliest opportunity."

Around him, the town was waking up. Here on the steps down to the little harbour, sunlight was twinkling on the ripples. The light breeze blew across the water from the direction of Troy on the other side of the narrow passage that separated the Gallipolis Peninsula from the Anatolian mainland. "I swear I will not set foot again in Asia," he said. "If I keep that promise to myself, I may make it back alive."

He saw a young woman with her mother, awkwardly climbing down the steps to where he was at the water's edge. He tried a warm "Kale Hemera!" one of the few phrases he had learned in Greek. The two women froze, the girl screamed, they fled up the steps as if pursued by a demon the blood drained from their faces. He knew he was the demon, a demon with a smiling face.

To the Greeks, the Catalan Company were now quite simply that, the enemy.

Three more days were required for the survivors from Adrianople to return. Luckily, they were strapping young men who had never sustained a major injury before, for whom this was their first major campaign. They were half dead with heat exhaustion, thirst and sunstroke when they finally stumbled into view with the morning sun scorching them from behind as they came from the east. It was clear they were the bearers of ill tidings.

"We are the last three alive. All the others are dead. Everyone has been killed in their sleep." They spoke in short sentences with rasping voices. "They were all drunk, except for us. We met some girls. They'd taken us up to this tower at the top of the city. We missed it all." They took it in turns to tell their story and, between drafts of water and pants of exhaustion, they told their tale of doom.

"Everyone else was drunk and asleep in the palace. We only escaped because the girls tied the sheets together so we could climb down." They paused. Then Ramón Alquer, exchanged glances with the other two. They looked away. He summoned up his courage to speak.

"The girls suddenly burst in and told us Roger de Flor had been killed not more than an hour ago, that we had to go," he said. "We were angry and wanted to go and help but they said the whole regiment was killed in an hour. We'd had our meal in the palace, then everyone else started drinking. Kor Michael's wife took Roger de Flor's wife, Maria Assèn, to a special chamber to get her away from Roger de Flor. Then Gircon, the leader of the Alans, killed Roger de Flor once he was in his bedroom. Kor Michael was nowhere to be seen, they say. But the signal was given after Roger de Flor was killed. They were all drunk and sleepy after the meal and the forced march. The girl said it was planned to happen like that. But the Greek army and the Alan mercenaries managed to keep it a secret till the signal came. They said they knew we'd drink too much, too soon. It was all over quickly. We've been walking ever since, sleeping and eating when and where we could."

All the commanders were speechless when they heard what the three young Knights, Ramón Alquer, Ramón de Tous and Bernat de Roudor had to say.

"You must not, under any circumstances, repeat what you have said to anyone. We will explain what happened," said Rocafort. De Siscar commented to Josep, "So Kor Michael did suspect something! But they got the wrong man! He allowed Gircon to kill Roger de Flor when the real threat comes from Rocafort or Arenós."

The story that was therefore decided on for the morale of the remainder of the Catalan Company was the following: these three were attacked in the bell tower and they defended themselves so valiantly that the Emperor's son said it would be a sin if they were to perish; and so he gave them his assurance of their safe conduct. These three alone escaped from the Adrianople massacre.

CHAPTER THIRTEEN

The news of the sudden but calculated murder of their leader on the thirtieth of April 1305 stunned and confused the Catalan Company. A rumour sprang up that they were going to be attacked by the whole army imminently, which caused panic not of course among the Almogavers themselves but among those who accompanied the Catalan company, such as the Catalan merchants and stallholders, preachers, barber surgeons, tailors, cooks and prostitutes. Contented previously to live in camps in tents around whatever fortress it might be, the non-combat contingent now insisted on being accommodated within the castle walls of Gallipolis, terrified now of the intentions of the local townspeople.

No one could really believe what had happened, or that it had been quite deliberate. With little instinct for plotting and scheming, the Almogavers could not fathom why the Greeks had behaved in this way and therefore attributed the tragedy to a colossal misunderstanding.

It did not take long for Rocafort to realise that the commander who took the lead now would effectively take over from Roger de Flor, even though Berenguer d'Entença outranked him completely and was *de facto* leader on Roger de Flor's demise.

"In any case, Berenguer d'Entença was appointed by the Emperor. What we must therefore ascertain is how much responsibility the Emperor bears for this act. Can we trust him or not?" Ramón Muntaner said to Josep one evening.

"We could send a deputation to Constantinople to break our oath of allegiance to the Emperor and free ourselves of our chivalric obligations," said Guillem de Siscar.

"I think it would be a mistake," responded Gisbert de Rocafort, Bernat de Rocafort's brother and lieutenant. "They are a bloodthirsty thieving bunch who will cut any deputation to shreds. They have no notion of chivalry like ours." Josep stifled a bitter laugh. Could he really believe in chivalry any more, he wondered.

"We are Almogavers! We cannot be cut to shreds so easily!" responded Dalmau Sant Martí.

"It's just a question of numbers! How big a force would be required to keep the Imperial Army at bay? Look at what happened to the fifteen hundred Almogavers who accompanied Roger de Flor," said Gisbert.

"They were drunk and their trust was betrayed. We will not make the same mistake again. If we send a deputation, the Emperor may apologise and explain it was all a terrible mistake. We could then renegotiate our payment and have a clear idea about what to do next."

"I have never heard anything so preposterous in my life!" shouted Gisbert de Rocafort. "Go if you wish to go but be sure that you will not come back alive. The tide has turned and even if Kor Michael acted without his father's approval, the Emperor is hardly likely to publicly declare it was all a mistake now the deed is done. I fear we are at war with the Empire and the longer we delay organising ourselves, the worse it will be for us."

Josep reported this conclusion of Gisbert to Berenguer d'Entença, who had still not publicly expressed an opinion about the matter.

"Let them send out a mission if they wish!" Berenguer d'Entença said. "It is true that it will confirm one way or the other whether the Emperor is for us or against us!"

"But what if they are destroyed my Lord?" Josep asked, shocked that the Grand Duke and a soldier of great experience should overlook this obvious possible consequence.

"They seem to believe they will be under diplomatic or chivalric immunity. So be it. They can do as they wish!" Berenguer d'Entença turned away to signal the conversation was over, in typical fashion. Josep stood there a moment at a loss as to what to do or say. Entença was certainly not behaving like a leader in the Company's hour of need.

"My Lord," said Josep, steeling himself and knowing he was clutching at straws, "I feel you should consider that whoever is seen to send the mission will be considered the Commander-in-Chief of the force," he argued.

"Let those who wish to follow me, follow me!" was all that Berenguer d'Entença said in reply, over his shoulder.

Consequently, the mission was fitted out to be sent from among Rocafort's men despite Gisbert Rocabertí's disagreement and was to be led by Dalmau Sant Martí, with Pere Lopis as the boat's Captain. They were to sail to Constantinople and a light twenty-oared lleny, smaller and faster - and less threatening - than a galley and in the presence of the Emperor, Ambassadors of the City of Venice and Pisa in Constantinople and the Captain of Genova in Pera, they would challenge the Emperor and accuse him of the offence that had been committed against them.

CHAPTER FOURTEEN

No sooner had the envoys been sent the following morning than the attack on Gallipolis that had been feared finally took place. Josep was with Ramón Muntaner at the time the shout went up and they took up the defence of the tower. However the gates of the town were still open as the squadron of Almogavers that had accompanied the envoys to their ship was returning and the aggressors, a brigade of Imperial army Turcopoles numbering five thousand or so and skilled in guerilla warfare on horseback, ambushed them and attacked them from behind as they came through the gates and many poured in. Taken by surprise, the two Almogaver regiments resisted fiercely but the force was well organised and the plan well executed and in less than two hours, a thousand more Almogavers lay dead, about a third their number. Gisbert Rocafort's prediction had been correct: it did not matter whether the Emperor approved or not of Kor Michael's actions, the latter was in command of the army and the crucial point to bear in mind was how the Company could best defend itself against his troops and how to organise an offensive to attack the Greek army in return. It was now a matter of life and death, kill or be killed.

Berenguer d'Entença rallied his men while Rocafort did the same with his and between the two regiments the tower was defended, the invaders driven out of the walls of the town, which was then stoutly barricaded against another attack. Meanwhile a squadron of about three hundred Almogavers pursued the repelled aggressors and inflicted significant damage on the force in retreat. Several of the Turcopoles were captured and brought back to the camp.

With the aid of interpreters, they were interrogated. Their

instinct was to lash out despite the fact they were in danger of being summarily executed.

"Perhaps that is the point," Berenguer d'Entença said. "They won't speak."

"Then torture them!" shouted Rocafort. "Use any means to get any information about future attacks."

"They will die resisting," said Berenguer d'Entença.

"Then so be it," shouted back Rocafort, grabbing one of the prisoners by the hair and thrusting his head back to expose his throat. The Turcopole warrior was already seriously injured. His arm lay limp by his side, his hand crashed, several fingers missing. He was bleeding heavily and was pale with blood loss. The sweat of the agony stood out in beads on his forehead and his eyes were bloodshot with pain and exertion.

"Tell us where the forces are or so help me God, I'll run you through with this very coltell of mine!" screamed Rocafort. So saying he put his face next to the captive and roared the same order and threat, which the interpreter conveyed as best he could. His quietness contrasted grotesquely with Rocafort's fury.

The man looked deep into Rocafort's eys, then with every ounce of strength that he had left, spat the contents of his lungs into Rocafort's face. Rocafort roared, then struck instantly. It was deliberately a slicing blow which left the man's carotid artery severed but did not cut all the way through the neck. Rocafort, still grabbing the man's head by the hair, now tilted the half-severed neck, allowing the blood to spurt out from the sliced artery. Checking to see the man was still conscious, he tilted the head forward on the neck so that the flow of the blood was stemmed but now seeped into the man's lungs. He started to convulse as his lungs filled with blood and he tried to cough his lungs clear.

"For God's sake man, kill him!" bellowed Berenguer d'Entença, knocking Rocafort's right hand so that the man's blood would spill out and he would die more quickly.

Rocafort let out a low growl and without changing the position of his hands at all, deflected Berenguer d'Entença's blow with his knee, which still had the greeve protecting it. The point of the greeve caught Berenguer d'Entença's hand cutting deeply into the palm. Berenguer d'Entença instinctively withdrew. Rocafort then took his coltell and lopped off the man's ears and sliced off his nose before he would let him fall to the floor and cough his last breaths out.

"You are a savage," hissed Berenguer d'Entença. "I've always known it. I will be avenged of this, mark my words!"

"I mark your words!" retorted Rocafort, imitating Berenguer d'Entença's aristocratic vowels and formal expression. "Go fuck yourself and stick your words up your arse for all I care. Come near me again and I'll peel you cock first you toffee-nosed piece of shit!"

He plunged his coltell into the now dead man's back, using the blood-sodden clothes to wipe down his weapon. Then aiming one blow at the remaining captive, he decapitated him.

"There's mercy for you, shit-for-brains! They weren't going to talk anyway so I've saved you the trouble."

Berenguer d'Entença launched himself at Rocafort and landed a crushing punch on the side of his jaw, which sent the man reeling. In seconds ten men were on Berenguer d'Entença and ten men were on Rocafort and the brawl was set to develop into a free-for-all.

"That will be all!" roared a voice Josep recognised. It was Ramón Muntaner, who literally jumped between the two men. "There's been enough slaughter here today without our two senior commanders tearing each other's throats out. How they would dance for delight if they could only see us now in Constantinople! Get a grip on yourselves, now, or we all die! We all have to get out of this mess alive. That's going to be hard enough without our two commanders lending the enemy a helping hand."

It was a mark of Ramón Muntaner's character and the respect he commanded that he was able to bring the situation under control. The two commanders knew instantly that what he said made sense but the situation was so volatile that had it not been for Ramón Muntaner, this explosion could have blown up into a full-scale conflagration. Both men faced each other bloodied and panting in a tense stand-off. Rocafort turned and stamped off.

"Mess with me again and I'll have you sent back in pieces," he shouted!

Berenguer d'Entença did not dignify the threat with a reply. What was clear was that they had both declared war on each other. At that moment, Berenguer d'Entença with his gashed palm and Rocafort with a smashed jaw were quits. Until the next time.

"We must keep these two as far away from each other as possible. We need a fort for each one," Josep said to Muntaner.

"I'll talk to Rocafort's deputies and suggest they raid north of here and see if they can establish a base somewhere," said Muntaner. "In the meantime, I'll aim to send Berenguer d'Entença's party south. That way, we might see the week out in one piece."

As soon as Berenguer d'Entença heard the proposal, he commandeered five of the galleys and said he was going to wage war on Constantinople. As the port was part of the walled structure around Gallipolis, this was quickly organised and the detachment had left by midday.

CHAPTER FIFTEEN

Scouts reported that night that the enemy were camped a league to the west of Gallipolis. There was no imminent danger but the following morning at dawn, Josep went to check the sentries only to find, during the night, siege engines had been moved to within two hundred metres, a distance of two crossbow shots, from the walls. Arrows now whistled past Josep's ears and one of the guards was struck in the chest, falling from the parapet to the ground. He shuddered, then was still. They were under siege.

In the meantime, messengers came from the Turcopoles opposite requesting the dead bodies of the two captives. At first Rocafort, undeniably in charge now that Berenguer d'Entença had departed, was in favour of shooting them dead from the ramparts. However, according to the interpreters, they said they had something that would interest him. A bloody sack dripping with blood was thrown to the floor.

"Who could it be? Everyone is accounted for!" Josep said.

"Too soon to have captured and killed Berenguer d'Entença, worst luck!" said one of Rocafort's deputies.

"Tell them to leave it ten metres from the gate and withdraw and we'll do the same with their bodies on that side," shouted Rocafort.

The gruesome exchange was organised and carried out. Shrieks were heard as the dead men's families recovered the bloodless corpses of their mutilated menfolk. Their cries and curses were drowned out as the gate was shut. In the privacy of the town's perimeter wall, just inside the gate, the bloody bag was opened. Now it was the Catalan company's turn to vent shock and horror.

"It is Lopis!" someone shouted. "They have killed Captain Lopis!"

Pere Lopis had been dispatched to Constantinople with Dalmau Sant Martí. He had been killed in flagrant contravention of the laws of civilised warfare when presenting accusations against the Emperor and formally breaking the oaths of allegiance to him, as the laws of chivalry dictated.

"You see the nature of the enemy?" roared Rocafort. "We cannot give them any quarter. They will cut us down as they have these emissaries, who travelled in the belief that they were safe because of diplomatic immunity and the laws of chivalry."

There was uproar. Lopis' wife came and hysterically recovered her dead husband's head. She was in such shock that she slipped into a coma that night and died before morning. Her last words were reported to have been, "Where do they have the rest of him? Promise me you'll find him, bury him the Christian way."Josep organised a small boat and set out to catch up with Berenguer d'Entença to apprise him of the dreadful news. When his captain skilfully caught up with him in less than a day, Josep also warned him the enemy were implacable and had abandoned all norms. Scouts with interpreters were dropped at various points along the mainland. There was no news. When finally they came to the town of Rodostó, a port up the coast from Gallipolis, where they needed to dock and take on more provisions, the local traders, despite whose side you were on, always keen to do a deal, fled as soon as they saw the Catalan *lleny* entering the harbour, next to the long sandy shore. Josep later could only imagine the panic that must have raced through the town driving the whole population indoors, men, women, children, young and old, able-bodied and crippled alike, scurrying away with suppressed shrieks of fear before the landing force arrived from the port area. Stalls still displaying their wares stood empty, inviting the Catalans to take whatever they wished. Food was cooking on white hot embers in the restaurants, open bottles of wine and half empty glasses stood abandoned on the tables. A lost child wandered aimlessly in the street, screeching hysterically, unaware of the source of the danger he could feel. He was mercifully ignored by the Catalans, who looked about them mystified as to what was happening. As they passed the child, a door suddenly opened, the child was plucked off the street, the screams continued, the door slammed shut, bolts were heard driven home as the house was barred again against the invaders. Silence returned but for the cries of the child, which were enough to mark out the town for destruction and doom.It was a hot, late afternoon at the beginning of June and the sun was burning the backs of their necks as they climbed the steps that lay between the harbour and the marketplace of the town. The town was well-to-do: there was a sense of civic pride in the place reflected in the well-kept gardens to the sides of the steps. The pruned trees, now in leaf as the year stood between spring and summer, felt to Josep like static symbols of the town, frozen with fear, silent behind barred doors, everyone hoping against hope that the intruders would simply leave. Spires of Greek churches were visible ahead and above them at the top of the steps. There was an isolated sound. A donkey braying. It was tethered to an arcaded hall, dark, damp, smelling of red meat and fresh blood. The donkey brayed not out of fear but out of boredom. It was tethered to the entrance to the meat market. Its feet were in blood. It wanted to move out of the blood but couldn't. It was stamping its feet as it brayed. The blood was being splattered all over the whitewashed walls of the meat market. Inside, it was deserted. The butchers had fled, too. Huge sides of beef hung on hooks. Pigs in pens grunted almost inaudibly: they sensed the strangeness of the silence more than the idiotic braying donkey. Semi-butchered joints lay on the long wooden slabs and there was a constant drip-dripping as the blood drained from freshly-slaughtered stock. The shock was visceral. Like an icy blade slicing through the base of the stomach. Their knees gave way and they momentarily lost control of their bowels and bladders. Near the centre of the market, the meat hung on the hooks at odd angles. It was pale, almost white and dry, showing it had been hanging there for some time. And it was lean. Little fat adhered to the flesh and the skin, the skin was pale and there was little or no hair, not to mention a hide and what hair there was was sparse and fine, not bristly like a hog's hair. The cuts were smaller than usual, somehow familiar, though impossible to associate with any creature normally slaughtered, butchered and hung on hooks for display in the meat market. Not heavy slabs but light joints, on light bones but awkwardly cut, as if the butcher had been in too much of a hurry, hacking through bone when the joint could be more easily severed, leaving oddly formed L-shaped pieces. The pieces dangled from the hooks, they had not been carefully hooked to help drain the blood or appeal to the buyer. Nor could they be easily moved around. The pieces simply hung there, flies were buzzing around them and they exuded an odd and off-putting sweetish smell. If it had been for sale, it had not proved popular. Yet all around there was evidence of the meat trade in full swing.

Josep sank to his knees and vomited in the gutter, then Berenguer d'Entença saw it too and turned in horror, clutching his stomach. Behind the pole where larger pieces were displayed there was a pile of what looked like blanched chicken wings and offcuts. Yet to the side lay the unmistakable shapes of feet, amputated at the ankle, precisely done work, each pair looking like a pair of shoes tidily left side-by-side outside a room to be stepped into on their owner's return. Above the pink-grey owner-less feet were suspended two remarkably similarly coloured legs, or at least the lower section up to the knee, into which nails had been driven carefully so that the limbs would hang straight down, directly over the feet they had been attached to. They were good shapely lower legs, with good muscle definition and bulging calves. Stout, athletic legs. There was the slightest breath of a breeze and the dangling legs, suspended from fine rope from the ceiling, twisted slightly in the breeze but curiously, such was the care of the design of the system of suspension, they did not sway from side to side and stayed directly overhead, as it were, or rather, above their feet. Looking back at the pile of chicken wings and offcuts, one could now clearly identify hands, ears, fingers surprisingly separated from hands given the scant care the artisan had elsewhere devoted to the butchery of the larger pieces of his gruesome task, apart from the feet and legs.

Josep vomited again. Next to the chicken wings and offcuts were the heads, barely recognisable because of the random way they lay strewn on the floor as if they were the part the butcher had shown least interest in or had abandoned first, it was impossible, impossible to imagine. Other unnameable parts littered the floor where the heads had been tossed carelessly in a pile, staining the once brown hair blood red or liver black, colours briefly witnessed before departure at the end of the day of fighting on the battlefield, human gore even the most carnage-hardy warrior would turn away from. All of this was displayed when normal people shopped for their meat; a display, an exhibition, an amusement. Josep vomited again.

Berenguer d'Entença had by now recovered and was giving orders for his men, all in a state of shock, to assemble some of the townspeople. A group was quickly gathered, they kept their heads down clearly and understandably panic-stricken that, were they not do so, they could quickly lose them. Water was demanded. The heads were washed. Twenty-six of them. Their owners were quickly identified by Berenguer d'Entença's men. It was the entire deputation sent from Gallipolis to Constantinople two weeks before. However, there was one notable exception: the head of the ship's Captain Pere Lopis was missing.

The riddle was quickly solved. Brisk questions and answers through the interpreter established the whereabouts of Lopis or at least that of his head, which Josep confirmed. The person who had seemed to become the spokesman for the huddled group of townspeople – whose knowledge was to Josep alarmingly detailed – was there even a hint of pride in his demeanour? Josep wondered – this well-built man with strong long-fingered, large hands, he said to Josep's amazement, he thought, pointing to the side of the chicken wings and offcuts, they might be his legs.

Berenguer d'Entença roared and with one movement grasped the man who all too late realised he had taken too much pride in his handiwork. True to the criminal instinct, this miscreant had returned too soon to the scene of the crime unable to resist celebrating it. One could almost say, Josep thought, there was something deeply personal in Berenguer d'Entença's rage, that even he was personally shocked by the depravity of the act. Berenguer d'Entença had the accused villagers bound and imprisoned on board his own galley and arranged for the body parts of the hapless mission to Constantinople to be collected and transported to Gallipolis, where they would be given a Christian burial. Josep admired his decency and restraint: he could have simply given orders for the town to be utterly destroyed in revenge but his instinct to do the right thing for his comrades overrode other considerations.

It later became clear he also wanted to find out who the perpetrators of this crime were in order to punish the guilty rather than punishing the whole town. Under interrogation, the main culprit broke down, giving names of men in the town who had assisted in overpowering, killing and dismembering the deputation. These men were duly arrested and imprisoned on board Berenguer d'Entença's galley. However, the names of others were given who were residents of the city of

Heraclea, a town twenty miles along the coast from Rodostó. This proved to be the last town the deputation had passed through the night before arriving in Rodostó and where, Josep and his companions learnt, the plan to commit the murder had actually been hatched. Berenguer d'Entença's five galleys consequently set sail immediately for Heraclea, which fell easily. Once the guilty had been rounded up, they were imprisoned together with their co-conspirators and taken out to sea. Here, they were read the charges in Greek, found guilty and condemned to death. They were then thrown overboard without any further ceremony, fifteen in all. Berenguer d'Entença resisted pressure to execute twenty-six, the number of Catalans in the deputation. He considered that revenge had been exacted and justice done on behalf of his murdered companions and that the episode was finished. It was not until two weeks later that Josep found out what the eventual fate of Rodostó would be.

CHAPTER SIXTEEN

In Berenguer d'Entença's absence, the situation for the Almogavers and particularly for the Greek population of the Gallipolis peninsular east of the River Evros became worse and worse. Revenge was all Rocafort seemed bent on, though it was a blind revenge vented upon any non-Catalan now, which involved the total pillaging of what had been known as the Thracian Chersonese in classical times, one of the great *bread baskets* of antiquity. Rather than conserve resources, stimulate trade, rebuild the local economy and take a handsome tithe of all produce, Rocafort set out only to ransack what he could immediately lay his hands on and take it back to Gallipolis. In Berenguer d'Entença's absence, Entença's fledgling camp at Madytos was abandoned and Gallipolis became the centre of Rocafort's personal diabolical fiefdom. Needless to say, the local population melted away by night taking what few possessions they could, heading for the Greek controlled towns west of the Evros River and from there north towards the Bulgarian hills. Yet the sight of the Almogavers dragging along a gaggle of captive girls was not uncommon. Nor did anyone comment on the fact that the numbers of these girls did not swell into a visible group contained somewhere in, or in the vicinity of, Gallipolis. Josep could barely bring himself to imagine the cruel fate they must have met. Not that it concerned anyone. The women did not talk about it, they looked sternly away when they saw the pitiful little flocks crying out to them in obvious pleas for help and mercy as women themselves. But they might as well have been squealing pigs on their way to slaughter so little effect did they have on those battle-hardened hearts. What disturbed Josep as much was the daily need to make believe the hell they lived in did not actually exist. At night, fires were lit, livestock slaughtered during the day was butchered and spitted, then roasted over the fires. Musicians would then strike up and there would be dancing, Almogavers would dance with their wives, flirtations that had been developing for weeks between the men under arms and widows, ex-lovers, mistresses who had accompanied the Almogavers, would burst into fast-burning romances. The groans and cries of rutting couples formed a back beat to the music, which grew wilder as the evening became night and the night wore on into early morning. And even when the fires for their own cooking had burned down, there still hung in the air the scent of charred pine and flesh, though what flesh was unclear. Pine was too resinous to be used in conventional cooking fires, so it was presumed to be the odour of torched farmhouses and smallholdings, together with the corpses of their occupants, slumped inside the houses on their floors where they'd fallen defending their homes.

Within three months or so, the countryside surrounding Gallipolis, formerly gentle green rolling hills and uninterrupted cornfields as far as the eye could see, was a scorched black brown or red, eerily unpopulated, branded by the vengeful occupiers with the smoking relics of rural residences in ruins.

Whichever direction one looked, a pall of smoke rose somewhere not too far off, the visible inventories of work for Rocafort of the Almogavers' daily toil. He was bringing the Thracian Chersonese low, this stone-hearted man, wrestling the area under his dominion, grinding it under his foot.

Stocks lasted through Christmas, an even more lavish affair than any ordinary night, with scant regard to the Nativity itself and its promise of renewal but the wind blew cold as the New Year was ushered in. They first ran out of firewood. It was arduous to scavenge semi-burnt beams from the torched dwellings in the area, though, had the work been organised systematically, plenty of high quality timber could have been salvaged for their fires. Yet as the host had had easy access to the firewood stored up in plenty at any of the hundreds of homesteads that dotted the peninsular, they had come to reckon on having an inexhaustible supply of easy-to-transport logs for all occasions at any time. Ramón Muntaner had endeavoured to persuade Rocafort of the desirability of clearing out all usable wood before setting fire to the local houses but the military imperative of "flushing out pockets of resistance" had made the well-ordered, well-stocked stores of comestibles spectacularly flammable and Rocafort's Almogavers veritably tore through the stock like fireflies taking pride in the speed of their work. These industrious imbeciles with no thought for the future beatled through the resources of the area – their own future resources – as if their reputations and lives depended on it. But the tipping point had come and the iron winter earth unwittingly paid them back for their wastefulness. So short did they become of firewood that their lives were now as threatened by chilblains and frostbite as they had ever been by a possible rising, among the tumbledown masonry in the blighted landscape, of a secret army of resistance fighters, impervious to hunger or cold themselves. The guerilla force that Rocafort swore would launch a counter-offensive of course never appeared. But the monitoring gave his troops plenty to do.

CHAPTER SEVENTEEN

As Ramón Muntaner was the Quartermaster General, Josep stuck close to him and made sure his own trips focused on securing provisions. They were now simply subsisting. Yet these journeys were becoming so long as to be unfeasible. By way of example, simply providing the animals with fodder enough to last the sorties there and back was unsustainable and supplies dwindled daily. The diet of the force and its several hundred hangers-on and camp followers consequently changed as less wheat became available for bread. The livestock became more undernourished day by day, more of it was slaughtered as it produced less meat although more of it was needed as there was less bread to eat. And the increase of meat in the diet led to an increase in the demand for wine.

"We cannot be expected to eat this tough old meat without plenty of wine to wash it down!" was a common opinion among the ranks. Having devastated their sustainable resources they proceeded to devour their irreplaceable resources. Put another way, they started, devouring themselves.

"You have brought this force to be very edge of ruin!" was Entença's opening remark when finally, after what seemed like a whole term in Purgatory, the ex-grand duke unexpectedly returned a little short of a year after he had gone. Even between Josep and Ramón Muntaner there was only a murky understanding of how Berenguer d'Entença had managed to extricate himself from the avaricious clutches of d'Oria. Yet it seemed the tentacles of power reached far enough at least to save Berenguer d'Entença's life – this part was the most opaque of all Berenguer d'Entença's vague narrative – in the northern

Italian seaport city state of Genova. Berenguer d'Entença's aristocratic credentials were utterly top-notch of course, he reassured everyone, but even so, having access to the kind of money needed to raise such a ransom hinted at his having found a battery of aristocratic business associates, keen to invest if the return was well-assured. Perhaps he had even managed to entice royal patronage. Rocafort could only dimly perceive the aristocratic connection but to think royalty would take an interest in this, in his opinion, failed military leader, was beyond his imagination. He was quick to grasp conspiracy and hatch his own plots to ensure his own ascendancy yet when required to plan strategically or to peer into the inkier depths of international intrigue he was utterly incapable, not imagining how he could ever really be affected, for good or ill, by such machinations. That was his downfall.

The return of Berenguer d'Entença, together with his force of five hundred Neapolitan mercenaries, had the effect of splitting the Almogavers force into two factions again.

One was clearly loyal to Rocafort and occupied the stronghold of the Castle of Gallipolis, the adjoining castle port, with the remains of the galleys scuttled and half-submerged in the shallows next to the steps up to the Castle. This party included Rocafort's brother of course, Gisbert de Rocafort, together with the three knights who had managed to escape the Adrianople massacre, the two Ramóns, Alquer and de Tous, who were inseparable and their companion, Bernat de Roudor. A fourth knight, Guillem Peris de Caldes, was a childhood friend of the latter. Each knight commanded a squadron, a unit of some ten provincial knights, and eighty or ninety Almogavers, of which one was the Almogaten, the Almogaver commander. Those who gravitated towards Berenguer d'Entença were basically the knights who, or whose fathers, had accompanied him in Sicily and Naples during the Sicilian war, Ferdinand Gorí, Eiximen Alberò, Martín Lograu, Pere d'Erós and García Gomis Palacín.

All of the Company had Catalan roots, except for Rocafort, who came from Valencia but he was keen to stress his family had moved there only during the reign of King Jaume I. He claimed that his father and grandfather had served the King, the latter with distinction at Gallinera in 1258, after which the family had been given land outside the city of Valencia. Rather than serving with an aristocratic family, the Rocafort family had carved out a good living as mercenaries but had not worked their way up the social ladder. Rocafort spoke Catalan with a southern accent, without the neutral vowel that so distinguishes the Catalan of Catalonia Vella, Old Catalonia, north of the Ebre river, from that of Catalonia Nova and Valencia, which had remained in Muslim hands much longer. These subtle differences of pronunciation lent variety to the force and gave the colour that was attractive to those who believed in the Almogaver ethos, who had served as in the northern Pyrenean foothills as in the hills around Granada. It was a matter of pride to Berenguer d'Entença with his title, royal connections and ancient family, that his accent was unmistakeably upper-class and he exaggerated these aspects when he spoke to Rocafort or within earshot of him, just to remind him always of the social pecking order; just as he winced every time Rocafort opened his mouth. Of course, Rocafort reacted to this linguistic peacocking by stretching out his neck as far as he could, so to speak, and speaking in a strangled accent to offend the sensibilities of Berenguer d'Entença.

It was therefore natural that the two factions kept as much to themselves as possible. Berenguer d'Entença's followers were accommodated in the fine town houses around the Market Square. Josep and Ramón Muntaner, being in charge of the gate house and the stores, were accommodated next to the warehouses at the castle gate.

But life was not without its lighter moments. Guillem Peris de

Caldes was one of those people who naturally bring fun and humour with them. He was nominally one of Entença's men but had volunteered for the job of Dog Officer, responsible for controlling the stray dogs in Gallipolis, under Rocafort's command. These dogs prowled hungrily around the cattle, occasionally picking off young or sick animals. He was effective in this task as he knew he could not possibly destroy all the dogs he found, a pointless and time-consuming task, as they were too numerous and more would come where others had been destroyed. But he was able to drive them out of the city gates daily, knowing his efforts were keeping the dogs at bay, protecting the livestock and therefore making a valuable contribution. He was a good-natured, good-looking man, with copper-coloured hair, which he wore long, a large nose, a strong chin and an expressive mouth, which almost always wore a smile. He was funny, gentle, polite and especially popular with the women and girls, some of whom had been given puppies he'd found. "So long as you keep them at home, why should Rocafort be any the wiser?" he would say. What appealed to the girls most about him, Josep and Ramón Muntaner concluded, was his easy-going manner. He was strong but he was also flexible, good to talk to and funny. He was also firmly single, which made him even more alluring. But he seemed impervious to the charms of the many beautiful girls and women in the camp. In fact, some girls even thought he might just not be interested in that sort of thing as it would complicate his life and encroach on his freedom to roam. He simply enjoyed his own company. The task of dog catcher was made easier as dogs are gregarious creatures that form packs to hunt better as well as for the company, warmth and protection. Find one and it would eventually lead you to the pack, was the cornerstone of the wisdom of Guillem Peris de Caldes.

It was Josep who spotted the dog for the first time. He was struck by the unusually rich thick red-brown coat of the dog, which was in prime condition. It was clearly a male and all its movements were muscular but measured and graceful. It also had a very trusting nature and came to Josep immediately when called, snuffling his hair as he crouched down to pat him and nuzzling him with his long brown muzzle. There was something bear-like about him, the brown coat, the long muzzle, the big feet and muscular movements and Josep suddenly realised looking into these strangely intelligent, sensitive dark brown eyes whom he reminded him of.

"Of course, you look just like Guillem Peris de Caldes!" he said.

Ramón agreed with Josep but reminded him Guillem had a job to do and that he'd better see if the dog could lead Josep to its pack.

Josep and Guilly, as Josep decided to name him, after Guillem, strode off, both of them proud to be with each other, good-looking males in the prime of life. But the dog lead Josep to no pack. Every time Josep asked where his companions were, he cocked his head to one side and jumped up with both paws on Josep's chest, as if to say: "You are my companion now, I do not know who else you mean. Yet Guilly never tired of searching, almost as if he were searching for something – or someone.

Josep was seriously taken by Guilly but allowed himself to be overruled by Ramón Muntaner.

"He's a lovely animal Josep but he's a dog and dogs are not allowed in the camp, as simple as that. Why do you not introduce him to Guillem. He's a good sort. He won't do him any harm and then you can both decide what to do with him."

"You know, that's a splendid idea!" replied Josep happily. "You're always so logical and sensible, Ramón, I cannot possibly keep him...," he broke off.

"... and it wouldn't be permitted for you to keep him here, we're right at the city gates. The sight of a dog here would be very likely to attract all the other dogs in the area,"

Muntaner finished his sentence. "If the dog problem became any worse, can you imagine what Rocafort's henchmen would do? Guillem has requested the task, do not force Rocafort into taking it from him."

So Josep went off to find Guillem. The result was engraved on his memory forever after. The two, man and dog, took one look at each other and became inseparable. It was as if they complemented each other perfectly and Guilly, being an intelligent dog, required little training to perform his task of Chief Dog Sniffer. He made Guillem's work so much easier as he unerringly led him to the other packs of dogs every time. Then with his commanding manner, Guillem was able to round the dogs up and escort them out of the city gate in no time. There was not a nook or cranny the dog did not know intimately within the month. Hidden recesses in tumbledown houses overgrown with foliage and vegetation were no safe bolt-holes any longer. In Guilly went and out came a mother and litter. Added to this natural olfactory ability was his boundless enthusiasm and energy for his task. For every ten paces Guillem took, Guilly took two hundred, thereby scouring entire neighbourhoods of Gallipolis in the time it took Guillem to walk along the main street, Calle Major. Yet Guillem was officially under Rocafort's control and was therefore answerable to him. Though Rocafort's force outnumbered Berenguer d'Entença's, Entença had, in point of fact, been nominated Grand Duke, equivalent to the rank of a senior general, and therefore outranked Rocafort, who was the Commander of an Almogaver regiment.

Perhaps still testing the water, Entença still had not challenged Rocafort but it was clear from the atmosphere in the camp that the times had changed, judging from the fact in any case that the nightly parties were now more interspersed and not so wild. Rocafort, never a great communicator, wore a constant frown now, a brooding look. He made it clear he was watching everything and commented on everything he saw. As a result, it did not take long for it to come to Rocafort's attention that Guillem had effectively adopted a dog.

"What is that bloody idiot thinking of? He's supposed to be getting rid of dogs not adopting them!" Josep heard him say. It was unclear who had told Rocafort. The garrison was a microcosm rife with petty rivalries, jealousies and vendettas. Rumour had it a certain young lady, whose amorous advances towards Guillem had been rebuffed, feeling scorned, had taken advantage of the opportunity for revenge by reporting the situation to one of Rocafort's Almogatens. The rumour then began to circulate that Guillem had scorned the love of a young lady for the company of a dog- and a male dog at that. The amount of mirth that was squeezed out of that joke showed not only how desperately boring life in the garrison had become but also how much wine was being consumed nightly. For a week, Rocafort's soldiers split their drunken strides at Guillem's expense, doubling their normal alcoholic intake as finally they had something to laugh about.

Yet even Rocafort found he was taken with the handsome hound and Guillem, faced with losing Guilly and, apart from his company, also his valuable help in his task, was only too ready, in fact, delighted, to hand the dog over to Rocafort, who promptly justified his new ownership, blatantly untrue though it was, by claiming he had discovered him and he was now the company's lucky mascot.

Matters soon became so complicated that it was actually difficult to pinpoint the origins of the situation as they unfolded then.

The fact of the matter is that beauty seldom goes unnoticed and often excites jealousy. The beautiful attract beauty, so when Hatche first appeared at the gates of the camp speaking Turkish no one could understand what this astonishingly beautiful young woman wanted.

No one could fathom why such a beautiful woman would put herself at such risk when in the whole countryside around her, unmentionable barbarity was being visited on the Greek female population.

Perhaps that was it: the fact is she was not Greek and did not speak Greek. She turned up at the city gates one morning, repeatedly asking the same question. She was pointing to her own green brown eyes and dark brown hair making woofing and panting sounds and generally imitating a dog so well it was obvious what she was talking about. When the soldiers saw her, they couldn't decide whether just to mock her and drive her away from the gates or stand and watch her. She was enchantingly graceful, seemingly fearless and funny in an earnest sort of way that was so artless and open that it was both lovely and disarming. It was quite impossible to ignore her.

Ramón Muntaner, always pragmatic, brought her to Josep's attention.

"We're going to need a Turcopole translator," he said into his cupped hand dissimulating a cough, as if aware he could be ridiculed by the soldiers for taking her seriously even for a moment.

"Josep, if you can take your eyes off her for just a moment, we need to find a translator or march her off the grounds or lock her up but we cannot have her causing the guards to swoon around her! We'll be made a laughingstock not to mention the wives and women folk when they get to hear about her. Josep, are you listening to me? Josep, for God's sake!"

"Er, yes, Ramón, of course I'm listening to you. Yes," he said, unable to tear his eyes off the woman. "She's obviously talking about a dog. But look Ramón, when she imitates its face and mannerisms, she does it so well she almost reminds me of someone…"

"Or some...thing," Ramón said with emphasis, trying to snap him out of it.

"What?" asked Josep, still paying more attention to the woman than to Ramón.

"Oh, forget it, I'll go and get Guillem. He is the one responsible for dogs after all!"

"Yes, and do not forget the Turcopole translator" he said utterly missing the point. "I'm fascinated to know what she's trying to say!" Josep replied. Ramón momentarily glanced at him then scowled again. Josep was lost.

"Josep this is official business, not a circus act!" But even to himself he sounded silly and over serious. He must have known it was going to end badly, Josep later thought, but Josep did not pay any attention at the time and off Ramón marched to find Guillem.

The young woman took Josep and a handful of Almogavers down to the shore in front of the town and showed them the lateen-rigged *lllaüt* she had come to Gallipolis in. She kept gesticulating towards the port on the other side of the Hellespont, Lampsaki, and continued her act suggesting she was looking for something, presumably a dog and she had followed him across the narrow neck of water and needed to know urgently if he was in Gallipolis.

CHAPTER EIGHTEEN

When they returned to Gallipolis, they found Ramón Muntaner, Guillem Peris de Caldes and Rejep, the Turcopole translator, waiting for them sternly. They had left the gate unguarded. Once they had been thoroughly dressed down for dereliction of duty, Josep spoke up for the other Almogavers saying they had followed the Turkish girl and explained what they understood from her mimicry."For God's sake, let's get this sorted out once and for all before Rocafort gets to hear about it or the Greeks launch an attack while the men are enraptured by this girl and her pageantry!" he said gruffly. Guillem adopted for once a countenance of deep concern and all looked around them for the girl. Yet she couldn't be seen. They looked around the gate, along the outside perimeter wall, some even went down to the boat they guess she'd come in but all to no avail. Then a shout went up from the gatehouse and everyone rushed back to where they had been twenty minutes before. Hatche had been found curled up in a recess behind the heavy iron-reinforced wooden gate, where it swung open and was housed when open. As she brushed off the sleep from her face and hair and came to her senses, she looked like a bundle of colourful rags on the floor. She'd obviously fallen asleep during the hubbub following the soldiers' telling-off and unable to hold anyone's attention and overlooked for the moment, had slumped where she had stood, overcome with drowsiness. As she struggled to her feet, she once again had an almost hypnotic effect on the people gathered around her. The moment she and Guillem saw each other, there passed between them something like a wave of recognition, Josep later thought, and Hatche immediately began addressing him, in quieter, less desperate tones, as if she knew he of all people would be able to help her. Josep was amazed. He had not seen that kind of empathy between two people since he had experienced it himself many years before with Queen Constança. The thought reminded him in a flash of the hope and excitement of his early years, his love for the Queen and his utter devotion to King Pere, his dreams as a young man with Alba. Then he thought of Lali, a bitter-sweet pain stabbed his heart and everything his life had become flashed before his eyes. He staggered to steady himself. These two people, despite the misery of the situation they all found themselves in, with its wanton destruction, depravity and pointlessness, seemed to be held in a plasma that allowed them to communicate with each other, it seemed, beyond words.

Ramón Muntaner, ever the practical one, and, Josep later thought, the one with the most to lose, was the first to dispel this astonishing instant rapport manifesting itself to him, too. He had not been immune, Josep thought later to himself, he just saw clearly how it was going to end.

Sure enough, Ramón instructed the Turcopole to translate and it was as Josep and Guillem already knew, that the girl, whose name was Hatche, had been pursuing a lost dog for some days and had actually crossed over from Anatolia in Asia to the Gallipolis peninsula in Thrace, Europe, in pursuit of her beloved pet. Josep was really taken with the poetry of the idea. But the most extraordinary fact of all was that everyone present knew by now from the descriptions and imitations Hatche had been giving that the dog she was describing was Guilly.

When Guilly was finally brought in and dog and mistress were reunited, the dog let out a series of triumphant *whoofs* that reverberated around the walled town. Guilly's bark had by now become so familiar that it was instantly recognised. Moreover, it was the excited, playful bark he gave when he found what he was looking for. Everyone burst out laughing instantly and it made everyone feel so good!

"He's been searching for her since he came here!" said Guillem in utter bewilderment.

"And she wouldn't give up on him, either," added Josep.

Despite her tears, Hatche was laughing and hugging Guilly, holding his head to her lovely breast and kissing him with delight. Nor was it to anyone's surprise when, after a few days of Hatche returning to the boat she had arrived in to sleep at night, she and Guillem actually became the couple everyone thought looked so good together, inseparable, of course, from the dog.

All good things must pass. And just as beauty attracts beauty so does it also attract envy and lust. No sooner did Rocafort notice he'd seen less of Guilly in the past few weeks than various individuals, jealous of Guillem and Hatche's good fortune in finding such a lovely ideal partner, whispered information in his ear and, once the water was tested, further details about the extraordinary and indeed romantic events that had come about as a result of the appearance of the Company's mascot. Mean by nature and easily disgruntled, Rocafort lent them a willing ear.

"It isn't right to have a Turkish woman in camp. They were our enemy and they still could be for all we know," Josep heard Magdalena complain. But he remembered she was one of the young widows who had showered attention on Guillem to no avail.

"He has effectively taken what rightly belongs to you as our leader!" Josep heard one of Rocafort's officers say to him in his headquarters in the Castle, where every whisper carried. Josep had not been spying but had gone there on official business to see Rocafort and had quite innocently overheard.

"They say she's a real looker, my Lord, though she's obviously just a common girl, a Turkish girl at that!" Josep heard another of his men say. Rocafort was silent. That was when Josep became truly alarmed. Garrulous in the way people are who feel uncomfortable in silence, Rocafort was incapable of dissembling that he was considering carefully what his men were telling him. Josep was paralysed with indecision. Should he reveal himself, he might be accused of having spied on Rocafort's counsel. Yet if he were to leave, how could he defend his friends, people who had afforded him some respite over the past few weeks and made life in the camp bearable for once.

"Normally, I take no interest in the captives the men bring into the camp. They are their chattels and they have the right to dispose of them as they see fit. This, however, is a matter of principle. The women of the camp have to be considered and their sense of propriety must not be offended. What are the intentions of the couple? Do they plan to marry? They cannot continue living in sin. Have them brought to me at once to explain themselves. I must also consider my own dignity in this matter and preserve my rights."

He leered horribly and obviously at the men around them and they started laughing and joking.

"You have to keep your own end up, after all, my Lord!" said one.

"You have your reputation to consider," said another. As soon as Josep could leave, he went as discreetly as possible to the couple's rooms next to the old gatehouse. Neither Guillem, Hatche or Guilly was there. Trying to calm himself, Josep decided to take a walk along the battlements of the camp, thinking he could return later and all would be well. He started walking and allowed his thoughts to wonder wherever they wanted to. What had Rocafort meant by *"preserving his rights and dignity"*? Josep's mind rebelled against the prospect of Rocafort forcibly submitting Hatche to his will. Guillem would never allow it in any case. He would die fighting if it came to it. But in that case, Rocafort could do as he pleased with Hatche.

But why would he put himself in such danger and dispose of a good soldier in order to seize Hatche? Surely he wouldn't be so stupid. Yet twist the scenarios whichever way he might, Josep kept imagining Guillem struggling with Rocafort and Hatche's face etched with shock and horror. He had walked a good mile by now and was at that part of the wall that was least visited, where were stowed goods belonging to the Company that were no longer being used or were being stored for future use. Amid the smashed cartwheels, broken weapons, sacks of spare clothes, broken tents, stacks of rotting animal fodder, there was a shiny object among the debris. The sun was going down and Josep checked there was no one else around as guards would come soon to take up positions for night watch at dusk.

Josep climbed down from the battlements on the weathered blocks that acted as steps, carefully checking his footholds so as not to make too much noise. Checking again that he was alone, he approached the object and picked it up. It was a beautifully decorated charm on a necklace. It was strung on a simple leather strap but the charm was of diamonds mounted on a rose made of gold and looked Greek, not Catalan, French or Italian.

He heard a soft thumping sound as of something heavy but soft falling on something solid. It was coming from the other side of the wall, beyond where he had been walking. He had an instinct that whoever had lost this necklace, had only just lost it and was desperately trying to find it. Objects like this were quickly found and pocketed. He climbed up onto the battlement again and lying flat on his stomach pulled himself over to the side of the camp wall so that he could see down the other side.

CHAPTER NINETEEN

It was as if Rocafort had become possessed. He said nothing except to those closest to him and was rumoured not to have slept since the day he killed Hatche. Rumours circulated that in the dead of night when sleep finally descended on him he awoke with a start after a few moments' slumber whispering her name. Some say he was haunted by her spirit. Others, that he would drink himself into a stupor and have imaginings, during which he would rant and rave, though his closest advisers denied these rumours, claiming he was busy making plans for the Company's next move. There was no doubt, in Josep's mind, however, that he was suffering from new emotions for him: namely, remorse and regret. There was no doubt he was singularly and solely responsible for the unlawful killing of two innocents who had every reason to protect themselves and each other. How could he possibly continue to exercise leadership over the force in those circumstances? When Josep commented on these ideas to Ramón, his old friend looked him square in the eye.

"We have to be on our guard now more than ever, Josep, he will suspect everyone, will see plots everywhere, will deal with threats mercilessly. We must stay out of his way as much as we possibly can," he whispered.

Consequently, Josep and Ramón busied themselves rebuilding the wall furthest from Rocafort's quarters, without venturing to the part of town where Entença's regiment, which had cut itself off almost entirely from Rocafort now, were garrisoned.

Rocafort's next hapless victim did not take long to appear. When Josep saw Gombau, two thoughts passed through his mind: firstly, he was the man he had seen piling up the freshly killed bodies of the Greek female prisoners for disposal on the cart; and secondly, he thought he might know something about the diamond necklace he had lost.

When he now saw him standing next to Rocafort's brother Gisbert, answering the charges made against him, he saw in his hands the necklace with its beautiful, diamond-encrusted pendant, twisted around his stubby, powerful fingers. Sadly, however, the image of the women's bulging eyes forced the thought of jewellery out of Josep's mind.

It was unclear what form of execution Rocafort would choose for his victim. What was clear was the man was already as good as dead and he knew it. He had his head down, his hands being tied behind his back and he was being held on either side by two powerful Almogavers who clearly felt no kinship for him. In an act of depraved, grotesque showmanship, Rocafort was forcing this man to stand though his legs kept failing him. He had an absent air about him as if he had already taken himself off to another place in his mind so that he was only answering the questions put to him with grunts or monosyllables. It was an utterly pathetic, unedifying spectacle, like all executions Josep had seen, he reflected, bizarre, pointless and inhuman in its controlled cold barbarity. Luckily, it did not last long. Various witnesses testified loud and clear they had seen him leave his post when Rocafort was attacked by Guillem Peris de Caldes . Therefore, the man was found guilty as charged by ten Almogatens in Rocafort's company of abandoning his post, a court martial offence punishable by death. Many hurled abuse at the condemned man when the sentence was announced. Presumably, they wished to show their leader they acknowledged and agreed with his administration of justice. Josep and Ramón secretly exchanged a look as if to say: "There but for the grace of God go we!" as a noose was fitted around the man's neck, he was lead to the nearest tree and strung up. He kicked a couple of times and died quickly, to the disappointment of many in the crowd, who jeered and laughed, shouting comments like "He got off lightly!" and "Let that be a lesson to you!" and other examples of gallows humour. Rocafort's eyes were riveted to the scene, sweeping over the faces of all there assembled, taking in all the faces, all the details, nodding at the various utterances as if drawing energy from the event. He presented himself as their man. "Here I am, your leader, protecting you from evil!" he seemed to be saying, rather than, as Josep saw it: "Do you see how easily I can break you?" It was a tacit exercise in intimidation and the knot in the stomach everyone experienced was recognition of the fact. Josep looked steadfastly forward, with as inscrutable an expression as he could manage on his face, then when the ordeal was over and silence briefly descended, punctuated only by the creakings of the rope, he marched off as stiffly and formally as he could, making sure to make eye contact with no one.

"Where would Rocafort's next victim come from and what would the crime be then?" Josep wondered to himself. It was clear to Josep and Ramón that Gombau's real crime was simply being too close to Rocafort. From his shaky answers, it was nonetheless now clear to Josep his voice was the voice Josep had heard encouraging Rocafort to exercise his Dret de Ciuxa with Hatche. Had he not claimed he was doing it all so as to satisfy the womenfolk who were jealous of her? Perhaps this advice had convinced Rocafort that raping Hatche was desirable to him not only physically but also politically. Yet look what had happened to Gombau as a result of giving his advice. He was also the one responsible for killing and disposing of the Greek female prisoners. That policy was now at an end. The women in the camp, Josep felt, would not tolerate it for long after what had happened to Hatche. Gombau had been responsible for coordinating that policy and his elimination removed the evidence, wiped the slate clean, at least in Rocafort's mind. Lastly, though few but Josep and Ramón Muntaner now remembered, it was Gombau who'd been sent to summon Hatche. By executing him, Rocafort was easing his own conscience. The man who had delivered Hatche up to him had to die for his alacrity in carrying out his orders. In Josep's mind, Rocafort was merely continuing his policy of devouring everything, including now those around him. The question in Josep's mind was how many others he would destroy before he finally destroyed himself.

Josep's despair and disbelief at this turn of events was further compounded by the decision of Berenguer d'Entença to leave Gallipolis.

"You'd be well advised to do the same!" Berenguer d'Entença said. "In your own words, the man is descending into lunacy and the only way to keep safe from him is by putting distance between him and us. There are still a couple of towns three days' march from here that can be besieged for supplies. I shall base myself either at Madytos or Megarisi. Join us if you wish to."

Yet though the prospect of escaping from the madness of Rocafort was compelling, Josep rightly figured that Berenguer d'Entença somehow increased his risk of attack from Rocafort as he could now pose a physical threat to him. Nor had Josep yet forgiven Berenguer d'Entença for refusing to take him back to Italy when he was transported to Genova. Lastly, Josep was with Ramón Muntaner in Gallipolis. No matter how bad the situation got, Josep was sure that Ramón with his common sense and imperturbability represented his best chance of survival.

Berenguer d'Entença's departure depleted the town's manpower significantly making it feel more prone to a possible Greek counterattack. There was no formal notice of departure to Rocafort, which he took as an insult because he felt the omission diminished his standing.

Rather than acting as a catalyst, Entença's departure in no way affected the monotony. Days turned into weeks as usual, where nothing of importance happened. Daily raids were made into the surrounding area which resulted in little gain. Josep simply kept his head down and worked assiduously with Ramón Muntaner whose task as quartermaster of the host occupied all his time as consumption continued to exceed supply. Rocafort reduced his immediate circle to four or five, yet their daily allowance of wine and food was not cut, nor was food or wine ever left over. Rocafort was beginning to look more and more bloated. His face had become jowly, the skin on his cheeks sagged, his eyes were permanently bloodshot. His burly physique lacked the exercise it had grown accustomed to over the years and he became visibly heavy on his feet, a result of his growing obesity and alcoholism. On several occasions, he would not be seen for days on end, leading to speculation that he had died or was seriously ill. Then he would reappear with a hollow show of aplomb, conduct a meaningless raid, come back and order a camp dinner with extra food and wine for everyone, despite Muntaner's protestations that the camp could ill afford it.

CHAPTER TWENTY

November 1306

Just when Josep thought it could get no worse, Rocafort scraped the bottom of the barrel even for him. He had always helped himself to the best of the booty, his notion being that he thereby shored up his own prestige though, of course, this caused deep resentment among those not cowed by fear, or corrupted by toadying or whose intellect was still intact. However, one night he got exceedingly drunk and tried to take the wife of one of the soldiers. Needless to say, a fight broke out between Rocafort and the Almogaver in question. The Almogaver, a younger man, neither drunk, nor in poor physical condition, was far superior in arms to the now lumbering Rocafort and threw him so that his weapon flew from his hand. As the Almogaver, blind with rage came in for the kill, Rocafort covered his face with his hands and cried out for mercy. The soldier stopped and turned away in disgust. Rocafort from behind kicked him from the ground between his legs, felled him and drove his own coltell into his throat. When the wife, because of the fight, came screaming to her husband's aid, Rocafort, wheezing heavily, took out the dead man's coltell, pulled back her head by her hair as she knelt over her dead husband and slit her throat.

The shock was visceral and through Josep's mind flashed images of his childhood. Bru Miret was cutting Josep's own umbilical cord with his coltell, he knew this couldn't be a memory but it was part of his psyche now. Yet the monster standing but feet from Josep now who had just slit an innocent woman's throat looked so much like Bru Miret as he had come to look over the years, filthy, bestial, savage, that for a couple of moments the two images blended in Josep's mind. The fragile thread that linked the happiness of his childhood with his present was finally severed. As winter drew on, Ramón Muntaner experienced more success in restraining the excessive appetites of Rocafort and started laying the ground that would later convince him that it was necessary for them to leave Gallipolis and the Thracian Chersonese altogether as food stores were dangerously low. It was therefore planned that they would move west across the Evros River and head towards the Kingdom of Thessaloniki.

Early one morning, a visitor arrived for Josep. He arrived with his own galley and his papers were in order, so there was no alarm. He was neither Greek, nor Genovese, nor Pisan, so Josep was mystified especially as the visitor had not wanted the messenger, the sentry on duty at the main gate, to tell Josep who he was, preferring for Josep to wait until he saw him to find out.

"Josep, Josep, Josep, it is so good to see you! My word, you've grown into a handsome man and there's no denying it! How many years is it since I have seen you? It must be..." The voice, though deepened and mellowed with age, was instantly recognisable as that of Jacques de Molay.

"It was the night of the Sicilian Vespers. We had attended the Easter vigil in the Capella de Santa Agata in the King's Palace..." said Josep, struggling to hide his confusion and consternation. He somehow felt appalled to see him there, as if he were looking at a ghost.

"How sharp your memory is..."

How fresh the memory still was of the humiliation Josep had endured at Jacques' hands just outside the chapel! He could still remember the collision between them, the jolting concussion of the accidental blow to the nose, the shock causing the red wine to spill out of Jacque's goblet, Josep's blood in great splashes hitting the floor of the Palau at the same moment.

"Twenty-four years have passed my Lord, it was the night before my sixteenth birthday and I am now forty years of age," he said gathering his wits and disguising his feelings of horror.

Jacques came to him and embraced him closely. There was warmth in the embrace Josep had not expected and when Josep looked at him, the older man did not avert his gaze, as he had the last time he had seen him. Josep looked into his eyes and found the man behind them wearier, more perplexed and less overbearing than he had been when he had last seen him.

"My Lord, do you realise you are approximately twenty years my senior? Therefore, you were my age now when we last saw each other."

"My goodness, it is a lifetime since I last saw you, my boy! So much has happened. So little has been achieved. I believe that is why I have been recalled by the Holy Father."

"I have not followed the latest developments of Templar diplomacy in the Middle East, my Lord. I knew that you were based in Famagusta, in Cyprus, not far over the sea from Acre in Syria. I heard you had rescued many people from Acre, wealthy and important people among them, and had met Roger de Flor."

"What a genius of a man! What a remarkable person he was, Josep! Did you have the pleasure?"

"Briefly, my Lord, all too briefly!"

"His death was a tragedy. It took all of us – in the Middle East – by surprise," he paused on the words Middle East.

"Do you mean his death was not such a surprise in some circles?" Josep asked.

"Josep, little escapes the attention of the Holy See, the Holy Father has the most developed network of contacts and communications in our world and often the most able people."

"Do you mean they might have connived in his assassination?"

"There is no knowing what their plans and ruminations are, Josep. Their methods are inscrutable, their representatives whiter than white, it is their agents who are the perpetrators of these acts, which often coincide with the interests of the great Lords of temporal power."

"There is only one great power, my Lord, and that is France," replied Josep.

"Quite so. And thus the papacy wished it to continue, yet conflict has arisen since the new king, Philip the Fair, the fourth of that name, assumed the Crown. Where the peace was signed between King Jaume II of Catalunya Aragón and King Charles of Naples at Anagni, in 1295, seven years later, the King of France's henchmen, led by a certain Guillaume de Nogaret, attacked the Pope and held him hostage. He died not long afterwards."

"I had heard, my Lord, that Pope Boniface had died but did not know he had been attacked, as you say. And I know Guillaume de Nogaret, at least by name, from many years ago when I met him in the company of the Count of Foix."

"Yes, Josep and I was notified of that meeting. Do you not remember being interviewed by Ramón Berenguer de Belvís, Commander of Monzón and being told to be more circumspect?"

"I remember the interview well my Lord."

"I'm sure you resented it enormously at the time!"

"Had I not had such respect for the Templar in question and yourself my Lord, I might have turned my back on him and left."

"My goodness, Josep, how alike we are! I am sure you have since learned to master your temper and use it to your advantage. I'm afraid it is a lesson I still have to learn and

I have alienated many people as a result of the wrong word, even the wrong look over the years. Yet isolation – and I have known periods of isolation in Cyprus over the years– isolation and silence train the spirit. Temper is superficial, a symptom of the vexation caused by troublesome company, the desire to neutralise irritants. Truly the great players do not lose their temper. When they move, they are silent, invisible, decisive – and deadly. You realise you have lost only when it is too late to reverse the situation."

Josep turned and wondered what all this was about. Why had Molay come at this moment, welcome though it was? What was the connection between Guillaume de Nogaret and Jacques? Clearly, it had something to do with Jacques' position in Cyprus and he guessed, with the Pope.

"Why have you been summoned to Rome, my Lord?" Josep asked.

"Because our strategy with the Mongols has come to nothing. The Mamluks are stronger than ever and there is a race for the control of the Crusader states between the Papacy and the King of France. The Pope feels that the intervention from the military orders could be more effective if they were combined."

"A combined force of the Knights Hospitaler and the Knights Templar could strike more effectively from Cyprus on behalf of the papacy for example," Josep concluded.

"Precisely but the French crown are no longer interested in the Crusader States. Their policy in the Empire of Rum, as the Mamluks and Turks call the eastern Roman Empire, is to regain a Latin Emperor in Constantinople. A powerful Almogaver army frustrated their ambitions in the time of King Charles of Anjou and does so again. The French in order to further their ends aim to neutralise the Almogavers."

"Hence the assassination of Roger de Flor," said Josep.

"In my opinion, they managed to persuade the Co-Emperor

Michael that Roger de Flor was in cahoots with the Duchy of Athens."

"Which also suited the Duchy of Athens, of course," Josep replied, remembering conversations he had had with Entença when he first arrived in the Roman Empire. "Who else will the French try to eliminate?"

"This is dangerous talk, Josep. We will talk again later when we can be more discreet. Suffice to say it is too dangerous for you to remain here. I've come to take you home!" the old man said.

Their boat had been made ready for departure. Josep was insisting that he should take his leave correctly of Ramón Muntaner.

"He will understand Josep"

"He might worry!"

"Let him. He'll conclude when you're not found with your throat slit in a ditch that you went with me but the more quietly we go, the better, as I'm sure you understand."

They slid out of the harbour and Josep did not even glance back at Gallipolis as they left. He knew Muntaner would come to the right conclusion and would not resent him for taking the opportunity to leave. Had he been offered a place, he probably wouldn't have taken it. He still had work to do, making sure the rest of the Catalan Company survived. He was already involved in plans with Rocafort to move on. He would be responsible for coordinating this with Entença. The fact was that Jacques had come to rescue him, he was like some demi-God intervening to save the situation when all hope had failed. How fortuitous, Josep thought, that he had not accepted Entença's invitation to join him. How would Molay have found him then? This man, so central in his life, with whom he still had so many unresolved issues, who had caused him so many problems but made his strange life possible, had now come on purpose to save him. For all his faults, he thought, it did not get much better than that.

As they sailed out of the Dardanelles, Jacques seated himself more comfortably opposite Josep.

"Now we can speak more freely. It's only easy to see in hindsight Josep but whoever appears a stronger future leader of the Almogavers will be eliminated first, in my view. The elements are probably in place already waiting for the moment to strike. If the action has the backing of the French king, it will be coordinated by Guillaume de Nogaret, the King's Chancellor. You are also at risk from this man as my protégé. If they have you they can blackmail me. Hence, I had to remove you," Jacques said almost apologetically.

"As you can see, I was reluctant to leave!" replied Josep.

Jacques de Molay smiled politely at the joke but he was being deadly serious now. "The French Crown has always despised Catalonia and Aragón, an upstart Crown, in their own opinion," he said. "Yet their last king married into it and junior branches of the same Capet line have now married its princesses and vice-versa. It was one of the results of the Wars of the Sicilian Vespers, as you know. You would imagine that this would have settled differences and brought the two Crowns closer together. However, the resentment still simmers. Naples, in theory loyal to France, is drawn now to both Aragón and Sicily and by association with the Crown of Catalunya Aragón, to Majorca. Each Crown has its own ambitions and secret agenda. All the smaller ones could benefit from a fief in the Duchy of Athens, while the French in turn plot to bring down the Greek Emperor with the help of the Duchy of Athens. This is what the French do not consider. They always underestimate their competitors. I believe we shall see all these Houses make their moves soon. Blood is about to be shed in Thrace again. I think Majorca will play an important role."

Josep thought about this for a moment. It was an interesting idea. "If I follow you correctly," he said, "you mean Majorca is the only Crown whose leadership Rocafort could possibly accept, as he hates Sicily for banishing the Almogavers and Naples because of his own personal conflict with King Robert. As for the Almogavers, they would be delighted to have the crown of Majorca assume control of the Company," he said.

Jacques de Molay nodded but raised a finger. "All the Almogavers except Rocafort, who will do everything to frustrate the attempt."

"Why do you say that?" asked Josep.

"Because he wants it for himself!" replied de Molay.

Josep nodded. "So where does Entença fit into all of this?" Josep asked.

"A very good question. I believe Berenguer d'Entença, who is after all still Grand Duke, will seek the Emperor 's support in establishing a Greek state in the Duchy of Athens, perhaps even replacing the French House of Guy La Roche as the Duke of Athens. That would totally frustrate any French designs on Constantinople."

"But who is backing Berenguer d'Entença?" Josep asked struggling to understand the bigger picture.

"Well, this is just my personal theory but I believe Berenguer d'Entença has the backing of the Crown of Catalunya Aragón in the person of King Jaume himself" replied Jacques.

"Revenge against France for years of war between 1282 and 1295?" Josep said, catching the idea now.

"Exactly. Also, out of loyalty, at the end of the day, to his own Royal House, he would continue the policy of his father King Pere the Great and redeem himself for the shameful peace of Anagni."

"The question is whether the French Crown will be able to persuade Rocafort to eliminate Berenguer d'Entença before

Berenguer d'Entença eliminates him," Josep said.

"The right pretext will have to be presented to Rocafort. Simple: kill or be killed. Secondly the right moment. Thirdly, get someone else to do the dirty work so that you can reap the benefits with a spotless reputation!" the old Templar said, seeing the scenario in his mind's eye.

"But who could control people to that degree?" Josep asked somewhat amazed at the intricacy of the planning involved.

"Only a madman or one terrified out of his wits would attack and kill Berenguer d'Entença, effectively in cold blood," replied de Molay. "But the right moment, carefully chosen so that the killers are at their most lethal, will be chosen, mark my words. Then the success of the plan depends on luck, a factor that cannot be controlled. The best laid plan can unravel in a moment if luck goes against it."

CHAPTER TWENTY-ONE

He spoke with such clarity and conviction that Josep was impressed by him in a way he had never been in his childhood. He had been, he now thought on reflection, a bon-vivant; jovial, convivial, fond of drink – too fond of drink perhaps. Sometimes, as he all-too-well remembered, it went to his head. Thinking about him suddenly made him think of his mother and his heart jumped in his chest.

"My mother! I am thinking of my mother!" he said for no apparent reason. "I hope she is well!" he said and lapsed into silence, bemused by his own outburst.

"I know that she is alive and well," Molay said, attentive to every sound he made.

"And Lali then?" Josep's voice was sharp with surprise, tinged with fear.

"Josep, Josep, Josep! She's fine. Would I not have told you already if I'd known she was not? All your family are well and in good health."

"But I did not know you knew anything about any of them!"

"Do you think it is just by accident that I happened to call by Gallipolis at great risk to myself and this ship to see if you were still here?" he said. Josep was speechless.

"Josep, if I know this, do you not think I know the situation of your wife, your mother and your children, too? I know I'm expecting a lot from you and haven't given you much time to adjust to the newness of your circumstances but I thought our conversations made it clear you had been in mortal danger and needed to be evacuated immediately..."

"I beg your pardon? I'm a man of forty!" Josep replied. "I'm capable of looking after myself!"

"Josep," said de Molay very calmly. "Do not be offended. You were no more than observing events any more, let alone protecting yourself. The campaign as we have been saying has gone into its last phase now. Death and destruction will follow, as we said last night, until the Almogavers find a new direction. That is why I came to rescue you."

Josep's head and heart were so full of conflicting emotions at that moment that he could not reply. He was so relieved to hear his mother and Lali were all right it almost wiped out any other consideration or emotion. But it also revealed the poverty into which his powers of analysis had fallen.

"Is my life really so seriously at risk?"

"If you agree Rocafort and Entença are intent on killing each other, how many others do you think will die next to them? Either man dies and there will be a bloodbath caused by hysterical attack or feverish defence, probably both. You do see that now, don't you?" de Molay said looking at him steadily.

"Yes," said Josep simply. "Christ knows what is going to happen to Muntaner."

"Muntaner has an excellent handle on the situation. He will find his way out of this."

"My God, I hope you're right. But it is true that he has always managed to stay out of the line of fire. He has always stayed out of the gross petty tragedies that have become increasingly common."

"Did you hear about Guillem Peris de Caldes and Hatche, his Turkish fiancée?" Josep now said.

"Of course! I heard a brief report about it and brought forward my departure from Famagusta as a result."

"You heard about it in Famagusta?" Josep asked in astonishment.

"Josep, come on! You're not making much sense. I can only suppose that you are in a state of shock as a result of all that is happening. But there's no need to get agitated. As I say, I have been following every single incident with the utmost attention for the past few years, your situation, your family's situation, the whole picture."

"Since when?" Josep asked.

"Since I arrived in Famagusta!" replied de Molay with a note of exasperation in his voice now that he found all the conversations until that point had been for Josep in some sense academic and he was only now adjusting to reality. Josep sat in stunned silence.

"But how could you have heard about Guillem and Hatche?

"From the very same messenger who reported Hatche's death to her family in Lampsaki, Josep. The Turkish are brilliant horsemen. Furthermore, they have guilds for the various offices that check standards in the work they do. The office of Herald is an extremely important one, combining the skills and qualities of horseman, pioneer, marksman and tireless loner: the same messenger who informed the Turkish girl's parents – Hatche you call her – I knew her as Ceylan of Lampsaki's daughter– the very same messenger, a week later, arrived in Famagusta with this news."

"But why would he bring the news to you?" Josep asked flabbergasted.

Jacques de Molly now laughed dryly. "Because I pay him to! Him and scores of others bearing information about anything that I think is important. And I know that the Emperor was sometimes using the same messengers, it did not matter that they were Turkish. He was delighted to hear how disastrously matters were turning out for you in Gallipolis, do not think that by being left alone you weren't being minutely observed!" the old man said.

"So everyone knew everything! Why did the Greeks not just come and finish us off?"

"You were isolated but still extremely dangerous. Anyway, they thought *"Let them just hack each other to pieces,"* as we were just saying. Apparently, Lord Michael at that point said *"and be forced to eat their own excrement!"* but that's probably apocryphal." He was laughing now. Josep looked at him in disbelief. The old man stopped laughing, his jolly face instantly falling into the heavy, jowly, serious countenance Josep was used to. He looked Josep straight in the eye.

"You'd got too involved, had you not? You were on the verge of picking up a coltell and killing him yourself, were you not?" The old man asked half mocking, half horrified.

"Yes, I was. Rocafort had destroyed every last vestige of honour and decency the Almogavers had. He had desecrated all my ideals, trampled on my deepest childhood notions of what the Almogavers were and represented."

"But it's not just the Almogavers., " said de Molay. "The fact of the matter is Josep, no matter who the soldiers are, soldiers are soldiers in the end, they go wild if they do not fight. Disband them immediately or they will start fighting anyone they can, even each other. That is why King Frederick disbanded them immediately after the war against Naples was over. That is why Rocafort left Sicily. But some people like Rocafort are just evil. Berenguer d'Entença was governor there, in Calabria working for King Robert of Naples. Rocafort after an unsuccessful siege that cost him quite a lot of money had relinquished a town called Castellofiore to Berenguer d'Entença's troops. They say Rocafort exacted a small fortune for it but King Robert was prepared to pay it to get rid of Rocafort. Anyway, everyone thought Rocafort had gone for good and people started drifting back to the town and life slowly got back to normal. But Rocafort returned one night in disguise and with false passes managed to get into the town and together with his company of brigands slaughtered the occupants of some of the better-off households, making off with the money he knew they'd had in the town all along. Then they left, committing mindless atrocities as they went, a girl meaninglessly disembowelled here, a child's throat slashed there, livestock cut down for the sake of it, barnes torched, for what? For nothing but the thrill of it, because they were soldiers and their blood was up and they did not have anyone to fight and Rocafort had a notion he deserved revenge because the townspeople had resisted his siege," de Molay said.

"How could Roger de Flor have taken on such a person?" Josep said in horror. This was the first time he had heard the full story of the personal conflict between Rocafort and Berenguer d'Entença.

"Roger de Flor alone could control him. He had the power, the wealth, the charisma, the ambition and the direction, he gave him a goal, somewhere to go to and carry on. He alone could lead him to what Rocafort considered, and Roger de Flor cleverly sold him as, his glorious destiny. This is the danger with great leaders. That in order to lead, they have to seduce.They have to know what to offer people to get them to do what they want even if they know they won't be able to deliver on their promise. Politicians do it all the time and normally, it's called charm. But actually, seduction is a better term for it because people fall for it completely but fundamentally, it's deeply dishonest."

"Thank God I stayed close to Muntaner!" Josep said.

"But now, not even Muntaner could protect you, Josep. He has the right instincts for staying out of the limelight, out of trouble, keeping his head down and going about his business, keeping the accounts going, turning a blind eye when there were practices he disapproved of privately but couldn't stop. Basically, he's a stoic. He did what he could when it was up to him and made sure he did his job properly. Without him as quartermaster the force would have imploded a good while ago but his focus and level head made him arguably the sanest of all the commanders."

Josep again looked at de Molay, whose features were as serene as his words were absolutely clear and true.

"*"How do you know all this?"* you are asking yourself, are you not, Josep?" the old man said, allowing himself a slight smile. "I can read the question in your face. I shall tell you how I know." He shifted a little on the bench rocking with the motion of the galley as it forged ahead.

"For years, I have dwelt on these puzzles, for years I have been effectively in isolation. Alone, no one to converse with, no one to check impressions with about these matters. The duties of Grand Master were onerous, it is true but they have a timetable that runs with the daily cycle of day and night, the sun comes up, business is done, the sun goes down, business continues a little after the sun goes down. Then the night takes over, until sunrise the next day. Apart from the hours of sleep, several hours a night to contemplate the affairs of the world, Josep, seven days a week, fifty-two weeks a year, for the past twenty years.

"So you knew Roger de Flor was going to be assassinated?"

"Not exactly but heads turned when he decided to return from Gallipolis to take his leave formally of Lord Michael in Adrianople. It was too good an opportunity for Lord Michael to miss. It showed the blindness, arrogance and impetuousness that had assaulted de Flor's reason. The Emperor had given him Anatolia as a state within his empire to get rid of him and attempt to pay his exorbitant costs. The Imperial Court couldn't believe it. Lord Michael was apoplectic with rage. Remember he'd had his headquarters and army in Anatolia when the Almogavers first arrived. It was an enormous slice of the cake to give away to this interloper."

"So the Emperor Andronicus plotted Roger de Flor's death with Lord Michael?" asked Josep shocked at the duplicity he'd always heard denied.

"No, I'm not saying that. But Lord Michael like a good soldier brilliantly seized the initiative, used the invaluable element of surprise Roger de Flor had handed to him on a plate and decisively put his plan into action. He even got Girgon, the leader of the Alan mercenaries, whose son Roger de Flor was blamed for killing, to do the dirty work. A whole regiment of unarmed Almogavers were slaughtered in an evening and to show you how fast word spread, no sooner had the news reached Constantinople than every Almogaver, unarmed as they were in the Emperor's city, naturally, was slaughtered too." "I was blinded too," replied Josep. "I did not see what was happening before my eyes, nor did I understand what was going on outside the camp. It was as if the world had disappeared beyond the gates." "Staying well out of your way, very wisely. But of course, the world carries on. Plotting your downfall in Paris, Athens and Constantinople. I had a vested interest in taking a detour to Gallipolis, however." Josep looked at him perplexed and dumbfounded.

"I should explain," de Molay said, banishing the smile playing on his lips. "Forgive an old man his little games."

CHAPTER TWENTY-TWO

The seascape was awash with mist. Distant islands basked like hulking behemoths readying to submerge completely. High wispy clouds fled a wind that tore into Josep's face. And the sea was so dark, darker than wine, darker than the darkest black at the centre of the eye of any beast, darker than the sky at night because the sky has the stars to light it. The sea, the sea, *thalassa, thalassa, thalassa*, like the sound that it makes, seductive but savage, endlessly churning, seething, shifting, mercilessly greedy of anything that falls into it but yielding resentfully to men's prowess in taming the waters, constantly battling with the timbers of the boats, madly smashing against them, mournfully parting before the thrusting prow. Josep felt ill and intimidated by the sea, now just as at so many other times in his life, as if somehow there were a personal debt involved, either owed to him by the sea or owed by him to the sea. But he always felt the sea wanted to swallow up something he loved, or someone. Josep's eyes stung out on the deck, his hair flapped round his face, whipping his eyes, as he looked up at the lateen sail full to bursting in the late October gale. What was this scourge he carried inside himself that the sea reminded him of? Or was it him himself the sea wanted? Was there some logic to the thought that this was reasonable, after all, that somehow he too belonged to the sea or would in the end belong to it?

"We're going at some speed!" he shouted with his usual bravado over to de Molay as he appeared on deck. He, by contrast, stood stoutly by the mainsail, needing only one arm to steady himself while Josep hung on with white knuckles as the galley careened left and right, rose and plunged. It seemed at moments she was going to flip backwards then she would lift sickeningly to the right or left and the keel would bring her smashing down flush with the horizon then woozily dipping underneath it.

"I always feel the sea is wild and full of spirits," he shouted bravely.

"I know what you mean, isn't it marvellous? Especially here in the eastern Mediterranean where the spirits are old and resentful, vengeful still despite their descent into oblivion. Who remembers now the gods of the Sea People who invaded Iberia from Sardinia and Corsica now thousands of years ago? Perhaps they are like the Great Gods that Greek culture wiped out but are still worshipped in parts of Thrace and Samothraki. Yet as we pass Limnos, Lesbos, Chios, Andros and Tinos and approach the Cyclades, those Great Gods, the *Megaloi Theoi*, become more distant still. Yet who now cares to honour even Poseidon, the upstart King of the Sea, when upon the churning deep?" The old man broke off. The effect on Josep of this diatribe, worthy and erudite though it was, was to unsettle him further still.

"I do not really follow what you're saying but let's pour libations if it will do the needful to get me back safe and sound on dry land," Josep said.

De Molay roared with laughter and gave Josep a great bear hug. "I was not mistaken in rescuing you, my boy. I have dreamed of it so long and you are well worth it. You are a disastrous sailor but does it deter you from setting out to sea? You are a warrior of ideals, a conviction soldier, who would rather lead a placid life among his family but did it deter you pitching in with the Almogavers for one last great adventure? You force yourself into exaggerated shows of bravery even though your heart is somewhere else!" de Molay once again expounded.

"My heart is in my mouth right now, to be honest with you, and my stomach has taken its place. How I loathe rough sailing!" he shouted. The Templar once again roared and clasped him to him.

"You see, in that we are different. I have always loved it."

"Are we not different in many other ways too?" asked Josep, now seeing many dissimilarities at this dire moment, at the jaws of death itself.

"I hope not, for that is what brings me to ask a great favour of you. It is why I came to get you." There was a long silence.

"Speak, speak," said Josep quietly, dreading in his heart of hearts what this favour might be and entail for him.

"Josep, let me tell you that I leave you a free man to decide on your own fate. I will not force you to do anything against your will. I have decided how I shall end my life but I am still not free: I am too visible. I have the eyes of the world's most powerful men on me, perhaps even at this moment. One never knows by whom one is being observed. My crew are loyal Templars, to all intents and purposes, at present at least. But every man has his price and the moment we have contact with another ship or make land our secret can be shared."

"Then let's not be boarded or make land!" said Josep simply.

Jacques de Molay looked at him hard. "That is very generous of you, Josep, especially when you are obviously feeling so wretched at sea. But let me explain myself fully first before you commit yourself. We have enough provisions to reach Catalunya without docking to replenish stocks or for any other foreseeable reason. I have so much to accomplish and so little time," he began.

"But what is it that you have to do so urgently?" Josep asked.

"I have to negotiate with the most powerful man in the western world. But before I do so, I need to build up collateral."

"You're speaking in riddles, Jacques. I'm sorry I do not follow you."

"The future of the order and my own future are at stake Josep. The King of France wants to merge the Orders of the Temple and the Hospital to create a new order. As Grand Master of the Templars, I cannot allow that. Our mission is simply too different from that of the Hospitalers. Besides, I believe it is simply a ruse to appropriate our treasure."

"How?" asked Josep.

"By appointing himself the head of the new order, the King of France would be in control of the Templar treasury. He would then be in command both of policy and finance. That way he could develop his plans for French hegemony in the east as well as in many other parts of the world without the interference of anyone."

"Except for the Pope," Josep countered.

"Even the Pope would find it difficult to counterbalance such power. In any case, being at the head of such a powerful order would make the King unassailable in France. Even if he is not already, he would then be without doubt the strongest monarch in Europe."

"So, how do you intend to negotiate with him?" asked Josep, feeling uncomfortably that this might be where he somehow came into the picture.

"I need to gather all the Templar possessions that I can and remove them from his reach."

"How do you intend to do that?" Josep asked feeling foolish that he was asking so many questions but again impelled to do so as he sensed his role in all this was on the point of being revealed.

"That is where you come in, Josep. I want you to help me move everything to Miravet and then quite simply I want you to put as much of it as you can on board one ship and take it to a safe place," de Molay said.

"But you know that I am no sailor! The idea of another sea voyage right now fills me with dread. Added to that, how long would I be away from Lali? I haven't even seen her yet!" Fear and doubt suddenly crowded in on Josep and he turned away.

"You're making this very difficult for me," he muttered.

"Josep, I understand how you feel. I know you've been separated from your wife and family now for three years. I know how desperately you want to see them."

Then Josep suddenly understood.

"But I owe you my life."

De Molay looked at him now with a look of such ineffable tenderness that it stopped Josep in his tracks.

"Josep, you are the only one who can help me now. Nobody knows your whereabouts now. We left Gallipolis so discreetly, only Muntaner and the guard on duty at the time know I was there and Muntaner will not reveal this to Rocafort unless asked. Rocafort may not even notice that you have gone, so there is little chance that this information will be passed on to the French crown. You have therefore effectively become invisible."

"But I thought you said I was in danger of being kidnapped by Guillaume de Nogaret and used as a pawn to blackmail you!""Indeed, indeed, Josep, but you're no longer there and nobody knows where you are, so the problem disappears. Any number of things could have happened to you. And even if de Nogaret connects the two of us, he would have to conjecture wildly to guess our intentions or be an even greater spy master than I take him for."

Josep looked at de Molay wanting to be convinced.

"You can move with total ease and secrecy and there is a bond of trust between us that is unimpeachable."

"Where are you going first?" Josep asked with his characteristic directness.

"I have to do what people expect me to do and head to Marseille. There I'll be able to gauge the seriousness of our situation and take appropriate action.

They both looked out from the ship.

"Where exactly are we?" Josep asked.

"We are heading southwest, just ahead to port we have Crete, the Peloponnese to starboard and we are presently passing Paros and Antiparos on the port side and Sifnos and Milos on the starboard side, all islands in the Cyclades."

During the following days, the two men laid careful plans for achieving de Molay's objectives. Jacques was to join Josep in Barcelona, by which time the Grand Master would have arranged for the transport of all the possessions in the houses of the Larzac region. He had been based there when he first met Josep's father and mother, namely, at La Cavalerie and La Couvertoid, names that had taken on special significance for Josep because of their association with his parents. These possessions were in Burgundian lands belonging to of the Holy Roman Empire, they did not belong to France, yet they were conveniently close to their huge neighbour.

"But first, your mission will be to return to Rennes-le-Chateau and once again convey greetings from the secret community of Cathars there to the community in the mountains," de Molay said.

"You mean in Artiga de Lin?"

"I do indeed."

Josep shuddered. "I was nearly killed in Es Bordes," he said. "I only escaped from there by the skin of my teeth."

"Yes, I heard about that, Josep. The community there revere

you all the more because of it."

"I'm surprised they're still there!"

Josep couldn't be sure but he thought he saw a shadow pass across the old Templar's face, which made him look away and shift slightly uncomfortably.

"You can burn a man but you still cannot break his spirit. Those people are as strong as their beliefs and these things endure," de Molay said.

"But how shall I transport the goods from Artiga de Lin to Miravet?" asked Josep, changing the subject. He was not in the mood for de Molay's oblique comments.

"I trust in your resourcefulness. It is not a journey you are unfamiliar with, after all."

"But I haven't done it since I was sixteen years old."

"I have every faith in you my boy," de Molay said, smiling gently at him again.

Over the next few days, Josep and Jacques also talked extensively about the three years Josep had been in the eastern Roman Empire and Thrace.

"I cannot say I warmed much to the people of Constantinople," Josep was saying. "They have a magnificent city, beautiful golden statues, monuments dating back hundreds of years, the greatest church outside Rome in the whole of Christendom, the Hagia Sophia, but they are among the most unfriendly, least communicative people I've ever met."

"It's called siege mentality," replied Jacques. "They are so used to being surrounded by enemies that they suspect everyone, even each other, and want to have nothing to do with anyone who is not from the Empire. It's very introverted and in that kind of atmosphere, tradition and ceremony become all-important and snobbery flourishes."

"Yes," replied Josep, "they say the language has become very static as so-called authorities imposed canons of usage or acceptability on it."

"They've also completely turned their backs on the Greek classics, the Homeric epics, the histories of Xenophon and Thucydides, the philosophy of Plato and Aristotle as collectively the work of pagans."

"Apparently, for them it's not politically correct to talk about that side of their history," Josep replied.

"Well, in a sense it is not their history as that side of Greece had passed a thousand years before the Emperor Constantine moved the Roman capital from Rome to the city that would bear his name," Jacques added.

"But little by little, over the centuries, their power diminished and their culture had to be preserved rather than being used as a means of expression and creation. What was dynamic became static and at the same time as power contracted, those in power toiled to control that power for themselves and created a way of speaking, dressing and viewing the world that is self-serving, narrow and worst of all for a culture, exclusive. It becomes trapped in a time bubble."

"Exactly. Interacting with the world in meaningful ways ceases to be attractive. Innovation, experimentation, creation, exploration, all the attributes of a thriving, dynamic culture start to be frowned upon and lose value in the culture. In the end, those characteristics disappear," Josep said.

"And the flame that once illuminated and empowered the culture sputters out," Jacques said with finality.

"I wonder how long it will take?" They both asked at the same time. They laughed then and chastised themselves for getting so serious.

"The Temple has not become static, Josep, do you know that?

What I'm going to tell you now is top-secret and you must swear to me that you will not reveal it to a living soul as long as I live."

"I swear," replied Josep. He followed de Molay into his private quarters so that they could talk more easily out of the gale but also in strict secrecy.

"Josep, so long as the Temple had its headquarters on the Dome of the Rock of the Temple of Solomon in Jerusalem, that is, between 1118 and 1199, when Jerusalem finally fell to Saladin, so nearly eighty years, the Knights of the Temple excavated the Temple of Solomon and with expert local knowledge we developed our own beliefs from the results of our research. We learned about the secrets of building, of mathematics, which underlie those secrets, the origin of those secrets themselves. These go back through the ages from the Muslims and Jews through the Romans, back to the great mathematicians of Greece and beyond the Greeks back to the Egyptians and beyond the Egyptians to the Mesopotamians and the Sumerians and the very origins of civilisation in the Middle East itself. The time scale is staggering, a continuous line of knowledge that stretches back four thousand years before Christ, that is older by a thousand years even than the oldest book of the Old Testament. We believe in Jesus Christ as mankind's saviour and our intermediary to God himself as we believe in the Trinity. But we the Templars also accept that the ideas of our church have existed in different forms for millennia. God, Yahweh, Allah, Brahma Atman, Jupiter, Zeus, Horus, Osiris, are all names of the same creative spirit of the universe. We within the order call him the Great Architect and he was known in ancient Mesopotamia as Hiram. He was the original builder. He was betrayed and killed by his own people, just as our own Jesus Christ was betrayed and killed. But just as Jesus Christ rose from the dead and ascended into Heaven, so also the ideas of Hiram did not die with him but live on in the marvels of the architecture that we are surrounded by. Just as Jesus was man and God and the son of God, Hiram was also human and divine and the son of God. We like the idea of the Great Architect but we stress that this is merely a description of God, in the same way the name God comes from the descriptive "One who is invoked." Therefore, the name of God itself is not sacred as it is merely descriptive and in the Order we therefore accommodate all other names for the divine that recognise the truth and benevolence of the divine, the creator of the universe, its principles and reality even though we cannot fully understand these things.

The ideas of sacrifice and death are central in many belief systems as they reflect the cycle of life. If all things must die, because death is part of life and is necessary so that new life has a reason for coming into being, by the same token, that which gives life, is life and is all-powerful, must also go through a stage of death in order to be reborn and regenerated. As the divine is all-powerful, this death is chosen. Therefore, the divine sacrifices the self for life to continue. Sacrifice is therefore central for regeneration. The crucifixion of Jesus is Christianity's enactment of this common element in religions and the crucifix is its symbol."

De Molay stopped there to check on Josep's reaction, to make sure that he was not lost, or offended that his faith was being discussed in these terms. Josep understood and simply said, "Go on."

So the Grand Master of the order of the Temple continued.

"All institutions have rituals or established practices. Around the Templars, certain practices grew up and developed over time. Understanding what I've just tried to explain or what the rituals of the Order are has never been a condition of entry into the Order and therefore certain rituals became mere repetitions without meaning. I tell you this because because what I'm now going to reveal to you will certainly shock you and I'm in a quandrary as to what to do about it." He paused.

"Why do not you just tell me and we'll take things from there?" Josep said.

The old man cleared his throat.

"Unfortunately, an ugly practice sprang up. Spitting on the crucifix. It became accepted as a way of acknowledging the crucifixion as one of many symbols of regeneration. The practice began before I became Grand Master and has existed as long as anyone can remember. I personally was appalled by it at first but accepted the practice as simply an eccentricity of the Order, knowing that eccentricity or at least idiosyncrasy, is common in all organisations, not least in religious ones. After all, cultural practices often seem strange to those outside a culture and even on an individual human level, each person develops a set of behavioural attributes which becomes unique to them, even characterises or defines them." He paused. Josep nodded for him to continue.

"I am not trying to justify the practice but its ugliness and apparent sacrilege are not what they appear to be, they only seem to be offensive. Symbolically, the practice was, in my opinion, a way of validating all other equivalent symbols of the same truth. It was an ecumenical act and a recognition of the way the truth and the light are celebrated in many other religions as well as our own."

"Why are you telling me this, Jacques?" Josep asked with characteristic simplicity. "Could it not be dangerous for you for anyone outside the Order to hear what you are saying? I understand completely what you have said and I believe absolutely in your honesty, sincerity and innocence as well as your devotion and holiness. But when I imagine you trying to explain these ideas, to explain a practice that seems utterly degenerate, I worry not for your immortal soul but for your mortal life. What you have said is so heretical that you could be burned at the stake both for the admission that the practise endures in the Order of which you are Grand Master and also for the beliefs you have explained as a rationale to understand the practice. In the eyes of any Christian community I know, whether Roman Catholic, Greek, even in the smaller, arcane Christian communities in Egypt and the Crusader states, the Paulicians, Manichaeans and Copts, these beliefs are clearly heretical and perhaps cannot even be called Christian anymore."

Jacques flashed him a look of indescribable anguish.

"I am sorry, my Lord," Josep said quietly, his colour rising. "I did not mean to offend or anger you." Jacques looked away then turned to Josep with tears in his eyes.

"Josep, you have not offended or angered me, it is just that you have said what I feared you would say." He walked over to Josep, raised him to his feet, then embraced him holding him very tightly and very close to him.

"The problem is that they know, Josep. And as Head of this Order, I am now required to be the symbolic sacrifice." He was shaking slightly and when he finally released Josep from his arms and Josep looked into his face, he could see that his cheeks were wet with tears.

"They will burn me alive at the stake!" he said in undisguised terror.

It was the most horrifying, hair-raising, prediction that Josep had ever heard. Yet his wits did not desert him and despite the horror, he managed to pull himself together.

"Jacques, as long as you do not reveal anything of what you have told me yourself, as long as you remain silent on all these issues, then you cannot be declared guilty of them, can you?"

"Do you think so? I cannot tell you how much your words comfort me, my boy," he panted, suddenly looking wildly at him. "Do you really think it is that simple?" he said shooting him a look of desperate hope.

Josep gathered his wits and tried to stay calm. "Unless of course they claim that your silence condemns you, but given the severity of the...," he paused.

"...the sentence...," Jacques continued for him.

"Yes, the sentence," continued Josep, "given the fact that the church itself would have to convict you of heresy and approve the application of the sentence by the legal organs of the state, the church will require verbatim evidence of guilt.

"Hence, the Dominican order has developed such skilful interrogation procedures to entrap the heretic and evince admission of guilt from the accused using set words and phrases that must be heard to come from the lips of the accused", Josep thought to himself, stifling the words.

"How much do they know?" Josep asked.

"The rumours have been around for some time. In any organisation, sooner or later, somebody becomes disgruntled or embittered enough to reveal the closest kept secrets. No," he said rising to his feet now, as if he wished to walk away from the person that he was. He started trembling again, breathless, overcome with panic.

"No," he repeated. "The cat is definitely out of the bag!"

"One thing is the cat and another thing is the cat's master. You do not recognise it, cannot describe it and even when described, it is unfamiliar to you."

"But Josep, I cannot lie, I am under oath!"

"You are not under oath until they put you under oath, my Lord, and the description of the wretched pest will have to be exact in all its particulars, otherwise to acknowledge it would also be to commit perjury."

The same harrowing look of hope suddenly distorted Jacques' face again.

"That's right, that's absolutely right. Whatever these traitors have said, if I have not seen exactly what they describe with my own eyes, I cannot confirm that it is true, as that would be tantamount to telling a lie. I must therefore hope against hope that the cat they've let out of the bag is a stray I do not recognise," the old Templar said looking off into the distance. Josep went over to him and put his hand on his shoulder.

"I'm terrified, Josep," de Molay said.

CHAPTER TWENTY-THREE

"You are sure about this plan, now, are you not, Josep? You will come back to me, won't you?" asked the old Templar. They had finally left Greek waters several days earlier and with a fresh Levant wind, were making very good time. The eastern coast of Sicily was visible, hazy in the distance.

"My Lord, of course I will, but before I go, there is one more matter I would like to discuss with you, yet it is deeply personal and embarrassing for me to do so."

"Speak young man," said Jacques simply, looking at Josep with great tenderness again.

"My Lord, I know it sounds absurd for a man of forty to ask these questions and you may feel me silly for being so preoccupied with them but you know that I never met my father and I need to know once and for all whether you knew him and if so, what he was like. How did my mother know him? How did you know him?"

"He was known as Guzmán. He was the ambassador of the King of Granada in the Palace of the King of England in Bordeaux. I was always travelling between Bordeaux and Larzac, your mother was always attending Sir Josep's wife and occasionally, Sir Josep had business in Barcelona. Several times, I accompanied your mother and Guzmán to Barcelona."

"What was he like?" asked Josep.

"You mean in appearance or character?"

"Both," Josep said too quickly, revealing his shame about his greed for any information about his father. He looked away in embarrassment from Jacques. Jacques as usual simply understood the look and put his hands on Josep's shoulders.

"It was only the affection of a friend for his friend's daughter. Sir John de Grailly knew your grandfather, of course. Hence, your mother fled but feeling unable to return home in her condition, she came to me."

"She came to you?" Josep asked.

"She was running out of money...and ideas. What does a young woman and a pregnant, unmarried woman at that, do in that situation? She waited till she knew I was in Barcelona, then came to see me at the Templar headquarters. It caused quite a stir, let me tell you. Many who have served their lives there have never forgotten it. That is one of the reasons you have always been so welcome there."

"Why, because I was the son of an English servant working in Bordeaux?"

"You do not give your mother credit, Josep. She was and still is a very beautiful woman. Luckily, some of the monks had met Guzmán and quickly pieced the situation together. But there was even a rumour," the old man started laughing, "that she and I..." He looked a little sheepishly at Josep.

"Were you in love with my mother?" Josep asked, grinning broadly in spite of himself.

"What do you mean *"were you"*? Had I not been a Templar already when I met your mother, had your mother not been in love with Guzmán,..." he broke off.

"You're still in love with her, are you not?"

"What's that?" the old man said pretending to be distracted.

"You're still in love with my mother, are you not?"

"Josep, it breaks my heart to admit it to you, but she has meant the world to me for years. But it couldn't be, so I put distance between us."

"You put distance between yourself and me, too!" The words slipped out before Josep could control himself. "You were the closest thing to a father I had and then you disappeared. Took me to school, away from my mother and then disappeared to the other side of the world. That's how it seemed to me."

"Josep, the last thing I meant to do was hurt you."

"I just needed a father!"

"I know you did," Jacques said. He paused. "I'm sorry. I could have been more of a father to you and stayed closer to your mother. But it hurt too much. So I chose my career and the Templars instead as a surrogate family."

Josep's eyes were smarting but he looked away. This was really hurting him, now, too.

"Why did you choose Clara to look after my mother?" he said as much to cover up his own emotion.

"Her brothers and I had served in Murcia. They had invited me to stay with them so I knew her. Clara was a natural healer, looked after me and those boys, was open-minded enough, I thought, to take Catharine in. And it was conveniently close enough for me to visit and to send money and send and receive communication."

"You chose well. Yet there is just one more question."

"Yes, Josep," the old man said earnestly, "Ask on!"

"Who killed Habiba's husband?"

A shadow passed over Jacques' face now and the blood drained from it.

"So much depends on it, Jacques. I sometimes feel as if my entire life could have been quite different had that event not happened."

"How so, Josep? Did we not have your best interests at heart?"

"I'm sure you meant well but if, as I think, it was Bru Miret and people knew it was, why was he ever allowed back into the family? Why was he not driven out and never forgiven? Was it because Habiba and her family were Muslim? Does that make it less appalling a crime?"

"Slow down, slow down, Josep! You're mixing up your anger and sadness at being sent away to school with an incident that may have had nothing to do with Bru Miret."

"Tell me you know it was not Bru Miret and I'll be satisfied."

"I cannot, Josep!"

"Did you not investigate it?"

"How could I?"

"You mean *why* would I!"

"Josep, we did as much as we could for him. He died in peace and safety. That was something. Life is full of tragedy."

"A murderer cannot be allowed to go scot-free," Josep shouted.

"Josep, so much time has passed."

"Certain moments never go away. What happened must be sorted out once and for all for my peace of mind, at any rate. It was a crime. It changed the course of my life. As a result, I was thrown onto my own resources, one moment I was fatherless, next I was without a mother, too."

"You were taken away for your own good, Josep."

"What, to be brought up a soldier, subjected to abuse and ridicule, made to feel even more an outsider and shown my place in Catalan society?"

"You are still very bitter about these things, Josep. What is it that really hurts you most about it?"

"I feel my childhood ended the night Habiba's husband died."

"But Josep, your time at Cavallers gave you a position, introduced you to solid Catalan society, gave you your future, equipped you with useful skills, intellectually and physically developed you, what more could you have wanted?"

"A childhood! For years, I rationalised the loneliness and dejection of my life by reminding myself I was alive while Habiba's husband and father were dead and that was the whole difference, that I should be grateful for my life. Now I see it was their death that robbed me of a normal childhood, with a family, friends in my own town, my own house to go back to at the end of the day. When I went home, there was always this atmosphere of angst, because nobody could get rid of Bru. And Bru was the only one who could have killed Habiba's husband and father. He would have killed any other competitor in the area. Why couldn't he simply keep himself away from us? But he always had to be there to sour the atmosphere."

Jacques nodded, carefully considering what he was saying. "Do you not feel any fondness for him at all, Josep?" he asked.

"It's a relief I haven't seen him for years. When I imagine how the so-called Expedition to the East could have been worse, I imagine what it would have been like if Bru had been there. It would have been even more excruciating. So, tell me. In your opinion, was it Bru or not?"

"Josep, I had my suspicions but it was not my business. Catharine and Clara drove him away."

"They forgave him in the end because he swore to Habiba that he was not the murderer of her men."

"You mean he swore a false oath?" asked Jacques, clearly horrified.

"If he killed either of them, what do you conclude?" asked Josep. There was a long pause.

"I'm sorry for the heartache I've caused you, Josep. I feel about you as if you were my son," Jacques said simply. Something dissolved inside Josep at that moment and he relented. His shoulders dropped and his face softened. He took a deep breath and breathed out slowly.

They looked at each other then, with equal measure of sadness and love, trying to make up to the other the loss each felt in his life.

"I'd be delighted to be your father, Josep," Jacques said. It was the right thing to say.

"In my mind, in a sense, you always have been, for better or worse," Josep replied.

"... and I've always felt about you as I imagine I would about my own son."

"I'd be delighted to be your son," Josep said quietly, looking out to sea, feeling the loss of his father ache in his heart next to the pleasure of the closeness he was finding with Jacques. A lump rose in his throat and when he furtively cast a sidelong glance at Jacques, he saw a tear escape the old man's eye as he swallowed and tried to hold back the tears. They looked at each other and hugged each other closely, perhaps as closely as father and son, closely enough anyway to be good enough.

"How are we going to get out of this mess?" asked Josep after a few minutes. There was new strength in his soul. Knowing how the old man felt about him fortified him. Warm energy flooded his veins, made his muscles stand taught, made his heart pound and his teeth clench with new resolve.

"What's certain is that I can only negotiate if I have the wealth of the Templars in safe hands. The French King might free me in return for it. If I do nothing, he will take it anyway. This mess is not my doing but as Grand Master I have to bear responsibility. In the eyes of the public, appropriating the treasure of a heretical order would seem reasonable. That being the case, I have to persuade the King to make a trade. My life for the treasure. That's why your role is so crucial, Josep. Before the King suspects anything, I have to move as much of the wealth of the Templars out of Paris as I can. Half will go to Rennes, half to La Rochelle. From Rennes it will go to Barcelona. From Barcelona to Miravet. I need your help in that side of things, Josep, and there is not a moment to spare"

Josep paused. "You know how grateful I am to you for rescuing me but can I not see my family, my dear wife, my children, my mother once more before I move on to the next challenge in my life?"

"Josep, the *llaüt* has been prepared for you to go directly to Barcelona. There is no time for you to visit your family. Two Templars will accompany you but will keep themselves to themselves. Address them only as brother, it will keep things simpler but they are there to serve you, Josep, sail the boat for you, lift, carry, work, so make good use of them."

Late afternoon was chosen for the transfer as the wind dropped at that time and there was a period of relative calm before the changing temperature as the sun went down caused the direction of the winds to change making the sea once again choppy.

It was time for Josep and the two brothers of the Temple to depart.

"We will talk more about these things in a month when we see each other again in Rennes, Josep."

"I think we will have plenty of other things on our mind then," Josep replied trying to smile. It seemed his new relationship with Jacques was not going to lead to tranquillity and contentment. At least, not for some time.

CHAPTER TWENTY-FOUR

Once again, Josep was amazed how quickly he could get used to his changing situation. He was in the Templar headquarters in Barcelona planning the next months' movements when he received a message that he had a visitor who was awaiting him outside. He thought this strange but once outside saw Clara and understood why. Women were not admitted into the Templar monasteries. She looked as she had when Josep had last seen her, if a little more tired than before but she was still strong and she beheld him in her calm gaze.

"I knew this day would come and come it has," she said. "I am proud of you. You kept your head, did you not?"

"I did, Clara, literally!"

"You did well! Many will not return, am I right?"

"You are right, Clara," Josep nodded. "Many good people among them."

"Was it as atrocious as we have heard?"

"I cannot imagine anything worse. How is it that you are here?"

Josep still desperately needed to see Lali but he could still barely believe he was sitting there with Clara. One thing he would have to make clear was that had it not been for Jacques' timely arrival in Gallipolis, he might not have been spared. But there was important and sad news.

"A message came from Jacques de Molay saying you would be in Barcelona so I came immediately, Josep. Bru has passed away." Clara said. He died but a few days ago, peacefully in his sleep. We are waiting to hear the will he lodged with the lawyers here in Barcelona. I do not think he could write. We must sign as we are beneficiaries."

Josep was surprised how shocked and saddened he felt. He rationalised that as effectively his uncle, he had been an adult in his life since his earliest childhood despite the torment he had caused during his life. But more was yet to come.

"Where had he been living? Not with you?" he tried to say as naturally as possible.

Josep saw Clara understood what he meant.

"He had been living in the town," she replied calmly. "We saw him occasionally but he was not comfortable with us." She managed a smile. Josep sensed she had to get through this as painlessly as possible and she was not going to get hurt about a man who, whatever he had been to her when alive, was now dead. She was made of strong stuff.

"He became a very private, quiet man in his last years, almost as if he were brooding over things. He did not seem happy to be honest."

The will did not contain many surprises. Bru's property was willed to Clara and there were small sums willed to Josep as well as to his mother. Neither Habiba nor Jacques was mentioned.

"The house was a tiny little place not far from the Castle in what is called Sota Ribes or Lower Ribes, as it is literally under the castle. It was full of booty as would be expected of a man of seventy who had spent his entire life earning his living as an Almogaver. He could have comfortably lived off the proceeds for another lifetime. The goods were easy to sort but suddenly one day while emptying the box under Bru's bed, something caught Habiba's eye. She shrieked and ran out of the house. I went after her but couldn't bring her back. I went back and picked up the mysterious object Habiba had obviously seen. It was the only thing on the floor at the time. It was an Islamic knife, simply but beautifully decorated with what looked like rubies and quartz. It was not very valuable but it was beautiful."

She paused. "It was her husband's knife Josep. The discovery has opened up all the wounds we thought had healed. It was never found when her husband was killed. It was assumed to have been stolen by the person who killed him. Her husband would have been holding it when he died, trying to defend himself. How was it Bru had it? He must have been his attacker and murderer."

"But he swore he was not," answered Josep immediately.

Clara looked away.

"What is it?" Josep asked.

"Josep, he never swore that to us, did he? I mean, we made him swear that to Habiba, did we not?"

"Yes that's right. That's why it was so important. He swore he had not killed Habiba's husband to Habiba herself. What difference does it make that he did not swear it to us?" Josep said slightly indignantly as, despite his ambivalent feelings towards Bru, the honour of his dead uncle was at stake and he felt he had to defend him.

"Josep," Clara said firmly. "Do you not see what this means?"

Josep shook his head. The old lady was now looking into the fire with a look of infinite sadness in her eye. Josep felt her pain. After all, this was the woman who had loved Bru and the woman over all women Bru had loved.

"It means Bru lied to Habiba, Josep."

"You mean he lied on oath?" Josep said, his worst fears confirmed

"He swore the oath to a Muslim, Josep. He felt he was not bound by the oath he swore to Habiba, Josep, because she was Muslim and he was Christian.

Josep was momentarily shocked at this but he was used to being shocked especially about things like this and he recovered quickly these days. He felt overwhelmingly sad for everyone involved, including Bru.

"That is why he could not live here, isnit? He thought about it all those years and realised he'd made a terrible mistake. He couldn't face Habiba."

Clara nodded. "I suppose so," she said quietly. "I do not know if I will ever be able to persuade Habiba to live with me again."

It was clear to both of them that Clara would not accept Josep's invitation to come and live with them in Sicily. He knew she would feel all the more strongly now that it was her duty to look after Habiba as long as she lived.

Jacques de Molay was impatient to further his plans when Josep returned to Barcelona to meet him as planned. A huge treasure was being amassed in the Templar castle of Miravet, containing all the objects of value that belonged to the Templars that could be moved, without distinction as to material, purpose or size. The only criterion was value. Anything that could be removed and kept out of the grasp of the French Crown was stored in Miravet.

It was the beginning of December already. Rain and wind lashed the countryside and deep ruts formed on the roads, making travel all the more difficult when Josep began his journey to Rennes. It was worth the journey. The treasure in Rennes was immense. Everything that could be sold had been sold for the highest price it could fetch. The result was a chest full of gold that could barely be lifted on to Josep's cart. In addition, a small chest was buried also containing a smaller but still considerable fortune in the parish church of Rennes. Inside the chest was a note explaining the origin and purpose of the treasure. The chest was then buried under the main altar of the church. Josep only found out about the contents of the note some months later. It would in the future make the church and its priest, famous and rich beyond all imagining.

Josep arranged for the treasure to be packed onto four mules which would accompany him to Vall d'Aran and the Cathar community in Artiga de Lin. He then passed through the old Languedoc Cathar strongholds of Puivert, Lagarde and Mirepoix, in each town quietly but instantly recognised, warmly welcomed, shown great but secret hospitality, given letters to give to friends and family in the secret community to which he was going, in each town adding more treasure to his store. Josep had to be careful to avoid Foix, of course, as the Count Roger Bernat de Foix was still alive and had sworn revenge on his jailers, one of whom for some years had been Josep though this was many years ago. As he travelled, Josep pondered on the nature of revenge, wondering how long a vendetta could be kept alive.

Jacques de Molay had chosen Josep well. Everyone remembered him, he remembered everyone in turn and delighted the different communities with his stories of his travels in the world, including a sanitised version of the Almogaver campaign in Greece, Turkey and Constantinople and the latest about the Templars and Jacques de Molay. He went north of Foix, to Pamiers, then cut across country on back roads towards Saint Girons. Between towns, he slept with his mules in some of the many caves of the region, often an unsettling experience, which he traced back to his fear of the Count of Foix and his followers, whose brutality he always imagined as savage, bestial, lupine. He would then remember his childhood sweetheart, Alba and her poor mutilated sister Bella. He realised he had blanked out the memory and rarely thought about it so wondered why he had started to do so again now. Somehow, he associated it with his time with the Cathars although Bella's murder had happened four years after he'd last been to the Cathar camp. Despite these feelings of fear and sadness, he always slept and, as nothing happened to him, he ascribed them to fatigue and loneliness. Yet he somehow also felt this beautiful land was imbued with the tragedy of its past and exuded its essence at night.

He was now leaving Cathar country and had only to get through the enemy territory of the Count of Comminges. Only when he had the town of Saint Gaudens behind him did he finally feel safe and he gladly headed south into the huge mountains of the north of Vall d'Aran, along the Garonne River once again.

He was deliberately so badly dressed that he attracted little attention. His donkeys were valueless and therefore, he thought, did not excite the envy of those few wayfarers that passed him. What is more, Josep had devised a cunning method of carrying the gold so that the bulging saddlebags were invisible. Instead of slipping them over the sides of the powerful pack animals, he had them strapped to the underbelly, chest and neck of the animals and, because of the cold, found the perfect excuse for using heavy woollen blankets to cover the backs of the donkeys. Unless the blankets were removed to reveal the leather straps crossing over the backs of the animals, really nothing of the moneybags could be seen. It was an ingenious system and Josep was proud of it. He estimated he was carrying about twenty-five thousand Barcelona sous, enough for a king's ransom, which he figured in effect is what it was. It would provide Jacques de Molay the chance to negotiate for his freedom.

Jacques had also chosen Josep well because he knew he was well able to defend himself. He was walking through thick woods now alongside the Garonne, taking shelter in caves as before when it rained and to rest. He preferred to walk from daybreak to dusk, then light a fire for himself in a convenient grotto as dusk fell. He'd set traps, which brought in a small rabbit or if lucky two, within the hour, once he'd identified the runs and burrows. Skilled with his bow, he was also able to shoot the occasional bird, pheasant, quail, more hen, wild goose and even once a small swan on the waters of the river, which was a veritable feast. Once cooked, all this meat kept for two days especially if salted, for which he carried a supply and he found he had plenty to eat this side and this height of the Pyrenees. He even managed to shoot a couple of juicy salmon trout with his arrows, which reminded him of dear Lali, who had taught him how to do it in Formentera. How he longed simply to finish this last mission, return to her and their family and live out the rest of his days in peace.

He had become absorbed in fishing, having set rabbit traps one afternoon and was standing on the riverbank over some shallows where he could actually see the fish aimlessly cruising around the pebbly bottom, prodding at the stones or seemingly content just to glide around, catching or swimming against the current. Those that seemed to hang motionless in the water swimming just strongly enough against the current to resist being swept downstream where his favourite prey and he'd had his eye on the great rainbow trout for a moment or two when suddenly there was a thud and he saw stars.

He fell face first from the bank onto a marshy area six feet or so beneath it, which provided him thankfully with a soft landing. Recovering from his initial shock, he put his hand to his head and felt the warm stickiness of his own blood between his fingers.

Strangely, he thought, nobody had followed up the attack. Presumably because he had fallen and gone silent, they took him for dead or at least unconscious or he was being observed to see if he would get up. He heard voices, strong French accents speaking Occitan. He couldn't understand them but there seemed to be the voices of three different men. One was keeping watch and chattered nervously in a high-pitched urgent voice. The other two seemed to be vainly shouting at the donkeys, trying, it seemed, to drive them forward. Perhaps their failure was frustrating the lookout, who became more and more frantic. Using his military experience, Josep quickly reckoned they were merely opportunistic thugs who had come across his mules by chance and had decided to steal them just for the sake of it. The animals were after all obviously next to worthless. His story had always been he was so impoverished he had nothing but them left to sell and was heading to market in Les to see what he could get for them.

Josep had fallen in such a way that he could see the lookout now. In fact, the lookout was now standing directly above him but as Josep was motionless, he was paying him no attention. Instead, he was looking back at his companions, practically shrieking at them to get the beasts moving, Josep guessed. Josep suddenly jumped up, grabbed the lookout around the ankles and pulled. The man had no time to regain his balance and therefore fell forward and Josep was on him in an instant, with his coltell at his throat. Though the man was squealing for his life, Josep knew he had the perfect trade-off. He could have killed the man easily there and then but he'd still have to deal with the other two. Instead he would use his prisoner to bargain with. Sure enough, the man's screams brought his two companions to the edge of the bank. Josep now had a problem. How was he to get up the bank with his prisoner?

"Both of you! Down here!" he suddenly shouted.

"Oh, sir, please spare us, we meant no harm," one said in more comprehensible Occitan. Josep's head throbbed and the man's wheedling tone and watery smile only angered him.

"Shut your mouth or I'll cut your friends tongue out before I cut his throat. Get down here now and bring down the rope from the mules, too."

The man who'd spoken quickly darted to the mule, unpacked the rope, then scurried over the edge, berating the other for not already having done so. Finally, the two others stood in front of Josep, one catching his eye ingratiatingly, pleadingly.

"Tie your friends' hands behind their backs!" he said to this one, holding the knife suddenly so close to his companion's throat it drew blood. He squealed and started crying wildly.

"You bastards, you'll let him kill me. I told you you did not know what you were doing and now it's me who's got to die for your stupid idea. I did not hit you sir, it was him!" he nodded in the direction of the third man. "I told him not to but he wouldn't listen to me." However, his companion tied the hands of the lookout and his companion very quickly, panting with exertion. Now that the men's hands were tied behind their backs, he motioned them towards a nearby tree.

"Right, all three of you stand around the tree, one, two, three," shouted Josep. The three men positioned themselves evenly around the tree as Josep indicated.

"Oh my God, you are going to flog us to death," said the third man, now seeking out Josep's eyes in entreaty. "Please forgive and spare us. Take our possessions, everything we have but spare our lives for God's sake!" he sobbed. Josep was no longer listening. Expertly holding the end of the rope under his foot, he rapidly made a loop with his free left-hand whilst still pressing the coltell dangerously against the man's throat, causing yet more squealing recriminations. He had by now soiled his trousers, he was so terrified of Josep, who was taking satisfaction in turning the tables on these three amateur cut-throats. He fastened the loop, held with a sailing knot he'd learnt in Greece, around the base of a sturdy branch and quickly proceeded to tie the three men to the tree so tightly they stopped pleading and fought for breath. He then tied the hands of the last man behind his back. There was plenty of rope, he was satisfied to see, for him to be able to leave them well and truly trussed up until someone should pass and decide to untie them. He then gagged all three and placed sacks over the heads of the two who tried to steal the donkeys. It would now be up to the lookout to somehow draw attention to their plight and persuade someone to help them.

"If I were travelling this way and saw you three, I'd spur my horse on. Catch up with me and I'll kill you without a moment's hesitation. You have no idea how lucky you have been this time. If I am attacked, I guarantee I will survive and shall hunt you down personally and take pleasure in cutting out your tongues, skinning you and burning you alive," Josep said for good measure.

He then cut their clothes from them.

"Perhaps your modesty will prevail even if your good sense doesn't. You will be less inclined to give chase until you find some clothes again. Good riddance and thanks a million for the warm welcome to the neighbourhood."

Josep left them weeping and shivering, went back to his mules, which had not moved and were still munching on their fodder and found three shire horses tethered nearby belonging to the men.

He had been walking until now but decided he could either kill the animals so they could be no use to his captives or take them and sell them at the fair in Les as he was intending to do with the mules. He felt he did not look much stranger now than he had when leading the mules to market and wondered why he had not decided to bring a horse and ride on horseback earlier.

"I'd have been more conspicuous and so more vulnerable in open country," he thought to himself. "Yet here a horse is a positive advantage and there are so few people around to see me, it makes little difference to my safety. I will be a target for attack only because I am alone as happened before. Besides I have these men's provisions, which are fresh and plentiful. I shall not sell the horses but when the moment comes, I'll turned them loose. I have no interest after all in any more money or attracting any more attention to myself than I need to but I must remove from my captives' reach any means of transport."

He was pleased with his plans and reasoning but his head was pounding now from the blow he'd sustained earlier. He needed to rest so he found a cave a little way up from the path and lit a fire. He found camomile in his bags, packed for the purpose and made an infusion of it, in which he soaked some cloth. He applied this to his wound, then used the light of the fire to rummage through the packs belonging to the men who had attacked him. There were several dry meats, which he had not had for the journey as the Cathars, being entirely vegetarian, had packed him bread, wine and cheese. He also found quality red wine in the men's bags. He allowed himself the luxury of a glass but counselled himself against having more in case his wound gave him problems in the night or he should find himself under attack again.

He was proud of how well he'd reacted to the attack; it had been a swift, intelligent solution. He needed his wits about him more than ever now, he thought, as he was wounded and he'd been attacked because he'd dropped his guard too much by enjoying hunting for his food. He would have to be more careful in future.

CHAPTER TWENTY-FIVE

As he travelled, he went higher and higher into the Pyrenees and the temperature dropped dramatically. There may have been vestiges of autumn still in the lower reaches of the Garonne as it spilled out into the rolling hills of Comminges but here, two days' journey he estimated from Les, a footprint left at the end of the day would be frozen solid the following morning. In order not to leave tracks, to maximise warmth and because he was starting to get lonely for company other than the sullen mules and lugubrious shire horses, he decided to start moving as early in the morning as he could and stop early afternoon, well before the sun went down. He was dragging brushwood behind the horses and mules to break up their tracks, though there was little he could do to disguise the huge piles of excrement left behind the pack animals. He had tried riding on horseback but found that if he did not walk, he became so cold he almost passed out once, so he decided to keep walking and therefore moving and set the horses free.

He finally arrived in Les one Friday morning. He had been out in the elements now for ten days since leaving Rennes and had not seen another human being since being attacked a week before. His clothes had turned to filthy rags from sleeping rough in the caves he'd used for shelter, his hair was long and tangled, his beard bristled with the ice formed from his solitary exhalations. The first person he saw was a well-to-do townsman saddling his horse outside the tavern at the entrance to the town. He gave Josep such a look of suspicion mixed with disgust that Josep stopped in his tracks, considered, then tethered his horse and marched into the inn. He got a room with a lock and key next to the stables so that he could react quickly should anything befall his animals and relieved them of the treasure, which he hid carefully under his bed. He washed properly for the first time since he'd been attacked. He then locked his room and went to the public room, with benches and tables for eating and a large open fire which was blazing. He was overjoyed to see food was being served and had a proper hot meal consisting of stew, bread and red wine. He did not attract any looks. He was now dressed himself like a well-to-do townsman, who had as much right and reason to be at the market as anyone else. He had decided to keep only one of the horses and buy the provisions he would need for the rest of his journey up to Artiga de Lin. He would also buy materials he thought might be scarce or unattainable for the Cathars in the mountains: seeds, agricultural tools of different types, sugar, salt, olive oil, flour and wine. He knew the Cathars ate simply but he concluded that in the community to which he was going, this simplicity was born out of absolute necessity and what he brought would be welcome and used sparingly and occasionally to vary the staple oat gruel and root vegetables diet they subsisted on.

Two weeks' travelling had taken him one hundred and fifty miles, he was able to ascertain now, and from about two hundred metres above sea level to two thousand, from temperatures of a few degrees above zero and the hint of early spring to sub-zero conditions where all was snow, slush and frozen ridges of ice.

"Where are you headed, sir?" he was asked by the innkeeper when he came to pay.

"I am visiting family in Salardú and wish to arrive tomorrow afternoon. I shall therefore be leaving before dawn." If he felt he was being followed, he would simply head on into that town and wait until it was finally safe to proceed.

He was secretly looking forward to seeing the Cathar community again. He had last been there if his memory served him rightly just after his nineteenth birthday. He looked down at his left wrist, still scarred from where it had been wrenched from the prison manicle that had held him, the mark now covered in thick hair. Lali had often commented on it over the years.

"Twenty-one years have passed, a lifetime," he said to himself as he left the tavern in Les in the freezing early morning after a few hours' sleep. He wondered whom he would find at the Cathar camp, whether there would be anyone who recognised him, whether the Perfect he'd known was still alive.

"The small children who played so quietly with me when I was last there will now have children of their own," he said to himself.

The night was crystal clear, not a cloud was in the sky, the stars twinkled and cheered him and he thought of Lali, Catarina, Lucio, his mother Catharine and the man he considered the closest person to a father he'd ever had, Jacques de Molay, on whose behalf he was undertaking this last mission, his own father, whose face he could now picture, and all the strange events surrounding the death of Bru Miret. He felt he was reaching the end of a story, that the Cathars were somehow the link between beginning and end but he did not know why he had that feeling. He now understood what had happened to his father, why his mother had not told him, because she simply did not know and it was less painful for her to forget than to remember something she did not understand. If he found that difficult to accept, he only had to remind himself that he had not been able to recover the memory either.

"Grief cuts our memory and guilt cauterizes the wound!" he said to himself, looking down again at his left wrist and the scar around his left hand. He couldn't quite figure out why that reflex seemed to make sense. Did he always cause himself damage when he tried to break free? "No, nothing comes without a price," he thought, "that is the point. Either you damage yourself or someone else, whether you mean to or not, but damage is always done."

His mules were so laden now that progress was slow and unless fed large quantities at regular intervals, they stubbornly refused to move. Calculating rapidly, Josep dug in once more in the late afternoon just outside the town of Es Bordes as he did not wish to attract any attention to himself when he came close to Artiga de Lin. He had to get past the castle at Es Bordes where he had been imprisoned all those years ago. He shuddered at the memory. He had to hope against hope that the mules would keep moving. In the end, when he set out in the middle of the night, he found a route he remembered that took him a mile or so behind the castle into the deepest woods along a track next to the mountain ridge. Freezing, exhausted and anxious, Josep was prey to all sorts of quasi-supernatural and paranoid imaginings. As the wind whistled around him, he constantly had the impression he was being watched as, he reasoned, all small animals, rodents and canine alike, would be wary enough to keep their distance yet equally curious to observe briefly who this person was with his mules in tow. Hardly anyone ever passed along these ridges, torn as they were by the bitterly cold north Tramuntana and north-westerly Mistral wind from the Guyenne and Languedoc plains and the Atlantic coast. Savage gusts howled at the lone horseman threatening to unseat him. The eyes of the small animals around Josep flashed in the bright moonlight as they made way for cover and kept out of the way of this highly unusual stranger. Josep kept his pace steady, knowing each pace took him closer and closer to the Cathar community. When at length he arrived, Josep found out he had as usual been observed by his friends long before he realised he had even entered their domain and had been therefore perfectly safe.

"The night guard," the perfect told him. "We have shifts to police the area. Each man over the age of twelve does two shifts every week. We watch all night, every night, without exception. We are so skilled and quiet, not even the small animals that so alarmed you mind or even notice us. We were here long before they were born. We are now part of this landscape," the Perfect said.

"So nothing has changed here, as I hoped," Josep said. The Perfect, twenty-five years older than when Josep had last seen him, seemed to have aged but a few years.

"The same moon shines as shone the last night you were here, Josep. The stars have remained the same, the ridges and rocks have withstood the heat of twenty-five summers, the cold of as many winters, the landscape remains the same, adorned by passing shadows, caressed by shifting winds," the Perfect said. Josep had a feeling of timelessness. It relaxed him deeply.

"It is so good to be with you. I feel the most difficult part of my journey is over. I have never come to you from the French side. I was attacked once and nearly lost my mind with loneliness and the cold," Josep replied.

"You are more than welcome here, Josep. You always bring us tidings of our lost brethren, infrequent but, without you, non-existent."

Josep was struck again by the clarity of this old man's ideas.

"I have brought you much more than that!" Josep whispered, smiling. Despite himself, the old man's eyes flickered with unaccustomed curiosity and Josep was thrilled in his heart to find that there were gifts that he could bring to the Cathars that were welcome.

Josep and the Perfect talked all the short day and into the small hours of the night.

"You must remember the hell on earth we were made to pass through by the Catholic church in France, Josep. On account of our beliefs, we were massacred like plague-infested rats, all captured and burnt alive in our thousands in the villages of Languedoc you have passed through. What more evidence of the existence of the evil of this world do we need to validate our beliefs? How can so-called civilised men not only roast a child alive but stand passively by hearing the mounting screams of innocent families as their hair flares up like brushwood and the fat in their flesh hisses out of their blistering cracking skin? What demons can ever eat meat again after the reek of roasting human flesh has once entered the nostrils? Killing any creature is against our faith, even for food, let alone as an act appropriate for the glorification of Divinity. Where was the gentle fisherman, the blameless son of a blameless woman and the humble carpenter in all this? How can such crimes be committed in the name of a loving God? Forgive me but your God is now as much a prisoner of those who wield power on Earth as were our brethren who were sacrificed to give up their land. You say Jacques de Molay will freely give himself up to the French Crown. I do not mean to alarm you Josep but his fate will be that of our brethren. They will burn him for heresy, mark my words." The Perfect lapsed into silence.

"Perfect, where can he run yet maintain the dignity of his order? He would have died in battle for its honour, he cannot betray his order now. He knows sooner or later he will fall into the hands of the French king but he will not give himself up or become a fugitive. Nor will he allow himself to be easily convicted. I believe he will twist and turn like an eel amid their interrogation and make the process as long and drawn-out as possible. The longer he can make the trial last, the longer we have to negotiate an honourable release for him." Josep said.

"The French king will benefit simply from eliminating the Temple. All its possessions will belong to a new order that will inevitably be under the control of the French Crown. The financial experience of your Templar fellows who preferred to recant and stay in France will be put at the disposal of the French Crown, all the networks and contacts will be maintained, credit will flow as before, as the French Crown will now be the guarantor. If the French king so wishes, he can launch another crusade against the Muslims. He will have the means and the penetration," the Perfect explained looking steadily at Josep.

"In which case, why should Jacques de Molay have to die?" asked Josep.

"Because all this will happen behind the scenes once Molay has been removed from the picture. With his demise goes the organisation but so long as he lives, there will be doubt about his guilt. While a man still lives he can have supporters. Once he is dead, of course, and nothing remains of him, it is all over. All physical support for him will dissipate and other events will become more important. There is no doubt he will be remembered but he will be a spent force, zero, cancelled out. But that will not happen until and unless he is dead so the French king will not let him escape."

"But why, if Jacques knows this, does he impel me to make this journey to found a new order and collect a ransom for him?" Josep asked.

"It is a good question, Josep. The honour of his order is of paramount importance to him. His order will live on in the new order and his name will always be linked if not enshrined in it. He may not thereby gain the status of a prophet but he will definitely gain immortality. He and his old and new order will escape oblivion. For the establishment of the new order, money will be needed."

"So it is not to be used as a ransom after all?" asked Josep.

"For a while, perhaps. Jacques de Molay will hold it out to the French as a bargaining chip for his release. The King will have to go through the motions of contemplating the offer carefully before finally rejecting it. Remember, he is interested in the future profits he can derive from taking over the order not simply the present treasure. Besides, I understand the treasurer of the French Crown and the Temple are one and the same man and the treasure is even in the same place, is that not so?"

"That is right. The treasurer is Jean du Tour and the Royal Treasury is in the Templar headquarters in Paris," Josep confirmed.

"Then, if he has the cooperation of this monk, he has control of the Temple's finances. But again, it is a question of presentation: if he convicts Jacques de Molay of heresy, he has the right to confiscate the funds."

They continued talking through the night. As dawn crept upon them, the Perfect, laying down thick blankets next to the fire, invited Josep to rest a while. He left the hearth to debrief the night guard. Josep slept for several hours then awoke refreshed. The Perfect was waiting for him.

"We have a reward for your generosity, Josep and a dilemma we can resolve at the same time. Come with us tonight to Aïgualluts, where Amaury was killed. We have something to show you there that will be of great interest to you. And before we go on, take this. It is for Jacques de Molay. You must give it to him immediately you see him next." He handed him a small metal ball that unscrewed to reveal another small ball inside.

"What is it?" asked Josep.

"He will know immediately. In fact, he may well have thought of a similar solution after all those years spent researching ancient knowledge in the Holy Land. If he swallows the ball, he will die within several minutes. It is a peaceful sleepy feeling. Those brethren of ours who were wealthy enough had access to a similar drug. Not everyone died in agony on the pyres.

Under cover of darkness, three men led Josep back down the steep mountain passes to Aïgualluts, the frozen pool where the melt water flowing off from the glacier of Mount Aneto collects. Under the light of the moon, the Perfect crouched down by the side of the pool, took a stone, smashed through the ice, then braced himself for the cold and plunged his hand into the hole he had made in the ice. Several seconds later, he withdrew his hand from the freezing water, laying a hessian bag the size of a horse's nose bag on the quartz rocks that littered the area.

No sooner had he done this than his companions did the same, reaching into the inky water, then gasping as their forearms froze in the seconds it took to retrieve all ten bags. All the men now wrapped themselves up as warmly as possible and with the bags carefully stowed inside their clothing made their way back to the camp.

To Josep's astonishment, the bags once emptied out contained several pounds of diamonds, each one the size of a lemon pip.

"These gems have been in our possession for hundreds of years," the Perfect said. "Diamonds were considered valuable currency. If we were ever to leave the Languedoc, we could be sure to trade with them. They are lighter than gold and as valuable. Each one represents a family's life savings."

There was a sizeable heap of diamonds on the floor in front of Josep. He had never seen so many gems amassed in one place.

"This is part of the Cathar treasure, Josep. We have waited a long time for the right moment to use it."

"And you're just going to give it to me?" Josep said flabbergasted.

"It is useless to us here as you know. Besides it is only part. What we have managed to store in preparation for your coming."

"You knew I was coming?" Josep asked, his head spinning.

"A messenger was sent a month ago from the Castle of Ayerbe, by your old knight, Lord Pedro."

"My goodness! I haven't seen him for years. He was so badly injured after the attack on Girona. My life changed so dramatically after that that I had no contact with him." Josep dreaded being asked to explain what had happened to Bella Pinós de Benavent.

"We know everything that happened and have always accompanied you in your torment in our thoughts. We have not been in contact with Lord Pedro but Jacques de Molay has. He asked him to announce your arrival to us. He was one of the few people who could be trusted and his messenger was also carefully vetted and had a Templar background. He arrived exhausted a month ago."

"When the weather was getting worse," said Josep.

"But we accompanied him back as far as Benasque on his homeward journey. Lord Pedro also sends you his greetings," the Perfect added with a wry smile.

Josep was speechless. The Perfect continued.

"This as I say is only part of the treasure. We will take you to see the rest of it later on today but we risked a lot breaking the ice. We had to prove to you we have this hard currency."

"Harder impossible!" Josep quipped.

"Precisely. Practically indestructible, light, impervious to heat and with another even more astonishing quality. It is invisible."

"How is it invisible?" Josep looked down at the very real mound of sparkling diamonds before him. The twinkle returned to the old man's eye.

"You will see. In a few hours, all will be revealed."

CHAPTER TWENTY-SIX

Josep was awoken just after sunrise.

"We let you sleep again! You must be exhausted," said a young man Josep recognised who looked like Amaury. It was true, he had not had a full night's sleep since he'd arrived. He rubbed the sleep from his eyes. "What time is it?" he asked.

"About three hours after dawn. There was no point waking you earlier as the best time of the day to see the glacier is at midday when the sun falls directly onto it."

Breakfast was waiting for him and it seemed to him that the whole settlement was awaiting him. Young women he had not seen before peeped out shyly from behind the well-camouflaged entrances to their tree-trunk-and-branch dwellings. Young children shuffled past then disappeared into the trees. It was odd and slightly eery. Normally, there was no activity in the clearing, if that was the best way of describing the settlement. The centre of the settlement now familiar to Josep from a lifetime of visits consisted of the meeting hall whose walls were built of well-disguised timber between the trunks of large trees, the space inside large enough to seat ten people or so, the largest group ever assembled in one place in this Cathar settlement. The area to the front, back and outer side of the meeting hall was thickly wooded so that from a distance of only a few yards, the walls were all but invisible. No light emanated from within as fire was strictly limited to what was essential; namely cooking. Meetings were always held in the mornings when fire light was not needed. At dusk, fires were permitted inside dwellings but behind clay bricks and stones to reduce the light they cast at night. People went on guard at night once the sun had set, while others went to bed. The community existed practically in darkness during the winter and early spring months. During summer, there was more activity as the crops were harvested, root vegetables in patches scattered around in a variety of places to avoid notice.

The fact that someone had addressed Josep, therefore and had approached even if only fleetingly from behind their dwelling entrances or passed him as he stepped towards the meeting hall, was an event in itself. The Cathars did not assemble in public view. Yet he had seen three at once just now. Something was going on. This was more activity in the centre of the settlement than he had seen in a lifetime.

The Perfect drew him towards the meeting hall, closing the reed and broom entrance-covering behind him. It was so dim inside, Josep could barely see the Perfect but slowly his eyes adjusted again and he became aware there were more people inside the meeting hall.

"Josep, those of us here gathered will all accompany you to Aneto today. We have checked, do not ask how but we are experts at this as our survival as you know depends on it, we have checked that there will be no one around to see us if we all ten of us accompany you to Aneto."

Josep was mystified.

"You are going to show me something invisible?"

"Once seen, it will be impossible to hide it. It has been rumoured to exist for many years and has been sought ruthlessly by a few. If what we are to reveal to you today were known, Aneto would be overrun. So enough of words."

"Enough indeed!" thought Josep silently to himself. "This is almost garrulous for the Perfect in front of other people. He has talked to me at length one-to-one but I have never seen him utter so many words together to an assembled group since I was first introduced to the community all those years ago."

The Perfect was speaking again. "Please be aware Josep of the absolute trust we place in you."

"I hope I am worthy of your trust," Josep replied trying to be light. There was a brief murmur of Assènt from those assembled in the hall that made the hairs on the back of his neck stand up. They rose in one body and left the hall. The Perfect left last accompanying Josep.

They headed to Aneto by a route Josep had not known before, in which they were walking single file along very rocky terrain for a long time then entered a labyrinth of tracks and passages through the rocks, some covered up with vegetation for disguise and others not. Josep wondered how far away it was from the settlement and hoped this would soon end but felt, as his companions were utterly silent as they walked, that he could scarcely venture the question and scolded himself for his childishness. He reasoned he just was not used to it. Normally on these mountaintop sorties, he was either alone on horseback and rejoicing in the exhilaration of being amid beautiful if austere countryside, surrounded by majestic mountains, deep forests and views that went on infinitely. Or at other times, it was the dead of night and there was nothing to see but the moon and stars and the occasional illuminated eyes of startled curious animals. Being led like this, in almost ritual seriousness, along secret tracks and passages, with walls of sheer rock on both sides was quite claustrophobic and unnerving.

At last, they stopped walking and one by one started disappearing down potholes. Josep, unwarned and naturally claustrophobic, had to work hard to keep up with the rest and ahead of those behind him. Apart from his rising panic as the holes he squeezed into became tighter and tighter, in his haste as he scrambled and crawled alternately, depending on the height of the roof above him, he several times cracked his head on projecting edges and cut up his knees and hands on the sharp slate, granite and flint he encountered on the floor.

He was ready to explode with repressed fear, pain and anger when, suddenly, he tumbled out of the pothole onto marble-smooth stone and collided with the man in front of him. He looked down at his feet, which were bleeding of course, as were his hands and knees, to discover they were standing on a narrow shelf of perfectly smooth ice inlaid with interlocking pieces of jet-black slate.

"You will see why black enables us to see better, Josep, in a moment. These slabs were mined not far from here specifically for this purpose. They are frozen into the permanent ice in a way that unless the glacier melts, which at this point is unlikely, we will always have this platform to work on." He turned and left abruptly.

"To work on?" Josep nearly shouted, half in exasperation, half with the pent-up annoyance he had been feeling all morning.

"Look around you, Josep. What do you see?" he heard the Perfect ask from a distance. Josep looked at his companions and saw that they too were cut and bruised but were all gazing at the wall in front of them in awe.

"It will take your eyes some time to adjust. It is only possible to see at this time of the day with the sun arcing to the south and shining directly onto this part of the glacier, which, if I am not mistaken, is well-hidden and therefore unknown to all but the initiated." Josep's let out a snort of laughter as if to say, "You can say that again!" when he realised his ten male companions, of different ages, one or two in their late teens, one or two in their twenties, another couple a little younger than Josep, a couple his age and two more approaching the Perfect's age, were now quietly mouthing what seemed like the same phrase.

"Cathorum consolamentum."

With a small chisel and hammer, the Perfect now stepped

forward and carefully started tapping at the ice. Instantly something dropped onto the black slate. Josep picked it up.

"Now you see it. Before you could not, even though it was right in front of you," the Perfect said. Josep looked at the wall of ice, so smooth it looked polished and saw nothing. His companions were now chanting the same phrase as before very quietly, over and over, running their fingers over the smooth ice, tracing what seemed to be letters in the ice.

"Cathorum consolamentum, Cathorum consolamentum, Cathorum consolamentum," they repeated, some moving their fingertips in the shapes of letters from left to right, from right to left, upwards, downwards, diagonally.

"Today is the day of removing, brethren. Be careful to leave no evidence behind us," said the Perfect.

Josep put his hand on the wall of ice that extended ten feet to his left and right and was smooth from floor to shoulder height. He suddenly realised all the men were as tall if not taller than himself.

To all intents and purposes, they were invisible to the eye except when the light caught an edge and was refracted so that what had looked like the irregular shine and glisten of ice were in fact hundreds of letters fashioned by the diamonds. Josep looked down at his fingertips where he still held the diamond that the Perfect had removed. The air was now tinkling faintly with the sound of the small chisels and hammers. Each time a diamond fell, it was quickly spotted and put away safely.

"There are twenty-one letters in the phrase "Cathorum consolamentum, Josep and each letter is made up of ten diamonds. If you cannot see the diamond, you know it must be there because that is the way the cache was designed. The diamond must be there even if you cannot see it as it could not have fallen out as the glacier at this point never melts appreciably and, as we are now on the glacier, doesn't move in relation to the platform. The platform is built into the glacier. In time, access would have had to be found from another pothole. This pothole has lasted us twenty years now. But of course, this is the last time we will need it."

"How long have these diamonds been here?" Josep whispered in disbelief.

"The first one was embedded two weeks after "The Field of the Cremated" took place in Montsegur on the twenty-third of March, 1244, perversely coinciding with the beginning of spring."

"Today is the twenty-third of March!" Josep said, his mind again reeling.

"Precisely, we hope for a new beginning," replied the Perfect, but Josep did not hear him.

"So how did you escape? You're a Perfect. You were all burnt in Montsegur on that day," Josep asked in bafflement.

"Women cannot be Perfect, Josep! How old do you think I am anyway?"

"Of course, of course. Your mother was set free together with all the other brethren if they allowed themselves to be questioned by the Inquisition and swore an oath of loyalty to the church." Josep was speaking to himself as much as to the Perfect.

"My mother was with child at the time. She could not bear to take her child to the pyre even if she had been expected to," the Perfect finished.

"You were born sometime after the foundation of the settlement?" asked Josep.

"Not exactly. My mother gave birth to me on the twenty-third of March, the very day the mass burning took place. I predate the settlement by two weeks but I lived in Rennes-le-Chateau until I was six. Today is also my birthday. The day we celebrate our freedom. Today is a special day for many reasons. We will recover all our precious stones today, now that we have a use for them."

"How many are there?" Josep asked.

"Four thousand eight hundred and thirty. The ten men will each find two hundred and thirty phrases. It is easy to remember as it is ten times today's date. And in the bags of the settlement there are a further one hundred and seventy. That makes five thousand."

"And what is each one worth," asked Josep quite innocently.

"I was told the least one would fetch would be thirty Barcelona sous and a sou is a day's salary for a working man."

"Thirty sous!" Josep had to control his voice. "That's…," he did the calculations rapidly in his head.

"That's a hundred and fifty thousand sous! That's six times more than I'm carrying already! It's an absolute fortune!"

The Perfect nodded, picked up his tools again and together with the other man, started tap-tapping at the ice wall.

Josep couldn't get over the solidarity the Cathars' treasure represented. This was the entire fortune of the Cathars and a considerable one. It must have represented the combined savings of tens of thousands of people as he could not imagine that each and every family had been able to save thirty sous in a lifetime. After all, people did not save, they lived from hand to mouth and the Cathars weren't motivated by financial gain but an excess was occasionally inevitable and if organised could be put together with the extra coming from other families. Little by little, it was possible even for very humble folk to save if they co-operated and if there was one characteristic Josep could attribute to the Cathars in his experience of them over the years, it was the ability to live together harmoniously. If that was possible and living in peace together as a community is no easy achievement, then co-operating and managing to save by pooling resources was also possible. It made perfect sense. Far from saving for self-aggrandisement, wealth and power, saving enabled life to go on even in times of severe hardship.

"Was saving encouraged by the Cathar communities?" Josep asked finally, a little abruptly, as he and the Perfect had lapsed into silence a few moments before. The old man paused, lowered his tools and looked Josep in the eye.

"You may feel it contradicts what the Cathar stand for, because you know that we are not supposed to value wealth. You also know that we believe wealth to be at the root of much evil. But our resources were only ever used to rescue ourselves from what we call *malchance*. We have always lived as simply as we could but given that we are alive, we have to nurture the body, otherwise it degenerates in deplorable conditions, which is not our aim. We live in order to die a righteous death, to leave this vale of tears, to enter Cathar heaven. But we do not insist on complete abnegation of the body. The body needs sustenance otherwise it suffers hunger and ultimately cannot maintain itself. The body needs to be clothed for the sake of warmth as much as for personal modesty. Sometimes fire is needed for warmth. If there is so little produced that food and drink, clothing and fuel are not available, what can be done to minimise suffering? This is why we decided it was reasonable and dare I say even gentle, to save, to cover our basic needs when we could not provide for these from our labour. We have saved to make our journey through life towards death possible." The old man had not taken his eyes from Josep the whole time he had been speaking. He had been searching Josep's eyes, tracking his eyes, as if, somehow now, he had doubts about Josep's integrity.

"Perfect, be sure I have no desire for your wealth nor do I mean to question your reasons for saving and I understand completely what you have said. I did not mean to suggest there was some inconsistency between your beliefs and this practice. It is only that I am taken aback by how much the community has managed to save."

"These are the savings of ten generations of Cathars living in the Languedoc, Josep. It represents if you like the excess produced by tens of thousands of Cathars in their lifetime. I believe that you do not question our integrity but such a significant amount of wealth cannot fail to be noticed sooner or later both outside the community and inside the community. Therefore, these questions themselves have been raised among us, too. Some of our brethren have asked why we cannot occasionally use some of these resources to "minimise our suffering" here in this community."

"And what have you decided?" asked Josep.

The old man shifted uncomfortably and very quietly whispered in Josep's ear.

"This is a delicate subject. We will talk later. We have to talk later anyway. This is why we are here."

Again, the hairs stood up on the back of Josep's neck and he could not quite disguise his consternation and confusion. He blinked, noticed the old man held his gaze and was looking for consent and agreement.

"Of course, that is not a problem, Perfect," Josep said furrowing his brow and wondering what on Earth was going on. Why were the diamonds being removed, what were they going to do with them? It seemed his part in the process was more complicated than simply taking them with him on his journey to Miravet. Had the Cathars really been so precise in their calculations that they knew to the day when he would arrive, when he had not even known himself?

Then he reconsidered. After all, he'd been given little time even to rest since he arrived. They'd been told by Pedro de

Ayerbe's stewards that Josep was coming and had set their dates for the "Day of Removal" accordingly only quite recently. Had Josep arrived later than expected? And when had Pedro de Ayerbe's steward come? And Jacques de Molay? Josep couldn't believe Jacques would go to the trouble of journeying all the way to Ayerbe, a considerable distance from Marseille. Josep had assumed he was still in France gauging the seriousness of the situation the Temple found itself in. Was not that the real reason Jacques de Molay had returned in the first place? Would Jacques therefore travel all that distance just to ask Pedro de Ayerbe to advise a secret community of obscure heretics in the mountains that an acquaintance of theirs would be arriving? It did not make sense. He thought his arrival would simply be a pleasant surprise, he could bring them something useful, they would give him a share of their wealth for the Templar cause.

Even there, he ran into some confusion in his logic. What exactly was the Templar cause? Was everyone as aware as he was of the danger Jacques faced? Certainly the communities north of the Pyrenees in the Languedoc had given up their treasure without even discussion, had known Josep would come and what they were to do but Josep thought he was the only one who really understood why. Yet, the Perfect seemed to know something Josep did not and was also contributing significantly more than any of the communities north of the Pyrenees which were theoretically better able to contribute. That is, their entire fortune amassed over generations, unused and untaxed for the best part of seventy years.

One final thing Josep did not understand was why Pedro de Ayerbe had agreed to send his steward up into the mountains in the winter. The steward had barely survived the trip. What was going on that was so important? Jacques must have gone to visit Pedro de Ayerbe himself, otherwise Lord Pedro would never have agreed to help him. The two men barely knew each other as far as Josep knew. Yet Josep had become Lord Pedro's squire as a result of being sent to Cavallers all those years ago, which Jacques himself had personally arranged. Was the hand of Jacques behind that, too?

He reflected it was indeed possible. Jacques seemed to know and always to have known not just more or less what Josep was up to but exactly what he was doing, when, with whom and with what consequences. Hence, when Josep finally left Cavallers, he'd had the unnerving interview with the Commander of the Castle of Monzón, Berenguer de Belvís, who had warned him that his behaviour had been attracting unwelcome attention. Yet he was barely fourteen at the time! Was something being played out now that had begun nearly thirty years ago?

CHAPTER TWENTY-SEVEN

They had arrived at the glacier wall at noon and had been working solidly now for three hours. The diamonds had been inserted into the ice so carefully that they were difficult to remove. The ice itself was like iron and the simple chisels they had been using had quickly become blunter and blunter as the day went on. Yet finally the last diamond was removed, the diamonds were accounted for to the very last one, an astonishing feat, and it was time to retrace their weary steps back to the community in temperatures that were now dropping rapidly below zero. Josep remembered the scorching days of Gallipolis and tried to infuse his frozen aching muscles, fingers and toes with the memory of that heat. At least those memories distracted him from the pain and cold of his journey back and gave him some perspective on his present discomfort. Just as well. After four hours of scrambling, then walking in single file in silence in sub-zero conditions, they finally arrived back at the camp.

Josep was in no condition to talk by then and making his excuses, he hurried to his bed, not even pausing for food or drink. It was only the ninth hour but it felt like the small hours of the morning. Yet he knew he was in good shape when the next day he woke at dawn and felt perfectly fit and refreshed. His hands, knees and fingers were calloused and scarred but what concerned him most was his colossal appetite, as if he had not eaten for days. His stay here now was becoming more demanding than he had ever imagined. When he came to think of it, his diet had also diminished significantly since his arrival in the Cathar community and unwilling to wait until he was offered food, he rifled through his own provisions, which contained significant quantities of salted meat and wine. He drained a glass instantly, then more calmly began to eat and sip in order to restore his strength. After a good quarter of an hour, he was replete. He belched quietly and said under his breath, "Now that's something I wouldn't have done at the tender age of fourteen!" as he felt the effects of the wine on his head. Yet he also realised he was anxious. He'd dreamt about his situation all night. He lay down again for a moment to listen for any sign of activity in the camp but hearing none, dozed off again. He was awoken several hours later by the Perfect himself. He came bearing a large bowl of porridge with pine nuts and dried fruits of the forest, which Josep devoured. He felt guilty about his early morning feast then simply laughed to himself and decided not to say anything about it, or to reveal his secret store of food. He was considerably larger than anyone else there. There were a lot of them as tall, if not taller than he was but he was far more muscular than anyone else there, deep chested and with a slight curve of the belly. A lifetime of military exercise and generous rations were plainly visible in his appearance. He would need to keep eating extra portions if he were not to go hungry in the company of the Cathars. Yet he was determined to do so as he considered this was the source of the strength he had needed to accomplish his mission through the Languedoc and in the Pyrenees so far.

"You eat with relish," said the Perfect, smiling at the big man who sat opposite him. Josep, wrenched from his musings, smiled, nodding.

"This is really good and believe me, after yesterday, I seriously needed it."

"There is more if you want some," said the Perfect but Josep had enough self-respect, considering his private reserves, not to mention respect for the Perfect, not to oblige the Perfect to fetch him more food.

"That is good, Josep," began the Perfect. "Because as we discussed yesterday there are some important issues that we have to discuss."

"Go ahead!" said Josep a little too quickly. He feared it may have sounded flippant. Of course, he had been thinking about nothing else since they had last spoken but wanted to disguise anxiety in his voice.

The Perfect's eyes narrowed momentarily very slightly and his gaze penetrated deep into Josep's eyes, expertly tracking his eyes and unconscious flickerings of embarrassment and concealment. Josep returned his gaze with a relaxed smile as if to say he'd been expecting this, so please to begin.

The Perfect nodded, smiled, then locked onto Josep's eyes once again.

"Josep, these issues go right to the heart of our presence here and continued existence as a community. I will introduce you to all the members of the community later as there are many you have never met, nor would you ever have met their parents over the years. But you are considered, without wanting to sound flattering or ridiculous, like a hero to these people. You are among the few outsiders some have ever seen close enough to touch. You wear clothes that are unknown to us, you have so many small belongings, you smell of the wider world, you are obviously a man who knows well how to survive in the wider world and experience its pleasures."

Josep laughed self-consciously and exchanged a look of bashful puzzlement with the Perfect, who smiled back but kept his eyes locked on Josep's.

"That was an important preamble but it is only the beginning," was what he managed to communicate to Josep without words.

"Where on earth is this heading?" Josep thought to himself, slightly alarmed, naturally enough but doing his utmost to reveal nothing.

"Josep, there are people here as you can imagine, who have never known anything other than this community, people whose parents only dimly remember the wider world we came from as many years ago as I have been alive, these sixty-three years. I myself have no memory of anything outside these immediate environs. My mother does not talk of Montsegur, or her previous life. We are not, as a people, great talkers. We rise and sleep early, work hard for our meagre existence and expend our energy on concealment and self-preservation. Our visits to the glacier, occasional expeditions to Aigualluts, sorties to the Castle of Es Bordes, your visits, unexpected deaths like that of Amaury, these are the raw materials of the stories that we tell, these are the legends that stitch together our community. But just as fire can be smelt by the merest whiff on the wind, no community is truly hermetic. People are people and have real inner lives, dreams, imaginations, desires. Josep, our beliefs are not the same as those of our founders nearly seventy years ago. We have several families here whose women have had children at the age of twelve for the past six generations, can you imagine that? Six generations have been born and reared and aged here. When someone arrives from the outside, it is like a knife is plunged into the fabric of our lives, ripping it open, and the wild world floods in, bearing smells, sights and sounds strange beyond any imagination you may have. That is what it is like to live in relative sensory deprivation."

Josep was disturbed by the image of swords ripping into lives and understandably looked shocked and upset.

"Are we ruining your lives when we come to visit you?" he asked.

"That is a value judgement, Josep," said the Perfect with a slight dismissive gesture of the hand. "The fact of the matter is this: whether we want it to happen or not, the vitality of this community is beginning to ebb. The wider world is exciting and attractive. No matter how we, the elders, stress the danger, the third, fourth, fifth generation who have been born here know that we do not speak from experience but from what we have heard and has been passed down."

"But there are the oldest among you who do remember," Josep countered.

"There are presently five of them and they do not speak about these things, nor have they ever, in fact. Why revisit the pain? So, these conservative attitudes are not validated by them. They are placidly awaiting death, in accordance with their Cathar beliefs and wishes. They live according to their values and it is not in their nature to advocate some kind of Cathar inheritance. They live in the way they do simply because they are the way they are, it does not occur to them even to try to proselytise. Yet the younger ones know and understand little what happened on the pyres in the first half of the last century. They sense there is life in the wider world and they want to experience it. And that is only natural. People are not born with beliefs, beliefs are inculcated. If culture does not express itself fully and engage with others to demonstrate its difference, it begins to implode and its power dissipates. No one is being disloyal and we the elders have come to the conclusion that these are natural developments. We are now of the belief that all living things can change even if we still believe that in essence things never change, day and night, the passage of the seasons, the landscape, the cold wind on the mountain ridge, the wind on water. Yet beliefs are living. If they are not nurtured, they begin to perish. So, our community as a community is beginning to implode because the weight of the expectations, hopes, desires and passions of the people who comprise it is greater than the gravitas of the sense of community which unites it. And it is more than one man can do to alter this process, even if he wanted to. And that man is me. I have to make a decision for my people to continue our present existence here or move the community elsewhere."

"And that is where I come in," Josep said to himself, the scales falling from his eyes.

The old man noticed the momentary flicker in Josep's expression as the thought flitted across his mind. He now locked his gaze onto Josep's eyes even more powerfully than before. He was smiling faintly but there was such a magnetism to his gaze, there was such a force of request and requirement behind it that Josep could do nothing but open his mind to this leader's urgency. It made his throat contract with sudden anxiety and he coughed lightly. The old man was preparing to frame a petition yet Josep couldn't anticipate what he could possibly propose.

"Josep, will you lead us out?"

There, the question was out, simple, unequivocal, clearly phrased. There was no doubt about the meaning.

"Where?" Josep asked equally simply.

"This place is no longer a secret and is therefore dangerous. The community are willing to take the risk of finding a new home. They are excited at the prospect. Lead them to a new future with safety. Lead us as your father would have led us had he not died!"

Josep saw in a flash he was walking in the footsteps of his father who was considered worthy, despite his Muslim faith. Josep accepted it. His father had been loved and respected by the community just as he had obviously loved and respected it. What Josep's mind snagged on was the word safety. Where was "safety"? Could it exist anywhere? If he agreed, where would that leave him? Where could it end? He instantly envisaged his life immeasurably more complicated than it even was now, a simple mission transformed into a life-or-death flight of a whole community to a new future. There were so many questions but his mind suddenly cleared.

"What resources would I have, how many would I be taking and when would I know the mission was accomplished?" he asked quite simply, surprising himself with the straightforwardness of his question. Was he really contemplating taking this on? He felt a visceral pull, a surge of adrenaline, synapses connecting, sinews knitting as if his whole being, mental, physical and spiritual, the person he was for himself and for many others, his family, his mother and father included, his surrogate father, this man, this community, his past and present, all coalesced into one future statement of intent. Despite himself yet inside the universe within him, his being resoundingly answered "YES!"

Of course, faced with this response, which Josep couldn't possibly have anticipated from himself, the old man did not fail to notice the physiological echoes that could be read in Josep's face and body. There was utter calm in the Perfect's expression. Josep noticed and instantly felt calmed.
"Josep, you astonish me! There must be so many questions you want me to answer you. We have made no mistake in depending on you. I would be your main resource, Josep. I shall come with you and shepherd my people under your command. You know the financial resources we have. As you have said, they are several times greater than the considerable fortune you already bear." His inflection fell upon the word "bear."

"Perfect," Josep said calmly. "My mission was to deliver the treasure I've collected to the Templar Castle in Miravet. I now see my mission is broader and deeper, a heavy burden that I must shoulder. My question is how I can best minimise the liability"

"On horseback, Josep, and on foot, we will be vulnerable to attack. This has already happened to you yourself."

"How else do you propose to arrive at Miravet?" asked Josep

"You yourself once had the idea but have decided it is not

realistic."

"How do you know about my boat?"

"Josep as you know, our survival depends entirely on surveillance. Total concealment requires total surveillance. We admired all those years ago how well your boat was concealed. Under cover of darkness, several times, we have improved the durability and inconspicuousness of the stone and wood shelter you built around it. Your boat is still in perfect condition."

"You mean the boat is still intact and navigable more than thirty years later?" Josep asked once again in awe at the capacity of this community.

"Absolutely. It is in exactly the same condition as it was when you left it."

"You people are truly extraordinary. Is there anything you do not know or are not capable of?"

The Perfect allowed himself a brief laugh and smiled broadly.

"Josep, your astonishment does your modesty great credit. The boat was excellently constructed in the first place, the raw materials and expertise were excellent. Consequently, we continue to depend on you as our main resource. We will depend absolutely on your leadership."

"Then how do you propose that I should lead you, community, treasure and all, to Miravet in a boat barely big enough for myself?" Josep said a little too loudly as sudden confusion and panic flared in his breast.

The old man's eyes widened momentarily as he read Josep's reaction.

"Have you any idea how much of our fortune remains to us?"

"I do not understand what you mean," Josep said hesitantly.

"Nine tenths, Josep. We have invested five hundred diamonds

or roughly fifteen thousand sous in a riverboat to bear us to Miravet."

Josep stared at the old man for a whole minute before he could muster his wits sufficiently to speak.

"But I do not know anything about navigating a riverboat on a river. It would have to be pretty large to carry nearly ninety people and there is more than one river in question. There's the Esera, then the Cinca, then the Segre and finally the Ebre itself…"

"We've hired a Captain and a boatswain, too," the old man interrupted. "They await us at Benasque."

Josep stared at the old man half in disbelief, half in horror. But the logic of the arrangement was trenchant and incontrovertible. As he had imagined it so many times in his mind, for Josep it was the absolutely ideal way to get to Miravet. The safest, the fastest, practically the most direct way imaginable.

"Water will always find the shortest way," the old man said.

"Follow the river," said Josep, which was how exactly the same thought had found expression on his lips.

CHAPTER TWENTY-EIGHT

Not only was the ship finely built, it was also comfortably fitted out for the eighty-six people who comprised the Cathar community, ranging in age from babes-in-arms to the five elders in their eighties or nineties, among them the Perfect's mother.

Josep, who had ventured into Benasque, as if it were the most natural thing in the world, which in a sense for him it was, had no trouble locating the Captain and boatswain, who turned out to be none other than the two Templars who had assisted him in Sicily. Perfect planning once again. In fact, the two Templars had come to Benasque almost directly after leaving Josep in Barcelona. This was presumably why Jacques de Molay had urged Josep not to delay their return. They had been the ones responsible for commissioning the boat in Benasque in the first place.the previous year, making the journey specifically from Famagusta, where they were long-term members of the Templar community They were navigation and boat building experts and the boat had been two months in the building. She sat serenely on the quay by the meadow opposite the Town Hall in Benasque among several other craft.

She was a shallow-bottomed, two-masted sloop, handsomely-made and spacious with a hold strung with hammocks, divided into two areas, one for men, one for women, and ample deck space for the ninety of them. There was plenty of storage space as well as room both for the little livestock the community had and a stable on deck for five horses.

The Templar sailors dealt with the final stages of the purchase, the shipbuilder delighted with the deal he had made, which had left him quite a wealthy man. The Templars, on the instructions of the Cathar Perfect, had paid him exactly what he had asked and had agreed during construction on a number of expensive additions and refinements, which had pushed the final cost up considerably. The only extra condition imposed on the happy Shipwright was absolute secrecy. He was not to reveal by whom the ship had been commissioned or any other detail relating to the enterprise. All being well, he would receive one further final payment a year hence. The man could not believe his good fortune and never breathed a word. Under cover of darkness, the Cathar community had embarked. They had lived with so little under the wooded ridge above Artiga de Lin that when the moment came to leave, they simply left their everyday implements behind them in their tenebrous tree dwellings and walked through the night to Benasque, silent yet expectant.

By dawn, they were approaching Sahún, there was a fresh wind blowing, the families had settled below. They passed Graus, the nearest port to Pobla de Castro, where Josep had gone to school at Cavallers and Josep was aft looking behind at the trail the boat made, lost in thought, when the Perfect came up to him.

"Your small boat will be there for you should you ever need it!" he said. Josep looked at him and laughed. The Perfect had known about him at least since that day more than thirty years ago when he had made the raft with Pere de Queralt and Ramón Muntaner and the evil Bertrán de Solsona in his first year at Cavallers Academy. The old man knew him so well and had read his mind once again.

"Your father would have been proud of you," he said. The river journey took them past so many places that had been important in Josep's life that, had he wished to explain it, he would have had the perfect accompaniment. The third day found them now on the River Cinca. They passed the towering Templar Castle at Monzón, then the smaller Castle of Pomar de Cinca, up on its hill overlooking the town and the river, where Josep had witnessed the murder of King Pere's half-brother, Ferran Sanchis, when King Pere had still been the Infant, or Crown Prince. He shuddered as he relived the spasms of that drowning body, felt the cold waters of the Cinca slide under him and realised that that experience could well have submerged deeper memories in his own subconscious. Shapes and shadows slipping, shifting, sinking. Yet here he was being borne along, not according to his own will but because others had once more shaped his fate. By committing himself so firmly as always to his purpose, he accommodated perfectly the demands made upon him by others. Yet he himself still felt his life was somehow adrift, subject too much to the desires, plans and stratagems of others, pressing needs though he recognised them to be.

"From now on, I will assert my own direction in life!" he muttered to himself. "Once I have done this last thing for Jacques, then I'll live the life I want to by the side of my wife and children and I hope my children's children. I feel I have fulfilled all my obligations and that now I deserve this much for myself."

They sailed on placidly from Pomar de Cinca towards Fraga, the land around them the endless flat plane where the river was the only feature. The riverside was dotted with beautiful birch, willow, poplar, ash, reeds and rushes. The landscape started to change near Fraga abruptly rising to a plateau to the west to starboard in the direction of Castille and the low rolling hills around the river lulled them into a state of calm.

"Now that we have some time, let me tell you about your father," the Perfect said. "But I must stress that I do not know all the details."
"I have a feeling Jacques de Molay can furnish the rest," Josep said.
The old man smiled and nodded. "He was an honorary member of the Cathar Knights!"

"The Cathar Knights? What a contradiction of ideas!" Josep said in astonishment.

"You are right," the Perfect replied, "but we had lords and knights without strongholds in our towns, dispossessed by the likes of de Montfort in their lust for land. They could not bear to stand idly by as their homes and people went up in flames. They were called Faydits in our language, which means something like dispossessed and excommunicated at the same time. Your father respected their beliefs. Somehow he won their complete trust and was privy to their most secret plans. Their last meeting was at the town of Aguilar in Roselló, Rousillon in Northern French."

"What did they intend to do?" Josep asked quite bewildered by this news. There was a whole history and perspective here he had had no idea about at all. Even Jacques had never even mentioned it. The Perfect read Josep's thoughts correctly again and nodded sympathetically.

"I can understand this is all impossibly difficult for you to fathom and assimilate all at once. You see, I believe that no land was safe for us north of Perpinyan. They therefore may have planned tp move to English Aquitaine, where your father was ambassador of Granada. Or to Provence, which was outside French control as part of the Holy Roman Empire. They might have planned to settle in Catalunya, as we did in Artiga de Lin, or perhaps even Granada."

"Are there any here I can talk to?" Josep asked.

"Not of the lords and knights, no, they are all long dead. Some here knew of your father but prefer not to talk about these things these days."

Suddenly, the sailors had to work hard to stop the shallow-hulled boat scudding across the water and hitting the opposite bank as the rolling waters of the mighty Segre, issuing from the Languedoc Pyrenees and having flowed all the way along the eastern Pyrenees to Balaguer and past Lleida, now flowed into the Cinca and became one river. The boat's direction had to be controlled by long trailing oars attached to the rear of the boat. Further oars were lashed to both sides of the boat to fend off the riverbanks should the boat be swept too close to one side of the river or the other and all able-bodied people were instructed to man them until further instructions were given. The great currents swept the boat along as the River Segre became broader and broader until, at Mequinenza, the boat was almost impossible to control as it flowed tumultuously into the deep fast waters of the Ebre, so important it gave Iberia is name.

The boat actually moved sideways in the water as the mighty volume made it respond like a twig thrown onto the rushing floodwater of a spring river in spate. Yet calm was preserved, the two navigators skilfully ordering the community members in their different tasks. Finally, the direction of the vessel was righted and the trip began to normalise again but the Ebre even then was twice as wide and fast as the Segre had been and many times faster and wider than either the Cinca or the Esera.

In its magnificence, the Ebre felt more and more as if it were actually bearing Josep home, enabling him to sort out his deepest thoughts. He slept incredibly well, was treated like a hero by the community members, men, women and children alike. He had never received such attention and admiration. The nightmares he had become used to associating with sleeping when next to water stopped and he began to have dreams of his early childhood, his mother, Jacques and, he was not sure, but could it have been his father? Did he have memories of his father? Were his earliest memories returning to him? Had what was submerged gradually moved up from the deepest recesses to his conscious mind, which he could access perhaps not only in dreams but also at will? Would he one day be able to summon up memories of his earliest days in the company of his mother *and* his father? His heart beat wildly at the thought.

"You know you were the one who was chosen to lead us out, do you not, Josep?" The Perfect asked him on their fifth day on the water not far from Mora d'Ebre.

"No, I had no idea! I was just collecting the Templar treasure when...!"

"No, no, Josep," the old man cut in. "I do not refer only to recent developments but also to the origins of your relationship with us, perhaps even to your own origins."

"You're going to tell me next that you knew my father," Josep said half joking.

The Perfect gave him another one of those penetrating looks and something in his expression warned Josep to brace himself.

"I did not, Josep, but I know of people who did. Your Father and Jacques de Molay used to spend time together in Rennes-le-Chateau, just before you were born. According to our family members in Rennes, you know, the ones you brought the notes from, the Fabre family, you take after your father: Dark, hawkish nose, down-turned mouth, eyes that can be warm one moment yet cold the next. But if you had not been so warmly accepted by Amaury, we couldn't have trusted you so deeply."

"But our meeting was completely coincidental," Josep broke in.

"No, Josep, you were sent on your first mission to check on the border situation in Artiga de Lin, on the recommendation of Jacques de Molay to Lord Pedro de Ayerbe. As you were his Squire and Jacques was your patron, the Director of the College, Fray Domènech, was compelled to allow you to carry out the mission."

"But he was on the side of Ferran Sanchis. Why would he give the mission to someone loyal to the Crown Prince?"

"Why not? It would have seemed suspicious if he had not. Besides, the intelligence you brought back though valuable was confirmation of what was already known, namely that the French had occupied Vall d'Aran as far as Es Bordes."

"I'm glad they appreciated the information. I nearly died of cold and hunger getting it," Josep replied with a snort. The old man allowed himself a laugh.

"Amaury thought you were tremendous, so young and so capable. We even broke our own rules and allowed him to help you catch the rabbits you had for your dinner."

"I was faint with hunger," Josep said, clearly remembering how close he had felt to desperation.

"And I always agreed with Jacques that he had made an excellent choice! Capable and perfectly trustworthy!" the old man added.

Josep glanced at him. Was he working his way up to asking him another "favour"? Was it not enough he had agreed to accompany these people out of Vall d'Aran? As if reading his thoughts again the old man reassured him.

"I tell you these things so that you may understand better the forces at work in your early life, Josep. We were talking of Fray Domènech a moment ago, he had his own reasons for sending you. He was able to trail you. He was hoping you would lead him to the secret community of the Cathars."

"So why did he not succeed?" Josep asked.

"We were too well concealed, always aware of this danger, so they only got as far as Aigualluts, where Amaury was murdered."

"That has always puzzled me," Josep said his gaze falling to the floor, the memory of his friend's death clearly saddening him. "What was he doing there at the time?" he asked.

"Unfortunately for him, he had gone to check on the diamonds concealed in the ice at Aigualluts. He was found with a bag of diamonds on his person. The secret of the Cathars was almost out of the bag, you might say." The man smiled sadly.

"But when tortured to reveal where more diamonds could be found or where our settlement was, I have it on good authority, he died saying nothing. Literally disappeared in front of the eyes of his captor who was unable at the last moment even to take from him the bag of diamonds that he had secreted on his person."

"It was my uncle who witnessed the murder," Josep said, his head down, as if he were responsible.

"We know, Josep," the old man said, putting a hand on Josep's shoulder to reassure him.

"We also understand why a mercenary would not intervene to save him."

"Poor Amaury," Josep said.

"He died more quickly than you think, Josep. He had his ball of poison and managed to take it at the crucial moment."

"With his head being held under water, struggling for his life and desperate for a breath of air, how could he have put the ball into his mouth and swallow it?" Josep said in disbelief shooting the old man a look of incredulity.

"No, no, Josep. He'd had it in his mouth all along. He only needed to crush it between his teeth when he knew his situation was critical. You must remember, death for the Cathars is a deliverance from the world of evil."

Josep did not seem convinced.

"So why was he so ready to give up this life? Why are you not all prepared to commit collective suicide if that is what you are accusing Amaury of?"

Josep was clearly horrified to hear Amaury had been responsible for his own death.

"Do you disagree with his action so deeply Josep?" asked the

Perfect. "He was after all safeguarding his people, it was an action performed "in extremis". But you're right, it is shocking, it shocked his people, too."

"Hold on, how do you know he took poison?" Josep asked all of a sudden.

"We knew he had the poison ball lodged in his cheek. It was a common precaution for those going on dangerous missions."

Josep nodded. That much made sense.

"Secondly, when we found him in the Riu Jueù, his eyes were typically bulging."

"I thought that was a sign of suffocation!" Josep interrupted, again in horror at hearing in detail about his friend's death.

"It is, Josep but there was more definitive proof."

Josep looked questioningly at the perfect.

"His tongue was completely black. It is due to rapid necrosis. It affects the tongue, throat and nervous system in seconds. He passed out immediately, peacefully, much more peacefully than would have been the case if he had drowned. His heart had stopped beating even before his assailant realised he could be dead. His assailant may well have held his head under for several minutes before he could believe he was truly dead." Flashes of drowned faces and thrashing bodies swept through Josep's mind.

"Then his body was sucked down by the mysterious currents of the underground caves of Aigualluts. We knew about them as several of the passages we've used over the decades to get to and from the ice face were alternately dry and flooded."

"Who killed him?" Josep again interrupted the old man.

"It was Guillaume de Nogaret, Josep."

"Motive?" Josep asked, shaking his head.

"Amaury's refusal to reveal the whereabouts of the diamonds or our settlement. However, I do not think he meant to kill him, he wanted to torture him to reveal the whereabouts, then decide what to do with him."

"But when Amaury knew there was no escape for him, he opted for suicide?"

"Exactly. It's a reasonable choice given the circumstances." Josep shook his head in wonder at how coldly the Perfect could talk of Amaury's harrowing death.

"Many Cathars, you must remember, Josep, in similar situations, have behaved in the same way."

Josep remembered the capsule he'd been given to give to Jacques, found it in his pocket where he had sewn it into the fabric, fingered it and contemplated what he'd just been told. Would Jacques face a similar dilemma in the end?

"As I was saying, Amaury's death shocked the community. No one had died except of old age for decades, Josep. Death was met peacefully but *his* death reminded people of the terrible deaths of their family members long ago. It was awful. It tore the heart out of the community. It made people question why we were living in this way. His death, you might say, rang the death knell for the community."

"Yet you've waited this long?" Josep asked in disbelief again.

"All things have their due moment, Josep. Do you not recognise that as central to our philosophy yet?"

Josep shot the man a look expecting to see a rebuke in his eyes but saw that there was none, that the question simply reflected the Perfect's perplexity, no criticism of him intended.

"As I've said, in the absence of your father, you had been chosen to lead us out," the old man continued.

"All those years!"

"There was nobody else. You were the only one who knew us well enough and could be entrusted with so perilous a task. Our home had become a prison in the end, Josep. That is how people felt about it but all accepted it as there was no other option. Yet we looked forward to the day when you could come and deliver us."

Josep breathed in deeply and looked away from the old man, who sensed he needed his own space. The responsibility was overwhelming, Josep thought. Despite what he had felt so strongly a week ago, he now felt he did not want it. But what could he do? He couldn't abandon these people. A new feeling suddenly stabbed at his heart. It was resentment towards Jacques de Molay for not explaining what he had intended for him to do.

"Had Jacques explained this, I do not think I would have gone through with it," was the thought that crossed his mind. "This, and this alone, is payment enough for saving my life. When I arrive in Miravet, I am drawing a line. That will be the end of it. I owe it to my wife, children, family and myself." He pondered these things inwardly but said nothing to the Perfect, who sat, hunched up with his legs drawn up to his chest, lost in his own thoughts now.

Josep continued his inward conversation. So it had been Guillaume de Nogaret who had killed Amaury. And the motive was purely venal: he wanted the fortune. That also explained Bella's death. The man who'd accompanied Bertrán de Solsona was the same man who had followed him into the hills, whom he'd seen previously at Cavallers, all those years ago. Guillaume de Nogaret had known about Josep even when Josep was an innocent schoolchild, when Josep had accompanied his knight to the Count of Foix's castle. He had tried to knock Josep into the water in Navarra. His were the penetrating, snake-like eyes Josep had recognised, though seen for only a fraction of a second behind the grey hood. So much hatred. He would have tried to drown Josep or torture him to death to reveal what he knew about the Cathar treasure. He had been on his trail all these years.

"And he'll be on my trail now, that means," Josep said to himself, remembering what Jacques had said about de Nogaret when he arrived to rescue Josep from Gallipolis. He had missed Josep after all those years by but a day or two. If they were ever to meet again, one of them was sure to die.

CHAPTER TWENTY-NINE

In fact, Jacques had been awaiting Josep's arrival in Miravet. This was the end of the journey for Josep. He disembarked, took his leave of all on-board simply and without ceremony and walked up the steep cobbled road to the castle when he heard that Jacques was there.

They hugged each other warmly. Despite his anger at feeling that he had been manipulated by the Grand Master, Josep had also had time during the journey to reconcile himself to the reality that Jacques de Molay always had a plan, not all of which was revealed to anyone, let alone Josep and the outcomes for Josep were at least intended to be positive.

"You have saved an entire people," Jacques said when Josep revealed he knew he'd been selected for the task. "You were the right man for the job," Jacques added, "as is evident."

There was no point in Josep saying he'd been at greater risk of attack as he was carrying much more treasure than he'd expected. The fact of the matter was, as Josep well knew, that he had not come to harm on the boat. In fact, he had only been attacked when he had been alone, before he even arrived at the settlement. Arguably, the boat had been the safest way of travelling, not only for the Cathars but even for Josep himself. When he reflected on the journey from Benasque, he found it incredible that they had not been attacked, that the whole journey had gone so smoothly. It was certainly not how Josep would have organised things himself but he couldn't help feeling a secret admiration for the Grand Master's obvious excellent judgement.

"Josep, before we get into deep conversation – and I have much I need to discuss with you – you have a visitor."

Josep looked up in surprise. He couldn't believe his eyes and stared in total amazement for a moment, mouth wide-open.

"Ramón Muntaner! I cannot believe it." He jumped to his feet and grabbed him as if to make sure it really was him. "I cannot believe my eyes!"

"My dear Josep! How are you? I hear you've had quite a ride since we were last together!"

"I'm frankly a little surprised that you managed to get out alive yourself!" Josep said.

"You're very well informed, I see." Ramón laughed.

"I know absolutely nothing of what happened in the end, Ramón, only that Jacques has convinced me I'd be dead by now if I'd stayed there."

"Well, I very nearly died myself, Josep, but why would your life have been in danger? I was always there to look after you, I seem to remember."

"I see your sense of humour has not improved, Ramón. I was the one who persuaded you to keep a low profile after the Hatche incident!"

"I seem to remember "low profile" was exactly the expression I used, Josep," he said, raising his eyebrows to show he was still in jest. "But the situation did become very toxic!"

"Did Guillaume de Nogaret arrive in the end?" Josep asked now.

"Indeed he did, Josep. How did you know? He was not even in Gallipolis. He made straight for Christoupolis and made his base there."

"And did Berenguer d'Entença and Rocafort finally come to blows?"

Ramón was amazed. "I see bad news travels fast, Josep.

Rocafort's men killed Berenguer d'Entença," he said, his face unusually serious.

"It is just as Jacques predicted," said Josep. Now it was a Ramón's term to go slack jawed in amazement.

"Jacques believes Guillaume de Nogaret orchestrated the whole thing," said Josep.

Ramón shook his head. "But how could he have? He was only there a week or so before the fatal attack."

"He would have infiltrated Rocafort's troops and started rumours that Berenguer d'Entença was setting a trap for him!" Josep replied. The supposition was shocking, of course, and Josep would normally have behaved with more tact but this was Ramón he was talking to, they were in a safe place and the events he was referring to had happened several weeks ago now.

"We only knew Jacques had come when you disappeared, Josep, and we pieced things together," Muntaner said. "I am here to request ships from the Grand Master to evacuate the rest of the Company that wants to return home. He is the only one who can authorise that kind of expenditure and all other vessels are fully deployed. As you remember, Rocafort deliberately scuttled our ships to make sure we stayed. Jacques' arrival coincided with de Nogaret's departure from s'Atines, or Athens, as everyone else calls it."

"I am convinced Berenguer d'Entença was working for King James of Majorca." Jacques de Molay said. "That explains why his son, Crown Prince Ferran, was there. He wished to propose himself as the new leader of the company of Almogavers. You will remember King Jaume of Majorca had always had a complicated relationship with the Crown of Catalunya Aragón. Now it suited his nephew, King Jaume of Catalunya Aragón, whose vassal he was, to expedite this and thereby extricate Catalunya Aragón from the whole Almogaver Expedition to the East, which had become a catastrophe. That was Entença's mission, and, therefore, Prince Ferran of Mallorca was travelling with Entença. However, Rocafort rejected the idea because he still wanted to be the Commander of the Company of Almogavers. But de Nogaret's agenda was simply to cause as much instability as possible to the Crown of Catalunya Aragón and all its interests. In the end, it was brilliantly simple: convince Rocafort it was life or death, Berenguer d'Entença was coming to kill him." Josep said.

"But Rocafort couldn't possibly have known Berenguer d'Entença would come that day," Ramón said. "What is more, Rocafort's men had got up late the morning it happened. How could de Nogaret have anticipated that?" Muntaner asked.

"Anticipated? Jacques de Molay asked coolly. "He planned it. It's not so difficult. If you want a battalion to catch up another one, give one drink and food aplenty the night before and keep the other on its normal rations."

"Well, that is precisely what happened, Grand Master," Ramón said. "Rocafort's troops were near Alexandroupolis, about a day's ride from Christopoulis. We know de Nogaret himself was in Alexandroupolis the night Rocafort's battalion camped there because we have witnesses who swear they saw him there. From what you're saying, he'd come on purpose. We thought it was just a coincidence. Clearly, he made sure Rocafort's men were well entertained and that plenty of good food and wine were available. The soldiers couldn't believe it, they thought the hospitality was coming from the Greeks themselves. They did not know and still do not know that de Nogaret was behind it. We only found out later he was there but couldn't see why. Now it makes sense. The secret was the French crown was behind it. Anyway, to Rocafort's men, here were Greeks prepared to treat them like heroes, just like the early days before evrything started going wrong!"

"De Nogaret must have persuaded the Mayor of

Alexandroupolis to do this by saying they needed to delay Rocafort's regiment so that Entença's force could find and attack them," said de Molay. "Maybe, de Nogaret also told him Rocafort's force was full of the worst sort of Almogavers because they had accepted Turks and Turcopoles into their ranks."

"That would have made it sound plausible because that detail was true," Muntaner agreed. "Their ranks had been increased by a number of Turks and Turcopoles who offered themselves to Rocafort as mercenaries. After the incident with Hatche, they saw him as the stronger leader, even though the incident made them fear and hate him. Rocafort treated them with great suspicion and had them closely controlled but he knew that they were good troops. The following morning, Rocafort's troops got up late just as de Nogaret had intended, as you say, and he launched the second part of his plan. He must have started the rumour that the force in Alexandroupolis was under attack from the Turks and Turcopoles they had accepted into their numbers, who were actually in league with Entença and had betrayed them. Therefore Rocafort's brother, Gisbert and his henchmen, hungry for the limelight and even easier to provoke than Rocafort, threw on their armour and still pretty drunk came to within two hundred yards of Entença's force. Entença had gone to the head of the force to restrain his men as soon as he had heard they'd caught up with Rocafort. He had not even dressed for battle but was wearing ordinary clothes. From a distance, he looked like a Turcopole, light cavalry who wear no armour. Then a Greek messenger rode up to Gisbert at full tilt shouting that Entença was the Turcopole leader and he was ordering his troops to attack. They charged at him and ran him through with their lances. A fight then broke out between Rocafort's men and the Turcopoles they could see, together with the rest of Entenca's Almogavers, none of them armed and despite their protests and consternation, a hundred and twenty were cut down and killed instantly. Prince Ferran, who had been at the rear of Entenca's battalion, rushed as quickly as he could to the front and was immediately recognised as he was carrying his royal standards. He told Gisbert and Dalmau they had listened to false intelligence and made a terrible error Of course, that was the end of Prince Ferran's initiative." The Greek messenger they had listened to had simply slipped away when the fighting started and couldn't be found.

"He must have been one of de Nogaret's agents," said Josep.

Muntaner nodded. "But when Rocafort was told, he simply thought it had all been a terrible accident. His brother made it sound that way and no one thought to try to find the Greek messenger who had raised the alarm in order to interrogate him. The people in Alexandroupolis had no idea who he was either. The Mayor of Alexandroupolis was strangely taciturn about the incident repeating again and again he was not surprised the accident had happened as there had been Turks and Turcopoles among the force. Did you anticipate all of this, Jacques?"

"Not the absolute details, just the main strokes, based on complete intelligence." Jacques replied. "I can see you two have a lot to catch up on," Jacques said. "Please let us talk as soon as possible about the ships you need." He excused himself and left at that point.

Ramón Muntaner did not speak for moment. He was looking intently at Josep, with his head cocked slightly to the left, an expression halfway between surprise and pleasure on his face.

"This whole expedition has been a disaster, he said. "But you, Josep, you sound so different! You're more self-assured than you ever were. And you're right, we should have been there, too. However, provision also had to be made to evacuate the wounded from Gallipolis. We had managed to repair just one of the scuttled ships, refitted it and sailed it to Thasos, just off the coast from Christoupolis. I saw nothing of the actual fatal engagement."

"Jacques de Molay has been keeping a very close eye on the movements of the French king and his chancellor, Guillaume de Nogaret. He was convinced he wanted to ensnare and capture me, too," Josep said.

"Why would he want to do that?" Ramón asked.

"He wanted to hold me hostage. That way he could force Jacques to turn himself in."

"He would have done that for you?" Ramón Muntaner said looking steadily at Josep, clearly not at all sure about what was going on.

"I've found out a lot about our lives since we came back from the east. I've been very useful to him but, yes, he would have given himself up for me if it had come to that, I believe. I have a lot to tell you."

"Yes," Ramón agreed, "I believe you do."

CHAPTER THIRTY

The following morning, Muntaner bade Josep and Jacques farewell. Josep had brought him up to date and then proceeded to report to de Molay what Muntaner had told him the night before. The remaining Almogavers were becoming increasingly frustrated with Rocafort as their leader. Muntaner had also come to request King Jaume's instructions.

"Rocafort will have to be careful he does not now come too much under de Nogaret's scrutiny himself," de Molay said.

"De Nogaret is no longer there, my Lord. He has returned to France now they say."

"All the more reason, then," answered de Molay. "Yes, he's in Paris now, according to my sources."

"And therefore close to the King," said Josep. "They will be planning how matters will end," he added.

"Exactly. We're all going to have to be even more on our guard," replied the Grand Master. "I need to talk to you about the Cathars' and Templars' onward journey."

"Onward journey? Josep paused. "What has that got to do with me?" Josep asked horrified. This was news to him. He braced himself.

"I know you do not want to do it," Jacques said. Josep gasped in disbelief at the forthrightness of the old Templar.

"That is an understatement! The Perfect had to explain my father's role to persuade me to bring them down from the Artiga de Lin."

"But they are of course still in danger, Josep, as we were just saying and will be until they are out of the reach of the French crown. That was your father's mission after all!"

"It is one mission too far for me," Josep said despairingly, shaking his head. "I am increasingly worried about Lali, Catarina, Lucio and my mother."

"I understand your fears but believe me, the Cathars and their treasure are at greater risk than your family at the moment."

"Why can they not go into hiding here or hereabouts?" Josep said suddenly, sounding flippant even to himself.

"You know very well why not, Josep!" Jaques replied. "You know how extensive the King of France's network is and how it can extend into the very ranks of the army this side of the border. You have seen it yourself. Besides, the last thing they want is to go into hiding again."

Josep was looking away and had gone silent for a moment. Then suddenly he said, "You ask this of me knowing my family is in danger?" He turned sharply to face Jacques de Molay, shock and anger in equal measure registering in his eyes. His face was suddenly flushed and he was sweating.

Jacques de Molay sighed heavily. "I understand your anxiety Josep. You feel the net is closing around all the Templar networks and the Cathars too and that includes your family."

"Absolutely right! Is it so surprising that I should feel that way?"

"Hold your nerve, Josep!"

"Hold my nerve?" Josep spat out the words with sudden fury. "You talk to me of nerve? You have a nerve!" He was almost shouting. "You make me jeopardise my own safety and fulfilment of my mission, that is, to get home safely in one piece, in order to rescue the Cathars, which despite the subterfuge, I have done and now you request I jeopardise my family's safety with that psychopath de Nogaret around, in order to ensure the safety of the Cathars?" he was white and shaking.

Jacques de Molay grasped him by the shoulders and looked very hard into his eyes.

"Keep your voice down, for God's sake! Nothing will happen to your family at least until the time comes for me to give myself up, Josep, and when that time comes, I shall do so in a way that does not endanger your family."

He spoke again with such certainty and utter conviction that it was impossible not to be persuaded by him. He seemed as usual to see how everything was going to work out and Josep knew he had very good reason to be so sure of his own predictions.

"Josep, you have to see the danger to your family will come only if I do not surrender myself. At the moment, I am not the quarry either of de Nogaret or the French Crown. They are moving stealthily to seize all the assets of the Templars but they still do not know for sure the Cathars even exist, let alone that they have arrived with their treasure in Miravet."

"So what will happen when they find out?"

"Good question, Josep, because find out they certainly will. Word has probably gone to the French king this very morning."

"And of course, I have been seen with the Cathars."

"Yes, Josep."

"So they will be after me!" He said with less anger than fear now as the prospect started to sink in.

Jacques nodded. "You're only in danger so long as they know where you are."

"So you mean it's in my best interests to disappear?"

"Exactly Josep!"

"Any ideas?" Josep asked sarcastically.

"Where better than Scotland?" de Molay answered calmly without a pause.

"Scotland? Scotland?" Josep shouted. He grabbed the big man's tunic and pulled him to him. Jacques had to take a step forward to steady himself.

"Keep your voice down, Josep, for God's sake or really all is lost!" he said removing himself roughly from Josep's grasp.

"No one but you and I know you could be heading for Scotland not even Ramón Muntaner, not even the Perfect, no one. Nor does anyone know exactly where in Scotland you are heading, for that matter, as that's still a complete secret."

Josep was stunned and said nothing. He'd broken into a cold sweat and the hairs on the back of his neck were standing up. He felt like a fly trapped in a web and Jacques de Molay was the spider.

Jacques seized the moment's hiatus and pressed home his advantage.

"Save yourself, save the Cathars," he heard Jacques say. "Help me remove this treasure once and for all from beyond the French King's reach and I will be one step closer to ending things. But return to your family now and you endanger them, as I'm sure you see."

Deep anger and resentment now flared up in Josep's chest. He was paying dearly for his life being saved by Jacques de Molay.

"You knew you were putting my family at risk!" he growled through gritted teeth.

"Josep, do you not see that you are leading them away from your family! When you return, things will have moved on and you'll be irrelevant. I will ask nothing more of you, I swear to you but do this last favour for me, for the Cathars, for your father!"

Josep couldn't work out whether he was angrier now at this latest demand or the reference to his father or his family as irrelevant. For him, right then, his family were all that mattered. He could not see himself extricating them from danger otherwise.

"When do we set out?" he asked suddenly, very quietly, looking away from Jacques whose gaze he had held rock solid for the last few minutes. He was red in the face and tears of fury, fear and frustration burned in his eyes.

"Tomorrow, Josep," replied the Templar.

"Why should I believe they won't go after my family just for the sake of it? They are perverts and psychopaths!"

"Only when money is concerned, Josep." Jacques paused and took a deep breath. "They tortured Bella to death because they thought she knew about the Cathars."

"Then why shouldn't they do the same to my family?" he shouted.

"That is the point, Josep. You need to go with the treasure. On your return, you will be no use to them. They will want you now, now that you have the treasure when they discover all that has happened. The sooner you go, the sooner your family will be safe. If you and the treasure stay here, they may well consider using your family as hostages." Josep's face was white yet his eyes burned red.

"What an evil mess you have involved me in, Jacques!"

"You were always the best man for the job, Josep. I know you can do this. With this money, the Order can live on, elsewhere, with other folk but there will be continuity."

"Damn your Order and damn your concept of continuity. If you had not rescued me, my family would not be in danger now. How is that for continuity?"

"Josep, calm yourself. You know in the cold light of day that you have been enmeshed in this situation since you were little more than a child!" Jacques said now, a new tone entering his voice, cold and hard as ice.

"Yes, I do. Unfortunately, I do know that. You were the one who put me there. You were the one who had such great expectations for me. If I had had any idea this would happen, I would never have gone on the Catalan expedition to the east."

"Nor did I plan that you should go either, Josep. But I couldn't let you perish there either, could I? Nor could I explain all the details and stages of this mission to you in case you were captured. Now you have to follow the mission through to the end."

Josep said nothing but looked at the old Templar with such fury that the big man stepped back.

"Josep, they need a focus for their attention. You will be that focus but by the time they find out, you will be gone. You will leave the Cathars in Scotland and will return. Without the Cathars and their treasure you will be of no interest to them, nor will your family."

"They will track me down just to find out where the treasure has been taken!" Josep said shaking his head.

"They will already know by then. Their agents will make sure of that. And I will make sure that they know."

"You expect me to believe I can return from Scotland, rejoin my family and live in peace and safety" Josep said acidly.

"A sum of money has been put aside for you already. It is large enough to make a significant difference to an individual and his family but too small to be of any interest to the French crown."

Josep laughed a hollow laugh. He was beginning to feel like a fool. Jacques de Molay had it all worked out. Even his anger and resentment, his fear for his family and now his future financial security.

"And I will be free of all future obligations?"

The old man said nothing and nodded. Josep flashed a look at him and saw sadness in his eyes. Remorse stabbed at him. Despite the fury he felt towards this man, his heart flooded with pain when he remembered what fate was likely to have in store for the Grand Master. He was setting up the pieces that might well lead him to his own death.

"Josep," the old man said, "I accepted my fate when I took the post. When the moment comes, I will be the focus of their attention. Mark my words, all other considerations will pale."

Josep pushed into de Molay's hand the small cotton bag containing the pellet the Perfect had given him. "Keep this safe," he whispered barely audibly. "It comes from the Perfect. They will not detect it if you put it under your tongue. You will know what to do with it."

CHAPTER THIRTY-ONE

Of course a seagoing boat had been prepared for them and was awaiting them at Tortosa. They would leave from Port Fangós on the Delta de L'Ébre, as Josep had done en route to Sicily. Josep allowed himself to be swept along in the natural current of events and did not even enquire whether a buyer had been found for the riverboat they had travelled in from Benasque to Miravet.

Speed was of the essence and everything had been so well organised before Josep and his party had even arrived that, by the time they changed ships in Porto, courtesy of the Portuguese Templar headquarters there, top secret instructions as to their final destination were waiting for them with the Visitor of Portugal, who had come to bid them farewell.

Just as many years before, when King Pere the Second's fleet had left Port Fangós, heading it seemed for Sicily, the strictest instructions had been given, on pain of death, that the sealed directions were not to be opened until they were twenty miles out to sea, so likewise, not until Josep ship was twenty miles out from Porto was he permitted to break the seal on Jacques de Molay's directions for the ship that was taking Josep, the Cathars and their treasure to Scotland and a new future.

"My dearest Josep" the letter started, "By the time you receive this, you will be heading due west out of Porto and wondering what devilish adventures I have planned for you. Forgive me if my tone seems light but I rejoice so completely in my good fortune to have been able to count on you to see through this part of our plan that, as one who considers himself as close as a father could be to a younger man who seemed to him like a son, I will go to my grave celebrating the day that my path crossed your parents' path, bringing us all after great personal tragedy and loss, on all sides, to this day, when an Order and a People can be saved. And I have you to thank for that because without your inside knowledge of the community you protect, without the ease of communication you have established with the Perfect and without his and his people's utter confidence in you, their security and future survival would not be assured, as it now is. I now urge you to be completely secure in all your dealings with your sacred cargo.

Josep, not only are you delivering perhaps the last of the real Cathar people of the Languedoc into a new life and a new future but you are also ensuring the perpetuation into the future, the continuity of which we spoke into the coming years, centuries and ages, of a light that so deserves to shine but that was in danger of sputtering out. You will plant a seed that was thought to have been extirpated that will now prosper in and vitally contribute to a new community of brethren, in a new land, under a new name.

It was not my fate to have had a child Josep, nor was it my path in life to have had the love of a woman, but once and for all, I want you to know that I have loved both your mother and yourself as if you were my own family and in another life would have been content, utterly content to have your love, both as a husband to your mother and father to you, my son. Keep me in your love and remember me, as I will always remember you, with pride, only wishing to be at your side, no matter where you are.

Jacques de Molay.

Josep's instructions directed him, his ship and the new community to Ayre. They made land in late April 1307 at the small port at Dunure Castle. Brought to land by Templars from nearby Kilwinning, all members of the community and its treasure arrived intact. There had even been a birth aboard. Josep stayed with the community at Kilwinning, twenty or so miles north of Ayre, for a month. The Templars provided all they needed and the Cathars quickly settled into their new life.

Shortly afterwards, Josep sailed back uneventfully to his family in Trapani. Templar contacts being what they are, accommodation for the two brothers accompanying Josep was found without delay in Trapani itself. The town was beautiful and sleepy, still somnolent after the fierce summer heat, the air thick with humidity and the faint sweet smell of ripe grapes and *mosto,* as the harvest and winemaking season had begun. Josep managed to find a horse and made straight for Can Pere Josep, a few miles outside Trapani. He had considered landing further down the coast where he knew Lali had her fish salting shed next to the salt pans but had decided not to risk surprising her there as she worked. He considered that she would be better able to deal with the shock of seeing him again after these three years of absence if she was at home with the children. He calculated the children's ages quickly.

"My God," he said to himself as he rode along. "Catarina is twenty-three. She is no longer a child. How is she going to react to me? I've been absent for such a long time for her, all the time she has taken to grow from girl to young woman. She might resent me for delaying her plans for marriage. I wonder if she is still seeing the same young man as before. Her choice, whatever. As for Lucio, my goodness, he'll be twenty. What will he think of me? I have nothing to show for my five years away. I return as empty-handed as when I left."

He continued on his way, enjoying the simple pleasure of the open road in a way he had not done since his childhood, musing as he went, apprehensive and excited, and contented with this reintroduction into island life. The sun was still beating down, the silence was broken only by the sounds of insects buzzing, pigeons noisily flapping their wings taking flight, occasionally distant dogs barking. He was in the grounds now of Can Pere Josep, his horse ambling past vineyards that belonged to him and Lali, some harvested, others black and green, still weighed down by their heavy luscious load. He reached down and picked a bunch from a vine that faced south. Plump, firm, exploding with sweet juice, a more delicious grape he could not imagine. He was instantly excited about how good the wine would be from this harvest. The vines were well attended, the leaves vital, rubbery, green and perky, sour to the taste, also in prime condition. Lali had obviously been working hard to maintain them.

Suddenly he saw people working in the fields. He turned his head, not wanting to be identified, for some reason suddenly self-conscious, shy, as if he were an outsider.

He nodded now to the workers in the field, whom he did not recognise them and who did not recognise him but they paid him no heed. This was an untroubled land peace had finally descended upon with its blessings of endless days marked only by day and night, the seasons and the seasons' tasks.

Then of course it happened. He was recognised. It had to happen. One moment the workers were politely ignoring him, the next a worker did a double-take and stopped and stared, screening the intense sunlight with one hand straining to see clearly. Then in a body, the workers turned to him, the men removing their hats, the women bowing their heads. They clasped their hands in front of them as they paid him this simple token of respect. As he passed, he noticed one worker slip off, jump into the saddle of a horse tethered nearby and urge the horse on down what Josep presumed was a shortcut to the *finca*. His arrival would now be announced. He was glad that Lali would therefore be forewarned. They had so many things to say. But how sweet a homecoming was this? He could not imagine a more idyllic, bucolic late summer Mediterranean scene than this and his heart ached and beat wildly with excitement and pleasure and tears pricked his eyes.

"I'm back," he thought simply. "I'm home."

Lucio was the first to find him. He must have got wind of the news before the servant Josep had seen leaving for the *finca* had reached his mistress. He came trotting down the track that led from the main entrance of the *finca* raising a cloud of dust behind him, with a whole pack of his dogs at his heels. He shouted "Father!" and leaped up onto the saddle behind Josep with the athleticism and spring Josep could now only dimly remember of his own youth at Cavallers.

He hugged Josep tightly round the waist as the dogs went into an apoplexy of barking, disconcerting the horse, which started picking its way more slowly now as the dogs gathered round it. As Lucio told him about the dogs, the servant Josep had seen returning to the house trotted up and without even looking at Josep or Lucio, took the reins of the horse, started leading it and the dogs immediately fell into line behind the horse. Josep was impressed. This was a working household, the man leading his horse was used to this situation, presumably all travellers were treated to this overwhelming canine reception.

They were now passing the gate of the *finca*, there were the kennels to the left in a clearing in another lush, well-kept vineyard. To the right of the big gate, which was made of rough wood but was well mounted and solid on heavy posts with strong, deep red iron hinges, was a shady fig tree with plenty of room for a whole party of people underneath it. As Josep looked left now, as the path rose to the house about two hundred metres away, he could see the sea over the vineyards and tears came to him once again as he remembered how many evenings he had sat and wondered when, or even if, he would ever set eyes again on this dear smallholding. This sea was the same sea at the other end of which he had sat and looked out to the west at sundown and wished he could be closer to the rays of the setting sun as those very rays were setting on Can Pere Josep as they were setting on him, so many evenings, he couldn't even remember how many, it had become a ritual almost for him; and now, right now, the sun was setting and here he was.

There was a cry from the house as they rounded curve in the drive and Lali came running as fast as her legs could bear her from the house.

"Josep, Josep, it *really is* you!" she shouted as she came towards his horse. "I said to myself I wouldn't believe it till I saw it with my own eyes! and here you are! Why did not you let us know you were coming home?"

"I couldn't. It all happened so suddenly. I was at sea. I'll tell you later. It is all so complicated!"

"It matters not and your mother explained a lot when she arrived but the house is upside down, there's wine being made in the cellars and all sorts of bits and pieces lying around the place. It would be dangerous if there were any little kids running around the place."

Josep looked at her and with a wicked look in his eye.

"There are not, are there?"

Lali laughed with delight.

"None of mine and yours, anyway."

Josep stopped his horse. He was but fifty metres from the house now and he nimbly jumped down from the horse, grasping the hand of his son, who had moments earlier dismounted, to steady himself.

"My God, Lali, it's good to see you!"

He pulled her to him and held her so close she started coughing and laughing. As he looked in her eyes, he saw she was struggling to hold back the tears. Now she was pummelling his chest with her fists.

"I'll pass out if you do not let go a little bit!" and they both laughed out loud at her simple good humour. They were walking now up to the house. Josep could feel a slight limp in the way she walked but she did not seem to be in pain.

"How are you feeling, Lali?" He said suddenly amid the chatter and laughter.

"Oh, there will be plenty of time to fill you in on all of that. But I'm fine, as you can see, absolutely fine."

"You are fine to me," echoed Josep, a little joke they'd always had since the earliest days.

"Yes, I am!" she said smiling through her tears as they stood holding each other. Josep's mother entered with a look on her face as if to say she had been expecting him. They embraced quietly. The front of the house was then all opened up, the blinds were thrown open, all the doors were open, people were coming in and out, paying their respects to the newly returned master of the house. The sun's rays penetrated deeply into the house, revealing it in uproar.

"Are there normally so many people about place?" asked Josep.

"At this time of year, we're so busy with wine pressing Josep. It's non-stop work for a month and we've only been at it a week. Come and have a look."

She took him over the threshold and he blessed himself silently as he re-entered the house of his dreams, the one he seriously wondered whether he'd ever see again. He thanked God for his good fortune as he was taken around the two wine presses where an unknown girl was trampling the grapes in great stone tubs filled with bubbling, frothing grape juice and the girls rearranged their hitched up skirts, nodding a greeting to the master, "Signore Goodman", Josep heard, then mopped their brow and carried on pressing the grapes. One girl stepped out, clearly exhausted, her feet stained utterly purple with grape juice, unsteady on her legs after her exertions. Another finished washing her feet in a huge granite bath. Josep saw her feet were still stained from previous activity.

"This is a real *bodega*, an authentic winery, Lali," he said. "My goodness, things have moved on! And is there any chance of a drop just to try it?"

"But of course! Would you like last year's, or some from five years ago, when you left?"

"Could I try a little of both?"

No sooner said than done and Josep sniffed the glass he was offered. He tasted.

"Delicious but a little bitter," he said, looking into Lali's eyes. "Giving way to a round, sweet finish. This must be the vintage from five years ago."

"Correct!" Smiled Lali.

"And last year's?" Josep asked.

"A disaster. Too bitter to drink. No sweetness. Little rain. Little yield. The grapes shrivelled on the vines. A terrible year."

"Further east as well," Josep added. He and Lali were laughing. "Rough and bitter on the palate, undrinkable, utterly undrinkable."

"Was it so bad?"

"Words cannot begin to describe it."

"Then let it go! Try six years ago."

"Delicious. The year before I left."

"Little remains of that year but it was exceptionally good."

"What's the best vintage you have?"

"Try twenty years old," she said, hugging Lucio to her. That is the sweetest, strongest, most natural that we have. And we have a fine spirit from before we arrived. Twenty-three years old now."

"May I see?" he asked.

"We'll show you later. As yet, unavailable."

"Lali, are you now talking about our daughter or brandy?" Josep asked suddenly a little lost.

"Wait and see!" Lali teased.

Lali took him around the house then while Lucio tended to his horse. He was reintroduced to Luigi, the old servant who had worked the small holding before they arrived and his wife Bianca. They apologised again for the uproar the house was in, it was a very busy time of year but the wine had to be made now, it was very popular and provided so much work for the people round about.

As they turned, Luigi and Bianca greeted their daughter, a young woman in her early twenties. Josep disciplined himself not to stare because she radiated calm and beauty. He turned to comment on the good state of the walls and floors when he caught Lali's eye, her brow slightly furrowed, then a sudden widening of the eyes when she saw Josep's expression. Decent in not looking he might be but she could see he was quite overcome in the presence of this young woman.

"Josep," she whispered in his ear. "Do you not recognise your own daughter?"

There, standing before him, looking to the side now in slight embarrassment, muttering a barely audible farewell to Luigi and Bianca, with her hands clasped simply in front of her, was the most astonishing likeness of Lali Josep had ever seen.

"Catarina!" he whispered.

"Father!" she replied.

"Catarina, you have become even lovelier than you were when I left. I cannot tell you how much like your mother you are when she was your age."

Catarina smiled, blushed and looked away.

"You did not know me when I was her age!" Lali said lightly, then burst into laughter. They all laughed then.

"But look at you now, my dear, you are now a very lovely woman in your own right."

"Thank you, Father. You're looking well, too."

She approached him and kissed him gently on the cheek. She smelled faintly of roses.

Josep instinctively put his arm around Lali's waste, pulled her to him, kissed her on the cheek, too, then put his arm round Catarina's waist, drew his two women to him and buried his head between their heads, luxuriating in the rich heady scent of both their perfumes. He was home.

Josep had only been back three days when he suddenly had the sensation he'd never been away, chatting to the workers, his mother, Lali and the children. In fact, it was Lucio who reminded him he had been away at all.

"Would you ever tell us what it was like in Constantinople, Father? Is the Emperor the most wicked king in the world, as they say? My friends tell me he cannot be trusted after betraying Roger de Flor."

"Indeed," replied Josep, "I still do not entirely understand how that happened myself. My friend Ramón Muntaner will be able to explain the situation in Constantinople better than I. I'm sure he will pass by this way with my share, if any remains."

Ramón Muntaner did not take long to visit them on Sicily, bearing with him a small boat's worth of booty for Josep and also a messsage that Clara and Habiba were well. He himself was awaiting an appointment from King Jaume II of Catalunya Aragón, which Josep later found out through King Frederick's court network on Sicily was the Governorship of the island of Jerba, a Catalan possession off the north African coast, not far from Tunis and the Hafsid coast , where they had both served with King Pere in 1282.

CHAPTER THIRTY-TWO

Six years later, 1313.

As he had predicted, Jacques de Molay was captured, or rather, he awaited his captors, on Friday, the thirteenth of October, 1307. Josep knew this and where he was supposed to have been taken but for six years, Josep knew nothing more of Jacques. He had no contact with the Templars and did not even know if they still existed as an order. Then, one chilly November morning, Josep received the following letter.

Chateau Royale, Gisors, October 1313.

Dear Josep,

I hope this finds you well. I know that you know where I am and please be assured I am being treated well. So much time has passed since the events I need to explain to you now that it is difficult to gather my thoughts coherently in what must be my last communication to you.

If you are reading this letter, it is because I have the permission of your mother to tell you some things you may not have guessed about yourself and your parents.

Your Father, Guzmán, as you now know, was the ambassador of the King of Granada at the court of Henry IV of England in Guyenne, the English possessions in France, at Bordeaux. He was a man of exquisite elegance and taste, as was reflected in his choice of your mother as the woman he wished to spend his life with. Though I secretly shared his rapture at your mother's loveliness, I was because of my vows to my Order unable to act upon my deep feelings for her. Nevertheless, I was only too willing to spend as much time in their company as I could so as to be near her. It was I who arranged for your mother and father to meet each other after they had fleetingly seen each other only once. But one glance was all it took! They both became intolerably irritable with me until I was able to facilitate their meeting again, like spoilt children!

Josep, I cannot describe the two years we spent travelling between Barcelona, Larzac, where I was based, and Bordeaux. Perhaps they were the happiest times of my life, out on the open road, fulfilling a legitimate mission always but in the best company you could possible imagine. How we were not chastised for our high-spirited capers is beyond me! We were lucky and we felt free!

Gúzman was an exceptional man, Josep. He had the genuine innocence of spirit and gentleness of nature not to see any conflict between his own beliefs and those of any other creed, believing in love and beauty as the highest praise he could raise to God. In his company, it was impossible not to be enveloped in his warmth and he was able to evince these qualities in all those who had the pleasure of his company. It was in this spirit that he made such an impact on the Cathars and explains why the Cathar Knights planned their future with him.

Yet your Father was also shrewd and brave when it came to defending those for whom he cared and he was able to prepare an escape route for the Cathars from their secret hide-out in Rennes-le-Chateau, in 1250, ten years before he even met your mother, when the net of the Inquisitors in Languedoc tightened around them. Had it not been for his skill and foresight, those Cathars would have shared the same fate as the Cathars in Montsegur or the two hundred brethren of Quéribus, two years later, who were all captured and burnt at the stake. Those he helped to survive never forgot him, of course.

Josep, you were always an intelligent boy and I know that the reason I arranged for you to deliver the Cathars once and for all from harm has not escaped you. You were the ideal person, you who were his son! I know how proud your father would be of you and it would have been his wish that you were the person to help these persecuted brethren to reach safety. I knew they would follow you without a moment's hesitation, as they did. Your familiarity with them and the terrain in which they lived ensured your success. I hope you do not feel that I have negatively influenced your life over the years by preparing you for this role. You even managed to escape from Es Bordes Castle when you were captured! You surpassed even our most demanding expectations. I might add, it was also a measure of the honour of your Knight, Lord Pedro de Ayerbe, that, despite the deliberate deception we were obliged to use with him during your early days at and after Cavallers, when asked to help in the final rescue mission years later, he was only too willing, regardless of his ill health.

Your journey to Scotland I am reliably informed (I still have my secret collaborators, hence this letter!) was uneventful apart from the dreadful sailing conditions between Bilbau and Bordeaux in the Bay of Biscay and again off Arran as you approached Ayre. Dunure Castle was the perfect point to land as it is so secluded and on the road to Kilwinning. The help you received there from the Morays was arranged some years ago between myself and Knights of the Temple resident in Ayrshire and Dumfries. It was I who convinced the Morays they were distant cousins of the Molays. But more of that later...

Josep, I must tell you now that I believe that the origins of the family names of your father and mother and in my opinion, my own, are Muslim. One of the best guarded secrets in Spain is the origin of the name of Guzmán. You will see in a moment why this is so important. It will not have escaped your notice that the founder of the Inquisition and the Dominican Order was Domingo Guzmán, whose name is therefore held in reverence by the Catholic church. Those who persecute often do so as they feel they have the most to hide! Though Guzmán is one of the most important noble names of Spain, closely related to the Casa del Duque de Medina Sidonia, your father knew that the origin of the name Guzmán was his own name Qusmân, an Arabic name, and he was able to trace his ancestry back to the Qusmân who founded the Alcazar, later known as the Castle of Guzmán, in Niebla, near Huelva, in the tenth century. His branch of the family were the Lords of Hisn Atiba, the Castillo de Estrella, in a village called Teba, not far from Granada. Your Father, Yusef Qusmân, studied law in Granada and rose quickly in the court service of Abu-Abdullah Muhammad I, the first Nasrid King of Granada. I believe he intended to propose Granada as a future destination for the Cathar community. The delay was perhaps due to difficulties he experienced there in organising this. What an irony of history that your father and the psychotic monster who founded the Inquisition should have had common ancestry! As I have told you, it was believed your Father had died in the Straits of Gibraltar. I am not sure that that is the case. That is a matter only your mother can perhaps shed light on. However, when you were born, he was gone and, amid the grief and fear of the circumstances, to avoid problems if you were named Guzmán, your mother and I decided to call you Goodman, as it harked back to the Bonnes Hommes of the Cathars whom your Father so admired but was clearly similar to Guzmán. Your mother also liked it because it sounded so English. She was terrified someone would accuse you of being an impostor and claiming false name and credentials, so she invented this name, Goodman, for you, to protect you. The origin of your mother's name Morris is, I believe, Moorish. I thought for half my life the origins of Molay, Moray and Murray were also Moorish. I was wrong about my name but I had my reasons. You see, by the time Charles Martel defeated the Moors in Tours in 732, France had been the host to the Moors for a decade. People from different cultures inevitably meet and fall in love despite even war or differences in race and creed and have children. Love therefore clearly defies war sowing seeds where war has sought to destroy. Love is also a stronger force than faith no matter how much wealth and power there might be behind any particular church. The aim of religion is to control whether by conversion or conquest and thereby to preserve itself. But love conquers all though the aim of love is simply to protect. The founder of Christianity preached love not war. His message now falls on deaf ears.

In any case, the names of Morris and Molay I believed were thus established and the bearers of these names, among them your mother's ancestors, in time moved further north into England probably as members of armies just like their Moorish forebears but perfectly well assimilated now as French or Norman soldiers. In time, these newcomers became assimilated, in the case of your mother's family in England or moved on, as in the case of mine, I believed, further north still into Scotland. This belief as you will see was partly my undoing.

However, I wish to return to your father. He was a great source of information not only about his own personal family history. Do you remember from our conversation how influenced the Knights of the Temple were by Islamic mysticism and especially the myth of Hiram? He was also knowledgeable about both and discussed both at length with me and the Cathars from Rennes-le-Chateau. As a result, I feel he influenced their views as much as he did mine. The Hiram myth is the origin of the myth of the divine architect, which the builders of the original Temple of Solomon knew. Your Father was convinced that the Cathars were familiar with the myth and found it attractive. The shared asceticism and mythology have made the Cathars and the Templars kindred spirits faced with extinction, hence the origin of the Cathar Knights. Even those whose creed is harsh and simple prefer to avoid annihilation. In any case, everything evolves, everything changes in the end. Thus it is not unfitting that there are Templars who recognise that the end has come for our order and a new beginning is at hand. This I know is also the feeling of the Cathar community you have delivered. In isolation over the years in the wilderness their ideas changed as well and they now desire only to be allowed to live as they wish in peace. It is therefore not surprising that I have heard from Scotland that there is already discussion between the newly arrived Cathars and the Templars in Kilwinning to merge and found a new organisation called the Free Masons, membership of which will be based on belief in God but in a way that is ecumenical and open to all faiths; and also on the tenets of liberty, equality and brotherhood. How proud your father would be of such a development and your involvement in the origin of this movement! There is also something strangely fitting to the whole enterprise of the Freemasons in the Son of the Widow carrying on the Father's work, as is your case. You were the perfect person to enable all this even with respect to future projects!

As for myself, Josep, I feel I am an old man now and have to face up to my failings. My interrogator, Guillaume de Nogaret, is as cold as he is clever and calculating and he has managed to confound me on so many counts now that I know I am doomed. He has forced me to confess, I am ashamed to say, with only the threat of torture, that we as an order blasphemed, spat on the cross and stamped on an image of our Lord Jesus Christ. This is nonsense, because, as we discussed, the Order of the Poor Knights of the Temple of Solomon did no such thing as an order whatever some individuals may have done. I therefore later recanted this confession and face death as a result. These days, I am not so horrified as I was about the nature of my coming death. I am better prepared to die for the honour of my order as its Grand Master but I must confess my personal shame when interrogation started that I feared torture. Nogaret later reminded me of this in private and it was enough to rob me of my pride. He intended to crush my spirit. Yet I feel I go to my death bravely.

He also showed me that my belief that the Molays were related to the Morays is erroneous. For years, I endeavoured to prove that Molay and Moray were of the same root and that I was related to a certain Freskin de Moravia who emigrated to Scotland together with many Flemish and Normans from that part of Europe in the early twelfth century and established the ancient Royal House of Moray. This was the origin of the name Murray, the senior line of which became the Earls of Sutherland while another branch of the family became the Lords of Petty in Moray.However, recently de Nogaret has shown me evidence to the contrary. He has proved to me that Murray and Moray come from old celtic *Muireb* (or *Moreb*) meaning *sea settlement* and are entirely Scottish names in origin and existed as names before Freskin even arrived in Scotland. Secondly, he has documents that show that *de Moravia* was a Latinisation of these names that Freskin used after he arrived in Scotland not a former Moorish surname that he brought with him. And thirdly, he produced witnesses and documents that attest that Molay is a name, in its own right, in the Haute-Sâone, in Burgundy and therefore part of the Holy Roman Empire (as I knew too well!) and therefore nothing to do with the French, Flemish or Normans though all of them are generally in that part of the world. His intellect is razor sharp and when he revealed this detail, he made great play on the ambiguity of my expression, "that general part of the world," making me appear utterly ridiculous. He finally convinced those at that particular tribunal that I had always fantasised with being related by blood in some way at some time in the past to the Islamic world to bring me closer to the woman I could not have, namely your mother. By claiming a common Islamic heritage with her and your father, I presented a spurious kinship with her in an imagined happy Islamic family. The members of the tribunal that day could not contain their mirth and broke out in great guffaws at what he cleverly presented as my asinine stupidity.My undoing was well under-way by then. He proceeded to argue that I detested the French king so much that I was prepared to make an alliance with the Mongols against France and Christianity in the Levant. Yet, in his summation, he banished all levity and became more serious than I have ever seen him. He argued that I had become perverted by Islamic mysticism during my time in the Holy Land and was more interested in finding common ground with Muslims than in defending the Christain faith, which was my role as Grand Master of the Templars. In short, he destroyed my credibility not only as Grand Master of the Templars but even as a monk.

Josep, what can I say in my defence? I must tell the truth. He often overstated his case and played to the crowd like any good advocate but in essence, he was right. For as many years as I can remember, I have allowed myself to believe whatever made me feel closer to your mother and yourself. I plotted against the French and the Angevins with Emperor Andronicus of Constantinople, to aid your King, Peter II, not only because the balance of power was therefore better preserved in the Mediterranean at the time but also secretly because it seemed more propitious for your future in Catalonia, Josep.

It is true, as de Nogaret stated, that I did not pursue military opportunities as diligently as I should have after the second Fall of Acre, in 1291. From the relative safety of Famagusta, just across the water from Acre, I toyed with the idea of a military alliance with the Mongols so as to counterbalance a possible French alliance with the Mamluks in accordance with the intelligence I had received. However, I knew very well that neither Mongols nor Mamluks could ever be trusted allies of a Christian force so even the thought of co-operation was utterly futile and a dangerous distraction. People, military and civilian, die minute by minute in these conflicts.

Lastly, de Nogaret pointed out that I put your rescue from Greece above my duties in Famagusta when I left Cyprus for France, or as he put it, left "Cyprus with its backside in the wind." If you remember, this is where de Nogaret's interests and my own finally collided: he was behind the confrontation between the Catalan leaders Entença and Rocafort and wanted you dead. This detail was not even mentioned as it was irrelevant to the proceedings so it is not common knowledge and will be brushed under the carpet and never come to light. But he was especially vindictive when he made the accusation of dereliction of duty, as he formally termed it, catching my eye almost coquettishly (I have thought about the word carefully) several times to ram home the point personally to me. It was as if he got a thrill from skewering me and then watching me writhe.

In his summary, de Nogaret called me defeatist and that my policy was to allow the Muslims, whether Mongols, Mamluks or Turks, to thrash it out with each other for the Holy Land regardless of the loss of Christian lives there. For all these reasons, he concluded, I was therefore never even interested in amalgamating the Templars and the Hospitalers. In his peroration, he urged everyone present to conclude that as a person, I lived in a fantasy world, as a monk I had effectively broken my vows of chastity, that as a Christian, I was guilty of apostasy and as a commander, I was guilty of gross dereliction of duty on several counts.

Josep, if I have erred it has been in the most human of ways. You must know now how deeply in love with your mother I was and still am. It gave me pleasure to act as a father to you but also pain to know that you were not my son. Though I am unshakable in my faith and thoroughly committed to carrying out my duty as Grand Master of the Order of the Poor Fellow-Soldiers of Christ and of the Temple of Solomon, believe me when I say that in another life I would hold nothing more dear than to be at your mother's side as her husband and your father. I apologise if that sounds inappropriate or if my devotion to your mother or my own human failings ever stopped me from expressing my love and admiration for you, whom I have come to look upon as a son.

Josep, you have done your duty and are a credit to your mother, to your father, to me. Now you must do your duty to yourself and your wife and family. You know that I will argue for my order and for my life. But I will also die for the honour of my order as I was prepared to do on the battlefield countless times. That is my fate, which I embraced long ago. You are therefore to dismiss any thoughts you may have about rescuing me. I have chosen my path, which will include self-sacrifice if necessary.

It has been an honour to know you, your dear mother and your father. You have the looks of both of them, your father's eyes, your mother's expressions. They both live on through you and will do through your family and descendants. I desire now only to express as your benefactor, if you will allow me the privilege, even if merely symbolically, my wish to call myself father to you and how proud I am of you. Remember me.

Jacques de Molay

CHAPTER THIRTY-THREE

In the low, introspective days that followed the arrival of Jacques' letter, Josep and his mother finally had the conversation they should have had many years before. "Josep, there are so many things I haven't told you about your father and the circumstances of his death. He did not drown between Gibraltar and Morocco as I had believed but turned up out of the blue one day when you were three. I nearly died of fright when I recognised him! He'd been hiding near Can Baró, watching for me and waiting till he could attract my attention without being seen. I thought I was seeing a ghost at first. I shouted at him and asked him what he thought he was doing, playing such a nasty trick on us, I was not thinking straight, I was uncertain, but I'm sure you can understand why, can't you? It was such a shock and I'm so ashamed of how I reacted now. He said his ship had gone down off Gibraltar but he had made it to shore in Tarifa on a smaller boat and then the survivors when they arrived simply went their separate ways, glad to be alive. He managed to travel to Granada. That's where he hatched the plan." "What plan?" asked Josep breathlessly, his mind reeling at this new Catharine took a deep breath. "The day your father died, we had gone out in a small rowing boat he had somehow managed to get his hands on. He thought it was safer that way and that we wouldn't be seen and could talk. It was his idea not mine. It was romantic. We were both wearing the necklaces with the interlocking loops and I remember I was sitting with you in my lap, steadying myself with my right hand and you were touching the necklace. Anyway, he rowed away from Sitges northwards up the coast, never more than two hundred feet or so from the shore. I had not told Clara anything about him or meeting him again. We were busy making plans but then I said I did not want to move to Granada and he became angry." "Why was he angry?" "He thought I did not want to go because it was a Muslim city," Catharine said. "Is that true? Didn't you want to go because it was a Muslim city?" "Josep, you have to understand I'd only just found out that he was alive and I had only just settled down in Sant Pere de Ribes and was quite contented with my life. Then he told me he was Muslim. I just did not know how to react. I had thought it did not matter to me what he was but once I knew, I realised it did. "How is it possible that you did not know?" Josep gasped in disbelief. "It never occurred to me to ask him so I never did. Guzmán is a perfectly common Spanish name after all, he came from a tiny village called Teba, had a good position in Granada, the rest was not important to me, it did not make any difference. "How could you not know he was Muslim if he had a good position in Granada?" Josep asked. "I didn't think about it because it didn't matter to me and he was welcome at the English court in Bordeaux. That was good enough for me. Ignorance is bliss, and all that. I thought I'd find out in due course and we had all the time in the world. It did not matter. I realised I just still loved him." "So why did you not go to Granada with him?" Josep asked.

"It was all moving too fast! He was saying I could go there straight away without him, his family there would look after me, he would follow on as soon as he could," Catharine said, weeping now. Josep reached out and touched her to comfort her. It was horrible to see her so unhappy.

"Mother, you do not have to do this if you don't want to," he said. But she shook her head, blew her nose and dried her eyes as well as she could.

"I do want to, Josep. It is now or never," she said.

"Did you not believe him or trust him?" Josep asked, trying to understand what had happened and what was so hard for his mother to explain.

"It was not a matter of believing him, or trusting him, Josep.

You've got to understand I'd been in a similar situation when I was pregnant with you and after a month of wandering around, had ended up in Sant Pere de Ribes, thanks to Jacques de Molay's recommendation and I felt relieved and settled. Clara had reassured me so much about you when you were a baby, I really felt it was all possible, that it could work out all right, that everything was going to be all right. Then the man I had loved found me and turned my world upside down again in a matter of minutes and wanted me to leave my home again and wander into a new town completely on my own! He wanted me to go through a similar situation again. I cannot tell you how scared I'd been until I met Clara. I thought I was going to lose you, or I was going to die in a ditch somewhere giving birth to you, or we'd have to live rough and take our chances and you know what living in the hills is like!" She shuddered.

"So you couldn't travel together openly, is that what you mean?" asked Josep.

"Yes, that was a problem for him, I think. He thought that was dangerous and would attract too much attention to us, but we never managed to talk about that. He got annoyed with me because I said I needed time to decide what I was going to do and that it was a huge decision to take from one moment to the next. I did not even really know where Granada was, let alone how I would get there without him, how I would find his family, how they would react to me and how they would look after me. But I had not said I wouldn't go! I just had not agreed immediately and said what a great solution that was to all our problems. But listen to me now because I've thought about this long and hard over the years. His family name was in fact Qusma later Gusma, the original name that the Spanish Christian surname Guzmán comes from. Can you imagine what would happen if the roles were reversed and a Muslim woman came to a great Christian city, like Barcelona or Bordeaux, saying that she was looking for such and such a family and saying that this little boy was their son? It would cause such a scandal! Where would the poor woman start for one thing, who would she turn to if there was a problem, which, with the best will in the world, there almost certainly would be."

She was looking steadily at Josep now. "We were in the boat, as I say, and were on the point of talking it through, I thought, when the accident happened. All these thoughts were flying around in my head and I was dumb-founded, I did not know what to say! I guess your father came to the wrong conclusion about my silence, he became exasperated or impatient or whatever, I never found out because he suddenly stood up and at that moment, a small wave hit the boat. He snatched at something to hold onto but lost his balance and fell over the side of the boat and struck his head on the side of the boat as he fell. He let out a cry and that was the last I saw or heard of him. I panicked, I stood up with you in my arms and of course, lost my balance immediately and the next thing I knew, I was in the water, too! It was as much as I could do to grab hold of you and swim to shore with you. Do you remember passing that point on the Llobregat river where Jacques told us that story of the Lady of the Wells, do you remember, the day after we'd left Ribes to take you to school? You know, the story about the lady who drowned when her hair got caught in the reeds. I remember I suddenly thought, "I am the Lady of the Wells!" I have remembered that for all these years but it was not me who drowned but my would-be husband. But I'd been trapped all those years all the same because I'd been hiding my guilt not only about his death. I'd also been trapped by feeling guilty about the accusation I had levelled at him in my own head, that he had died and abandoned me. But he had not. He came back for me. Then there was an accident."

Josep hid his head in his hands.

"I thought the dreams of drowning I have always had were just dreams. It seems they are connected with a memory," he said.

She looked down, a picture of dejection and misery. "I did not want to burden you in this way but I could not hide it from you any more," she said.

"I did not understand so I made you tell me. It is not your fault," he said.

He could see the lifetime of guilt and remorse she had been through. How difficult it must have been for her over the years to live with the truth of what had happened, to stay positive, to try to live her life! How complicated the situation was to explain and how understandable that she had simply preferred not even to try to explain it! Who would she have told, anyway? The fact was it would be agonising for her not only to have to explain it, but she would also have to convince people she was telling the truth. It was all so complicated. But at the time, Josep thought, the events simply happened one after the other. Time is relentless and unforgiving in that way, he thought: what seems perfectly normal, when you come to explain it years later, sounds totally implausible. But it was also totally reasonable that he had wanted to hear it all. He had made her remember what she would rather have put behind her because he had to know.

"Grief cuts our memory and guilt cauterizes the wound!" he said, remembering thinking that once about Bru Miret. Catharine nodded.

"We try to forget and put things behind us so that we can carry on and live our lives," she said. She looked at Josep gently, pulled his hands down from his face and put her own hands around his face.

"But after all these years, do you know what conclusion I've come to, darling?" Catharine asked. She was seeking out his eyes. Josep looked into her eyes so deeply he could see the blue-brown stars of her irises. It reminded him of Lali.

"I've learned, Josep, lost as I have been without the only man I've ever loved, distraught that I was maybe responsible for his death, I've learned that we have to move on, that life is for the living. These negative thoughts connect us with the deceased but they also weigh us down. His death was an accident, Josep, that is all there is to it. Despite all the remorse I've been through for all that I lost when he died, I've also learned I was not in any way responsible for it. Just as he was blameless for what happened to me in my life, I'm not guilty either."

"You can forgive yourself, can't you, that is what you mean, is it not? Josep asked. Catharine nodded.

She fingered the necklace with its interlocking loops that she always wore, in a daydream. Josep saw that she was now thinking about what had happened to the other part of the necklace that Josep's father had always worn. It had disappeared with him. It was gone.

"If Jacques loved me so much, why did he not come for me over all those years?" she asked suddenly.

"I suppose he somehow felt unworthy of your love," Josep replied.

"Are you like that?" she asked him. "I think I am just straightforward in those things. I cannot understand it. I am not made that way. I love fiercely so I hang on to what I love. That is why it has been so hard for me to let it go. For me, my love is all one. It cannot be split up and left behind," she said.

"But if he had?" Josep asked.

"One has to take that chance," she said. "But, yes, I think I would have accepted him. Fortune favours the brave, as they say, and it is also true about love!"

"Be true to your heart," Josep said but he knew as he said it, he also knew love does not always win.

They sat holding each other in silence for a long time, smiling and listening to the simple sounds of nature around them, feeling they had reached the end of a long journey and they could now greet the future with hope, love and joy.

THE END

EPILOGUE

Epilogue.

In 1309, the Catalan Compay overthrew Rocafort, handed him over to Duke Robert of Calabria, who held him hostage in one of the castles Rocafort had pillaged during the aftermath of the War of the Sicilian Vespers. Entença's prediction he would and should be punished for this came true from beyond the grave. Rocafort was never released and within the year was starved to death in his cell. The Company crossed into the French Duchies of Greece, went on to take Thebes and finally crossed into the Duchy of Athens, defeating the army they met there at the Battle of Cefis in 1311. The Catalan Company then ruled the Duchy of Athens for seventy years.

Ramón Muntaner retired from his post as Governor of Jerba, settled in Valencia and in 1325 started writing his account of the Catalan Expedition to the east (or Constantinople), the Chronicles. They are written in lively, graphic, medieval Catalan and are a brilliant evocation of the period and the original inspiration for this book. Muntaner died in 1336. Pere de Ayerbe, Josep's Knight in this book, married twice. He became the Seneschal, or Lieutenant, of Aragón. He died in 1318.

Kilwinning is the site of the First Masonic Hall in Scotland and there are Templar graves in the cemetery. Templars did fight with Robert the Bruce at Bannockburn but the Cathar community and treasure mentioned in this book are, as far as I know, fictional. Rennes-le-Chateau is a fascinating historical town in Languedoc with Cathar roots and mystery.

After seven years of captivity and inconclusive evidence of

heresy, Jacques de Molay was finally executed on the pyre on the 18th of March, 1314. Guillaume de Nogaret had died the year before. Poisoning was rumoured but never proved. Apparently, his tongue in death was black. The French Crown never acquired part of the Templar treasure. Jacques de Molay died bravely and quickly after cursing the Royal House of Capet, of whom King Philip the Fourth was the last monarch. The French King died shortly afterwards, followed rapidly by his own son, both within a year of de Molay's death. Plague then ravaged France.

AFTERWORD

HISTORIC PREAMBLE 1285-1294
SPOILER ALERT

In October 1285, King Philip III of France died in Perpignan, in the territory of King Jaume of Majorca, King Pere's treacherous brother. King Jaume then fled from his palace in Perpignan abandoning his wife and family. King Pere sent a fleet against Majorca under the command of his eldest son and heir, Alfonso, but, infected by the same plague as had just killed King Philip of France and knowing he was dying, he swore an oath that he had attacked Sicily merely to defend the rights of his family, as his queen, Constança, was heir to the throne of Sicily, and he had no hostile feelings to the Church. He was given absolution and his declaration was naturally interpreted as a statement that he would return Sicily to the Pope. He died in Vilafranca del Penedès on November 2, 1285.

King Pere II of Catalunya Aragón was known as the Great. Like his father, he was a man of stature and strength, an expert knight and more than a match for Charles of Anjou in single combat. He was also a clever and cautious ruler who displayed patience and that he could wait for his opportunity to come. To have defeated Charles of Anjou, the Kingdom of France and the Roman Catholic Church at a time when his own realms were far from united was a great achievement. By his will, his eldest son Alfons became his heir, to be followed, should he be without issue, by his second son Jaume, who received the kingdom of Sicily, to be followed in the succession, failing issue, by the remaining adult son, Frederick. King Pere II left one other son, Pere, and two daughters by his wife, Constança.

The elder daughter, Isabel, became Queen of Portugal, while the younger, Yolanda, married Robert, Duke of Calabria and Prince of Naples, grandson of Charles of Anjou, later to be the King of Naples. This marriage set in motion a series of marriages between the sons of King Pere to princesses of the Crown of Naples, which eventually eased the problems caused by the Catalan invasion of Sicily. However, this process, resulting in the Peace of Caltabellota, 1302, did not conclude until nearly twenty years after his death, as can be seen, and a terrible amount of blood was spilled in the meantime.

At the time of King Pere's death, Alfons was sailing to Mallorca with Roger de Llúria to conquer Majorca. This was not a difficult task as the inhabitants had suffered under the oppression of King Jaume of Majorca, Alfons's uncle, and Alfons was regarded as a liberator. In 1286, Alfons summoned the Estates of the Realm to Zaragoza for his own coronation ceremonies. However, he found the Aragonese nobles against him because they complained that he had already assumed the royal title while en route to Majorca before he had received the crown from them and taken the coronation oaths with them, all of which was regarded by the nobles as an infringement of their rights. Alfonso replied he had only used the royal title because the Catalans had already addressed him in that style. But this dispute was only the prelude to a lengthy series of discussions and recriminations spread over several years. The basic question of the Kingdom of Catalunya Aragón and the crown of Aragón was how united a crown of three realms could be and whether it could be ruled by one king.

Alfons was soon on the northern frontier, as the ousted King Jaume of Majorca was preparing forces near Perpignan for an invasion of Catalunya. He also had to defend his kingdom from Castile. When Alfonso X of Castile died in 1285, his brother Sancho had assumed the crown usurping his nephews, Fernando and Alfonso, the Infantes de la Cerda, whose father Fernando was heir to the crown but had died in 1275. The two young princes had been protected for years by King

Pere II and now by Alfons. This was because their mother, King Fernando's widow, was King Pere's sister, Yolanda. King Sancho entered into an alliance with the King of France, meaning that Alfons now potentially faced an invasion from Castile, from Navarra, whose queen, Joana, was married to the King of France and from the north Catalan county of Rosellón, which Jaume still considered part of his Kingdom of Majorca.

Alfons was also engaged in other important matters of foreign policy. During his father's lifetime, he had been betrothed to Eleanor, the daughter of Edward I of England, but the Pope had forbidden the marriage, as Aragón was then excommunicated because of Pere's invasion of Sicily. Alfons' fierce reputation held him in good stead with the King of England, Edward I, who was keen to pursue the marriage of Alfons to his daughter. The resulting alliance would have mutually protected both the King of England's Guyenne possessions (notably Bordeaux) and the King of Catalunya Aragón from attack from France and Navarra. All preparations for the marriage in Barcelona were made ready for 1291. However, the night before the celebration of the long-awaited ceremony, King Alfons suddenly and mysteriously died. He had developed a swelling in his groin, which had spread its contagion through his body and in the morning he was dead. Some blamed the fact that he was marrying so late in life and that his continuing virginity was too much for his body to bear. But others, once the disappointed wedding party had left Barcelona for England via Bordeaux, pointed to his will as evidence that his virginity was unlikely to be true. In King Alfons' last will and testament, he provided specifically for a young woman named Dolça, with whom, it was said, he had been romantically involved for some years.

Alfons had spent his entire reign outside Sicily as King Pere's will had stipulated that Prince Jaume was to become King of Sicily. In fact, Jaume had been crowned King of Sicily in Palermo before Alfons had been crowned King of Aragón in Zaragoza. However, the whole situation was thrown into further turmoil when King Jaume of Sicily left the island for Barcelona to succeed Alfons after his sudden death. The new King of Catalunya Aragón acted promptly against a combined attack on his kingdom by Sancho the King of Castille and an alliance as before between Prince Charles of Valois, the French King's younger brother, and the Pope. Hungry for a kingdom, the present Prince Charles of Valois renewed the crusade against Catalunya Aragón, as in the time of King Pere. King Jaume II, like Alfons, faced war, therefore, on various fronts: in the west of Aragón with Castille; on the frontier between Aragón and Navarra; on the frontier between Rosellón and France, where the invasion had happened in King Pere's time; and the continuing war against the House of Anjou, Kings of Naples, over Sicily. Even though old King Charles of Naples, arch-menace of the Mediterranean and instigator of all King Pere's problems, had been dead longer than King Pere, his son, Charles the Lame, now King Charles II of Naples, continued to demand that the island of Sicily be returned to him as part of the dual crown of Sicily.

Troops were sent to King Jaume II to guard Aragón against invasion from Castille. Among their leaders was Prince Pere, the king's youngest brother, who was only twenty years of age. Queen Constança, anxious and powerless in Sicily, had lost her husband and eldest son in ten years. News came a month later that her youngest son Pere had now died in battle.

The situation was complex. King Jaume II was under pressure from within his kingdom to relinquish Sicily to his younger brother, Frederick, whom the Sicilians wanted as their king. His marriage with Isabelle of Castille had been annulled by the Pope on the grounds of consanguinity so he was free to marry again. Achieving peace and stability in the western Mediterranean eluded him. Yet he knew he held all the pieces in his hand. The coming year would be crucial. He could achieve more stability but at what price could he secure peace? This is the point at which this book, Book Three of the

Chronicles of the Forgotten Kingdom, begins.

Printed in Great Britain
by Amazon